PRAISE FOR THE LADY DARBY MYSTERIES

"[A] history mystery in fine Victorian style! Anna Lee Huber's spirited debut mixes classic country house mystery with a liberal dash of historical romance."

—*New York Times* bestselling author Julia Spencer-Fleming

"Riveting. . . . Huber deftly weaves together an original premise, an enigmatic heroine, and a compelling Highland setting."

—*New York Times* bestselling author Deanna Raybourn

"[A] fascinating heroine. . . . A thoroughly enjoyable read!"

—National bestselling author Victoria Thompson

"Reads like a cross between a gothic novel and a mystery with a decidedly unusual heroine."   —*Kirkus Reviews*

"Includes all the ingredients of a romantic suspense novel, starting with a proud and independent heroine. . . . Strong and lively characters as well as believable family dynamics, however, elevate this above stock genre fare."   —*Publishers Weekly*

"[A] clever heroine with a shocking past and a talent for detection."   —National bestselling author Carol K. Carr

"[Huber] designs her heroine as a woman who straddles the line between eighteenth-century behavior and twenty-first-century independence."   —New York Journal of Books

"[A] must read. . . . One of those rare books that will both shock and please readers."   —Fresh Fiction

"One of the best historical mysteries that I have read this year."

—Cozy Mystery Book Reviews

Titles by Anna Lee Huber

A WICKED CONCEIT

ANNA LEE HUBER

BERKLEY PRIME CRIME
New York

BERKLEY PRIME CRIME
Published by Berkley
An imprint of Penguin Random House LLC
penguinrandomhouse.com

Library of Congress Cataloging-in-Publication Data

Names: Huber, Anna Lee, author.
Title: A wicked conceit / Anna Lee Huber.
Description: First edition. | New York: Berkley Prime Crime, 2021. |
Series: Lady Darby mysteries
Identifiers: LCCN 2020050723 (print) | LCCN 2020050724 (ebook) |
ISBN 9780593198445 (trade paperback) | ISBN 9780593198452 (ebook)
Subjects: GSAFD: Mystery fiction.
Classification: LCC PS3608.U238 W53 2021 (print) |
LCC PS3608.U238 (ebook) | DDC 813/.6—dc23
LC record available at https://lccn.loc.gov/2020050723
LC ebook record available at https://lccn.loc.gov/2020050724

First Edition: April 2021

Printed in the United States of America

1st Printing

This book is dedicated to the medical workers of the COVID-19 pandemic and all previous pandemics: the physicians, surgeons, nurses, respiratory therapists, speech and language pathologists, technicians, researchers, scientists, janitors, midwives, apothecaries, and more, who risk their lives, stepping into the unknown—into the front line of the battle— to save lives and search for effective treatments and a cure.

Thank you.

A BRIEF NOTE ABOUT PANDEMICS

When I first began writing the Lady Darby Mysteries back in 2010, and decided to set the first book in August 1830, I always hoped the series would last long enough for the characters to reach the year 1832. But while I was aware that my characters would eventually have to wrangle with the cholera pandemic that struck Britain beginning in late 1831, I had no idea I would be writing about it while experiencing a new pandemic in our time.

That being said, the methods used for controlling a pandemic and treating a disease like cholera in 1832 were very different from those we now use in 2020. Our science and medical knowledge have progressed immensely in the 188 years since then, and so readers should be aware that the methods and thinking described in this book will not resemble what we have experienced during the COVID-19 pandemic.

PROLOGUE

Be sure to taste your words before you spit them out.
—SCOTTISH PROVERB

FEBRUARY 1, 1832
EDINBURGH, SCOTLAND

I blamed it on the salmon mousse. That, and my preoccupation with the stilted conversation around my sister's dinner table that evening. If my stomach hadn't been struggling to digest all the rich food I'd ingested and my mind hadn't been turning over my uneasy reconciliation with my sister, I felt certain I would have noticed the man before he stepped out of the shadows.

My husband, Sebastian Gage, pulled me to a halt, for the man clearly wasn't a servant employed by the town house from whose stairwell he had emerged. The night was too cold, and the likelihood of someone wandering by too slim for him to be a thief waiting for some hapless victim to stroll through this part of New Town. Most of New Town's inhabitants would have been huddled inside their carriages to travel to and from their evening entertainments.

Gage and I had decided to walk because our home on Albyn Place was less than five minutes by foot from my sister's in Charlotte Square. Not only did using our equipage for such a short journey seem more of a fuss than was necessary, but at seven months heavy with child, I welcomed the chill of a brief evening stroll, and the benefits to my constitution, especially after a large meal.

I clutched my ermine-trimmed claret pelisse tighter around me, my arm unconsciously coming to rest over my rounded stomach in protection. Even when the man rounded the railing which separated the stairwell leading downward from the pavement, allowing the faint light of the streetlamp on the corner behind us to reveal his features, I didn't relax my guard. For while I now recognized him, the fierce glitter in his eyes did nothing to reassure me he meant us no harm.

"Oot for an evenin' constitutional, are we?" Bonnie Brock Kincaid bit out, his words no less menacing despite their seeming innocuousness.

"Returning home from a family dinner." Gage's eyes narrowed. "But you already knew that."

Bonnie Brock had told us once that nothing happened in Edinburgh without him knowing, and that seemed to prove true in the Georgian splendor of New Town as well as the cramped and fetid wynds and closes of Old Town, particularly when it came to me and Gage. The previous spring he'd deployed men to observe me and report my movements, and since our return to the city the week prior I'd begun to suspect his men were at it again.

Gage studied our surroundings to our left and then our right. "Where are Stumps and Locke?"

Bonnie Brock's ever-present henchmen and bodyguards appeared to materialize out of the misty darkness, but my attention remained firmly fixed on their leader.

It had been nine months since I'd last seen the ruthless and charismatic head of Edinburgh's largest criminal gang. Nine months since he'd been poisoned and almost killed by a revenge-mad enemy from his past. Gage and I had departed Edinburgh soon after the culprit was apprehended, and while I'd known Bonnie Brock had made a full recovery, my last memory of him was a weak shadow of his normal self.

From what I could view of him through his open greatcoat, his body had regained much of the weight and muscle it had lost. As always, he seemed underdressed for the cold of a Scottish winter, sporting well-tailored but simple garments and no neck cloth. But I'd realized a year ago that he chose to sacrifice warmth for ease of movement and ready access to the weapons tucked about his person. His tawny hair brushed his collarbone, much like a lion's mane, and concealed the puckered scar which ran from his hairline down across his temple to his left ear.

Though I knew it would irritate him for me to refer to our last meeting—to those days when he was as weak and helpless as a kitten—I couldn't let this moment pass without saying something. "I'm relieved to see you appear as fit as ever."

His brow puckered as if suppressing some emotion, either further vexation or something softer, but no less cutting. "Aye, weel, looks like you're in fine health as weel." A roguish glint lit his gold-green eyes as he let them dip lower to my abdomen. "I see Gage has been an attentive husband."

In the past such a comment might have made me blush, but I could tell Bonnie Brock was resorting to crassness in order to distract from his own vulnerabilities. I'd suspected as much in the past, but now I knew it. And when neither Gage nor I rose to his bait, his scowl deepened.

"What do you want, Kincaid?" my husband demanded.

I had a fair guess what this was about, but I wanted to hear it from Bonnie Brock himself.

He strode closer until Gage lifted a hand, warding him off. His mouth twisted. "What's the matter? Worried I'll stick a dagger in your side and run off wi' your bride?"

"No, but I *am* worried you carry the cholera, and I'd prefer if you didn't infect my expectant wife," Gage replied sharply, his voice brooking no argument.

At these words, some of Bonnie Brock's ferocity diminished, recognizing as well as we did how dangerous such a thing would be.

Cholera morbus, which had run rampant through Russia and the countries surrounding the Baltic Sea, had arrived in Britain in October. From Sunderland, it had spread north and south largely along the coast, arriving in Edinburgh just before Christmas. With Old Town's squalid rows of tenements packed together cheek by jowl, with naught but a narrow wynd or close separating some of them, it was no wonder that the disease had gained a foothold there. The air was often foul, at best, and the food consumed by its residents sometimes barely edible, while the wide streets and airy squares of New Town, with their spacious Georgian town houses filled with a healthy, well-fed populace, had thus far escaped the worst of the infection.

By all reports, the cholera was much worse than the minor outbreak of typhus that the lower denizens of the city had faced the previous spring. As overrun as the infirmary had been then, I could only imagine the difficulties they were facing now. Of course, cholera morbus could also kill more quickly. Sometimes in less than twenty-four hours. The numbers in which people were dying were frightening, although the reports from Glasgow, London, and places on the European continent seemed to suggest that Edinburgh had thus far escaped the worst.

Gage settled his arm protectively around my waist. "Speak your peace but at a distance. And do it quickly," he added as gust of wind whipped down Charlotte Street, ruffling the tendrils of hair which had curled so artfully around my face earlier in the evening and now threatened to come unmoored from their pins beneath my bonnet.

"Who did ye tell?"

"Who did we tell what?" Gage countered.

"Who did ye tell aboot my past?" Bonnie Brock growled in his deep Scottish brogue.

I frowned, sharing a look of confusion with my husband, neither of us having expected to be accused of anything. But it was evident that Bonnie Brock was perfectly serious, and one look at Stumps and Locke told me they were equally furious.

"Is this about that book?" Gage replied.

It was the wrong thing to say. Bonnie Brock's nostrils flared, and Stumps and Locke each took another step toward us, their muscles tensing as if in preparation for doing violence. My breath tightened in my lungs, and I had to resist the impulse to back away, to turn and run.

"*Who* did ye tell?" Bonnie Brock's voice crackled like a whip.

Gage stepped in front of me, holding out his arms to ward off both henchmen. "Now, wait one minute! We don't have anything to do with that book, if that's what you're insinuating. Neither of us has told anyone *anything* about you or your past. Why would we?"

"Why, indeed?" the hardened criminal drawled, not believing us.

Gage lowered his arms, perhaps realizing they would do little to ward off any impending blow. He would be better served to lower his center of gravity and prepare to dodge around their fists to land a punch of his own. Or even better, draw the pistol concealed in his greatcoat pocket.

With that thought, I began to pull the strings of my reticule as unobtrusively as I could. But Bonnie Brock noted the movement, and he knew me too well.

"I wouldna do that, lass."

My fingers stilled as he stared pointedly at the beaded bag which concealed my Hewson percussion pistol. It had been a year since I'd taken to carrying it.

"The last time ye pointed a gun at me, things didna go the way ye hoped." His eyebrows arched, reminding me how swiftly he'd disarmed me and backed me against a wall. "And before ye make the mistake o' thinkin' the distance between us will spare ye, let me disabuse ye of the notion that any o' us is unarmed." He drew aside his greatcoat to reveal his own pistol, and I knew better than to think that was the only weapon he carried. He likely bristled with knives.

I lowered the reticule to my side, inhaling a deep breath to try to settle the quaking in my stomach. Regardless of the assistance he'd given us in our past inquiries, and the tentative friendship that had sprung up between us, Bonnie Brock had also displayed ample evidence of his capability for violence. On more than one occasion he'd made it clear that no matter what had occurred between us in the past, if we crossed or threatened him, or someone he cared about, he would not hesitate to harm or even kill us. There was a reason he succeeded in controlling the largest Edinburgh gang, and despite his Robin Hood–like reputation among the lower classes, it was not because of his compassion.

I had feared that his show of weakness the previous spring when he was poisoned would sour our relationship. It was one of the reasons I'd been so glad Gage and I had departed Edinburgh soon after, giving Bonnie Brock time to regain his strength and salvage his pride. After all, for a man in his position, used to wielding power quickly and sometimes brutally, any sign of weakness could spell death.

But this was different. If he was speaking of the book, then this was an accusation of betrayal. Or perhaps it was all wrapped up together. Either way, if we didn't make him see reason now, we might not live long enough to have the chance.

Straightening my spine, I met his irate glare. "We don't have anything to do with that book, Brock," I stated evenly, reminding him he'd urged me to call him thus the last time we'd spoken, hoping the intimacy it implied would pierce through his haze of fury. "We hadn't even heard about it until our return to the city a week ago." My lips pursed, allowing some of my own aggravation to shine through. "If we had, do you honestly think we would have permitted the offensive insinuations the book made about *us*?"

This seemed to give him pause, but only for a moment. "I dinna ken. Maybe ye were betrayed as well."

I shook my head at the irrationality of this remark. "Then we would be the first to reveal the author for the fraud he is."

Not that it would make a bit of difference. Society often chose to believe what it wished, and the more scandalous the better. Bitterness flooded my mouth, for this was something that at least my sister and her husband used to understand. Now, that didn't appear to be the case.

After a particularly vexing end to our last inquiry and the failure to see real justice done, Gage and I had decided to take a respite from the investigations we often undertook until after the birth of our child, just as Alana and Philip had urged. And yet our return to Edinburgh had still been marred by gossip and speculation. The turn of the new year had seen the publication of the book titled *The King of Grassmarket*, which alleged to tell the true story of the city's most infamous rogue, one Bonnie Brock Kincaid. Many might have viewed the book as merely a continuation of the tendency begun some years earlier in publishing to print rather romanticized histories of notorious criminals. These highly fictionalized accounts had shown to be popular, and novels such as *Paul Clifford* and *Eugene Aram* had been devoured by a public eager for more.

So it was no surprise that Edinburgh had proven to be fertile ground for the publication of the adventures of one of its most intriguing and perhaps mysterious citizens. After all, few people knew where Bonnie Brock had come from or how he'd seized power to build his gang of criminals and amass his wealth. He had preferred to keep it that way.

But for all its similarities to those other novels, there were two notable differences about *The King of Grassmarket*. First and foremost being that Bonnie Brock was still alive and at liberty to move about the city and perpetuate further instances of the crimes the book accredited to him. All of the cutthroat heroes in the other books of this style had been either executed or at least tried for and convicted of their crimes and sentenced to transportation. And secondly, that the author had chosen to use a nom de plume, hiding behind a fictional identity which, thus far, no one had been able to strip away.

Clearly Bonnie Brock was intent on doing so. And deathly earnest about it, if the intensity of his threats to us were any indication.

Outrage surged through me at the affront of him believing we would have betrayed his secrets so easily. "Truthfully, we questioned whether *you* might be the author. After all, infamous or not, your reputation seems to have been enhanced, and what better way to control the narrative of your life." I narrowed my eyes. "Not to mention the fact that I suspect you find it devilishly funny to watch all of Edinburgh speculate on whether *you* might be the true father of my child."

Not only was it insulting for the book to insinuate there had been any sort of relationship between Bonnie Brock and myself—or rather the character Lady Dalby, a thinly veiled allusion to me—but the fact that it purported to question my child's paternity was both outrageous and completely preposterous. I would never have been unfaithful to Gage. Not to mention the fact that I had last seen Bonnie Brock in early May, while the baby had been conceived in July on Dartmoor in southern England, four hundred fifty miles away. Thus making the rumor impossible.

"I dinna need my reputation enhanced," he snarled, striding yet another step closer so he was almost level with Gage. "Nor do I want the attention." He scoffed. "As if bein' followed aboot by newspapermen and pursued by a flock o' foolish ladies is beneficial to my business."

I wasn't surprised to hear the latter, for two days prior Bree, my maid, had pointed out the column placed by "a certain lady" in the *Caledonian Mercury* inviting Bonnie Brock to visit her one night. It was so absurd that it was almost laughable.

"And noo Maclean's sniffin' around again." He turned his head to scowl blackly at Gage, as if he could be blamed for Sergeant Maclean, our friend with the Edinburgh City Police, doing his job. However, he spared no sympathy for the difficulties this book about *him* had caused *us*. "I dinna have anythin' to do wi' that pack o' lies!"

"Except it's not all lies," I ventured to say, knowing it would earn me further ire. "Otherwise, you wouldn't be so determined to figure out how the author learned about your past."

"What of some of your exploits it describes?" Gage challenged. "The thefts. The body snatching. The time you broke out of jail. Were any of those true, too? Because we knew nothing of those. Certainly not in such detail."

Bonnie Brock's gaze slid sideways to meet Locke's before he admitted begrudgingly, "Some o' 'em."

The entire book was a disquieting swirl of fact and fiction, but too many of the more obscure particulars were true for us to believe they'd been cobbled together from what little was publicly known about Bonnie Brock.

"You've read it, then?" he asked.

Gage's expression turned wry. "Once we heard about the characters Lady Dalby and her charming partner, Mr. Gale, and the foul assertions made about them, we could hardly ignore it."

For not only had the book called my child's parentage into question, but it had also alleged that our interactions with Bonnie Brock had not been entirely law-abiding, or in the public's best interest.

"Then who do *you* think wrote it?"

Gage shook his head. "We don't know. Surely, you know better than we do who's been privy to all the particulars about your life." His gaze shifted to Stumps, who didn't seem to appreciate his making even this subtle accusation. The ruffian lifted his broad hands, cracking his knuckles loudly.

"It's no' Stumps or Locke," Bonnie Brock replied. "Or Maggie." His sister. His eyes scrutinized Gage's impeccably dressed figure.

My husband scowled. "We already told you it wasn't us. Now, are you going to let us pass?" He stretched his hand back toward me, pulling my arm through the loop made by his. "I'd like to escort my expectant wife home before she takes a chill. Or shall we call for help when this carriage approaching drives by?"

True to his threat, the clatter of wheels against the cobblestones could be heard in the near distance. It would be a matter of seconds before the carriage was upon us.

Bonnie Brock continued to glare at us for a few more heartbeats. Long enough to make me wonder if he truly did intend to harm us. But at the last moment before the carriage swept around the corner of Albyn Place, he relented with a grunt and a nod. He pivoted to the side, melting back into the shadows. "You'd better be tellin' the truth," he threatened as Gage urged me forward. "For if I find oot you've lied . . ." He left his words dangling, the implied threat worse than anything he could say.

I turned my head to meet his hard gaze as we passed.

"We're even noo, remember," he mocked. "I owe ye nothin'."

I struggled not to react, especially knowing I'd forfeited the last favor he'd thought he owed me to his sister, Maggie, before we departed on our honeymoon. After all, finding the pocket watch that had wreaked such havoc in his family, and set off the chain of events that had altered the direction of his life, had been more about saving the residents of Edinburgh from the mayhem that seemed to follow in the watch's wake than protecting him. In the past, Bonnie Brock's strict adherence to the rule of quid pro quo had initially seemed beneficial but then had proven to cause us more trouble than it was worth. I hadn't wanted to leave the city, not knowing when I would return, and leave Bonnie Brock feeling indebted to me. I'd decided it might be dangerous to hold such a thing over him for so long, but perhaps I'd been wrong.

Gage and I strolled quickly up Charlotte Street, and I pressed close to his side, both for reassurance and for warmth. We approached the patisserie at the corner which, even at this hour, scented the air with the smell of sweet breads and puff pastries. In the week since our return, I had already become well acquainted with the owners, Monsieur and Madame Lejeune, for I could not seem to pass their shop without stopping inside for a macaron, a profiterole, or a mattentaart. Even now, after eating too much salmon mousse and roast pheasant at dinner, my mouth still watered as we hurried past.

As we turned the corner, I risked a glance behind us, and finding that neither Bonnie Brock nor his lieutenants seemed to have followed us, I breathed a sigh of relief. The lamp outside the door of our town house was lit in anticipation of our return, a halo forming around it in the mist. Gage hastened us across the street toward the welcome sight. But I could not move as swiftly as him in my condition, and when I clutched my left side, feeling a stitch, he checked his pace.

"Well, I hadn't expected that," I murmured, breaking the tense silence once I'd caught my breath.

"Perhaps we should have."

I looked up to find his brow furrowed in frustration, part of which I knew was directed at himself for not anticipating such an action on Bonnie Brock's part.

"Maybe," I conceded as we leapt over the foul ooze at the edge of the gutter. "After all, we know how secretive he is about his past. But really, how could he think we were the authors, or the informants, when the book contains such foul insinuations about us?"

"He's very angry. And that anger is making him lash out blindly and perhaps recklessly." He pulled us to a stop beneath a streetlamp just steps from our door, turning me to look at him. "Kiera, I don't want you speaking with him alone."

"You don't have to tell *me*. Not that I trusted him before, but I certainly don't trust him now." I nodded back in the direction we'd come. "Not after that confrontation."

Though I strove to deny it, I still felt shaken from the encounter. I'd witnessed Bonnie Brock's temper in the past, but never like this. Never with the complete absence of any of his usual sense of humor. Never when I wasn't certain of his control. In the past, his actions and emotions had always been measured and deliberate. This time, he'd seemed one false word or one false move from snapping. And the glimmer of leniency, of even the indulgence he'd seemed to extend toward me, had all but vanished.

Gage's pale blue eyes softened with understanding. He wrapped his arm around my waist, guiding me toward the door as I leaned my head against his shoulder. "One thing is for sure. He's not going to rest until he discovers who betrayed him." He turned his head to stare beyond the brim of my bonnet as we climbed the steps. "I just hope for their sake it was worth it, because men like Kincaid believe justice is dispensed by the end of a knife, not the word of the court."

Given the results of our last inquiry, it was difficult to argue that Bonnie Brock was entirely wrong. That being said, I wasn't about to abandon the rule of law. "Then maybe we should be trying to find who betrayed him before he does. After all, we have a bone to pick with the author as well."

Gage's reply was interrupted by the opening of our town house door. Our butler, Jeffers, stood on the other side, waiting to greet us and take our outer garments. It wasn't until we'd both changed out of our evening attire, with the assistance of our maid and valet, and we were settled in bed that he could answer.

"Perhaps you're right," he said, pulling the cornflower blue and ivory counterpane over his legs. However, his voice was cautious. "But we'll need to do so without Kincaid finding out."

I arched my toes toward the warmth generated by the heated bricks swaddled in cloth and tucked into the bottom of our bed. "You don't think he already expects it?"

From the surprised look Gage cast my way, it was obvious he hadn't considered such a possibility.

My muscles began to relax as the warmth seeped into them, and I sank deeper into the pillows. "He knows we're inquiry agents. And incurably incapable of leaving a question unanswered."

"Then you think tonight's confrontation was about more than just finding out whether we were the snitchers?"

My lips curled at his use of street slang.

"That he *hopes* we'll begin an inquiry?"

I shrugged. "It makes sense." It also might explain why the altercation had been so menacing, lacking any of his usual wit and finesse. Maybe he'd sought to manipulate us into helping him, even unwittingly, with his ferocity.

It was possible I was deluding myself with such thoughts, but I found myself comforted by them nonetheless. I didn't want to believe that Bonnie Brock would harm me or mortally injure Gage. I didn't want to believe that the scrap of fondness for the criminal which had taken root inside me went unreciprocated.

Gage crossed his arms over his chest, grudging respect twisting his lips as he called the crafty rogue a rather unsavory name.

"I'll take that as a yes?" I asked, smothering a smile at his rancor.

He huffed a sigh. "Yes. But mainly because we might be the only ones who can save the fool from the end of Kincaid's blade."

I hoped we were equal to the task. Otherwise, we might find ourselves pitted with the law directly against Bonnie Brock Kincaid, and I was confident we wouldn't like *those* consequences.

CHAPTER 1

Normally a visit to the Theatre Royal was a pleasure, particularly when my brother-in-law, the Earl of Cromarty, granted us the use of his private box. Gage and I could settle into the seats deeper inside with our hands clasped together and enjoy the play, shielded from some of the prying eyes of society by the swathes of red drapery. Whether the performance was Shakespeare or an adaptation of Sir Walter Scott's novels, there was always something of artistic merit to appreciate.

But this was no normal visit, and no normal play.

For perhaps the dozenth time since asking to use their private box the day before, I wished we could have found a way to discourage Alana and Philip from accompanying us. Though in the past the unflinching support of my sister and her husband had been a bolster to me, lately it had become a burden.

No, that wasn't quite right. I would always be grateful for

their love and care through all the difficulties of my scandalous past. That would never change. Rather their attitudes of mind toward it had. While in public they still displayed their unwavering support, in private their impatience had begun to show.

"What is the world coming to?" Alana grumbled as we entered the box. "A fortnight ago Philip and I came here to see *A Winter's Tale* and now we're here to view this . . ." she gestured with her playbill ". . . drivel." She sank into her chair, allowing her white fur boa to drape elegantly around her shoulders. Her lavender gown was the latest in fashion, with a wide flounced sleeve, a matching ribbon stomacher, and round bows marching down the skirt in rows and across the shoulders. Her chestnut hair, two shades lighter than my own, was dressed high on her head in braided loops and accented with a spray of flowers.

Meanwhile, I'd been forced to alter an older gown of azure blue to accommodate my ever-expanding waistline. I made no complaint. My maid, Bree, and the seamstress I'd hired had done a marvelous job. I had never been vain about my appearance or paid particular attention to what was fashionable. Although I admitted to a faint twinge of uncertainty seeing how puffy my face looked in the mirror in the morning, and I was growing tired of how awkward I now felt in my own body.

Gage helped me into my chair before sitting beside me, looking as astoundingly handsome as ever in his dark evening attire. The artfully tousled curls of his golden hair glinted in the light of the wall sconces, accenting his healthy bronzed complexion and finely sculpted cheekbones. "Yes, well, we're not here to judge the quality," he replied to Alana's comment. "Merely the content."

She glanced over her shoulder at Gage and narrowed her eyes in scrutiny, perhaps wondering, as I was, whether he was growing just as irritated with their carping. "We're well aware that you and Kiera had no control over the publication of *that book* or the production of this play," she retorted, turning back toward the stage. She twitched her shoulders, adjusting her posture. "Though I'm sure you realize you would never have been at risk to be included had you not had dealings with that man."

I rolled my eyes, not caring if Philip or Alana saw me. Of course we knew it. And if we hadn't, she'd already reminded us of it at least three times.

As if recognizing this, Philip reached across to rest his hand over Alana's in her lap. "They know, darling. Let's not rub salt in the wound."

Her shoulders tensed and she arched her chin in the air, but she listened to her husband and controlled her tongue.

I knew Alana was only worried about me. Her biting comments had begun after I'd been injured from a near tumble down a flight of stairs during our last murderous inquiry. While we'd made up from our quarrel, her feathers were still ruffled, particularly by this latest development—the adaptation of *The King of Grassmarket* into a play.

And the Theatre Royal's rendition wasn't the only one. With the book's rampant popularity, theaters all across Edinburgh—perhaps all across Scotland and even into England—had taken notice. Soon each theater's resident playwrights were racing to produce a script and compose music to accompany the flash songs in thieves' cant cleverly alluded to in the pages of the book. Versions of *The King of Grassmarket* were already being staged at the Adelphi, the Grand, and at least half a dozen minor theaters and penny gaffs for the working classes. In fact, while we waited for the curtain to rise at the Theatre Royal, Bree and Anderley—our intrepid and capable lady's maid and valet—were on their way to one of the more respectable minor establishments to view another version of the play.

I cast a glance past Gage's shoulder at the audience packing the theater and then turned away, doing my best to ignore the hundreds of eyes in the other boxes eagerly fastened on us, undoubtedly whispering about our appearance. My fingers plucked at the embroidery adorning the skirt of my gown, anxious for the performance to begin. Then it would at least be easier to pretend I wasn't being sliced to ribbons by vicious gossip.

Gage reached over to still my hand, threading his fingers through mine. "You've faced worse," he murmured in encouragement.

I inhaled a deep breath, releasing some of the tension coursing through me. "I have."

"And then you were alone. At least, this time, we're together."

I smiled softly. "Yes. You're right."

His pale blue eyes held mine steadily as he lifted my hand and pressed his lips to the satin of my glove. I could feel the warmth of his breath even through the fabric.

As the orchestra began to tune their instruments, my attention shifted back to the stage, though I kept Gage's hand clutched in mine. Nerves fluttered in my stomach, and I knew a moment's uneasiness about precisely what sort of story we were about to see depicted. But seconds after the curtain rose, everything fell away, and I became absorbed in the play.

It unfolded in three acts, the first focusing on Brock Kincaid's childhood. It opened with his birth and the abandonment of his father—a shadowy figure not named in either the book or the play, but implied to be from the upper class. A musical number sped us through the relatively happy years of Brock's childhood, and the multiple lovers and protectors his mother took to support them, as well as the birth of his half sister, Maggie. Though the play did not shy away from the fact that his mother had essentially been a *chère-amie*, or kept woman, it portrayed her with much more sympathy than the book. This worked to great effect, making her death scene far more emotional and devastating to Brock, who at thirteen years old was made an orphan with a three-year-old sister to care for. Tears flecked my eyelashes at the fear and anguish of the characters.

The first act ended with the betrayal Gage and I had learned about the previous May. Brock's unscrupulous neighbor, Angus Douglas, had maneuvered to have him wrongfully imprisoned for stealing a costly pocket watch he coveted. A pocket watch that rightfully belonged to Brock. Brock was thrown into jail and Maggie was taken in by the Douglases, who in their benevolence forced the young girl to perform the meanest of chores in their inn and sleep in the frigid attic, rousing the audience's anger and affront at such an injustice.

When the curtain fell after the first act, I knew I would be hard-pressed to find a single member of the audience who had not softened toward Brock. The playwright and the young actor playing the notorious criminal had managed to squirrel their way into the audience's hearts in a way that even the book's author hadn't been able to. So much so that from the moment the adult actor playing Brock strode onto the stage at the start of the second act, our allegiance remained unswayed despite the fact that he was noticeably harder and more intense, but also possessed of his dashing persona.

Five years had passed, and Bonnie Brock had adopted his infamous sobriquet, been released from jail, collected his sister, and begun to build his criminal gang, using the contacts and skills he'd learned while imprisoned. I found it interesting that neither the book nor the play attempted to speculate on how exactly he'd come by his nickname, only that it had emerged during his first stint in jail. The closest the book came to addressing it was the inclusion of a scene where Brock had viciously wounded a man for daring to deride him for it. The play had wisely chosen to omit that.

Just as they had omitted almost any mention of the body snatching undertaken by Brock and his gang. At the start of his criminal career, stealing bodies from the graveyards in and around Edinburgh to sell to the anatomy schools had been some of his most lucrative trade. Theft, housebreaking, illegal whisky distilling, and smuggling had initially been smaller enterprises, though they were now the gang's predominant sources of income.

The playwright was plainly attuned to the mood of the people and understood how unpopular resurrectionists had become, particularly given the crimes perpetrated in this very city three years prior by Burke and Hare—body snatchers turned murderers. Illegal whisky distilling, on the other hand, was practically viewed by the Scottish as a patriotic duty given the unpopular prohibition of all but the largest of Scottish stills from making whisky in 1814. Bonnie Brock's gang's ability to smuggle whisky from the illegal Highland distillers down into Edinburgh and other parts of Scotland had been part of what cemented his reputation as a Robin Hood–type figure.

That and his generosity to the lower classes in Old Town and his care for widows and children who would otherwise go without. I'd heard tell that none of his employees need fear for their family should they be killed or sent to jail, for Brock made sure they were cared for. Sergeant Maclean of the Edinburgh City Police had long complained that even when they were able to arrest him, they were never able to keep Bonnie Brock locked up for long. The citizens of Edinburgh would muddy the evidence against him or send someone else to take his place in the blame. They didn't want Brock brought to justice, for it was a justice they didn't believe in.

However, true or not, a jail scene in the second act proved to be one of the most exciting parts of the play. Where normally the action of the scene was set in one room or space, the stage had been divided into the cross-section of a jail, with compartments for four cells, two up and two down. At one climactic moment, Brock escaped from his shackles and scampered toward the fireplace, where he had earlier been seen scraping away at the brickwork. He dislodged the bars blocking the chimney flue and then clambered inside, disappearing from the audience's view, only to emerge from a hole opening in the floor of the cell above. From this chamber, he busted through the door and then climbed out the window to emerge on the flat roof of the jail.

But one trip through this course of obstacles was not enough. Brock declared he'd forgotten his blanket, and my heart lodged in my throat as he proceeded to retrace his steps in reverse back to his original jail cell. He collected his blanket and then made the trek for a third time, to the audience's gasps and exclamations. When he returned to the roof, he ripped the blanket into strips, tied them together, and climbed down the side of the building to freedom.

While impressed with the entire performance, including the novel staging, I was also disheartened. This was no slapdash melodrama. It was a rip-roarious success. And likely to run for weeks if not months on end. The book had already been popular, but this play would launch it to even greater heights.

When the second act ended, I wanted nothing more than to remain in Philip's private box, such were the nerves swarming inside me. The third act would be where the thinly veiled characters portraying Gage and me would make their entrance. But at just three weeks shy of the baby's projected birth date, I could not avoid the ladies' retiring room a moment longer. Especially not when the imp inside me had been pummeling my insides for the past half hour. Anticipating my dilemma, Gage escorted me from the box before the curtain had even fallen.

Once I was in a more comfortable condition, and my every thought wasn't focused on making it to the retiring room before I embarrassed myself, I could hear the murmured conversations of the women congregating on the other side of my private partition. Some were cooing over how dashing Bonnie Brock seemed, though whether they were talking about the man himself or the actor who was playing him, I couldn't tell. They didn't seem to differentiate. Just as they didn't seem to fully grasp the fictional aspects of it being a scripted play and not reality.

"Who do you think his father is?" one lady asked.

"I heard he's some member of royalty," her friend answered.

"Lady Jersey told me he's a foreign dignitary," a third woman added.

I rolled my eyes, suspecting Lady Jersey knew little better than anyone else, though she would never admit it. The next few comments were lost to the rustling and resettling of my gown, but as I reached for the door handle I clearly heard the next question.

"Do you think it's true, then? Was Lady Darby his lover?"

I stilled, not so much surprised to hear they were gossiping about such a thing as that I was trapped here, forced to listen to it.

The ladies continued to speak about me using my courtesy title. I'd long since ceased requesting acquaintances to call me Mrs. Gage instead, for such an appeal merely baffled society. They couldn't understand why I would willingly relinquish the title granted to me by marrying my first husband—Sir Anthony Darby—that I was permitted to continue to use by courtesy, if not right, when I'd wed my lower-ranked second husband. But then most of them did not fully grasp what I'd suffered during my first marriage, and I was not going to illuminate them.

"Why would he be interested in a woman like Lady Darby?" Scorn dripped from the second lady's voice, which I now recognized belonged to Lady Wilmot. I was more surprised by her presence in Edinburgh than her disparaging opinion of me. After all, she was close friends with Lady Felicity, the woman

Gage's father had chosen for his son's bride. That Gage had possessed a different opinion and chosen me instead had been a source of heated contention between father and son for months following our nuptials.

"Men must see *something* in her," her companion declared, before adding wryly, "Sebastian Gage married her, after all. And we all know his taste is unassailable."

I could practically see Lady Wilmot's eyes narrowing at this taunting insult to her and Lady Felicity.

"She's dangerous," the first woman supplied confidently, as if she knew of what she spoke. "Unpredictable. Ghoulish even. Men like to dabble in that sort of thing."

Having heard enough, I decided it was past time to make myself known. Giving my skirts one last twitch, I stepped into the larger area of the retiring room just as Lady Wilmot responded.

"I suppose that could explain it. Though I do hope Mr. Gage won't live to regret his weakness." The glint in her eyes as she scrutinized herself in one of the long mirrors made it perfectly evident that she hoped that very thing.

I nodded to the woman passing by me to enter the partition I'd vacated. That older lady's eyes dipped to somewhere near the level of our feet, but I kept my polite smile firmly affixed. Then I lifted my gaze to boldly meet Lady Wilmot's in the reflection of the looking glass, refusing to be cowed. Her expression revealed not an iota of remorse, though the first lady who had spoken—a simpering blonde—gasped and scampered farther across the room as if she might be worried I would lash out at her.

I ignored them all, crossing to the washbasin and murmuring my thanks to the attendant, who smiled shyly at me as she poured the water from an ewer slowly over my hands, so as not to splash the costly fabric of my gown. This was easier said than done when one looked like one had swallowed a large melon. Out of the corner of my eye I saw Lady Wilmot pivot as if ready to do battle. I'd already apprehended that there was nothing to be gained from confronting her, but neither was I going to run away.

I dried my hands on the proffered towel and stepped closer to one of the mirrors, adjusting the rolls of curls at my temples before turning to depart. All this was done while failing to even acknowledge the presence of Lady Wilmot and her friends, a move which was certain to exasperate her. And true to expectation, she stepped forward just as I was within six feet of the door.

Unfortunately for her, my cousin Morven chose that moment to enter the retiring room. At the sight of me, she gave an exclamation of pleasure. "Kiera!" She embraced me, allowing one arm to linger around my neck and the other against my stomach. "Oh, my dearest." She gave a fond shake of her head. "How much longer now?"

I exhaled a deep breath. "Dr. Fenwick says at least three weeks."

"And each one of those will feel like a year," she commiserated, already having three children of her own. "Though I vastly preferred the sensation of being akin to Humpty Dumpty than the first two months of making friends with the chamber pot."

My lips quirked. "True." I'd endured my share of queasiness at the beginning, although nothing compared to my poor sister, who'd suffered for nine torturous months with each of her children.

"I'm afraid that's the travail of being in the family way." Her gaze flicked over my shoulder. "You begin your journey hunched over a pot in London and end it waddling across Edinburgh." That this statement had been made for Lady Wilmot's benefit was obvious; otherwise, she would never have emphasized the location of the conception. The fact that it had been in Dartmoor and not London was beside the point. Both were hundreds of miles from Edinburgh and Bonnie Brock Kincaid.

"Are you here with Alana and Philip?" Morven asked, threading my arm through hers and pulling me toward the door before I could answer. "I'll accompany you to their box. I haven't yet had a chance to respond to your sister's invitation to dine tomorrow evening."

An impromptu dinner party she'd insisted on arranging for my and Gage's benefit, regardless of my feelings on the matter.

"Did I divine that situation correctly?" she leaned closer to murmur, her dark hair brushing my shoulder. "Lady Wilmot and her companions appeared bent on making trouble."

"Yes, thank you."

We paused before Gage, so that he and Morven could exchange greetings, and then he fell into step behind us as we made our way down the corridor toward Philip's private box.

"Morven," I murmured, waiting for her to glance at me. "Could you not mention Lady Wilmot to Alana?"

Morven's topaz eyes turned shrewd, deducing why I wished to keep it from her. "I know how much she's always hated seeing you taunted and belittled."

"Yes, but that's no longer her responsibility."

Morven's smile turned gently reproving. "Kiera, we never outgrow an obligation to defend our family. You, of all people, know this."

I sighed, conceding her point. "Yes, but you can't deny that Alana takes greater offense than most." I scowled. "And she'll only see it as another stick to beat me with."

We reached our destination before Morven could reply, but I trusted she would abide by my wishes. She might be closer in age to Alana—after all, they'd debuted together—but they had never deliberately allied against me. Perhaps because Morven also knew what it was like to be the youngest child. Her two older brothers had been protective of her throughout their child-hood and, at times, still were.

I looked on as the two of them embraced and then teased each other mercilessly, as they'd always done. They tweaked each other's curls and laughed over something one of their children had said.

Perhaps feeling they were leaving me out of the discussion, Morven turned to draw me closer. "Well, I'm glad to see Kiera looking so radiant. I'm sure I was never so in the pink when I was entering the final weeks of my confinements." She smiled approvingly at Gage. "You must be taking good care of her."

"Yes, but I do wish she would take it easier," Alana inter-jected. "There's no reason to go traipsing about town on walks as she does. Not with the cholera in the air."

I frowned. "I hardly think a stroll through the Queen Street Gardens or a trip to the theater would be considered 'traipsing about town.'" Particularly as those gardens were located less than a block from our town house. "In any case, Dr. Fenwick said physical activity is good for me and the babe. That there is no reason to fear catching the disease in a place like Queen Street, so long as I'm temperate and consume the correct diet."

Alana's mouth pursed. "Yes, well, of course I esteem Dr. Fenwick. He attended at the birth of my wee Jamie."

And likely saved Alana's life after a fraught and difficult de-livery. Dr. Fenwick wasn't considered one of Edinburgh's finest physician accoucheurs without good reason, after all.

"But that doesn't mean he knows everything."

I bit my tongue, holding back an acerbic response. I knew Alana was merely apprehensive for me, especially after the trials she'd endured bringing her last two children into the world. It was the manner in which she was expressing those concerns that rubbed me raw. I'd grown tired of her brusque and disdainful comments, and if not for the flicker of the lights signaling the beginning of the third act, I might not have restrained myself.

But my nerves began to flutter in my stomach, recalling me to my dread of what was to come. I offered Morven a distracted farewell, then gripped Gage's hand tightly in mine as the murmur of voices throughout the theater softened and the curtain began to rise.

CHAPTER 2

When the actress playing Lady Dalby strode onto the stage, I found myself holding my breath. Despite all the thrilling events that had come before—chases across rooftops, daggers drawn at a whisky drop, fisticuffs, and even a scene where Bonnie Brock and his men had eluded capture by wearing women's clothing—this was the moment I was most anxious about. As the scene played out, I could feel some of the audience members in the boxes across the theater dividing their attention between watching me and watching the play. Thus I was determined to display no discernible reaction.

I was relieved to discover that the actress sported flaming red hair—nothing like my own more muted chestnut tresses. She also spoke with a slight Scottish brogue—one which I had never possessed. Mr. Gale, likewise, looked unlike Gage, with dark hair and a sartorial style that was far more ostentatious than my husband would ever adopt. I assumed that once again the theater was wisely observing their bottom line, eager to avoid any potential defamation lawsuits we might bring against the play.

Lady Dalby brazenly waltzed into Grassmarket seeking Bonnie Brock and demanding he answer her questions about his involvement with an investigation she and Mr. Gale were conducting. I found it curious that both the author and playwright had made this error, that neither knew that Bonnie Brock and I had first met when he had abducted me in my carriage. An event they would surely have made use of had they known. But that they did know our meeting had ended with the notorious criminal asking for my help in locating his sister, Maggie, who for all intents and purposes had been kidnapped.

In the course of lending Bonnie Brock our assistance, the play affectingly showed Bonnie Brock falling in love with Lady Dalby, while her affections were torn between the two very different men. In the end, once Maggie is saved, it's clear Lady Dalby's heart is inclined toward the criminal. But having realized he cannot protect her no matter how hard he might try, Bonnie Brock chooses not to fight for her and instead sends her away with Mr. Gale.

Out of the corner of my eye I could see Gage scowling, not so much at the play as the sounds of a woman weeping in one of the boxes near ours. A swift glance around the theater showed me she wasn't the only person moved. Several ladies dabbed at their eyes with their handkerchiefs. If nothing else, the Theatre Royal's rendition of Bonnie Brock's story had cemented him in the minds of many as some sort of dashing and roguish tragic hero. A fact that Gage was obviously displeased by.

For my own part, I felt conflicted as I allowed Gage to escort me from the box after the play ended. On the one hand, this version of the story had downplayed some of the more scandalous implications made about our relationships with Bonnie

Brock, but on the other, it had also left out many of the more dangerous and unsavory truths about the criminal and his gang of cutthroats. Neither the book nor this play was a true representation of Bonnie Brock or his life, and within that fiction lay the seeds of trouble.

I schooled my features into an expression of bland courtesy as we approached the lobby of the theater, where the mass of society streaming from their boxes congregated to wait for their carriages. Recognizing the need for Gage to remain by my side, Philip peeled off to collect our party's wrappings. But even with my husband and sister flanking me, they could not shield me from the slings and arrows of whispered speculation and disapproving glares.

I couldn't help but roll my eyes at one such matron, who had been rather infamous in her younger days for her number of affaires de coeur. It was all quite ridiculous how society believed what it wished to and conveniently forgot what it did not. If I'd learned anything from my time spent with the Duchess of Bowmont, it was that society would write your narrative unless you refused to let them. While my feelings about the duchess and her family were conflicted after the murder investigation we'd conducted at their estate in January, I had to agree she knew how to weather a scandal and turn it to one's advantage.

My gaze snagged on the form of a man standing across the lobby. I pulled Gage and Alana to a stop as the man passed behind a pillar, trying to locate him again, wondering if my eyes deceived me. My nerves tightened at the possibility that he might be here, that I'd practically conjured him with my thoughts of his mother, and yet Lord Henry had not sought us out as he'd promised to do. As he promised to do *months* ago.

"What is it?" Gage murmured in alarm.

"I thought I saw . . ." My words trailed away as I strained my neck, finally catching another glimpse of the man. But though his hair was the same auburn hue, he wasn't the duchess's son. "I thought I saw Lord Henry Kerr," I finished flatly, struggling to hide my disappointment and irritation.

"Returned from escorting his brother abroad," Gage replied sharply beneath his breath, leaving out the words so evident in the glint of his eyes. His brother the murderer. For the Duke of Bowmont had exerted his privilege to have the charges against his fourth acknowledged son dismissed while Lord John Kerr was spirited away rather than face the consequences. It was true there had been extenuating circumstances behind the murder—ones that might have made the homicide defensible—but Lord John's failure to appear at the magistrate's hearing had soured both my and Gage's belief in justice.

Yet it wasn't these facts that made me so anxious about seeing Lord Henry. Rather it was the secret I'd uncovered about him just hours before he'd disappeared to escort his brother from Scotland. A secret he had begged me to allow him to reveal to Gage, swearing to do so as soon as our inquiry was solved. That he had left me a note of apology, pleading for my forgiveness and promising to visit us in Edinburgh as soon as Lord John was settled abroad, had not assuaged my irritation. Every day that passed without his arrival made my anger burn hotter. For I had now found myself in an impossible situation, and all because of him.

"Yes," I murmured fretfully, already anticipating how furious my husband was going to be when he learned Lord Henry was his half brother and that I had known this fact now for nearly two months.

Gage's gaze scrutinized my features in concern, driving the dagger of guilt even deeper. "Surely you're not concerned for his safety?"

"No, I . . ." But I couldn't think how to finish my sentence.

"Because given his motives for committing murder in the

first place, I doubt Lord John would harm any member of his family."

"Well, let's not discuss that here," Alana snapped, impelling us forward again and saving me from making another bumbling response.

But we only managed to take two more steps before we were accosted by a gentleman reeking of cheroots. I recognized his smug dissipated countenance from an investigation we had conducted a year before. I hadn't liked him then, and time had not improved my impression of him.

"Lady *Dalby*," Lord Kirkcowan drawled. "Er . . . excuse me." He flashed me a nasty smile. "Slip of the tongue, Lady Darby. Fancy meeting you here." His eyes cut toward Gage. "And with your faithful husband beside you." The way he said it made it sound like Gage was some sort of hound. Or perhaps he meant to imply that I was faithless. Whatever the case, I was not going to be cowed by such an odious man.

"Good evening, my lord," I said before Alana could speak for me. I glanced over his shoulders, pretending to search. "But where is your delightful wife? I should so like to greet her." Though I had not been in Edinburgh the previous autumn when it was aghast with whispers that Lady Kirkcowan had finally summoned the courage to leave her feckless husband, gossip traveled far and wide in upper-class circles.

Not taken in by my guileless smile, he narrowed his eyes. "I'm afraid she's at our country home."

This was a lie, for I also knew that his estate was mortgaged to the hilt. Anything of value that had not been directly entailed had been sold to pay his gambling debts. No, Lady Kirkcowan had returned to her father's house with their three children, likely with naught but their clothes and the jewels I had contrived to have stolen before privately returning them to her a year ago so that she would not be destitute when Lord Kirkcowan lost their remaining property on the turn of a card. She had correctly surmised that her husband would not pursue them or attempt to retain custody of their children, especially given the fact that he had no money to pay for a nanny or governess to look after them.

"Then I shall have to write to her."

He could make no reply to this without revealing his falsehood, so his gaze shifted to Gage, his mouth twisting cruelly. "And what did you think of the play? I found it illuminating, myself."

But Gage was not to be goaded either. His features exhibited nothing but the bland insouciance he often adopted in public, and he replied in a bold, clear voice for the benefit of those people surrounding us who were not making any effort to hide the fact that they were eager to hear his answer. "Yes, I suppose in terms of the disposition, habits, and moral character of a criminal there was much to be gleaned. And the performance was quite entertaining, even if a great deal of it was purely fictitious. But I can't help but wonder if such a play isn't a trifle irresponsible."

"Irresponsible?" one gentleman who had been listening in leaned closer to ask. "How do you mean?"

Gage turned to address him calmly. "Well, as I understand it, versions of *The King of Grassmarket* are being performed in theaters all over the city, even minor revues and penny gaffs." He glanced about him, showing that he was conscious of his entire audience. "And while I doubt there are many here who would take the words to heart, I fear that those who are impressionable might be swayed to think Bonnie Brock Kincaid's actions heroic and not criminal, and so be inspired to follow the same path."

That this had been true before the publication of the book and the staging of the plays, albeit to a lesser degree, I knew for a fact. But if the versions performed at the minor theaters were in any way similar to this one, that influence could broaden.

Impressionable boys and frustrated young men who might otherwise have eschewed such unlawful behavior might decide theft was not so terrible an action. That if Bonnie Brock and his men committed such acts and were lauded for it, then why shouldn't they be also?

I could tell I wasn't the only one contemplating these thoughts by the gasps and whispers rippling through the crowd. That Gage's intent had been to turn the focus of discussion away from the characters based on us and toward this moral conundrum was obvious, at least to me, though hopefully not to everyone else. Even Alana appeared aghast by the idea.

"Malcolm begged to be allowed to attend the play with us this evening," she confessed as Gage managed to maneuver us through the crowd and closer to the doors where Philip intended to meet us. "And I nearly relented, despite the lateness of the hour." Her nine-year-old son could be very persuasive when he wanted something. "Now I'm glad I didn't."

"Alana, I hardly think a play would compel Malcolm to live a life of crime," I argued. "He's more intelligent than that."

"Is he?" she demanded to know.

I opened my mouth to protest, but the look in her eyes made me stop. The play had been filled with dashing acts of derring-do and thrilling chases, and all had ended—save one—with a night of camaraderie with his mates, gathered inside a pub or around a fire, drinking and singing and laughing. For a young boy who loved to run, leap, climb, and arrange battles with his toy soldiers, such a life must seem grand.

Before I could form a response, Philip appeared, and we were all occupied with donning our coats and wraps against the chill of the March evening. Once Philip's carriage could escape the tangle of traffic in front of the theater, the drive to our house in Albyn Place was short. As we said our good-byes, Gage helped me alight from the carriage and climb the steps to our door.

"Good evening, Jeffers," Gage told our upright and restrained butler as he took his gloves and hat. "I trust you've had a quiet evening."

"For the most part, sir."

We both paused in removing our outer garments, looking to Jeffers in curiosity.

He retrieved a letter from the table behind him, holding it out toward me. "This arrived for Mrs. Gage while you were out."

I slowly reached out to take the missive, though Gage and I could both tell from his expression that he had more to say.

"It was delivered to the servants' entrance by Mr. Locke."

I sighed. One of Bonnie Brock's right-hand men. We hadn't spoken to the inveterate rogue who was causing us so much trouble since he accosted us on the street seven weeks prior. No doubt he'd discovered we'd attended the play at the Theatre Royal and had something to say on the matter.

"Have Bree and Anderley returned yet?" I asked him.

"No, my lady."

I wasn't surprised by this, though my aching back wished differently. "Send them up to the drawing room when they do. And will you have tea brought up," I added, smothering a yawn with my hand.

His shrewd gaze softened. "Of course, my lady."

"Thank you, Jeffers."

Gage pressed a hand to the small of my back, guiding me up the stairs to the drawing room at the front of our town house. A fire had already been laid in the hearth, casting flickering shadows over the wallpaper patterned with delicate yellow twining roses and the sage green and daffodil upholstered furnishings. I sank into the walnut settee, sliding a pillow behind my back to help alleviate some of the pressure.

"The chairs at the theater are not very comfortable, are they?" Gage asked sympathetically.

"They're torture," I confirmed. At least for a woman in my condition. By the end of the play, I'd nearly given up and stood in the back of the box. Only the knowledge that such a move would have been seen by the other audience members as an indication of my agitation had kept me in place.

He sat beside me, urging me to turn and sit forward, and then began to knead my lower back. "Here, darling?"

I groaned in relief. "Yes." For a few moments I ignored Bonnie Brock's letter and gave myself over to the bliss of having my tired, aching muscles rolled and rubbed. "I will tell you one thing," I said, draping my arms around my abdomen. "This child likes music every bit as much as his or her cousins."

"Oh?" Gage murmured as I leaned my head back against his shoulder.

"Every time the orchestra began to play, he started to pummel my insides like he was performing one of those Russian Cossack dances we saw at the Adelphi in London."

He chuckled, his breath warm on my ear.

"*You* can laugh. I'm the one getting my internal organs beaten to a pulp."

He wrapped his arms around me, placing his palms flat on my rounded stomach below mine. "Now, see here, little one," he chastised, pressing lightly into the skin. "Be kind to your mother. I know it must be getting rather tight in there. But you've only got a few more weeks to go. So let's be a good little chap."

As if to protest this, the baby suddenly lashed out with a firm kick. We laughed.

"You're going to have to work on your tone of authority or this baby is going to run roughshod all over you," I teased.

A rap on the doorframe signaled Jeffers's return with the tea tray, and I settled back against the pillow as Gage volunteered to pour out. I paused to examine the seal on Bonnie Brock's letter, noting again that it was stamped with the crest of Clan

Kincaid—a castle with an arm rising out of it and brandishing a sword. The words *This I'll Defend* arched across the bottom. Not for the first time I wondered whether he'd stolen the signet ring that made this mark from the laird of the Kincaid clan or if someone from his mother's family had given it to him.

I broke open the seal and unfolded the missive to reveal the words written in Bonnie Brock's neat hand. As always, he was brief to the point of rudeness, his letters formed with an arrogant slant.

Enjoy the play? We need to talk. Queen Street Gardens. Tomorrow. Sunset. Bring Gage if you must.

I frowned, trading Gage the paper for my cup of tea. I sipped while he perused the contents with a scowl.

"That man is like a canker."

"Yes, and a particularly irksome one, at that."

He dropped the letter on the table. "I wonder if he's seen any of the plays about him."

"I have to assume he has, simply from natural curiosity. After all, the characters based on us only appear in the third act, and *we* couldn't resist discovering for ourselves how we were portrayed."

"True," he conceded.

We could pretend all we liked that we'd attended the play purely as a matter of research—as we still hadn't uncovered who the anonymous author of the book was or who was the source of their information on Bonnie Brock—but the fact of the matter was that plain old curiosity had also been a strong motivating factor. We had also finally convinced the publisher to meet with us the following day, and it behooved us to be armed with as much information as possible before doing so. Not that I anticipated him being willing to share such a closely guarded and lucrative secret, but perhaps he would let something useful slip.

"In truth, I enjoyed the play more than the book," I admitted after taking another sip of tea. "The story arc was much more . . . satisfying."

Gage arched his eyebrows. "That's because there was one."

I turned to gaze into the crackling hearth. "The book was rather a hodgepodge of anecdotes, wasn't it? Some true, some not."

"It was insightful of the playwright to recognize this and shape it into a genuine narrative. That's what made it so much better."

The elements had all been there. They just needed the finesse of a real storyteller to mold them into an elegant curve. The play's narrative had shown that Bonnie Brock's driving desire was to try to regain the security he had known in childhood before his mother had died and he was wrongfully imprisoned. To make himself and, by extension, his family untouchable. That his sister—his only true family—had then been abducted, and he'd required help from outsiders to rescue her, had served as his moment of crisis. So that in the end, he realizes that even though he runs the largest gang in Edinburgh and is arguably one of the city's most powerful men, he still cannot guarantee the safety of those he cares for. Which leads him to give up the woman he loves—Lady Dalby—believing his rival for her affections will be better able to protect her.

It was very affecting, and I couldn't help but wonder if it was made all the more so by the fact it might be true. Everything but the romance between him and Lady Dalby, that was. For while Bonnie Brock held me in some sort of affection, not for one second did I think he considered me his soul mate, as the play would have us believe. Incontrovertibly, in my case, that honor belonged to Gage alone.

"The playwright was also astute enough to leave out most of Bonnie Brock's history of body snatching, recognizing how unpopular such crimes are," Gage continued, unaware of my thoughts. "Especially in this city," he added under his breath, clearly thinking of Burke and Hare, the notorious murderers who had sold no less than sixteen bodies to the local anatomists for dissection. That we had once been attacked in Grassmarket by a mob holding similar suspicions about me because of the scandal surrounding my late first husband must have also entered his thoughts.

Sir Anthony Darby had been one of Britain's most renowned anatomists, as well as sergeant surgeon to the king. When we had wed, he was in the process of writing a definitive anatomy textbook for medical students. What neither my family nor I had known until it was too late was that he had married me almost solely for my talent as a portrait artist. He'd forced me to produce detailed illustrations of his dissections for his book so he wouldn't have to share the credit or the royalties from its sales. Like all men of his field—who were perpetually in want of fresh cadavers—he had been forced to do business with body snatchers. A fact which had made the discovery of my involvement as a gentlewoman with his macabre work even more shocking and scandalous.

"The playwright also avoided falling into that quagmire of corruption the author implied Bonnie Brock was involved in," I said, passing Gage my cup.

"In truth, I wasn't certain how the Theatre Royal would handle that. I expected the minor theaters and penny gaffs to leave it out. No need to muddy the water about who their hero is. But the New Town audience is not as enamored of Kincaid as the rest of Edinburgh. More tea?" he asked, gesturing with my cup.

I shook my head. "I'm just glad the play left out that ridiculous drivel about Lady Dalby and Mr. Gale taking bribes." I exhaled in frustration. "Though I wish it had also left out that ridiculous drivel about a relationship between Lady Dalby and Bonnie Brock."

"Yes," Gage replied tightly. He had leaned forward to place our cups on the tea tray and continued to fidget with the dishes there, keeping his face averted from mine so that I couldn't read his expression. He couldn't be happy about all of the play's romantic insinuations, and the more lurid claims in the book had infuriated him. But he seemed determined not to discuss them.

I knew he didn't blame me, just as I knew he hadn't questioned my faithfulness for even a second. But that didn't mean he wasn't struggling with the repercussions.

I reached out toward him, but before I could speak, he determinedly turned the subject.

"One thing is crystal clear. The author of the book is an amateur. Oh, Nathan Mugdock, whoever he is, can formulate a paragraph well enough, but he doesn't possess the insight or ability to spin his words into a cohesive story."

I sank back, considering what he'd said. "You're right. Even the best nonfiction books are able to do that, not merely recite a list of facts or events." I looked up at him. "Then we've been going about this all wrong. We're not looking for a professional writer but someone inexperienced." I sighed in weary frustration. "Which makes the matter that much harder."

CHAPTER 3

G age touched my hand in commiseration. "To be fair, your idea to compare the writing in *The King of Grassmarket* to that of known authors had merit."

It had also had the added benefit of keeping me safe at home and away from the more cholera-ridden areas of Edinburgh while he ventured out to make inquiries, but I had agreed to such a scheme willingly, so I could hardly complain now.

"I hadn't thought to analyze the structure."

Neither had I, and with all the hours I'd spent poring over other texts and novels, it was something which should have occurred to *me* sooner. Of course, I'd been examining sentence structure and phrasing, not character arcs and themes. "What's done is done," I conceded with as much grace as I could muster. "Now we can hope your efforts have borne fruit."

"And sooner rather than later," he agreed, his gaze dipping to my rounded abdomen. A tender light entered his eyes. "It would be nice to have all this resolved before the birth of our child."

I couldn't argue with that. A gentle smile curled my mouth. One which flattened at his next words.

"Did I tell you I received a letter from my father earlier today?"

The warmth spreading through me abruptly turned to cold. Lord Gage and I didn't have the most congenial of relationships, and while we had seemed to find a new common ground before my and Gage's departure from London in December, my subsequent discoveries at Sunlaws Castle had changed that. "Did he?"

But rather than darkening as I'd anticipated, my husband's brow seemed to lighten. "As you know, I expected a tirade," he told me. "But he was remarkably understanding about the allusion to us in the book."

I blinked in shock. "He was?" A shock I could be excused for feeling, given the amount of contempt my father-in-law had heaped over me in the past for my scandalous reputation.

"He was." One corner of Gage's mouth quirked upward. "I think it helps that he can count."

Meaning that Lord Gage was well aware I hadn't conceived until long after we'd departed Edinburgh. I wasn't certain I was comfortable with my father-in-law contemplating such things, but in this case at least, I was glad of it.

"Then . . . he didn't berate you for your poor choices?" I asked. A familiar refrain from his father.

The corners of his eyes crinkled with amusement. "Well, I wouldn't go so far as that. He is my father, after all. He definitely bemoaned the situation. But he seemed to direct most of his hostility toward the people foolish enough to give any credence to such a tale about the extreme level of our supposed involvement with Bonnie Brock."

I nodded, still feeling bemused by Lord Gage's measured response and my husband's reaction to it. Since I'd met Gage, there had been a significant strain in his relationship with his father. One that I'd gathered had been there almost since birth. But since our time in London, matters had improved. The shadows that lingered in Gage's eyes when he spoke about his father were not so deep, their depths no longer fathomless. His lips no longer constricted into a grimace. I had even seen him smile over an anecdote shared in his letters.

All of which would have made me overjoyed, but for the secret I was keeping from him. I felt the weight of it settle in my gut like a lump of coal—black and fetid and combustible.

Just like dozens of times before, I ordered myself to tell him. I summoned the words to the back of my mouth, but then I couldn't force them out. Instead they sat there, crowded in my throat, choking me.

If only I hadn't promised Lord Henry I would let him tell Gage. If only I'd ignored that promise the moment Lord Henry had departed with his brother. Then I wouldn't be stuck in this impossible situation.

From the moment I'd discovered that Lord Henry was Gage's half brother, I'd known my husband would be tremendously hurt by it. At the time Lord Gage would have slept with the Duchess of Bowmont, conceiving Henry, he would have been wed to Gage's mother. And Emma Gage had been in love with her husband, even though she only saw him for about a fortnight each year, as he was off captaining a ship in the Royal Navy during the wars with Napoleonic France. Perhaps because of that.

Gage had adored his mother, stoutly defending and protecting her from a very young age, even from her own family. When he learned that his father had betrayed her in such a manner, he would be devastated, and the reconciliation that had begun between father and son would be utterly blighted.

All of this had been running through my mind when I initially hesitated to tell Gage the truth he rightly deserved to hear, and so I had sought to soften the blow, waiting for the right moment to tell him. Except there was no right moment. It had been foolish of me to think there ever would be. Gage's fury and disillusionment over the way matters had ended during our last inquiry had given way to new frustration at the discovery of the publication of *The King of Grassmarket*. And the longer I waited to tell him, the harder it became to do so.

Now two months had passed, and I still hadn't told him, and the realization not only that doing so would hurt him but that my keeping it from him for so long would also inflict another wound and possibly damage the trust he placed in me, held me immobile. The truth was, I didn't want to tell him. To cause him pain. To face the repercussions. But I also didn't want to face his anger.

I knew Gage would never intentionally harm me. I knew it to the depths of my soul. But I was not yet far enough removed from the years of abuse I'd received at the hands of my first husband, and those memories lingered below the surface, affecting me in ways I didn't always seem to be able to predict or control. I mistrusted anger, even in Gage, and then hated myself for feeling that fear at all.

Something of my agony must have communicated to Gage, for his brow furrowed in concern. "Don't worry, Kiera. My father isn't blaming you this time."

"Well, that will be a novelty," I replied with a weak laugh.

Unable to continue to meet his searching gaze, my eyes dipped to the ribbon trim of my bodice, which I plucked nervously.

"Is something wrong?"

"Of course not," I replied, forcing my hand back down to my side. But I could tell Gage wasn't convinced. "I'm just . . ." I cleared my throat, searching for an explanation. "Your father . . ." I was interrupted by a rap on the door, and I leapt on the fortuitousness of the timing, for I still had no idea how I was going to finish that sentence. "Come in!" I called, relieved when Bree and Anderley stepped through the door.

Ignoring the look Gage aimed my way, telling me he would bring up this discussion again later, I smiled brightly at my maid. She looked lovely in a willow green gown I had given her, which she had reworked to fit her more petite frame. However, her sparkling whisky brown eyes were noticeably dimmed, and I couldn't help but wonder whether it was because of the play or the man standing behind her. When she cast a glance over her shoulder at Gage's valet, setting the upswept curls of her strawberry blond hair bobbing, I suspected I had my answer.

Anderley was the dark foil to Gage's golden good looks. With his height, coal black hair, and olive skin, he had never failed to receive attention from the maids of the homes we visited. I'd thought Bree to be immune to his charms, but some months past I'd been proven wrong, and the pair had embarked on a tentative courtship.

Truth be told, it had been far from smooth. Bree's moods seemed to vacillate between euphoric and infuriated with remarkable speed for a person who had always seemed so eventempered before. For the most part, I had chosen to keep my own counsel, for the few times I had attempted to ask her about their relationship had been met with firm rebuttals. Gage never spoke of it, so I suspected he'd done the same. But I couldn't help but wonder how much Anderley was affected by their courtship's highs and lows. If he was perturbed at all, I had yet to see it. Though, in all fairness, I would be the last person to whom he displayed such emotions.

"No ceremony," I declared when both servants appeared prepared to stand and deliver their reports rather than sit in the giltwood armchairs. I urged them into the seats, determined that the sooner we discussed this the sooner I could retire, and the sooner Gage would be distracted from my uneasiness. "How was the play at the Grand?"

"First of all, the reports about the cholera appear to be true," Anderley declared as he settled in his chair, adjusting his deep blue frock coat. The subtle look he exchanged with Gage made it clear this was a subject they'd discussed at length earlier. "The number of cases seem to be diminishing. At least, here in Edinburgh."

"That's true," Bree remarked. "The mood o' the audience was lighter than I expected, even before the play began. And I overheard several women talkin' aboot how no new people had fallen ill in their tenement in o'er a fortnight. Ye could sense their relief."

A relief I imagined we all shared. But Edinburgh *had* been one of the first places that cholera morbus had appeared in Scotland before spreading on to the north and the west. The disease was now rampaging through parts of Glasgow, and the numbers of sick were already far greater there.

In any case, no place seemed to be completely safe. Not even small villages, which had reported their fair share of disease. Cholera had reached the east end of London in late January, and the newspapers had reported Paris's first flux of cases only a few short days ago.

"That sounds optimistic, but regardless, we'll continue to remain vigilant," Gage declared. An assertion none of us were going to argue with.

Anderley nodded, then inhaled a deep breath as his eyes locked with Bree's in what I could only term a speaking look. "Then, I'm sorry to say the play was a rousing success."

Bree's shoulders hunched as if trying to retreat from the truth. "Aye. I'm no' sure I've ever seen the like. At least half the crowd had already been to see it before. Some o' 'em even started singin' along wi' the actors."

"I heard one chap tell his friends he'd seen it half a dozen times, and he'd caught a handful of the plays and gaffs at other venues."

"I can't say I'm surprised," I admitted, meeting Gage's eyes. "The play at the Theatre Royal was also a remarkable success. You should have seen the mother's death scene. There practically wasn't a dry eye in the house. And the staging of the jailbreak scene was nothing short of revolutionary."

"Not to mention the swordfight with Maggie Kincaid's kidnappers," Gage supplied.

"The Grand's version had its fair share of fisticuffs and violence, as well. Along with a storm created by special effects, a ghost scene . . ." The corner of Anderley's lips quirked. "And not one but *two* defiant speeches decrying the aristocracy's suppression of the poor."

Given the fact that the Grand's audience was composed of people from the lower and merchant classes, this wasn't entirely unexpected. Nor was the fact that such a thing was left out of the Theatre Royal's script.

"Aye, but I think the main draw is the banter and the music. Over and over, in the streets, I heard people repeatin' some o' the choicest phrases and singin' the more memorable tunes. The drinkin' song from the second act seems to be the favorite." She began to hum a few bars.

"Good heavens," I gasped. "I heard a lad singing that inside the Lejeunes' patisserie just the other day. Something about . . . *nix my dolly?*"

"Aye, that's the one. 'Tis a catchy tune. Probably more so because it's in thieves' cant."

Anderley's fingers drummed against the arms of his chair, revealing more of his restlessness and agitation than perhaps he realized. "All the theaters and gaffs recognize what a windfall Bonnie Brock's story is, and they're going to keep competing with one another for their share of the audience and profits as long as the interest lasts."

"Which could be a very long time," I murmured in resignation.

"What of the story?" Gage interjected. "Did it adhere closely to what's in the book?"

Once again, Bree and Anderley exchanged a look.

"Yes and no," Anderley replied somewhat hesitantly. "I suppose it followed the general narrative of the book, but there were also parts that were heavily . . . embellished."

I wasn't certain I liked that word. *Embellished*. It gave me a sinking feeling. I could tell from the tone of Gage's voice that he didn't like it either.

"Embellished how? Did they mention the corruption?"

"No. No, they didn't touch on that."

"What about the body snatching?"

"They mainly skirted that issue, as well."

Much like the Theatre Royal, they understood what played well with their audience and what did not.

Gage arched his eyebrows. "Then . . . ?"

Anderley cleared his throat, seeming to look to Bree for help, but she merely scowled at him. "Well, the venue being what it is, and the audience being less inhibited . . . I suppose you could say the dialogue was a bit . . . bawdier."

My gaze flicked to Bree's furrowed brow and back. "Just the dialogue?"

"Er, well . . ." He cleared his throat again. "Mainly."

What exactly this meant was unclear, but given Anderley's discomfort and Bree's displeasure at his mentioning it, it was easy to deduce that this bawdiness pertained to the alleged romantic relationship between me and Bonnie Brock. That sick, swirling feeling began again in the pit of my stomach. I knew I should ignore it all. After all, what was there to be done? But the ire and aggravation etched across Gage's face made it difficult to disregard.

"And did the characters Lady Dalby and Mr. Gale look like us?" Gage demanded to know.

"Not particularly," Anderley replied.

Which meant the theater hadn't gone out of its way to make the characters *not* look like us.

Gage turned to stare into the hearth, aggravation tightening every muscle of his six-foot-two-inch frame. Meanwhile, Bree continued to glare at Anderley across the expanse of the low table. But it wasn't his fault. He was merely the messenger.

"Well, at least now we know what we have to contend with," I said. "The Theatre Royal and others like it might choose to omit some of the more titillating elements of the book, but it appears the minor theaters will not balk at it."

Gage exhaled a deep breath, releasing some of his frustration. "And neither will the gaffs and any traveling shows. In fact, I expect some of them to be outright lewd."

Anderley nodded in confirmation.

More often than not, when the manager of a theater company was fined or prosecuted for lewdness or indecency, it was one of the makeshift, pop-up penny gaffs or a traveling company of players moving from county to county—for obvious reasons. It was far easier to evade the law when one's play could take place in a different location every night.

"What of the production and audience in general?" I broke off, grunting as I adjusted the pillow at my lower back. "Did anything occur to you that might help us uncover the author's identity? For instance, differences in interpretations between what the book describes and what the playwright and actors chose to portray?"

I was curious to hear their thoughts. For some reason the book had given me the impression that Mugdock had not actually lived among the people he described. Despite his intimate knowledge of Bonnie Brock's past and vivid descriptions of some of the more lurid elements of his life, I felt quite certain Mugdock had never been a member of Brock's gang or even a rival one. For all its insight, at times the story devolved into either bland prose or gross caricature, making me suspect Mugdock was unfamiliar with what he was describing, and so had chosen to either ignore it entirely or manufacture the ambience out of whole cloth.

In contrast, many of the members of a minor theater's company had likely lived and grown up among the streets of Old Town, if not in Grassmarket itself. They knew the streets and wynds, the sounds and smells and textures of its walls. They intimately understood many of the experiences Bonnie Brock had endured, and they would have corrected any inaccuracies, either consciously or not, found in the book.

It was clear from her troubled expression that something had occurred to Bree almost immediately, though it took her a moment to find her words. "Well, I dinna ken how they depicted him at the Theatre Royal, but one o' the things that most struck me was how ruthless they portrayed Bonnie Brock. They certainly dinna shy away from it."

Anderley crossed his arms over his chest as he considered this. "He was very much the relentless, unbending, almost brutal man he's purported to be. And yet this did not repel the audience. Far from it. They seemed to find him even more heroic because of it."

"Aye, the lass on Anderley's left actually forgot to keep makin' coo eyes at him whenever the actor playin' Bonnie Brock was on stage," Bree drawled sarcastically.

His lips compressed slightly, letting me know this wasn't the first time she'd mentioned the girl and her cow eyes, and I wondered if this was the source of contention I'd sensed between them when they entered the room.

"They *did* stress how he has his ain code o' honor," Bree added, returning her attention to me. "So it was verra clear why he was ruthless when *he* deemed he had cause to be." She tilted her head in thought. "And considerin' how cruel and unforgivin' life, and even the law, can be to those who havena been born wi' all the advantages, I suppose his code o' honor is better than none. At least wi' him they ken where they're at and call that fair."

Bree made a valid point. A point she and Anderley were both familiar with. After all, Bree had entered my father's service as a kitchen maid, where she had been abused by the cook, nearly being crippled during her worst beating. At the discovery, my father had fired the cook and hired a surgeon to attend to Bree, but the damage was done, and to this day she still limped when the weather was cold or rainy. Whereas Anderley had been born into an impoverished family in Italy and sold to a padrone, who had promised his parents he would teach him a trade. But rather than an apprenticeship, Anderley had found himself essentially a slave, one of the hundreds if not thousands of Italian Boys haunting the streets of London and other cities in Europe, performing and hawking wares for their padrone masters. That he had run away from his padrone and saved Gage from a trio of ruffians, and then Gage had taken him into his service, had been part providence and part courageous perseverance.

Neither Bree nor Anderley had been responsible for the terrible situations they'd found themselves in. Servants were to mind their superiors and suffer whatever "reasonable" correction they meted out—a term which gave room for considerable latitude, sometimes with tragic consequences. That no one had recognized sooner how beyond "reasonable" the cook's punishment of Bree had become was horrifying and sadly all too common, while officials often ignored the existence of the Italian Boys—as they ignored the existence of many of the country's poor except to throw them into the workhouse for vagrancy—or accepted bribes from the padrones to look the other way. They had no one to champion them, particularly as they were foreigners, and so they were left to fend for themselves the best they could.

The world was filled with far too many people like Bree and Anderley, tumbled into terrible circumstances not of their own making. But by another twist of fate, Bree might have ended up dismissed from her job as a cripple, left to beg on the street, and Anderley could have found himself scraping an existence from whatever meager employment he could find, or worse, turned into a hard-hearted padrone himself.

It was a fact I had found myself wrestling with more and more often of late, especially after the stark injustice of the class divide illustrated by our last case. And because I was about to bring a child into this unfair world. Gage and I spent so much of our time and effort in the pursuit of truth and justice, and yet, at times, all it seemed to do was reveal how dubious and unjust the world truly was.

We had all fallen silent, lost in our own quiet contemplation until Gage spoke. "Anything else?" At some point his gaze had dipped to my rounded belly, perhaps also considering the world our child was being born into. His eyes lifted to meet mine, and his lips curled faintly upward at the corners, offering me a brief but bolstering smile.

"The vaults," Anderley replied. "Where Bonnie Brock supposedly stores his contraband whisky."

"Yes? What about them?" Gage asked.

"They look nothing like the author describes them in the book."

"Aye," Bree agreed. "I hadna' thought o' it before, but the way the author speaks aboot them in the book doesna make much sense, does it? 'Specially no' after I've seen more o' what they actually look like onstage."

"I wondered about that when I was reading it," I admitted. "The vaults are mostly enclosed underground, aren't they? A dark, dank, rat-infested labyrinth of chambers."

"Aye. No' the place you'd choose to hang aboot longer than necessary."

And yet, in the book, Bonnie Brock and his men had often plotted and caroused in the vaults when Brock owned multiple buildings throughout Edinburgh, each far more suitable to such activities.

The vaults had been created when the South Bridge had been built over the gorge of Cowgate to connect High Street with the University of Edinburgh in the 1780s. All of the arches of the bridge except for the one under which the street of Cowgate traveled had gradually been enclosed when tenements had been allowed to be built abutting the viaduct. The shops along the length of the bridge above and the buildings adjacent had then built extra floors within the arches, further dividing the space into storage rooms for their buildings.

However, the construction of the bridge had been rushed, and the surface never sealed, leading to flooding in the vaults. Soon after, legitimate businesses had abandoned its use, and it was taken over by less savory enterprises, as well as the most desperate residents of Cowgate. One could only imagine how appalling conditions must be in that damp, sunless world and what desperation those forced to dwell there must feel.

"It's clear the author has never actually been down there," Anderley surmised.

"No, he hasn't."

I turned to look at Gage, alerted by something in the tone of his voice. The almost derisiveness of its certainty. I glanced at Anderley, realizing he hadn't compared the author's words to the scene in the play. Bree had been the one to do that. Anderley had stated it as if he had firsthand knowledge. Which more than likely meant Gage also did.

A sharp lance of horrified fear streaked through me. "When have you been down in the vaults?"

He blinked rapidly, and I could tell he was considering lying to me. I narrowed my eyes letting him know I was not going to be fobbed off.

"Last year," he admitted. "Actually, that's one of the places Sergeant Maclean took us to search for Kincaid."

On that fateful night of my first encounter with Bonnie Brock, when he had appropriated Philip's carriage outside the Theatre Royal with me inside. I frowned in remembrance of that event, and the fact it had been missing from both the book and the Theatre Royal play. I couldn't help but wonder what that meant, if anything.

However, Gage evidently thought my glower indicated anger. "Darling, we never went deeper than a few rooms. Which was more than enough, I assure you." He took hold of my hand. "We were purely there to ascertain Kincaid's whereabouts."

I nodded distractedly. "Of course."

"We should tell them aboot his father," Bree murmured to Anderley.

I had been on the verge of excusing myself to retire, but her words made me sit taller. "Did they speculate on his identity?"

"No' explicitly," she replied. "But he had a cane wi' a gold lion head at the top, and Bonnie Brock's mother called him Leon."

But was that truly his name, or purely an inference on their part? After all, Bonnie Brock's unruly, tawny hair was often compared to a lion's mane. Had he inherited that trait from his father in fact, or did it merely make a pleasant fiction?

I remembered then that Maggie had told me once that her brother looked nothing like his father. But once again, had that been the truth or merely misdirection?

CHAPTER 4

I lay on my side, staring into the shadows gathered at the edges of the room, when the door to the dressing chamber clicked open behind me. Closing my eyes, I feigned sleep as I heard Gage cross the room and then remove his dressing gown, tossing it across the bottom of the bed. It seemed wrong not to wish him a good night, but I didn't want to face his questions. Not tonight.

He stubbed out the candle on his bedside table, and I waited for the familiar weight of his body to slide beneath the covers. When it didn't come, I found myself straining to hear any sound of his movement, but he seemed to still be standing at the side of the bed, perhaps staring at me. It made the breath I was already struggling to keep deep and even hitch inside my lungs.

"I know you're awake, you know." Amusement softened his voice. "Otherwise you'd be snoring."

"I do not snore," I retorted.

He chuckled, perhaps at my so easily revealing my ruse. "Normally, no. But for the past few weeks you have."

"That's the fault of the baby."

"Likely," he conceded, sliding under the covers. "Is it also the fault of the baby that you decided to pretend to be asleep?"

I frowned. "I'm tired, that's all."

"I see. So you're not angry with me for visiting the vaults?"

Turned away as I was, I couldn't see his face in the faint moonlight filtering through our bedroom drapes, but I could tell he was goading me to roll over. "Of course not. I understand it was Sergeant Maclean's decision to take you there." I adjusted the pillow clasped between my knees to ease the pressure on my hips. "I was startled because you'd never told me before, that's all."

"Well, it's not precisely a pleasant confession, and the topic never arose."

I suppressed a snort of derision because I was certain I'd asked where they had searched for Bonnie Brock that cold night in January of the previous year, the perfect opening for him to have mentioned the vaults. In any case, it hardly mattered now. Though I soon wished I'd raised the issue when next he spoke.

"Then you must be avoiding talking about my father and his letter?"

My muscles stiffened, and I wanted to curse, for Gage had surely noticed, having shifted closer to me in the bed. "I thought we'd finished that discussion."

"Kiera, something is clearly bothering you," he demurred, his long body curling around mine as he combed back the loose tendrils of hair clinging to the side of my neck with his fingers. "I know Father hasn't always been kind, that he's unfairly held you responsible for the scandals in your past, but he seems to have recognized his folly. Not that he'll ever apologize for it. But at least he's no longer ready to believe the worst."

"I'm not worried that your father blames me," I snapped, desperate to stop him from talking about his father. "Or rather, I suppose I was. A little," I amended. "But I'm not anymore."

"Then . . . what is it?"

I struggled to find my words, torn between telling him a lie and the truth. But neither would spring to my lips. And the arm he had draped around my chest suddenly felt less like a comforting anchor and more like a weight holding me down. It tightened around me, and for a moment I worried I couldn't breathe.

"You know I don't blame you, don't you? For Bonnie Brock. For the book. For people being foolish enough to believe such nonsense. For any of it."

"Yes," I replied, though I was less certain than I sounded.

I felt the baby move, perhaps sensing my agitation, and reached down to press my hand over the place where his or her tiny hand or foot was punching or kicking.

"Then . . . do you blame me?" his voice rasped.

The unspoken pain behind those words clutched at my heart, momentarily obliterating every other concern. "Oh, Sebastian," I murmured as I awkwardly rolled over to face him. There was nothing graceful about turning from one side to the other when you were heavy with child. I cupped his jaw in my hand, feeling the scrape of bristles, and pulled his face closer to mine. "No, Sebastian, I don't blame you. How could I? Neither of us could have seen this coming."

"Maybe." His eyes ached with earnestness. "But it is part of my duty to protect you . . ."

"From an unseen, unimagined foe?" I challenged.

"From everything."

I gripped his jaw firmer, pulling his mouth closer to mine so that all he could see were my own eyes gazing back at him in the darkness. "Rubbish. Stop talking nonsense." I brushed my nose along his in a caress. "You protect me perfectly well, and you know it. Any better and I would kick against the traces."

I felt rather than saw the corners of his mouth quirk upward in a reluctant grin. I pressed my lips to his, pouring all my love into that single kiss before pulling back so that I could gaze directly into his eyes again. "There is no blame here. Not for any of this."

His hand clasped the back of my head, pulling my lips back to his, and I had no desire to resist. Not when his kisses had always had the power to overwhelm me, and he couldn't ask me questions with his mouth otherwise occupied.

I was surprised to discover that the offices of Thomas W. Rookwood, Publisher, stood just off North Bridge Street, across from the City Markets and but a short distance from the Theatre Royal. It was a tidy little building sandwiched between a linen draper and a counting house. Not grand by any means but certainly respectable.

The black lacquer of our carriage gleamed in the morning sun as Gage helped me descend to the street. Once safely on the ground, I turned to survey our surroundings while Gage issued instructions to our coachman. Church bells chimed the hour in the distance while carriages clattered past us in the street. Despite the cholera still plaguing parts of the city, the markets bustled with customers. After all, people still needed to eat and purchase other supplies.

Stalls brimmed with everything from potatoes and parsnips to baskets and leatherwork. The scents of stone and sun-baked earth swirled with the brine of the seawater sloshing about in the oyster cart parked to one side of the entrance. Oysters being a cheap and popular meal among the residents of Old Town at any time of day, the owner was doing a brisk business, while the beggar opposite was not. He waved sheaves of loosely bound papers above his head, hollering in a barely distinguishable broad Scots, "All the latest ballads for a penny! Includin' 'Nix My Dolly.'"

I turned back to look at him at his mention of the popular

flash drinking song from the Grand's version of *The King of Grassmarket*, and catching my eye he fluttered the sheet music toward me. "'Tis popular wi' all the ladies."

Gage reached for my arm, hustling me away. We crossed the street to the publisher's office and were greeted upon our entry by a man of approximately thirty, whose hair had nonetheless already turned almost entirely a silver white.

"Lady Darby, Mr. Gage, you are verra welcome," he assured us with a pleasant smile and a gentle Scots brogue as he ushered us inside, offering to take our coats and hats. "I'm Daniel Heron, Mr. Rookwood's assistant. He's ready to receive you, if you'll come this way."

He led us through the oak-paneled office past a series of worn wooden desks, each one bare and polished to a gleam save one, which was cluttered with stacks of paperwork and half-empty cups of tea. The air smelled pleasantly of lemon polish and ink, though this abruptly ended at the door to Mr. Rookwood's office. It appeared that the distinguished publisher possessed a remarked fondness for tobacco.

"Come in, come in," he called, closing an ornate box sitting on the mantel over his hearth next to a golden ormolu clock topped by a globe before he rounded his massive desk. He was a rather stout, barrel-chested fellow with naught but a few tufts of gray hair clinging to the sides of his head, behind his ears. He clasped the pipe he was evidently so fond of in one hand, though it was fortunately unlit, as he reached out to shake Gage's hand with the other. Truth be told, I was beginning to feel a little green from all the residual smoke that had saturated the room. Something that Gage noticed as Mr. Rookwood turned to greet me.

"Would it be possible for us to open a window?" he asked as the publisher pressed my hand in welcome, though he seemed unable to lift his eyes from my rounded belly.

"Hmm, what? Oh, aye," he replied, startled into meeting my gaze. "Quite right. Quite right." He offered me a tight smile and then bustled across the room to help Gage. "Allow me. There's a bit o' a trick to it. Sticks sometimes."

I sank into the armchair nearest the door, hoping the air would circulate quickly and the alley beyond didn't contain something even more fetid.

"Noo," Mr. Rookwood drawled around the pipe clenched between his teeth as he slapped his hands together. He returned to the leather chair behind his desk, which was cleared of all papers except a shallow pile on each of the far corners. "What can I do for you?"

"We understand you're the publisher of *The King of Grassmarket*," Gage began, sinking into the seat beside mine and lacing his fingers casually over the flat abdomen hidden behind his ice blue waistcoat.

"Aye, and before ye go on," he cautioned, leaning forward to set his pipe in a dish at his elbow. "I ken who ye are and why you're here." He raised his hands in a staying gesture. "I told Mugdock from the first that he shouldna be usin' your names, but he wouldna be budged. It took me threatenin' no' to publish the book before he agreed to at least change a letter in each o' your names. Even so, 'tis obvious he's referrin' to ye."

Frankly, I was shocked to hear him admit all this. Did he not realize we could sue him for libel, and his admission was as good as a confession? Or was he counting on us not doing so and, by admitting to the association without provocation, hoping to soften our opinion of him? Craftily, the scurrilous accusations made about us in the pages were mere insinuations. Rather than charge us with our sins outright, Mugdock had allowed the reader to draw his or her own conclusions, though the implications were clear. Such a fact made the charge of libel more difficult to prove.

Mr. Rookwood sat deeper in his chair. "But you'll have to take that up wi' him."

"Gladly," Gage replied with a stern look. "Who is he?"

Mr. Rookwood shook his head in feigned regret. "I'm afraid I canna tell you that. Signed a binding document that I wouldna divulge the author's true identity." He nodded toward the door. "No' even to the police. And believe me, they've tried."

I turned to Gage, uncertain what to make of the publisher's disclosure. But if my husband found the police's involvement curious, he didn't let it show, maintaining the same level, unyielding stare.

"And what is it precisely you risk should you reveal this Nathan Mugdock's alias?"

A vee formed between Rookwood's brows as his chest puffed up like an irate robin. "My reputation, for one. My honor. And . . . a large portion o' the profits from the sales o' *The King o' Grassmarket*," he grumbled before gesturing broadly with his hands. "But before ye go offerin' me money, ken that my honor isna for sale. Bribery willna work for ye any more than it worked for Bonnie Brock Kincaid. And your threats willna either." He crossed his arms over his chest as if in illustration.

But Gage wasn't so much impressed by this display of outrage as intrigued by what he'd revealed. "So Kincaid *has* been here?"

"Aye. Thrice. Each time wi' a larger bribe and a meaner threat. But I have no kin. Least none within a hundred miles o' Edinburgh. And should Kincaid go lookin' for trouble among my relations, he'll get more than he asked for in return. So he's only got me to menace, and I dinna frighten easily. I've faced doon enough bluster in my day, and killin' me willna give Kincaid what he wants."

Perhaps, but there were less extreme measures Bonnie Brock could take. Pain could be an astonishingly persuasive method for making people talk. Sir Anthony, my first husband, had known this well, and I was certain Bonnie Brock did, too.

All that being said, and his protestations aside, I wasn't convinced the publisher could not be persuaded to divulge Mugdock's real name. It was more that no one thus far had stumbled upon the right inducement. But until we discovered it, perhaps he would be willing to cooperate in a less straightforward manner.

"Have you met Mr. Mugdock?" I asked.

Mr. Rookwood's gaze shifted to mine, and a shrewdness entered his features. "I assume ye mean in person, but I'm no' gonna discuss that. Let's just say that Mugdock and I have a healthy correspondence."

"Our scrutiny of this Mugdock's writing leads us to believe he's not your typical writer," Gage remarked almost offhandedly. However, I knew from experience that the suppression of his voice's inflection during an interrogation was conversely proportional to his interest in the answer to his question. "In fact, this is likely his first book of fiction. And yet, he's obviously educated and well read."

"Yes, he's a bit of a conundrum, isn't he?" I replied, playing along with my husband's gambit. "He's evidently familiar with Edinburgh, but there's something inauthentic about his descriptions of the lowliest of places and the perpetuation of the crimes described. It makes one wonder how he came across his information about Bonnie Brock. And why he seems to have a vendetta against him."

"A vendetta Kincaid now seems to be turning back on you."

A gleam of reluctant admiration lit Mr. Rookwood's eyes as he observed our exchange and absorbed Gage's pointed statement—a blunt reminder of the threats he faced. "Seems you've worked oot a great deal for yourselves," he said, but whether this was confirmation of our deductions or he was humoring us, I couldn't tell. "I willna deny that at times I wonder whether publishing Mugdock's book has been worth all the trouble. Oh, aye, it's made a tidy profit. But the threats and harassment I've been left to face while he hides behind a false name have been more than I bargained for." The hand resting on his desk tightened into a fist and then released abruptly as he exhaled. "But what's done is done. And I'll no' dishonor myself noo." He turned his head aside. "'Specially no' for the likes o' a man like *Mugdock*."

This more than anything before made clear the state of the relationship between the publisher and author, and it was both a hole to be prodded and a difficult problem to surmount. For while Rookwood might eventually be convinced that revealing Mugdock's true identity wasn't dishonorable—particularly after all of the unsubstantiated allegations he'd made in his book and the trouble he'd caused him—Rookwood would abhor having to concede anything to the man, making that contract a thorn in all our sides.

"Mugdock," Gage ruminated. "That's a rather odd choice for a nom de plume, is it not?"

Rookwood shrugged. "'Twas his choice. I've no idea why he chose it."

But perhaps it might unwittingly tell us something about him.

I allowed my gaze to trail over the papers on the desk and then down to the rubbish bin sitting next to one of the cabriole legs perched on crisply carved claw-and-ball feet. It was overflowing with foolscap, but one document resting near the top caught my eye, for I'd seen a playbill just like it. "You've been to see the play? At the Theatre Royal?"

Rookwood broke off from whatever he had been saying to Gage and turned to me with an aggrieved sigh. "Aye. Three nights past."

"Did the Theatre Royal pay Mugdock for their use of his book?" Gage queried.

Rookwood chuckled as if Gage had said something humorous. "Nay, lad. Theaters dinna pay for the use o' an author's material. Least no' unless you're Sir Walter Scott and likely to sue them wi' the sympathy o' the entire bloody nation." He shook his head. "Nay. Most authors receive nothin'. Unless the theater manager happens to feel guilty. But even then 'tis only a single payment in exchange for the author's endorsement in their advertisin'." He reached out to pick up his pipe, but seeing my eyes following his movements, he left it in the dish. The stale air inside the chamber had cleared, but it would rapidly grow rank again if he began to smoke. "Nothin' for it but for the author to take it in stride."

"And did Mugdock? Take it in stride?" Gage clarified.

Rookwood's placid good humor returned to irritation as he tapped the desk with a single finger. "Nay, wanted to sue 'em all. And when I told him I wanted no part o' it, that he would go that road alone, he threatened to sue *me* for breach o' contract." A feline smile curled his lips. "Except he'd no' anticipated the book bein' made into a play, and so his contract didna cover it." He gestured toward the playbill in the rubbish bin. "The Theatre Royal made him a handsome offer, but the fool refused to endorse it because o' the changes they'd made. So he . . . *we* . . ." he amended ". . . received nothin'. And yet the play still runs. And a spectacular success it is."

Gage and I shared a speaking look.

"Do you know which changes he was displeased with?" I asked, turning my head so that I could breathe more deeply of the cool breeze wafting into the room.

Rookwood scoffed. "Anythin' that made Kincaid look like anythin' better than the cur and charlatan he'd determined to portray him to be. Except he forgets that's no' how most o' Edinburgh sees him. And the showmen are savvy enough to appreciate what makes a profit."

"Then Mugdock truly does have a vendetta against Kincaid," Gage surmised.

"That much is obvious from the book, isna it?" His eyebrows arched high on his forehead. "But the question remains, does he also have a vendetta against *you*?" His gaze dipped to my rounded belly. "Or are ye merely a convenient pawn with which to illustrate Kincaid's depravity?"

I couldn't answer that. Not without knowing who Mugdock was. But his attack of me and Gage certainly felt personal.

Gage arched his chin, giving the publisher a long look. "What do you think?"

"That I dinna ken," he replied measuredly. "But I *can* tell ye that, whatever his motivations, he doesna like ye. No' one bit."

CHAPTER 5

Even though the sun had not yet set, the shadows had already begun to deepen beneath the screen of winter trees surrounding the garden. Elms, limes, horse chestnuts, and laurels lined the gravel paths, which crunched beneath my slippers. Gage and I were already dressed in our finery for the dinner party my sister was hosting that evening somewhat unofficially in our honor, and so we did not wander far from the defined trails. But I still took extra care not to muss the hem of my celestial blue dinner dress of gros de Naples.

Bonnie Brock had not specified in his message which of the three sections of the Queen Street Gardens he wished to meet us in, but I could only surmise he meant the westernmost segment as it stood closest to our abode. It was also perhaps the easiest to sneak into. The eastern garden, being the oldest, possessed the most mature trees, and the central garden had been planted with a thick perimeter of greenery. Though the gardens were private, with the residents in the surrounding terraces of town houses possessing keys to their gates, none of them were terribly difficult to trespass upon. All one had to do was pick the rather rudimentary locks or scale the five-foot-high rod iron fences. For a man like Bonnie Brock, both of these tasks were child's play.

As the sun dipped behind the skeletal trees and buildings to the west, the warmth of the day all but dispersed. A cool breeze wafted down the back of my neck, and I clutched the fur collar of my cloak closed beneath my chin to block the chill. In another hour, the temperature would dip so low that we could see our breath lingering in the air.

Silently, Gage guided our steps toward the crescent-shaped shrubbery near the center of the west garden, fashioned of holly and yew. A formation I could smell almost before we saw it upon rounding a thickly wooded turn in the path. As we approached the broader sweep of lawn that adjoined it, we swiveled to peer around us, searching for any sign of the roguish criminal or his henchmen.

"There he is," Gage murmured, drawing my attention to the four figures descending the gentle slope of the terraced edge of the garden along Queen Street.

As always, Locke and Stump shadowed Bonnie Brock, but I was surprised to find his sister, Maggie, also following in his wake. Being a foot shorter than her brother, she scrambled to keep up with his ground-eating stride. As they moved closer, I was relieved to see that the formerly waif-thin girl had gained some much needed weight over the past year, though it was less than I'd hoped. Her lips curled in a shy smile as they drew near, further softening her knife-sharp cheekbones, and I returned the greeting before focusing on Bonnie Brock's sullen visage.

"Well, what have we here?" he drawled with almost spiteful pleasure as he came to a stop some eight or ten feet away without Gage even having to remind him to maintain a distance because of the cholera. His gaze drifted over my fur-trimmed cloak and Gage's dark evening attire. "We havena interrupted your plans for the evenin', have we?"

"Of course not. We're on our way there from here," I replied briskly. We might have agreed to meet him here now for the sake of expedience, as in the past Bonnie Brock had shown he could make himself quite the nuisance if we did not obey his requests, but that did not mean we were going to wholly alter our plans for him. "Now, why did you want to speak with us?"

"You. 'Tis always only you, lass."

That this was stated with the intention of riling Gage was certain, but while I felt my husband's arm flex beneath mine, he did not rise to the bait.

"You saw the play?"

He already knew the answer to this, but I responded anyway. "Yes."

"Then you ken what a bloody spectacle it is," he practically growled, glancing off to the right and then the left. "As is the show your servants saw at the Grand."

That he should also know where Bree and Anderley had been wasn't truly unexpected, though I couldn't help but feel irritated that he was not only having us followed but also our staff.

"As we understand it, that version is rather bawdy." I spoke softly, clipping my words with disapproval.

His gaze shifted to Gage before settling back on me, a smile lurking at the corners of his lips. "If you think that one's bawdy, you should see some o' the gaffs." His gold-green eyes glinted with savage delight. "Apparently, you're no' the type to keep quiet."

Blood rushed into my cheeks at the implication of what that meant, both for me and for the scripts of those penny gaffs.

Gage took a warning step toward the rogue. "You're deluding yourself, Kincaid, if you think I'm going to stand here and allow you to insult my wife."

"Och, you thought that was an insult? How verra tellin'," he sneered.

Gage lurched forward, and I was forced to restrain him, lest this meeting dissolve into a violent scuffle. One which would more than likely end with my husband stabbed.

"Enough!" I snapped. "Quit behaving like a child," I scolded Bonnie Brock. "Tell us why you asked us here or we're leaving this instant."

His brow lowered. "I ken you're meetin' wi' Maclean tomorrow."

That he held this bit of intelligence was more surprising given the fact that Gage had prearranged the meeting with Sergeant Maclean himself. Was Brock reading our correspondence?

"He's goin' to tell ye that there's been a rash o' crimes. That they're inspired by the book and the play."

"Which, in turn, means they're inspired by you," Gage supplied, following this to its logical conclusion.

He scowled. "But my men and I got *nothin'* to do wi' them. We've done nothin' different than we did before." He looked about him once again, and I noted Locke and Stump doing the same, as if they expected trouble. Maggie shifted anxiously from one foot to the other. "Truth be told, we're actually doin' less. Layin' low since Maclean and the other pollies have been bayin' for our blood," he groused, and then stabbed his chest with his finger. "'Tis no' my fault the bloody play chose to romanticize my life."

I studied Bonnie Brock's drawn countenance. This entire affair obviously infuriated him. Someone he trusted had shared intimate details about his life, and they'd been turned into fodder for the public's entertainment, to the monetary benefit of some unknown writer. And because of it, not only were his gang's activities now under even greater scrutiny, but other criminals were encroaching on their territory, thinking to claim the same glory without understanding the cost, and besmirching Brock's reputation in the process. There was much to be enraged by.

But I also noted something I hadn't expected. All of this seemed to genuinely trouble him. Beyond anger, beyond disgruntlement. The shadows around his eyes, brackets about his mouth, and wariness of his surroundings denoted a deeper level of uneasiness and, dare I say, distress.

My gaze flicked to Maggie, who stood just beyond his shoulder, to the side, nibbling her thumbnail, her long brown hair trailing over her shoulder in a braid. Even her presence here seemed to speak volumes, for in the past he would never have brought her along to such a meeting. Perhaps he was grooming her, so to speak. Allowing her greater freedom and control. But I didn't think so. Rather, I thought he was most concerned about keeping her close. Keeping her safe. Maybe the playwright working for the Theatre Royal had been more perceptive than I thought.

However, Gage was not as sympathetic.

"Such an inconvenience," he scoffed. "Do you honestly expect us to believe you're not the least bit pleased by all of this fame and adoration? At the moment, you're the most celebrated man in all of Edinburgh. The police may be after you, but in the eyes of everyone else, you're a figure of fascination and intrigue."

Brock arched a single eyebrow.

"And yet you're trying to tell us you despise the attention." Gage shook his head derisively. "You're doing it up much too brown, old chap. I *know* you must be enjoying the allegations being made about the child Kiera carries."

"Well, then, you'd have it wrong," he retorted. "I might wish you to the *devil*, but I'd no' see Kiera harmed." His gaze met mine squarely, the gold-green depths swimming with unspoken words. "Though I daresay the bloodthirsty wench could best anythin' thrown at her."

I swallowed the lump rising in my throat, affected more by the words he hadn't said than those he had. At this point, the appellation "bloodthirsty wench" was more of a term of endearment, as often as he'd used it to describe me.

"Mr. Rookwood informed us that you've been harassing him," Gage said.

Bonnie Brock's brow furrowed into a low vee, making the scar running down his nose stand out white. "Aye, and I'll continue to do so until he tells me who bloody Mugdock is," he snarled, using far stronger language.

"There are other ways to get the information besides threatening him," I proposed.

"And ye dinna think we've already tried those?"

"Of course, but I'm not certain you were aware at the time of the most effective points with which to pressure him."

His hands clenched into fists at his sides. "Nay, but I *will* be."

I frowned. "That's not what I mean." I tilted my head. "What if I told you we could get the name without doing the man any sort of violence? Would you let us try?"

His gaze switched back and forth between me and Gage, weighing the veracity of this statement, and perhaps his willingness to trust such an assertion. Gage didn't help matters by scowling at the man so contemptuously. After all, I was almost as determined as Bonnie Brock to uncover the identity of the man who had so callously besmirched my name, and I knew Gage's resolve must be heightened as well.

As if recognizing this, the inveterate rogue nodded, though his gaze trailed to the side as if he'd heard something. I followed it, but in the falling darkness I couldn't see anything to cause alarm.

"Aye," he said, turning to go. "But dinna take long. Word is Mugdock has written a second book." His eyes hardened with fury. "And this one is even more damagin' than the last."

I turned to Gage in shock. A second book?

"Where did you hear that?" Gage demanded to know even as Bonnie Brock and the others began to melt away into the shadows of the overarching trees.

"I have my sources," he replied, and then they were gone.

"Do you think it's true?" I asked softly, clutching Gage's arm tighter.

He exhaled a long breath, telling me he was more anxious than he'd wished for anyone to realize. "I don't know. Maybe." He turned our steps back down the path leading toward the gate opening onto Wemyss Place. "Kincaid's sources do seem to be enviously accurate."

I frowned at the trees lining either side of the trail, their trunks and branches fading to a darker gray against the gloom of twilight. "I wish Rookwood had told us about this sequel, but I suppose it's not surprising. And he wonders whether publishing the book has been worth all the trouble," I jeered, repeating his words. It must have been if he was willing to publish another one. "To think I actually felt a little bit sorry for him."

"Yes, well, speaking of sympathy, Kiera." Gage waited until I turned my head to look at him. "Don't give Kincaid any more than he deserves."

I opened my mouth to object, but he cut me off.

"I saw the way you were looking at him after he tried to tell us he and his men aren't responsible for the rash of crimes inspired by the play. The man is not blameless in any of this. He might not have wished for his life to be turned into a melodrama, but he *is* responsible for the crimes and exploits that inspired it. And undoubtedly whatever vendetta the author is out to repay."

My first impulse was to protest that we couldn't know that Bonnie Brock had done anything to deserve such revenge, but then we also couldn't know that he hadn't. The fact was, he had done many things worthy of reprisal in his lifetime, no matter his personal code of honor. That code was not the same as the rule of law, and I was under no delusions that he hadn't committed dozens of crimes, including smuggling, theft, housebreaking, body snatching, assault, and murder.

We'd long lamented the necessity of cooperating with him, believing it was better to work with the devil we knew than the devil we didn't, but now I wasn't so sure. Particularly now that we'd found ourselves dragged into the solder mill of public opinion with him. And typically, because I was a woman, my reputation suffered the most.

When the scandal had erupted around my involvement with Sir Anthony's dissections, I'd bemoaned and berated the unfair treatment of me in the newspapers and among society's gossips. But now that my unborn child was being implicated in such slander, I felt fury supplanting all other emotions. How dare they speculate on the conception of my child. It was not only insulting but also absurd. Yet another example of society's swift criticism and condemnation of those who persisted in living their lives outside the prescribed manner deemed acceptable by our culture's rigid standards. And I had never colored inside the lines. Not completely.

I clutched Gage's arm tighter as he steered me around an anomalous rut in the well-tended path. "Oh, I know Bonnie Brock is far from blameless. Believe me. And he undeniably enjoys tweaking your nose and causing me to blush." I gave him a chiding look. "You really shouldn't rise to his bait. Not when you already know he's going to attempt it."

"I shouldn't defend my *wife*?" he retorted, determined to take offense.

"Not when we're well aware the scoundrel never follows the rules of decorum and never will, and our meetings with him are a necessary evil. In that instance, it seems we willingly sacrifice some of our right to take umbrage."

His lips flattened in vexation.

"Besides, what exactly did you intend to do back there if I hadn't stopped you? If you'd thrown a punch, he or one of his men would have likely retaliated with a knife. And what of the cholera, and the distance you've been so insistent we maintain from the worst areas of Old Town?"

He stiffened, perhaps realizing for the first time that in his anger, he'd forgotten his admonition that we remain a safe distance from the man and whatever contamination might hover about him from the areas still afflicted with the disease.

We strode in silence for a few moments. Whether because he'd thought my questions were rhetorical or he didn't wish to admit he was wrong, it eventually became apparent Gage wasn't going to respond. So I pressed on, finishing my initial thought.

"All that being said, I don't think that means Bonnie Brock is enjoying any of this." I grimaced recalling the storm of emotions I'd seen reflected in his eyes. "In truth, he seems disturbed by it all."

"Of course he's disturbed, Kiera," Gage snapped. "All of this attention has *disturbed* his normal mode of operation, and now he might actually have to face the consequences of his actions."

"That's not what I meant."

"Oh, I know what you meant. I can't believe you're defending him!"

"I'm not!" I protested, a knot forming in my gut. "I'm simply pointing out the fact that he's not relishing the attention, as you seem to think."

"I *think* he cares for nothing but what's in his own best interests. And in this case they do not align directly with our own. It would serve you well to remember that."

That had been just as true in previous circumstances involving Bonnie Brock, and yet Gage hadn't felt the need to remind me of it. I never strayed from the mark, even if I might have bent it more than my husband might have wished a time or two. It infuriated me that he was insinuating that fact now.

"The ability to feel empathy for another person—even a criminal—is not a weakness, Sebastian," I bit out in a low voice. "Nor does it necessarily make you susceptible to manipulation."

My use of his given name should have alerted him to how earnest I was, but he continued almost as if I'd never spoken. "Just as it would serve you to remember that he's well aware of your fondness and compassion for his sister, and not above using it to his own ends."

Was that why Bonnie Brock had brought her with him? Clearly that was what Gage thought, but I struggled to accept that his reasoning was so calculated. At least, not purely so. Rarely were people's motivations so straightforward. More often than not, they were muddied by multiple impetuses—some conscious and some less so. Bonnie Brock's vigilant demeanor seemed to confirm he was keeping his sister close to protect her, but that might not be the only reason.

Either way, there was no winning this argument. Not when Gage's pride had been pricked. I tried to summon my empathy for him now, to draw him out, but it had temporarily deserted me. A wound to my own pride, I supposed, as I felt great satisfaction in my ability to read people so accurately. It had proven to be a great asset in the portraits I painted, as well as our inquiries. But in this case, identifying the splinter in my own eye didn't make it any easier for me to relinquish it.

CHAPTER 6

We traversed the remainder of the short walk to Charlotte Square in chilly silence. A chill which was not assuaged by my sister's reception to her home.

"Good heavens, Kiera, you're almost late," she chided, standing in the hall beyond the entry where Figgins, their butler, was helping us with our outer garments. "I expect the other guests to arrive at any moment." She gestured me forward impatiently as she scrutinized the plaited pattern in loops of satin braid on the bodice of my celestial blue gown, as well as the ribbon band of its waistline affixed high to accommodate my condition. "Yes, this is lovely," she proclaimed, reaching up to fluff the feather draped over my velvet toque headdress. "Oh! But why are your cheeks so florid? Don't tell me you walked?"

"It's scarcely two blocks," I countered.

"But in this chill? And in your advanced state?"

I scowled. "I'm perfectly healthy, Alana. As I told you, Dr. Fenwick assured me that walking is good for me *and* the babe."

My sister's lips pursed as if she'd tasted something tart. "That may be, but I hardly think he meant under these circumstances."

"Then what circumstances, pray tell, could he mean? We live in Edinburgh in March. Temperatures could hardly be balmier."

"Perhaps we should adjoin to the drawing room," Philip interrupted before his wife could utter a retort in front of the servants.

Alana inhaled as if to continue and then broke off, whirling away to stamp toward the room he'd indicated.

Philip finished shaking Gage's hand and then offered me his arm. "You look lovely, Kiera."

"Thank you," I replied, my affront softening under his regard and the genuine affection reflected in his eyes. While we hadn't initially been close, Philip and I had always rubbed along quite well together. I suspected it was because he did not demand that I be agreeable or entertaining, as many gentlemen of his status expected. Rather, he had been understanding and kind about my distraction and unsociable behavior, recognizing that my strengths did not lie in charm and small talk. Though perhaps he hadn't realized I was conscious of it at the time, I had recognized how he'd made an effort to discuss the things I was interested in, namely art. When he'd not wearied of this, I'd grasped what a good man he must be, and how very much he must have loved my sister.

Something that the evidence bore out when the terrible scandal broke following Sir Anthony's death, with the revelation that I had been the illustrator of his dissections. Philip had become one of my most stalwart defenders, taking me into his household without batting an eyelash, and even moving me to the seat of his earldom in the northern Highlands to escape the worst of society's slander. Because of that, I would be forever grateful to him—for his support and protection during the worst months and years of my life.

All in all, I was incredibly fond of my brother-in-law. But there were times when his high-handedness, his rather aristocratic insistence that he knew best riled my temper. He was the Earl of Cromarty, after all, and accustomed to people complying with whatever he suggested. And for all that, I granted him some compassion and clemency for being a supportive husband, I couldn't help but loathe how he sometimes encouraged and even gave greater leverage to Alana's little tyrannies. I hadn't forgotten how Philip had encouraged his wife to believe they knew what was best for me, or how he'd supported her efforts to persuade me to quit with my investigations at Sunlaws Castle when this quarrel between us had begun. He seemed to be working to help us mend the rift now, but he wasn't innocent in its inception.

As we approached the door to the drawing room, Philip leaned closer to murmur in my ear. "Be gentle with her. She's worried about you. What with the gossip, and the play, and your being so close to your confinement, she's very concerned."

And I wasn't?

Though I hadn't spoken, the thought must have flashed in my eyes, for the corners of his mouth curled in commiseration. "I know she looks it, but she's not as strong as you, Kiera. Few people are."

I was left speechless, unable to form a reply. I had always considered my older sister to be one of the strongest people I knew. Perhaps because, for as long as I could remember, she had always been such a strong presence in my life. Our mother had died when I was eight years old and Alana was twelve, and from that moment forward, my sister had tried to take on the role of mother to me and our brother, Trevor. With the exception of my art—which only I controlled—and the three horrible years of my marriage to Sir Anthony—in which he had controlled everything—for better or for worse, Alana had been the drive behind all my other decisions. She had always seemed such a force to be reckoned with that it had been easier to comply with her wishes than argue over every detail, especially if I didn't deeply care one way or the other.

That is, until Sebastian Gage came along. Since then, my confidence had blossomed, and I had begun to pay less and less heed to Alana's opinions.

Even so, I had never considered the fact that I might be more resilient. It was true, I'd weathered far more horrible things than my sister had. And while I'd trembled and bent considerably, I'd never yet been broken. But I'd always been under the impression my sister was stronger because she'd never allowed herself to be put into those situations in the first place. Maybe that thinking was flawed. Maybe I didn't give myself enough credit. And maybe I expected too much of Alana.

I watched as she paced toward the fire burning in the hearth and then pivoted to return, the rich crimson satin folds of her skirts nearly snapping with the movement. Her hands were clasped before her, and yet they fidgeted minutely, as if demanding to escape the other's grasp.

Philip was right. Alana *was* anxious. I should have noticed it before. And I might have had I not already been so irritated with Gage, and had my sister not immediately launched into criticism.

Knowing Alana, she had expended a great deal of effort to make this dinner party a success. She'd conceived of it some weeks prior, after her return to Edinburgh and the discovery of the publication of *The King of Grassmarket*, thinking to bolster our reputations. I hadn't been of the opinion that such a move was necessary. After all, nothing had stopped society from believing what it wished in the past, and those people who knew and loved me and Gage would already realize the allegations the book made were untrue. But Alana had been insistent, so I hadn't stopped her.

However, Philip's words made me think that perhaps her anxiety wasn't about the success of the dinner party, but rather the entire state of my affairs. With this insight, I felt the tight ball of injury and affront I'd continued to nurse since our argument at Sunlaws Castle two months past begin to loosen. I knew Alana had only ever wanted happiness for me, and while we might disagree on what that happiness might entail, I could appreciate her goodwill. That she now worried that the insinuations made about me in the book and play threatened that happiness and felt anxious to help remedy it only spoke well of her.

I crossed the room, prepared to make peace, when she suddenly plopped down on the spring green sofa where Gage had elected to sit with one ankle propped over the other knee.

"Don't you think your wife should take more care?" she demanded. "Walking in this weather hardly seems conducive to her health."

I stumbled to a stop, feeling as if I'd been delivered an underhanded blow. Alana knew how protective Gage was of me. How he struggled against his impulses to keep me wrapped in cotton swaddling. Especially now that I carried his child. For her to appeal to him in such a manner simply to get her way was a rotten, dirty trick.

I glared at her.

"Kiera will do as she wishes," Gage retorted before giving a humorless laugh. "I certainly can't stop her."

I transferred my outraged gaze to my husband, wanting to demand of him just what he meant by that. I followed his requests when they had merit, and never took action without thoughtful deliberation, or put myself at risk unless there was very good reason to. I was nothing if not reasonable.

Unfortunately, the first of Alana's guests chose that moment to arrive. Figgins hesitated in the doorway, clearing his throat before announcing them. "Lord and Lady Kinnear."

Alana leapt up at once, her face transforming into a welcoming smile without the least trace of the rancor that had marred it a moment before. But I was not so gifted in such things. Gage knew this. His gaze darted to mine briefly as he rose from the sofa, his public mask of relaxed charm falling into place.

I inhaled a deep breath before turning, attempting to affix a pleasant expression on my face, or at least something that conveyed indifference, but I feared I faltered. The feel of Gage's solid presence at my shoulder, his warm hand splayed across my lower back, steadied me, but I could tell the damage was already done. Lady Kinnear was a notorious gossip, and the vicious delight glinting in her eyes left me in no doubt as to whether she'd overheard Gage's remark.

The party had scarcely begun, and Alana's efforts were already failing. This did not bode well for my reputation or our reconciliation.

Though I knew Alana would scold, I couldn't resist sneaking upstairs away from the party for a short time. Three hours of feigning goodwill and making pleasant small talk, while still minding my tongue, had given me a ferocious headache. If I didn't sit quietly for a few minutes, I feared I might do something regrettable. Like slap the feral grins off Lady Kinnear's and Mrs. de Quincey's faces.

And so it was that I managed to steal four entire minutes of silence before my cousin Morven peered around the door into my old bedchamber to find me seated on the settee before the dormant fire. Her dark, gleaming hair had been swept into the high bows on her head now fashionable among society, the rich color accentuated by the lilac silk and white crepe of her gown.

"Good heavens," she exclaimed upon finding a gray cat perched precariously on what little room remained in my lap. "I do believe that is the most rotund feline I have ever seen."

"Yes, well you would be just as round, too, if you had children sneaking you treats all day." I smiled down at Earl Grey, who arched his chin to give me better access to scratch it. He had once been a mouser at Blakelaw House, my childhood home, but had managed to worm his way into my heart with his loyal, undemanding affection. He'd had a knack for finding his way into places I didn't wish him to be, but when conversely I needed him most. A knack he still seemed to possess.

Morven rested one hand on the door while planting the other on her hip, her enormous blond-lace-trimmed sleeves nearly touching the bedframe some feet away. "I thought he was *your* cat."

"He was, but the children were so fond of him, and he them, that I decided he would be better off here."

"Perhaps for his self-consequence, but not for his health," she quipped.

"Did Alana send you to find me?"

The manner in which she scrutinized my features told me I hadn't done a good job of masking my irritation with my sister. "Your husband, actually. He thought it might look too conspicuous if he slipped out. Said I would find you either here or in the nursery."

My lips curled reflexively that he knew me so well. "The children are asleep."

She advanced into the room, reaching out to pet the top of Earl Grey's head. "I suspected. Alana always was better than I am at finding nursemaids who can make the children mind. Oh, now you're in heaven, aren't you?" she crooned to the cat. "Why'd you name him after the prime minister?"

I shrugged. "It seemed to suit him. And he's gray."

I looked up to find her face alive with amusement.

"Is that funny?"

"It is, actually. But I'm more amused with you, hiding up here with a fat cat."

I frowned. "I'm not hiding. I couldn't care less what those gossips think. Though I know Alana wishes me to be more civil than to tell them that to their faces."

"That's not entirely true," she replied much too reasonably. "But in any case, they're not the people you're hiding from." Her eyes lifted to bore into mine. "Are they?"

I didn't respond. There was no need to. She already knew she was correct.

Morven shook her head and resumed her petting. "For all that you two are the closest sisters I know, you can be remarkably obtuse about each other."

I glowered at her, uncertain whether I should take offense.

"Have you tried talking to her?"

"When I can get a word in edgewise between her reproaches."

Morven sighed and stood upright, crossing her arms over her chest. "Have you told her you're investigating the anonymous author of *The King of Grassmarket*?"

I paused in my ministrations of Earl Grey, who whined in protest before sinking his head onto the mound of my abdomen. "How did you know about that?"

"Jack saw you entering Rookwood Publishing this morning, so it stood to reason that's why you were there."

It was my turn to sigh, this time in aggravation.

"Given the fact she thinks you're taking a respite from investigating, don't you think you should inform your sister before she finds out from someone else?"

"Finds out what?" Alana demanded to know as she entered the room. Her gaze riveted on me before dipping to my lap. She cringed. "Oh, Kiera. I know you love that cat, but now is hardly the time to pet him. Your skirt will be covered with hair, if not ruined from his claws."

I resumed petting him in silent defiance.

She huffed. "Now, what am I not to find out?"

Morven turned to me, her eyebrows communicating both an apology and an insistence I be the one to tell her.

"Gage and I are attempting to uncover the author's real identity." There was no need to specify which author, for there was only one writer on all our minds at the moment.

I braced for anger and umbrage, but Alana surprised me by nodding in hearty agreement. "Good. He should be held accountable for his spurious accusations. And so should his publisher."

I blinked in astonishment. Something that my sister found as vexing as Morven found humorous, covering her mouth with her hand.

"Stop gawping at me like a fish," Alana ordered. "This is a case of libel, not *murder*." She turned toward the mirror, adjusting the gold bracelets at the end of each of her long tulle gigot sleeves, and straightened the wide collar of her gown. "Now push that cat off your lap and come back downstairs before *all* the guests remark upon your absence. Thank heavens you have your condition to make excuses for you." She paused at the door to issue one last parting shot. "And quit scowling at your husband, or next we'll be hearing rumors of your unhappy marriage and what precisely led to such a state."

Alana had scarcely disappeared before Morven burst out laughing. "My apologies," she gasped. "But your face! You should have known how your sister would react, you ninny. Is she not as ferocious as a Greek fury whenever one of her loved ones is threatened?"

Morven was right. Alana had always been fiercely protective of her family, including me. Whether she was defending me from a young lord trifling with my affections, the ridicule of society, or the barbarous slander printed in the newspaper, my sister had always been one of my staunchest supporters.

Which was why her most recent actions and criticisms had

been so bewildering and hurtful. I could appreciate that she was anxious for the safety of me and my child. I could even understand why she would suggest I temporarily withdraw from taking part in any murderous inquiries. What I couldn't accept was her determination that I should retire from assisting Gage in his work as a gentleman inquiry agent entirely and forever.

She knew what pride I'd taken in discovering I was skilled at working out the complexities of my and Gage's investigations, and the sense of purpose I derived in wrangling the truth into the light and bringing justice to those who had been wronged or murdered. At least, those were the hoped-for aims, when the great and powerful didn't step in to prevent it, as with our last inquiry. But at least, in that case, we had prevented the blame from falling on someone innocent.

That she should brush my feelings and accomplishments aside in her single-minded effort to impose her will by forcing me to conform to the familiar mold pressed upon every upper-class lady—a mold I had never fit—was both baffling and distressing. I had always been able to rely upon my sister's unwavering, rock-solid support, but now, when I needed it most, I found that it was built upon sand.

CHAPTER 7

Two hours later when I was finally able to sink into the plush leather seats of our carriage, I could not repress a deeply weary and deeply relieved sigh. Though the distance to our home was short, I could only feel grateful Gage had summoned our coach, for the prospect of walking even a block seemed unbearable.

Gage turned to me with a sympathetic smile, reaching out to help adjust the warm fur collar of my cloak. "For all that your sister professes to be concerned for your health and that of the baby, she seemed remarkably blind to your fatigue."

"I imagine she was punishing me," I replied, too tired to summon the hurt and anger which so often accompanied my thoughts of Alana lately.

"Punishing you? But why?"

I smothered a yawn. "For not complying with her wishes. For trusting Dr. Fenwick's advice over hers."

"But that doesn't make any sense."

"I know," I answered sleepily, rolling my head to the side against the squabs to peer out the small part in the window curtains at the Georgian town houses lining the square. Most of their windows were dark, their occupants having long since retired.

I heard our coachman give the order and then we were rolling forward on the short journey to our home on Albyn Place.

"I apologize for my earlier comments."

I turned to find him gazing down at me in remorse.

"I know you're not blind to Kincaid's flaws or his manipulations. And you're right, your ability to empathize has proven useful in the past."

His expression of regret was at once unexpected and welcome, soothing some of the ache in my heart. I lifted my hand to his face. "None of this is easy, is it? And I don't blame you for your anger or frustration with Bonnie Brock. He is the crux of the problem, even if he isn't directly responsible for the book or the plays being written."

"Yes, but that doesn't mean I should turn that anger and frustration on you." His expression turned sheepish. "Or express it in the manner I did before your sister."

A pang of guilt twinged in my chest, for part of me knew I deserved that anger and frustration, simply for a different infraction. The words to voice the truth about Lord Henry's father bubbled up inside me, clamoring to be spoken. But the fear that was still lodged in a dark corner of my breastbone edged them aside, and instead I found myself voicing another thought entirely. "What did Philip have to say?"

Shortly before our departure, my brother-in-law had asked Gage into his study for a private word. I naturally assumed it was about our current inquiry or the predicament of *The King of Grassmarket*, but I was wrong.

Gage turned away, and I lowered my hand as he gathered his

words. "Apparently, the prime minister and his fellow cabinet ministers believe the only way they can circumvent the Tory opposition and ensure the success of their third attempt at passing a Reform Bill in the House of Lords is by creating a considerable number of new peerages. Thus inundating the House of Lords with pro-reform votes with new Whigs."

There had been staunch Tory resistance to the previous two efforts to pass a Reform Bill, despite its approval in the House of Commons and immense popularity among the general population. A number of violent riots had even broken out after the defeat of the second attempt the year before.

"But only the king can create new peerages," I said.

"Yes, and the king may balk at taking such a drastic step. Though it's not without precedent. But Earl Grey and the other ministers are considering it nonetheless."

I waited for him to continue, for I could tell from the firm set of his mouth that he had more to say. Philip, as the Earl of Cromarty, had a seat in the House of Lords and was intimately involved in a number of parliamentary matters, namely the Scottish Reform Bill, which would hopefully soon follow the passage of the current Reform Bill that only applied to England and Wales. But while Gage was a great friend and confidant of Philip, he didn't normally concern himself overmuch with political matters except when they applied directly to us or the implications of our inquiries.

"Philip said my name had been put forth as a potential candidate." The words seemed to be pulled reluctantly out of him, and then his tone turned slightly bitter. "That my assistance to my fellow countrymen, and my wisdom and discretion, had not gone unnoticed."

"You're thinking of Sunlaws. How the Duke of Bowmont used his wealth and power to ensure that his son didn't face any distasteful consequences."

His eyes shifted to meet mine, frustration at the injustice still prevalent in our society churning in their depths. "How can I not? Particularly when they want to know if I can be counted upon to toe the party line."

Which my honorable husband would sooner eat glass than do if the measure he was supposed to vote accordingly on was against his principles. And I loved him for it.

A warmth spread through my chest at this sure knowledge, and I reached for his hand where it clenched in his lap. "Did you voice your concerns to Philip?"

"No. But I told him I needed time to think on it."

Our carriage pulled to a halt in front of our town house door, placing a temporary hold on our conversation. But once we'd been divested of our outer garments and Gage had looped my arm through his to escort me up the stairs to our bedchamber, I readdressed it.

"You support the Reform Bill," I began, already knowing his answer.

"I do," he confirmed. "It's high time one was passed."

The chief objectives of the act were to extend the franchise of male voters, greatly increasing the size of the electorate, and to redistribute the boroughs which represented seats in the House of Commons so that they better represented the population. In the current scheme, some boroughs were made up of upward of twelve thousand electors, while others—the so-called pocket boroughs—consisted of as few as twelve. These pocket boroughs were often controlled by high-status patrons, usually noblemen. And some patrons had as many as a dozen of these boroughs in their pockets.

"Then, I imagine you'd like to help ensure its passage."

"Of course. But not if it comes with more strings attached."

I nodded, understanding his position. "Though, of course, there's nothing they could do once you've been given your title.

I mean, it's not as if they can take your peerage away once it's been granted. Not unless you commit treason." Which Gage would never do. "So they can hardly stop you from voting as you wish. And they *shouldn't* fault you, not so long as you help the Reform Bill to pass."

He didn't reply, his gaze remaining trained on the steps before us as we climbed. What thoughts were running through his head, I couldn't tell. Perhaps I'd shocked him with my suggestion, but the truth had to be acknowledged. If he agreed to the scheme, he accepted no obligation except to the passage of the Reform Bill, and he could make that clear to Philip if he chose. Anything more would slowly eat away at Gage, and I couldn't bear to see that. But maybe that wasn't all that troubled him.

"Or do you hesitate for another reason? Perhaps you don't wish to take on the obligations of a title and a seat in the House of Lords. At least, not so soon."

Eventually, Gage would inherit his father's barony, but as Lord Gage was still hale and hearty, I did not anticipate that being imminent.

His gaze shifted to meet mine, and I could tell I had hit upon something.

"I don't wish to pressure you to do anything, Gage. You must know that. But you *are* an intelligent and charismatic man." Two traits he'd inherited from his father, who unfortunately was much more of a Tory than a reform-minded Whig. "You could do some good in Parliament, and there is a great deal of important legislation being debated as of late."

"Philip tells me another attempt at an Anatomy Reform Act will be put up for a vote this summer if not sooner," he replied.

A bill which had long had implications for me, as it would alter the archaic and inadequate system for supplying corpses to medical schools and anatomists, making the unclaimed bodies from workhouses available for dissection rather than simply the small number of condemned convicts executed each year. A solution which was not perfect, as it seemed to criminalize the act of being poor, but was better than the current situation which necessitated the trade of body snatchers and gave impetus to resourceful criminals. Men like Burke and Hare, and the London Burkers, who had found a way to avoid the hard, dangerous work of digging up freshly buried bodies by instead murdering people off the street and selling them to the anatomy schools.

"I know you don't care about having a title. In our line of work, they can often bring as much trouble as benefit. And neither do I. Well, I suppose that's not strictly true," I conceded as we paused outside our bedchamber door. "It would be nice to have society stop calling me Lady Darby by courtesy." Our closest friends and family knew how much I loathed the reminder of my first husband. I much preferred Mrs. Gage, even if it was several rungs down on the social ladder.

I reached up to gently grasp the lapels of his black evening coat, compelling his pale blue gaze to meet mine. "The point I'm trying to make is that I believe you are more than worthy. And so did your grandfather."

Gage's relationship with his maternal grandfather, Lord Tavistock, had been nothing short of tumultuous, but in the end they had made their peace with each other. Lord Tavistock had even admitted to writing to the king, urging him to grant Gage a title on his own merits. We had expected nothing to come of the matter, particularly as Gage's father was a great friend of William IV and unlikely to agree with such a suggestion. He preferred to keep his son and heir under his thumb as much as possible, and having him granted a title separate from his own would blunt much of that power. But this scheme of Earl Grey's added another dimension to the matter. Lord Gage was shrewd and calculating, and there was no doubt he would prefer to have his son granted a title rather than someone over whom he might have no sway.

Gage's expression tightened with remembered grief at the recent passing of his grandfather, and I lifted a hand to cradle his warm cheek.

"The decision is yours. I will support you in whatever you decide."

He pulled my hand from his face and placed a gentle kiss on my palm. "As of now it's merely a threat. The king may very well balk at the suggestion. And even if he doesn't, if the Tories catch wind of the scheme they may sooner relent than have the House of Lords flooded with Whigs."

"I know, but it speaks highly of you all the same that they asked Philip to approach you," I reminded him as I stepped back, reaching for the bedchamber door. "Though I'm certainly not surprised," I added, tossing a flirtatious smile over my shoulder.

The corners of his mouth lifted in an answering grin and then he turned his feet toward the door to the adjoining bedchamber where Anderley would be waiting to help him with his evening attire. I found Bree waiting for me as well, my night rail already laid out across the counterpane covering our four-poster bed.

"Good evening, Bree," I proclaimed with a weary sigh. "Will you help me out of this dress first?" I requested, turning my back to her. "It was comfortable enough earlier this evening, but if I have to wear it another minute, I think I shall scream."

"Too tight, m'lady?" she asked as her deft fingers began their work on the buttons.

"Perhaps a little." I rested my hands over my rounded belly. "Another week or two and I suspect I shall not fit into it."

"Aye, bairns do grow right quickly at the end."

"I suppose I shall have to consider remaining home in the evenings after the first of the month," I acknowledged as equably as I could manage. For I possessed no gowns larger than this one.

"Ye could always try wearin' that set o' stays Lady Hollings-worth brought ye."

I glanced up at our reflection in the mirror to discover that her eyes twinkled with teasing. "No, thank you. Honestly, I don't know how Caroline stands it."

I knew Philip's aunt, Lady Hollingsworth, meant well, but the elaborately boned stays she had gifted me which covered the body from the shoulders to below the hips, compressing the body into a more slender line, seemed more akin to a torture device than an article of clothing. She had insisted her daughter wore one and found it helpful. If that was the case, I could only feel pity for Caroline, who had wed our family friend, Michael Dalmay, a month after Gage and I were married and was also now expecting. I found it more likely that Caroline donned it when her mother visited her and Michael at their estate north of Edinburgh, and the rest of the time it sat tucked in a drawer. At least, I hoped so.

I allowed my shoulders to slump as the gown loosened. Bree reached up to remove the velvet toque from my hair before pulling the satin gown up over my head. In short order, I found myself enveloped in my lace-trimmed nightdress and indigo dressing gown, and seated at my dressing table while Bree pulled the pins from my hair and then began to plait it. I fidgeted, finding it difficult to find a comfortable position in which to perch, and she gently scolded me.

"I'll be done just as fast as I can, m'lady."

I exhaled a tired chuckle. "I'm no worse than my nieces and nephews, am I?" I gazed at my reflection. At the luster of my hair and the lush cleavage revealed through the gap in my wrapper, at the plumpness of my cheeks and the shadows under my eyes. "But no one warns you how awkward you'll feel in your own body or how disconcerting that can be."

Bree's expression softened. "Aye. My mam always said that was nature's way o' makin' ye eager for the birth." Her teeth flashed in a grin. "'Tis hard to be fearful when ye simply want the bairn oot o' ye."

"And you have seven brothers and sisters?" I verified, for Bree's stories about her family—when she could be coaxed to share them—were often rambling and slightly confusing. Every generation seemed to repeat the same names, and often cousins shared variations of those, so I became lost in figuring out exactly who was who.

"Aye. Seven who survived anyhow."

I looked up in surprise.

"My mam has had at least two miscarriages, two stillborns, and my sisters Colleen and Mary both succumbed to illness when they were still bairns."

Fourteen. Mrs. McEvoy had carried fourteen children, and yet barely more than half had survived. The thought made me go cold. I knew how high the infant mortality rate was, knew how dangerous giving birth could be as well. More women died in childbirth than by any other cause. Heavens, Alana had nearly succumbed twice because of hemorrhaging and blood loss.

Yet I refused to dwell on those facts. It was too great a fear to be faced and impossible to control. So I pushed it from my mind but for those moments when someone either oh-so-helpfully reminded me of it or inadvertently broached the topic. This instance was definitely the latter, for Bree still seemed unconscious of the effect her words had on me.

"And my older sister, Brigid, already has three bairns, wi' another on the way."

I forced myself to take an even breath before asking, "Do you wish to have children as well?"

"Aye, maybe." A furrow formed between her brows. "Someday." That she was thinking of Anderley was evident, but the contemplation wasn't pleasant.

I vacillated for a moment, wondering whether I should say something. But as soon as I opened my mouth, there was a perfunctory rap on the dressing room door, followed by Gage's entrance.

Bree finished tying the ribbon securing my braid with a sharp tug, even though she must have realized by now that my husband was to blame and not her knots for my hair coming undone in the middle of the night. "Will that be all, m'lady?"

"Yes. Good night," I bade her as she bobbed a swift curtsy and swept from the room.

I watched her go, still wondering if I should have said something.

"Let it go, Kiera," Gage warned lightly a moment after the door shut, reading my thoughts. He shook his head. "She'll not thank you for your interference."

He was undoubtedly right, but I still couldn't help feeling it was wrong to ignore her obvious discontent. Wouldn't I want someone to ask after me?

I grimaced. No, probably not. I was too stubborn and independent to appreciate it. And so was Bree. Aye, there's the rub.

The next day dawned wet and dreary, affording me an excuse to laze in bed rather than rise for my normal morning constitutional in Queen Street Gardens. Usually I enjoyed the quiet of early day, after the bankers and solicitors living in this part of the city had rushed off to their places of business and the rest still lay in bed. Much of the time it meant I had the entire garden to myself, save for Gage; or Peter, our footman; or occasionally Anderley. Truth be told, I found the necessity of such an escort somewhat tedious, but Gage fretted about me in such an advanced condition, so I didn't protest the precaution.

However, I was still tired from Alana's dinner party and several late nights before it, so the extra rest was welcome. It also gave me time to pen letters to my brother, Trevor, and my good friend Charlotte, Lady Stratford, both of whom I had been tardy in responding to. Nevertheless, by midmorning I was ready to venture forth for our meeting with Sergeant Maclean.

As during the times before, we joined him at the tea shop owned by his sister-in-law, Mrs. Duffy, on Princes Street. The shop was not yet open for business that day, but Mrs. Duffy let us in the door with a warm smile.

"Ah, Lady Darby, it does my heart good to see ye so full and healthy. No' long noo, is it?"

"Perhaps three weeks," I replied.

"That's what the physician said? Then, I'd say it's mare like five." She leaned forward confidingly. "The first bairn never comes on time." She turned to her brother-in-law, a teasing glint in her eyes. "'Tis why they're usually so stubborn."

"Dinna listen to her. She's clearly biased," Maclean protested good-naturedly in his thick brogue.

I couldn't help but feel myself relax in their presence, their playful banter revealing a genuine fondness. I'd yet to meet Mrs. Maclean, but if she was anything like her dainty, pale-haired, kindly sister, I was certain I would like her. Mrs. Duffy kept a tidy shop, with crisp white tablecloths draped over the eight small tables and tiny bud vases sporting fresh blooms. This time they were filled with sprigs of rosemary, thyme, and chamomile flowers. She was also a brilliant baker, and I could already smell her sultana scones baking in the kitchen beyond.

She grinned at my flared nostrils, aware of how much I adored them. "I'll be back in a trice," she told us, ushering us toward the table we normally occupied at the back of the shop, farthest from the windows.

Sergeant Maclean, on the other hand, was a former pugilist, and as tall and brawny as they came. His features were crooked from too many bouts in the ring. His nose had been broken multiple times in the past, and his smiles were stiff and awkward, not so much because he didn't do so often, but more because it seemed like his cheek muscles could only lift so far.

He waited politely as Gage settled me in my chair before sitting carefully in his own. I noted that he sported a new scar across his brow, and when he rested his hands on the table, his knuckles were as scabbed and scarred, as always.

"I can see you haven't grown lax with criminals," Gage jested.

His face darkened. "Nay. Least no' like Mugdock suggests."

Though Maclean hadn't been mentioned by name, *The King of Grassmarket* had implied there were officers of the Edinburgh City Police involved in the corruption scheme that Gage and I, or rather Mr. Gale and Lady Dalby, were a part of. And the only policeman we regularly collaborated with was Maclean.

Gage's own humor deserted him. "I hope you've had better luck than we have uncovering who this Mugdock fellow is."

Maclean shook his head. "The publisher isna singin', and we canna force him. Least no' yet."

"What does that mean?"

"The superintendent claims he's got a few tricks up his sleeve. Meanin' favors he can call in." He narrowed his eyes. "In truth, I dinna think it'll be hard to convince one o' his judge cronies that 'tis in the public's best interest to ken who's stirrin' up unrest."

"And by 'unrest,' I surmise you mean the rash of recent thefts," I speculated.

He turned to me. "Heard aboot that, have ye?"

"They've been commented upon in the newspapers," I replied. At least, in that morning's edition of the *Caledonian Mercury*.

He dipped his head in acknowledgment. "Aye, and most o' 'em are naught but a bloody nuisance."

Gage sat back in his chair, his brow creased in interest. "What do you mean?"

But my attention was diverted by the sight of Mrs. Duffy bearing a tray piled with scones, a pot of tea, and a bowl of clotted cream. My mouth began to water before she'd even set the items on the table. I listened with half an ear as I helped myself to the tempting fare. All my gowns might already be too tight for me in my condition, but that did not mean I was going to pass up these delights.

"A fair percentage o' the thefts have been perpetuated by lads who have ne'er been in trouble wi' the law before—lads simply playin' at bein' a criminal." Maclean sat back, crossing his arms over his broad chest. "One night, I caught three young lads—ages ten, eleven, and twelve—attemptin' to cut the glass o' a toy shop window so they could steal the toy cannons on display, and another two scamps burglarin' a snuff shop. Some o' these lads are from a class that *should* ken better. Just two days ago, a respectable shoemaker's son was arrested for robbin' an establishment near Tollcross." He suddenly leaned forward. "And the whole sparky lot o' 'em have been entertainin' one another at the police house by performin' bits o' that bloody play—singin' and dancin' for one another's amusement." He shook his head. "They've gone barmy for Kincaid."

"Or at least the tales of his exploits," I interjected between bites.

"Aye, weel, it's difficult to separate the two," he replied gruffly, adjusting the belt under his gray greatcoat to which his baton was strapped.

"Then most of the crimes have been petty in nature?" Gage asked, slathering a scone with raspberry jam.

"Aye, pickin' pockets or burglarin' houses." Maclean scratched at the dark bristles peppering his jawline. "But there's also been a handful o' more darin' raids. A week ago, one warehouse was robbed o' all its whisky by a gang o' ruffians, and the night watchman they restrained claims one o' the men was whistlin' that flash song from the play."

"Kincaid's men?"

It was a natural assumption, but based on Bonnie Brock's mood the previous evening, I already knew the answer.

"I dinna think so. 'Twasn't their style."

Gage's eyebrows arched in query.

"For one, the watchman was thrashed before they tied him up. Nowadays, Kincaid rarely resorts to such measures. If the watchman isna willin' to be scared or bought off, he's delivered a sound blow to the head to knock him oot. For another, they're more apt to rob the delivery caravan. That way they dinna have to find transport for the contraband or load it themselves. They simply steal the whole wagon." He grunted. "But the superintendent isna so convinced."

"A rival gang, perhaps?" Gage asked after taking a sip of the tea I'd poured out for him.

"Maybe. Whoever they were, they dinna behave like amateurs."

"Then why whistle 'Nix My Dolly'?" I felt the question had to be asked.

Maclean shrugged. "Maybe he was full o' himself, or maybe he didna ken what he was doin'."

Or maybe he had purposely wanted to direct the watchman's and the police's attentions toward the play and Bonnie Brock. Perhaps *The King of Grassmarket* was a convenient scapegoat for their activities.

Either way, it was obvious the boys and this more experienced group of whisky thieves were familiar with the play. So it was easy to see why the newspaper and police were drawing a connection between them, blaming the depravity of the plays, and consequently the book, for exploiting the public's moral weakness and inciting them to commit crimes. But while I recognized that the sensational tale had some part in inspiring and perhaps stirring their pluck, I couldn't help but wonder whether much of the motivation lay elsewhere. After all, the cholera had disrupted life in the more squalid sections of Edinburgh these past few months. There were many who must have found themselves in desperate situations. Would they have been so easily influenced and willing to resort to vandalism, theft, and assault if they hadn't already been suffering from poverty and hunger? I couldn't answer that, but I also couldn't ignore it.

"And then there are the jewelry thefts."

CHAPTER 8

Gage and I both paused with our teacups raised.

"Jewelry thefts?" my husband repeated. "We haven't seen any mention of those."

"Aye, because the superintendent wants to keep 'em quiet. For noo. But 'tis somethin' I could use your help wi'." He leaned against the table carefully, ever conscious of how much space he took up with his brawny frame. "We've had two burglaries so far. One at Sir Phineas Riddell's home in Moray Place." Which was located practically around the corner from our town house. "And the other at Lord Kirkcowan's home on St. Andrews Lane."

My gaze collided with Gage's upon hearing this startling pronouncement, both of us far too cognizant of our involvement with Lord and Lady Kirkcowan and their jewelry in the past.

"You ken somethin' aboot it?" Maclean pressed, not having missed the look that had passed between us.

"No," Gage replied indecisively. "But . . ." He set down his cup in the saucer with a gentle clink of the porcelain. "But my father asked me to investigate the theft of some of the Kirk-cowan jewels just a year ago. A diamond and sapphire necklace had gone missing." He glanced sideways at me. "At the time we'd wondered if the alleged theft had been contrived by Kirk-cowan in order to raise funds for his considerable gambling debts. But the necklace was found soon after."

It was found because it had never truly been lost or stolen. Rather, Lady Kirkcowan had hidden it away as security for her-self and her children when her husband eventually lost every-thing to the turn of the cards. Gage and I had wanted to remain silent about our suspicions that she was responsible, figuring the jewels were rightly hers, even if the law would have said that they were actually the property of Lord Kirkcowan. She had endured enough for them. But Lord Gage had been insistent that Lord Kirkcowan be told, and so I'd warned her ladyship before he could do so. That way, the necklace could be miracu-lously "found" at the back of a drawer.

But that wasn't the end of it. And while Gage had his own suspicions about what happened next and my involvement with it, he had specifically asked me not to enlighten him about the details.

I lowered my hands to my lap, lest their fidgeting give me away. "However, less than a fortnight later, the Kirkcowans' home was burglarized, and all of their jewelry, along with a few other portables, were taken from their safe. I was under the im-pression that none of it had been recovered. But perhaps I've been misinformed?"

Maclean studied me with interest, making me fear I hadn't effectively concealed my discomfort with this topic. "Aye, I'm aware o' the theft, but Lord Kirkcowan insists a number o' those pieces were soon after reclaimed."

This news caused me a pang of misgiving.

"Only to have them stolen yet again?" Gage's voice dripped with skepticism.

"Aye, I asked the same question myself. But numerous witnesses claim to have seen Lady Kirkcowan wearin' the gems as late as November."

"Just before she and their children left for her father's home in Lanarkshire," I noted.

The glint in Maclean's eye told me he was also already aware of this detail and its ramifications. "Aye."

I frowned, recalling my first encounter with Lady Kirkcowan. "How can we be sure the jewels weren't paste? Some of the best imitations are difficult to detect. And I know for a fact that a paste version existed of the diamond and sapphire necklace Gage mentioned. I saw Lady Kirkcowan wearing it myself."

"And yet Lord Kirkcowan insists they were real, and is outraged by the suggestion that a man o' his status would lie."

"So, he expects you to take him at his word and, I imagine, has the superintendent backing him, ordering you to abandon that line of inquiry," Gage surmised, not unsympathetically.

"That aboot sums it up." He reached for one of the last scones, bitterness twisting his mouth. "But that's usually hoo it goes when even a hint o' suspicion falls on a member o' *your* class. Which is where you come in."

I knew that Sergeant Maclean didn't blame us for this double standard, but I felt the shame of it nonetheless. "I could write to Lady Kirkcowan," I offered. "She would know whether the gems she wore in November before her departure from Edinburgh were real or fake. And I believe, under the circumstances, she would tell me the truth."

If those gems had been real, it would also give me the opportunity to find out why she had allowed them to fall back into her husband's hands after I'd risked so much to obtain them for her.

I'd even contrived with Bonnie Brock Kincaid to have the job done, granting him a percentage of the spoils if his gang stole the Kirkcowans' jewelry and placed the rest into my hands. When I'd then passed them secretly to Lady Kirkcowan, urging her to conceal them in a place her husband would never find them, I'd expected her to save the jewels for a moment when she and her children were in dire circumstances.

"I'd be grateful," Maclean replied, his gaze once again turning too keen for my liking.

I nodded. "I'll do so as soon as we return home."

"Do you have any suspicions who might be responsible for the thefts, *if* they're both, in fact, legitimate?" Gage queried.

"Aye," Maclean pronounced around a bite of scone, chewing and swallowing before he spoke. "Bonnie Brock Kincaid."

I'm not sure why I was surprised, for he was already uppermost in my suspicions. I supposed it was the certainty behind Maclean's tone and the stony look in his eyes. "You think he's behind the jewelry thefts?"

"I *ken* it. But thus far I've no proof, other than my gut and the knowledge that Kincaid's men are the only ones wi' the skills to snatch such a haul o' baubles wi'oot raisin' the alarm until they've long gone."

It was true. Bonnie Brock employed specialists in a number of areas—be it for their skills in lockpicking, stealth, surveillance, scheming, or fencing stolen goods. These men recognized that by throwing their lot in with Brock, they could focus on the tasks at which they excelled and be at less risk of getting caught—and better protected if they were—and still enjoy a fair share of the profits from their efforts. The members of his gang *were* the likeliest suspects for the job. They had certainly proven capable and culpable of such crimes in the past. But I couldn't halt the suspicion that this was all a shade too convenient.

Bonnie Brock was nothing if not shrewd and perceptive, and

now of all times was not the moment to draw any greater attention or ire from the police and the nobility by perpetuating such thefts. He had told me once that it was a dangerous game angering the wealthy and influential, and so he had always taken care to neither prick their pride nor execute his crimes against them too closely together. Nothing was more risky than giving the noblemen and gentlemen a reason to shift their normally self-absorbed focus to him. Not when they wielded much of the power. Instead he had played a fine balancing act from the shadows—skimming just below the surface of their attentions while still managing to abscond with an astonishing amount of money and loot. Stealing jewels from the nobility while already under heavy scrutiny because of the book and play seemed more akin to prodding a slumbering beast than maintaining a shadow game.

"Is there any reason to believe the theft of Sir Phineas's jewels isn't as straightforward as it seems?" I asked.

"I havena uncovered anythin'," Maclean replied, sitting back in his chair and crossing his arms over his chest again—a move that emphasized the size of his biceps. "Unless you ken somethin'?"

I lifted my hand to the pendant my mother had given me, fingering the amethyst that dangled from my neck, and shook my head. By the slight narrowing of his eyes, I could tell he didn't entirely believe me, but in this, I was telling truth.

"I've told ye before, I dinna like Bonnie Brock Kincaid. He should o' been hanged for his crimes years ago." He kept his gaze leveled on me. "But I can no' like a man and still respect him. Least for the good he *has* done for the poorest o' this city, and his resolve to keep his word. He has his ain sense o' honor, and expects his men to abide by it. That's more than I can say for the other gangs at work here." His voice grew hard. "But all the same, he *doesna* follow the rule o' law. Be careful ye dinna persuade yourself otherwise."

"I'm well aware, Sergeant Maclean," I responded tartly. "I'm in no danger of falling under his sway." I rested my hands on my rounded abdomen. "And lest you forget, I have the most reason to be furious with him for the trouble his association with me has caused."

"I would think your husband has greater reason."

A flush of anger swept through me.

"That is uncalled for, Maclean," Gage warned, sitting forward.

"For shame, Braden," Mrs. Duffy gasped behind us, apparently having emerged from the kitchen in time to overhear his remarks. "Noo, why would a sensible woman like Lady Darby want anthin' to do wi' a man like Bonnie Brock Kincaid when she's got a fine braw husband like Mr. Gage." She planted her hands on her hips, standing over her brother-in-law. "No' to mention the fact that *we* ken Lady Darby left Edinburgh in early May." She swatted him with the towel in her hand. "And *you've* got enough bairns o' your own to understand how the process works. Why, if Lady Darby were already more than ten months along, do ye think she'd be sittin' here wi' you? Nay, she'd be lyin' in bed, bein' dosed with whatever vile concoction the midwife thought would induce labor. I ken you're under pressure from the superintendent to nab Kincaid, but that doesna give ye leave to be so foul to her ladyship. Noo, apologize," she demanded as if he were a recalcitrant child.

I expected Maclean to refuse or at least grumble about it, but he did neither, giving me a fair idea of who ran Sergeant Maclean's household. If Mrs. Duffy was this strong-willed, I imagined her sister was as well. He turned to me with a puckered brow. "I apologize." His gaze flicked toward Gage. "Your husband's right. 'Twas uncalled for."

I nodded in acceptance, though I wasn't certain I would ever look at him as so firm an ally again.

Our leave-taking was strained, not least of all because I could tell Maclean still suspected I was concealing something from him. Gage promised him we would uncover what we could about the jewel thefts, and I told him I would inform him as soon as I heard from Lady Kirkcowan, but I didn't anticipate that the sergeant would be sharing much with us in the near future. Particularly not if the superintendent was exerting pressure on the police to see Kincaid finally hanged.

"I was under the impression that Lady Kirkcowan had retained some of her jewels," Gage remarked offhandedly after we returned to our carriage, though his gaze remained trained on the rain-soaked streets outside the town coach's window.

I studied his profile, wondering how much he wanted me to confess. After all, he'd previously insisted he didn't want to know the contents of the pouch Bonnie Brock had slipped to me a year ago, though he was smart enough to guess.

"I wondered the same thing," I replied obliquely. "And wouldn't that have been fortuitous."

Perhaps the last statement was a bit heavy-handed. It certainly drew his wry gaze away from the window. "I suppose we'll have to wait to hear what she says about the matter."

"Yes." I adjusted the fall of my cloak, avoiding his eyes. "I only hope if she *did* retain some of those jewels that she wasn't foolish enough to let Lord Kirkcowan know it."

"Indeed," Gage replied, and then repeated it more quietly as he turned away. "Indeed."

Reclining as I was on the chaise upholstered in daffodil silk near our window overlooking Albyn Place, I heard my sister's carriage pull up to our town house. So I was prepared moments later when she came bustling into the room, her cheeks flushed nearly the shade of her Parnassus rose gown and the curls framing her face wilted.

"Why aren't you upstairs? Where is Dr. Fenwick?" She glanced about the room as if I might be hiding him somewhere. Perhaps behind the drapes.

"Alana, he left a quarter of an hour ago," I replied, marking the page of the book I'd been reading with my finger.

Her eyes flared indignantly as she whirled to face the gold and marble ormolu clock perched on our fireplace mantel. "But you told me your appointment was scheduled for . . . oh." She broke off with a deflated gasp.

"Yes, two o'clock," I finished for her. "But it's now a quarter to three."

"Yes. Yes, I see that." She sounded flustered and reached up to pat her hair. Upon finding it was damp, she hurried over to the carved foliate mirror hanging on the wall near the hearth. The better to hide her frazzled expression. "I do apologize. What did Dr. Fenwick say?"

I studied her in puzzlement. "He's pleased with me and the baby. Says it will be a fortnight or more before I deliver. Alana, are you well? It's not like you to be late . . ." I glanced at the clock ". . . or confused about the time."

"I made a simple mistake," she retorted. "Am I not allowed?"

I frowned at her defensiveness. "Of course, but . . ."

"Surely he encouraged you to rest as much as possible now until the baby arrives," she proclaimed as she rejoined me, sinking down onto the edge of the giltwood armchair nearest me.

I smothered a pulse of annoyance. "He encouraged me to do what felt natural. To rest when I felt tired. To move about when I felt like moving. He said a bit of mild exercise was good for me and the baby, and would help the labor go more smoothly once it begins."

Her mouth puckered in displeasure through this recitation. "But he must have meant for you to do this moving about indoors."

"Now, how would that make any sense, Alana?" I replied, unable to keep the sarcasm from my tone.

She arched her chin. "It makes perfect sense to me. You simply parade from room to room. As you'll recall, that's the sole exercise we received two years ago when the winter weather was so harsh at Gairloch."

"Yes, but that was *Gairloch*! It takes an hour to traverse all the corridors in that monstrosity of a castle." I exaggerated only slightly. Philip's Highland estate along Loch Ewe was in no way small, having once housed a large portion of the Matheson clan, being added to in fits and starts down through the centuries.

I clamped my mouth shut and closed my eyes, hating that Alana had riled me when I'd just told myself I was not going to allow her to do so. Exhaling a deep breath, I spoke in a calmer voice. "Why am I arguing this with you? I'm following Dr. Fenwick's instructions. Instructions that seem perfectly sensible to me. And that is that."

"I'm only thinking of what's best for you," she bit out, her shoulders rigid and her lips beginning to quiver.

Softening toward her, I offered her my hand, hoping she would take it. "I know you're concerned for me and the baby. How could you not be after everything you endured giving birth to Greer and Jamie?"

She sniffed, lifting her hand to clasp mine.

"Nothing is certain. It never is with childbirth." I squeezed her hand. "But I'm doing everything I can to make sure this baby is born safely, and that includes following Dr. Fenwick's orders. The stronger I am when the time comes, the better chance I have. That seems logical."

"Yes, I can see that." She released my hand, searching for her handkerchief in her beaded reticule. "I simply wish you would stay home while you do it."

"Why? Because of the cholera morbus?"

She blinked at me blankly for a second. "Well, yes, partly."

But I could tell the risk of cholera had not been on her mind at all. In any case, I'd never heard of anyone taking such drastic precautions as keeping to their own home to avoid the disease, especially not here in New Town. The residents of this part of the city were merely told not to venture into the more squalid areas of Old Town. As for the public notices posted throughout Edinburgh, they touted such recommendations as eating whole-some meals regularly, abstaining from alcohol, keeping one's home and person clean, and avoiding unnecessary exposure to cold and wet. All sound suggestions, but nearly impossible to implement for the city's poorest residents, whose living condi-tions were dreadful and whose income was too paltry to afford more than meager fare. As for limiting their consumption of spirits, it was often the only way they could warm themselves.

"Then, why else?" I pressed.

She scowled. "Must I state it baldly for you?"

"Because of the book? But I thought you were in support of our efforts to uncover the author's real name?"

"Of course I am. But must you leave the house to do so?" She pushed to her feet. "Why must you always make a spectacle of yourself?"

My head reared back in shock. "I don't make a spectacle of myself."

"You do, whether you intend to or not." She took several ag-itated steps toward the door before turning to add, "Kiera, I have stood by you for twenty-six years. I supported your painting por-traits even when others said it was unladylike." Her voice grew tight. "I sheltered and championed you after Sir Anthony all but destroyed you as well as your reputation. I . . . I even encouraged your macabre interest and involvement in Gage's inquiries. *Ini-tially.*" Her gaze dipped to my abdomen, stabbing in intensity. "But you are about to become a mother, and it is time for you to grow up and accept life as it is. If not for your sake, then at least for your child's."

With this, she whirled about and strode from the room, leaving me too astonished to even attempt a response. I stared unseeing at the wall across the room as anger built inside me, raising a flush in my cheeks and a searing heat in my blood. But just as swiftly as it flared, it snuffed itself out, leaving me with a raw ache and a deep well of bewilderment and sadness. I had always looked to Alana for approval, trusting in her unfailing love and support. To hear now that she so sharply disapproved of me, of the person I'd become, cut me to the bone.

We were to attend a ball that evening at Lady Edmonstone's, celebrating Miss Imogen Drummond's debut into Edinburgh society, but when Gage returned home, he found me not in our bedchamber, where I should have already begun dressing, but instead in my art studio. Normally this meant he would have discovered me absorbed in painting, my hair untidily tucked beneath a scarf, and my hands and apron flecked with paint. But about a month past, I'd unhappily realized that I'd grown too ungainly to be able to continue painting. The fumes associated with my art—which had never bothered me much before—had also begun to make me ill. So I'd been forced to temporarily halt my artistic efforts. Fortunately, I could still draw with charcoal and had filled several sketchbooks with different renderings. But I missed the feel of my specially weighted paintbrushes between my fingers and the glide of the bristles across the canvas as the image I was attempting to capture sprang to life in oil and pigments.

That evening Gage did not find me sketching, but rather perched on my stool, staring at the half-dozen easels which propped up my partially completed portraits, each one still draped in sailcloth to protect them. I wasn't entirely certain how or why I had ended up in my studio, except perhaps because my art had always been my solace, my comfort. My constant when the world around me shifted.

"Kiera?" Gage murmured, pulling me from my thoughts.

I turned to look at him as he advanced hesitantly into the room, surveying its dusty contents, including the special set of shelves he had built for me the year before to store all of my supplies. In fact, I could smell sawdust clinging to his coat now, amid the scents of bay rum and his horse, telling me that one of the places he'd visited that afternoon had been the woodshop he occasionally used at a friend's estate a few miles to the north. This was his third trip there in as many weeks, and I knew he was constructing something, likely for the baby, but I didn't want to ruin his surprise.

"What did Dr. Fenwick say? Is the baby well?" Though he spoke calmly, I could see the strain tightening his jaw.

"Yes. Yes, the baby and I are perfectly healthy."

He exhaled a relieved breath, and I stood to wrap my arm around his waist.

"I didn't mean to worry you."

He smiled down at me before pulling me closer. "Then why are you up here, in a brown study?"

"How do you know I wasn't composing a painting in my mind?" I countered. I'd told him before that half the work was done in cognitive preparation before I ever set brush to canvas.

He reached out to clasp my chin between his thumb and forefinger. "Because you could do so in a much more comfortable setting."

"Perhaps the lingering odors of linseed oil and turpentine inspire me."

His gaze softened. "Perhaps, but they didn't stamp that furrow of worry upon your brow."

"How do you know that furrow indicates worry? Maybe it's a sign of concentration."

"Kiera," he chastised gently, halting any further attempts to distract him. His fingers fanned out along my jaw, the calloused pads of their tips lightly abrading my skin. "I can tell when something is troubling you." His pale blue eyes searched mine, but rather than reassuring me, his words only made me more aware of *all* the things that were currently troubling me. All the things I was currently keeping from him. As if sensing my unease, he added. "But if you'd rather not tell me, I won't pry."

I considered telling him about Lord Henry but then dismissed the notion. Not now. Not when I was already smarting from Alana's disapproval and rejection. I couldn't stand to face his as well.

"Alana was here today," I finally said.

He nodded, plainly trying to figure out where this was leading. "For your appointment."

"Yes. Well, she was supposed to be anyway." I frowned in remembered disbelief. "But she was late. Very late. And she didn't seem to even realize it until she glanced at the clock in our drawing room."

"And that troubles you?"

"A little." I worried one of the gold buttons on Gage's coat between my fingers, struggling to put it into words. "It's not like her. She . . . she was frazzled when she arrived. Yet it clearly wasn't about the time."

"She was probably just preoccupied with something. A matter with her children or Philip." He brushed his fingers through the wisps of hair that curled against my neck. "You shouldn't let it overconcern you."

I nodded without lifting my eyes, cognizant that I was stalling. As was Gage, ever attuned to the things I didn't say as much as the things I did.

"And what did she say?"

I peered up at him through my lashes, before focusing on his button again. "That I make a spectacle of myself." When he didn't immediately reply, I risked another glance up at him to find him scowling.

"And I presume this preluded another attempt by her to convince you to stop assisting me in our inquiries."

"It was more of a scolding than an attempt to convince me. But yes."

Gage huffed. "I thought you and your sister had made up. That she'd accepted that this is your decision to make."

I felt a pulse of annoyance. Was he being deliberately obtuse? He'd heard some of Alana's barbed comments. "It's more like she accepted our decision to take a respite from any murderous inquiries until after the baby is born as an indication that we agreed with her and would continue to do so."

"Kiera." He cupped my face in his hands, forcing me to look up at him. "You do not have to agree with her, and you are not wrong for it. In fact, I would go so far as to say you are very right."

"Then I'm not displaying a lack of maturity and motherly instinct by choosing not to conform?" I asked, both craving his reassurance and hating that I needed it. Shouldn't I be strong enough by now to know my own mind and stand firm in it?

"Is that what she said?"

There was no need to respond, for the answer was obvious.

His head dipped so that our foreheads nearly touched. "I didn't fall in love with you because you conform. I fell in love with you because you are instinctively, unabashedly, unequivocally *you*, with all your brilliance and eccentricities. And that is the woman I want our child to have as a mother. Not some diluted version of yourself, where you mute your vibrant reds and blues into conformist grays and browns."

I blinked rapidly as tears began to fill my eyes, and squeaked, "Really?"

He smiled that tender, private little smile that I knew was only ever for me. "Really."

His lips pressed to mine as if sealing a promise, and I returned the pledge.

"Now," he declared. "I suppose it's past time we dressed for Lady Edmonstone's ball." He trailed his fingers down my neck in a caress, his eyes turning languid. "Unless you've decided not to attend."

I sighed, fighting the temptation reflected in his eyes. "We really should attend. For Miss Drummond's sake." I swallowed. "And her stepmother's."

Gage nodded, understanding what I was trying to convey without the need for words. Sometimes I struggled with the realization that Lady Drummond had been dead for just a year. My friend had died before my eyes, overwhelmed by the final dose of the poison that had slowly been killing her. And if not for my insistence, her death would have been ascribed to natural causes and her killer never found. Her stepdaughter, Imogen, had been a great help during the investigation, and while away from Edinburgh I had kept in touch with her through letters. I knew the lonely, melancholy girl was anxious about her debut, and I wanted to be there to support her.

I admitted I was also anxious to shelter her. She reminded me too much of myself at that age. But while I'd had a loving father, an older sister, and a brother to look out for me, her father was uninterested, at best, and neglectful, at worse. He was also likely to sell her to the suitor who was the highest bidder. Yet even with my family looking after my best interests, I had still made the dreadful mistake of marrying Sir Anthony Darby. I feared that with her ethereal beauty and uncaring father, Imogen's fate might be even worse.

CHAPTER 9

My first impression of Lady Edmonstone was that of a brick wall—sturdy, stalwart, and unbending—and the deep red hue of her gown only heightened the comparison. But I quickly recognized that her ladyship also possessed a weak spot when it came to Imogen. It was evident in the gentle smiles she bestowed on her and the soft encouragement she provided as they greeted their guests. She was just the sort of sponsor the girl needed.

As Gage and I had arrived late, we were caught at the tail end of the receiving line, which afforded me the opportunity to observe our hosts. A cousin to the late Lady Drummond, Lady Edmonstone had been abroad with her husband when she died. But upon their return—from somewhere tropical, it appeared, from the looks of their bronzed skin—she had immediately sized up the situation and taken Imogen under her wing. Imogen had spoken highly enough of her assumed aunt, but this was the first chance I'd had to meet her.

Whatever Lady Edmonstone's other talents might be, she had been astute enough to recognize that the fashion for pure white in debutantes' debut gowns would never do for Imogen with her long wheat blond hair and pale coloring. The petite girl would have been washed out. Instead, she wore a ball dress of white *gaze d'Inde* finely painted in soft strips of color and worn over a pale pink satin slip. This enabled her to still appear chaste and demure, but not wan and sickly. Her hair was dressed high on her head in three full bows with a bandeau of large pearls draped over her forehead to match her diamond and pearl earrings, necklace, and bracelet.

Her ensemble put my gown of jonquil-colored aerophane crepe edged with sapphire blue satin entirely to shame, but that was as it should be at a lady's debut ball. As should the sparkle of happiness and excitement that glistened in her eyes. When she caught sight of me and Gage in the receiving line, I was touched by the added radiance she seemed to bestow upon us in her smile. Having only ever seen her wide, dark eyes filled with sadness, I was slightly dazzled, and I could imagine many of the young gentlemen in attendance felt the same.

"Lady Darby," Lady Edmonstone proclaimed warmly as she clasped my hand. "I'm so pleased you could join us." She cast a fond glance toward her charge. "As I know is Imogen. Especially with you being so close to your confinement."

"We're delighted to be here. You look absolutely lovely, Miss Drummond." My smile dimmed as I fought back a wave of sadness. "Your stepmother would have been so proud."

"Thank you, my lady," she replied. A look of silent commiseration passed between us, both a giving and taking of comfort, and an acknowledgment of the woman we would always miss.

Lady Edmonstone pressed the hand she clasped, drawing my attention. "I must thank you also. For everything you did for Clare. For not allowing her murderer to escape justice." She studied my features, and I scrutinized her in return, noticing she possessed the same watery blue eyes, the same high cheekbones as her cousin. But she surprised me with her next words. "She wrote to me, you know. About you painting her portrait. About your kindness. About her admiration for you."

I blinked back at her, mildly stunned, and uncertain how to form my response.

Fortunately, Lady Edmonstone didn't require one. "I'm glad she had a friend like you with her at the end." Her voice hardened. "Because, heaven knows, Drummond can't be relied on." Her gaze darted to Imogen and back. "But we shall not dwell on such unhappy things tonight. However, I will assure you that Eddy and I will be keeping a watchful eye over Imogen's future. Won't we?" she called to her husband, who stood on the other side of Imogen.

"What's that, my dear?" Lord Edmonstone replied, his voice wobbling with two decades of age beyond his wife.

But she had already moved on, making me suspect Lady Edmonstone controlled a great deal of what went on within their household. "I'll not have my niece married off to some lecher with deep pockets simply to please Drummond."

"I'm glad to hear it," I said.

"I knew you would be." Her gaze shifted to my husband in consideration, releasing my hand and taking his. "A sturdy, honorable man like Mr. Gage, or my husband." Her gaze flicked toward Lord Edmonstone negligibly before returning to Gage with a smile. "Yes, that's the way to go. Even a younger son with his own means would be preferable to a man of no character. Perhaps someone like Lord Henry." She turned to her niece, though I barely noted her next words, too distracted by the former. "I saw the way you flushed under his attention."

I hadn't been able to hide my reaction completely, though it seemed Gage was the only one to notice, almost certainly having felt the jolt that had traveled through my muscles. "Lord Henry Kerr?" I tried to ask as casually as possible.

"Yes. Do you know him?" Lady Edmonstone's eyes narrowed. "Oh, but of course you do. You and Mr. Gage helped to resolve that predicament at his father's estate some months past."

That "predicament" had been a murder committed by Lord Henry's own brother, but that was the least of my concerns at the moment.

"Yes, I shall have to ask after his family and how they have been getting on," I said, sliding down the line to greet Lord Edmonstone.

"You're thinking of how awkward it is that Lord Henry was practically Lady Drummond's lover, and now Lady Edmonstone is considering making a match of him and Lady Drummond's stepdaughter at her debut," Gage leaned down to murmur as we climbed the wide marble staircase leading to the ballroom. The immense chamber was ablaze with the light of three enormous chandeliers.

That was part of my discomfort, undoubtedly, though not all. But I wasn't going to admit that to Gage.

I turned to scan the crowd dressed in their finest silks and crispest evening attire as we entered the room. "A ball which Lord Drummond is undoubtedly attending, though he was absent from the receiving line." I worried my lip for a moment between my teeth before adding, "I suspect I should also warn Lady Edmonstone of Lord Henry's relationship with Lady Drummond since she seems to be unaware of it. Not that a match with Miss Drummond is entirely out of the question, but it would be decidedly . . . awkward." I repeated the word, being at a loss to find a better one.

I leaned to the side to peer beyond a trio of debutantes dressed in white at the familiar figure standing on the opposite side of the room, his auburn hair a bright spot among darker heads, and had a sudden inspiration. "Or maybe I should caution Lord Henry." What better excuse to speak to him without arousing my husband's suspicions, so I could demand he finally reveal the secret he'd forced me to keep.

Gage tightened his grip around my waist, pulling me to the side as Imogen and Lord and Lady Edmonstone entered the ballroom behind us. "Not before you grant me your first dance," he said into my ear as we all applauded for Imogen as her father stepped forward to lead her onto the floor beneath the glittering chandeliers.

The orchestra struck up the notes to a waltz, and we watched as the pair stiffly circled the floor for a dozen bars before Lord Drummond passed Imogen off to a young gentleman not of my acquaintance. And apparently one whom Lady Edmonstone disapproved of based on the glare she aimed at Lord Drummond. Other couples then began to take to the floor to join them, including me and Gage.

I always enjoyed dancing with Gage, particularly when it was a waltz and I could circle the floor in his strong arms. But dancing while being so heavy with child was not quite the same experience. There was certainly no possibility of our bodies maintaining the appropriate distance. I only hoped that if Gage sensed my rising vexation he attributed it to the clumsiness I felt in my condition and not my distraction over Lord Henry's presence.

When the waltz ended, Gage guided me to the edge of the room where we'd last spied Lord Henry, but he had since vanished. "I noticed Sir Phineas Riddell speaking to our hosts," he said in a low voice. "I'm going to try to learn what I can about the jewelry Maclean told us was stolen from Riddell's town house." His lips quirked in dry humor. "Maybe I'll offer him our services."

I turned to scan the room as he departed, pondering where

Lord Henry might have gone. I didn't spy him in the lines of the quadrille, but the ballroom was large, and the guests spilled into a number of adjoining rooms. Like at most soirees, there would be a gaming room set aside for the gentlemen, and the various retiring rooms to meet the guests' needs, as well as the dining room where refreshments could be found and a cold supper would be served later in the evening. I edged my way around the room toward the far door, refraining from asking those of friendly acquaintance whether they'd seen my quarry, lest such a request fuel more gossip.

At the door, I paused, wondering if he'd ventured into the corridor or simply to the other corner of the ballroom. The scent of warm negus, ham, and savories wafted down the passage to my right, telling me in which direction the dining room lay, and I decided it was as good a place to continue my search as any. Besides, no one would be surprised to find me there sampling the choice offerings at such an early hour, not in my current state.

In any case, the air was somewhat stuffy, and I wasn't the only one strolling in that direction. I suspected many had gone in search of a cool drink of punch or ratafia. Lord Kirkcowan was the lone figure moving counter to that flow and, unfortunately for me, determined to waylay me.

"Lady Darby," he drawled as his stride checked before adopting a decided swagger. "Venturing forth without your husband, I see." He paused before giving his next word a great deal of emphasis. *"Again."* His yellow tobacco-stained teeth flashed as if he'd just said something fiendishly clever.

If it would not have drawn more unwanted attention, I might have slapped the smug grin off his face. Instead, I merely replied in a disinterested voice. "Lord Kirkcowan." I tossed a negligent glance over my shoulder. "I thought you'd be in the gaming room. Why, you haven't found your pockets to let again, have you?" I tilted my head in mock concern.

He chuckled, his gaze flicking to the side as a lady and gentleman passed us with a look of interest. "Why, whatever are you talking about, dear *girl*. I'm on my way there now."

"I see." I blinked vapidly, not unlike the chit he implied me to be before leaning forward to whisper loudly. "Are you certain that's wise? What if they don't let you play?"

"Of course they'll let me play," he snarled. "Not that it's any of your concern, but my pockets are plenty plush."

I turned my head to smile at a trio of matrons. "Of course they are."

"They are, you pert piece of baggage!"

One of the matrons gasped at this insult, and they all turned to glare at him. Though I noticed none of them considered coming to my aid when he grabbed hold of my arm and pulled me farther away.

"Listen here, I'm on to a very lucrative enterprise now, and I don't need some meddling minx and her besotted husband botching it for me."

"Unhand me, Lord Kirkcowan," I demanded.

He pulled me even closer, looming over me. "Not until I make myself clear."

I knew he couldn't do anything more to me, not in the middle of a corridor filled with people, but my heart kicked in my chest nonetheless. "Unhand me," I ordered in an even louder voice, tugging sharply against his hold.

"You're the one who encouraged my wife to leave me, aren't you?" he hissed. "You put that bloody foolish notion into—"

"I believe the young lady asked you to release her," a familiar deep male voice intoned behind me. His words sharpened as he crowded even closer to me. "I suggest you do it."

I didn't have to turn to see who it was. I had just been searching for him after all, and now here he had found me. Just in time.

Lord Kirkcowan glared at Lord Henry Kerr for the space of but two seconds before abruptly releasing me, nearly flinging me back against Lord Henry's chest, whose hands lifted to the back of my shoulders to steady me. "Collecting quite the number of swains, aren't we, Lady Darby," he sneered before brushing past us.

I flushed at the implication but refused to be goaded into uttering any further protests. When I heard Lord Henry draw breath to do so in my defense, I turned to stay him. "He's not worth your words. And neither is anyone who listens to him," I added for the two debutantes slowly strolling past who were not even attempting to conceal the fact that they were eavesdropping. They blushed and moved on.

Lord Henry and I both fell silent, gazing at each other uncertainly. He looked much the same as he had in January—strong and handsome, but with the same air of sadness lingering in his silvery gray eyes. Before, he had still been grieving for Lady Drummond, but I now suspected he was also grieving for his brother John and the fractures John had caused in their family with his actions.

"Did he hurt you?" he asked, nodding toward my arm.

I lowered my hand from the spot I'd been rubbing where Lord Kirkcowan had grabbed me, grateful that the crowned sleeves hid any markings, though he had rather wrinkled the fabric. "It's nothing."

"Are you certain?" He turned to look over his shoulder. "Because I could fetch Mr. Gage . . ." His voice trailed away, as if just recalling the implication of that statement.

I arched a single eyebrow, inviting him to comment further, but he seemed at a loss for words again. However, I had found mine. "When did you arrive in Edinburgh?"

"Yesterday."

"I see."

He shifted his feet, having the grace to flush. "I set out for Edinburgh the moment I returned to Britain," he hastened to assure me.

"You must have traveled some distance to settle your brother abroad," I queried leadingly.

But whatever guilt and discomfort Henry was feeling did not goad him into hasty words, and he kept the location of his brother to himself. He took my arm, guiding me toward an alcove along the passage where we might talk with greater freedom without being overheard. "I suppose I should have called on you the moment I arrived . . ."

"As you promised," I pointed out, my chest tightening with repressed anger.

He nodded. "I know. But there was a letter waiting for me at Bowmont House from Mother, informing me of Miss Drummond's debut ball this evening. Knowing what you did for Clare, I wondered if you might be attending. And I thought . . . well, I thought that perhaps it would be better to know where things stood, so to speak, before I . . . before I called."

I stared up at him, fighting the shame and frustration that had been festering inside me for weeks. "You mean, whether it would be better to know if I had honored the promise you extracted from me, never dreaming I would be forced to keep such a secret from the man I love for over *eight weeks*?" I bit out in a low voice.

Henry seemed to grasp how furious I was, for he edged back a step. "You haven't told him yet, then?"

I was perilously close to swatting him like I might have done to my brother, Trevor. I supposed in that regard he was already acting like a proper brother-in-law. "No."

"I know I put you in an untenable situation, and I'm sorry for that. Had I known I would be escorting my brother to . . ." He broke off, correcting himself before continuing. Though I didn't know why he was so hesitant to share Lord John's location. It wasn't as if we were going to chase after him or that he'd be charged with anything if we were able to drag him back to Scotland. "*Abroad*, I never would have asked it of you." The genuine contrition softening his features, and the marked similarities to my husband that I could now see because I was looking for them, were all that kept me from raking him over the coals.

I crossed my arms over my chest. "You need to tell him. Tonight," I insisted, though my stomach twisted in knots at the prospect. "Then we'll simply have to face whatever the repercussions are."

I was referring to Lord Gage's subsequent reaction when he learned that Henry and his mother, the Duchess of Bowmont, had deliberately defied his wishes by telling his legitimate son, for Gage was certain to confront him about it. Lord Gage had threatened to reveal certain sensitive secrets he possessed about the duchess and her family if they ever told Gage, and I knew from experience how ruthless my father-in-law could be.

However, I was *thinking* about the repercussions to my own marriage. I turned my head to the side, staring unseeing at the flow of guests moving along the corridor between the ballroom and the dining room. Whether they glanced our way in interest I didn't note, being too absorbed in my own concerns over what my husband's response would be.

"He's going to be angry, isn't he?"

I nodded. "Lord Gage has not been the best of fathers. But Gage always believed that, at the very least, he was faithful to his mother. Whom Gage adored."

But Henry seemed to realize that wasn't the only thing making me so tense. "I'll do what I can to shield you. He need never know you know."

I smiled sadly at him. "I can't lie to him. If even I could. One look at my face, and he will realize I already knew."

"Then I'll make sure he apprehends the pressure I exerted on you to keep my secret. I don't want you to be held accountable for my unthinking actions."

Except I *was* accountable. My allegiance should be to my husband above all, especially when it came to something as important as the knowledge that he had a half brother. However, I'd allowed my empathy for Henry and my own fear over Gage's reaction to override my good sense, and for eight long weeks! Gage had a very good reason to be angry with me. A very, *very* good reason.

But I said none of this to Henry. First and foremost, because my concealing information from my husband was a matter to be dealt with strictly between us. And second, because I strongly suspected Henry was already going to overplay his hand in trying to shelter me. I didn't need him defending me any more strenuously and making matters even worse.

As if conjured by my own worries, I saw Gage striding down the hall toward us. He'd been aiming toward the dining room, but upon catching sight of me, he changed course. Even from such a distance, I could see that his brow was furrowed, and the normally graceful movements of his form were sharp and hurried. Either his interview with Sir Phineas had not gone as planned, or someone had made some sort of spiteful remark about the implications hinted at in *The King of Grassmarket*.

Unless he already knew about Henry. Though how, I couldn't fathom. Few enough people knew the truth.

Regardless, I must have tensed, for Henry peered over his shoulder at what had so unsettled me. He turned to face Gage's approach at my side, straightening his posture as if preparing for inspection. I spared a pulse of empathy for him, anxious to please yet braced for rejection, uncertain how Gage would accept his news.

Gage nodded to him briefly and greeted him by name, but it

was evident that all his focus was directed at me and something more urgent. "Kiera, I've just received word that Rookwood has been murdered."

This so startled me, and was so disparate from the words I'd expected to come out of his mouth, that it took me a moment to respond. "I beg your pardon?!"

"I've sent for our carriage and begged leave from Lady Edmonstone. I presumed you would wish to come with me?"

"I . . . yes, of course I do," I replied, struggling to comprehend and adapt. "If you'll excuse us," I turned to say to Henry as Gage pulled my arm through his and began to hurry us away.

His eyes were wide. "Of course."

I turned to cast one last glance over my shoulder at him as we hastened toward the stairs, and I was struck by the downcast look of his features and the drooping of his shoulders. However, he didn't so much put me in mind of a person whose confession has been thwarted, but rather a faithful hound sorry to be left behind.

CHAPTER 10

When we arrived at North Bridge Street, it was flocked with curious onlookers, some of whom appeared to have strolled over in their finery from the nearby Theatre Royal. Gage and I descended as close to Rookwood's offices as the carriage could maneuver without becoming hopelessly jammed in the traffic on the bridge. In the dim streetlights, winter shrubs dotted the grounds of the old Physic Gardens below, and in the distance I could just make out the hulks of the orphan hospital, Lady Glenorchy's Chapel, and Trinity College Church lined up next to one another. The air was ripe with the smells of coal dust, horse droppings, and the promise of more rain before dawn.

We wove our way through the crowd, Gage's powerful presence and his bearing of authority persuading most to move out of our way with little effort. As we neared the block of buildings across from the market, I noted the police wagon had been pulled up to the publisher's door. Whether that meant his body had already been removed from the scene, I couldn't tell, for a young constable halted us some ten feet away.

Gage asked if Sergeant Maclean was investigating, and we stood waiting as an even younger policeman was sent to fetch him. That the constable knew who we were and had also read or, more likely, been to see one of the plays based on *The King of Grassmarket* was obvious from the wary look he cast our way and the glances he kept stealing toward my abdomen hidden beneath my evening cloak. This, coupled with the antagonistic glares some of the other officers directed at us, gave me an uneasy feeling. I began to suspect we shouldn't have come.

Maclean had warned us the City Police were enduring criticism from their superintendent for not only failing to secure Bonnie Brock's imprisonment but also the implications of corruption alluded to in the book. Implications we were insinuated in. We should have known we wouldn't be welcomed. So I wasn't surprised when Maclean appeared less than pleased to see us when he exited Rookwood's office.

He gestured with his head, requesting that we step aside with him, though I suspected this consideration was done more out of respect for our rank than because of our assistance to him in the past. Particularly given the contentious manner in which our conversation had ended that morning.

"It's true, then?" Gage asked. "Rookwood has been murdered?"

"Ye canna be here," Maclean told us firmly. "This is a matter for the police. Ye canna be assistin' us. No' this time."

The two men stared squarely into each other's eyes, and some unspoken exchange occurred. One I was not privy to.

Gage was the first to break the silent standoff. "We had an appointment with Mr. Rookwood yesterday morning."

"I ken. And I'll have some questions to put to ye aboot that later, but for noo, ye need to go home." His gaze was as sharp as ever, but I thought I detected a hint of uncertainty in his voice as he spoke next. "Ye need to stay far away from this one, do ye hear?"

"Are we . . . suspects?" I hesitated to say the last word, but once the sentence was begun, I could hardly leave it dangling.

His jaw hardened as his gaze swung to me, pinning me in place, and I wondered if part of the ire he directed at me was resentment at my forcing him to state the matter bluntly.

"Did ye have reason to wish the man ill? Did ye have any cause to bear him a grudge? Have ye been outspoken in your dislike?"

There was no need to reply. We all knew that the answer to these questions was an unequivocal *yes*. That didn't mean we *had* harmed him. Maclean knew this as well as we did. But because we had motive to do so, we still had to be considered as suspects. At least for the time being.

"Noo, get her ladyship oot o' this oorlich weather," he ordered, pulling the collar of his gray coat up around his neck as he turned to go. "I'll be by to question ye in the morn."

That this was stated at least partially for the benefit of the constable loitering nearby, I had no doubt, but it still left an unsettling feeling in the pit of my stomach. In any case, it was clear we weren't going to get any answers to our queries that evening, so Gage bundled me close as we retreated down North Bridge Street toward our coach.

The damp I had smelled in the air moments earlier began to sputter from the sky in moist flakes—part rain and part snow. With my head lowered against the wind and my thoughts fixed on escaping the miserable conditions, I nearly missed the fact that our coachman was hailing us.

"You've a visitor," Joe called out gruffly.

It took me a moment to apprehend what this meant, for I didn't see anyone else lingering nearby, but Gage had grasped his implication immediately.

He scowled. "Just one?"

"Aye. I couldna stop him."

Gage lifted his hand, letting him know he absolved him of any blame. "This one's a particularly virulent midge. One we can't quite rid ourselves of."

That our guest would also have heard these comments, there was no doubt. In fact, I suspected that was why Gage had made them. He guided me forward, halting our footman, Peter, who stood rigidly beside the coach before he could open the door. Instead, Gage threw the door open himself, glaring into the interior at Bonnie Brock, who lounged in the corner of the rear-facing seat. Far from intimidated, the scoundrel arched his eyebrows, goading him.

I opened my mouth to warn Gage that Brock's lazy stance was deceptive. I knew from experience that he was braced to strike at any moment. But then I realized my husband would not thank me for issuing such a warning in front of the blackguard. It also might reveal more about my past interactions with Brock than I'd cared to share before.

In any case, Gage clambered up into the conveyance before I could speak, obviously unwilling for me to spend even a second alone with the criminal, and reached out to help me up after him. Between Peter's efforts and my husband's, I was soon seated on the plush bench across from Bonnie Brock, with the queer sensation that I'd already experienced this moment settling over me. Perhaps it was the manner in which Brock was looking at me, as insolent as the first time we'd met. Happily, the comforting weight of Gage's solid presence by my side soon dispersed the feeling.

He reached up to turn the light of the interior lamp higher while I shivered inside my damp cloak, wishing I had a hot brick to rest my feet upon. But there hadn't been time for such niceties as we rushed from Edmonstone House.

Bonnie Brock appeared as disheveled as ever, but this time there was less of an artfulness to it. His hair was still wet and pushed back from his forehead to reveal more of his handsome features than it normally did, as well as the puckered scar running from his hairline down across his temple to his left ear. His clothes were equally damp, filling the carriage with the scent of wet wool and linen, as well as the less pleasant stench of the mud caking his boots.

The two men couldn't have cut more different figures—one damp and disheveled, the other relatively dry and immaculately groomed—but both were not only dashing but also in their own way dangerous.

We waited until the door was shut and the step secured before anyone spoke, and then it was Bonnie Brock who cut straight to the heart of the matter.

"I didna do it."

"And yet here you are, haunting the location where the murder took place," Gage replied skeptically as the carriage began to roll forward.

His eyes narrowed. "Because I received word that Rookwood had been found wi' his head bashed in. Same as you."

I flinched, for this was the first that I'd been informed of the method of murder, but perhaps Gage had kept that detail to himself.

"But my men and I didna have anythin' to do wi' it," Bonnie Brock insisted. "Though that's no' gonna stop Mean Maclean and his pollies from tryin' to pin it on me. For all I ken, maybe the pollies did it themselves. They've certainly been hammerin' at my people hard enough, tryin' to convince 'em to turn against me." He shook his head. "Fools." But the manner in which his fist tightened where it rested against his knee told me that he wasn't as unconcerned as he wished us to believe.

Nevertheless, I had to concede that his supposition was

possible. Not all of Edinburgh's City Police were so honest, and even the most honorable might be driven to do immoral things if they thought it would be for the greater good.

But Gage was of a different opinion. "Not Maclean," he stated unequivocally. "*You* may not like him, but he's upright."

"Ye think so? Weel, tell that to the old woman whose nose Maclean broke because she wouldna let him search her rooms for her grandson. Or the peddler who had his cart smashed because he'd positioned it where another peddler who pays Maclean for the privilege normally does." He smiled jadedly at my shock. "Maclean's no better and no worse 'an the rest o' 'em. And the police are no better than any gang. The only difference is that their bribes and thefts are sanctioned."

"It's not Maclean," Gage repeated through gritted teeth. His face had reddened with fury, and it was apparent that any further such accusations would not be tolerated. "Besides, even if you didn't order it, how can you be so certain one of your men didn't decide to take matters into his own hands?"

Bonnie Brock's posture shifted from relaxed to threatening with lightning speed. "Because my men ken better than to disobey my orders, and I ordered that Rookwood no' be harmed. They ken no' to cross me."

"Like those men who ran off with your sister knew not to cross you?"

Bonnie Brock loomed forward, and the hardened rage stamped across his features was enough to make my blood run cold. That he was seconds away from stabbing my husband, I had no doubt. And fool that my husband was, I could tell that he was about to further bait him.

"Please, gentlemen," I snapped, shifting forward in my seat awkwardly and raising my hands to keep them separated. "Stop it!" I inhaled a deep breath before speaking again, hoping to smooth out the slight quaver. "This is getting us nowhere." I glared at Bonnie Brock. "Sit back, and let's discuss this rationally."

His gaze cut to mine at this directive, and for a moment I thought he would refuse, but then he slowly sank back against the squabs. Somehow the quirk of his mouth made his retreat seem less like a concession and more like a taunting measure, but I wasn't going to call him on it.

Gage was another matter.

"And you!" I turned my glower on him. "Stop prodding the bear, or get a longer stick."

I pressed a hand to my abdomen, ignoring his black look, and slid deeper into the carriage seat. "Now, tell us why exactly you climbed into our carriage uninvited if you're innocent of Rookwood's murder," I demanded of Bonnie Brock.

His eyes dipped to my abdomen, observing my protective gesture. "Because as soon as I heard Rookwood had been crashed, I kent what you and the pollies would think. It's true enough I threatened the quill. But I needed him alive. To tell me who bloody Mugdock is. Or at least how he got his information. Though Rookwood swore he didna ken that part."

I had no difficulty believing he spoke the truth, at least about not knowing Mugdock's real identity. The wrath that suffused his features when he spoke of the author practically turned his complexion purple.

"Besides, when I kill a man, 'tisn't wi' a clumsy blow to the head. And my men wouldna been so inept as to leave before the job was done."

Once again, I was taken aback by the implication of the previous violence he and his men had done, and also the knowledge he already possessed. Though I realized I shouldn't have been.

"How do you know all this?" Gage queried peevishly.

"I have my sources," he replied vaguely.

I'd long been envious of his system of runners positioned

throughout the city—boys ready to relay information to or for him at a moment's notice. But in this case, I suspected his informant might be a member of the City Police he'd bribed.

"What do you mean, 'before the job was done'?" I puzzled. "Was Rookwood alive when they found him?"

Bonnie Brock's green-gold gaze flicked between us. "Didna Maclean tell ye?"

I glanced at Gage, noting his tight jaw. Plainly he wasn't going to answer, so I cleared my throat. "Maclean wasn't willing to tell us anything." Realizing I was fidgeting with my kid leather gloves, tugging them tighter onto my fingers, I lowered them to my lap. "Apparently, we are also suspects."

Bonnie Brock's features flickered in surprise. "Aye, weel . . . Rookwood supposedly scribbled a few letters before he slipped the wind. A *B* and either an *a* or an *o*."

My eyes widened.

"Aye," he replied with a fierce frown.

Ba might be anything, but *Bo* could be the beginning of Bonnie, as in Bonnie Brock.

"And he was also clutchin' the torn corner o' some documents. 'Tisn't clear what they are, but . . ."

"The sequel," I murmured, following his thought.

His eyes glinted in answer. "And if that's true, then who kens who has it noo."

Or where it would end up.

"Perhaps that was the motive," Gage remarked brusquely, his arms crossed over his chest. "Stealing the sequel." He glanced to the side, peering out the window at the darkened streets of New Town. "Which doesn't exactly paint us in the clear. But we can't be the only ones who would prefer not to see the sequel to *The King of Grassmarket* published."

"Ye mean like someone else whose reputation was tarnished in the book?" Bonnie Brock speculated with raised eyebrows.

Which led us back around to their differing opinions about the honorability of Sergeant Maclean and the rest of the City Police.

I grunted as we clattered over a bump in the pavement. "Or a rival publisher," I pointed out before they began to argue again, but then I was struck by another idea. "A rival publisher might benefit twofold. One, by preventing Rookwood from publishing it, and two, by publishing it themselves."

"If they could discover the identity of the author," Gage reminded us.

"I'm no' sure they'd even need to do that."

I turned to Bonnie Brock with interest.

"I'm sure Rookwood told ye how determined Mugdock was to keep him silent. Made him sign that ironclad contract. So how is Mugdock goin' to protest the publication o' his sequel by another publisher wi'oot revealin' himself?"

"Through a team of barristers, but I apprehend what you're saying," Gage said. "In doing so, he's disclosing his identity to not just one individual but, between the barristers' staff and the courts, at least half a dozen people or more. Is he willing to risk that?"

"That reminds me," I said, rolling the button of my cloak between my fingers as I sifted through my thoughts. "Rookwood told us that, at first, Mugdock balked at his insistence that he alter my and Gage's names in the book, but later he relented, even if he only modified them by one letter. But if he was so adamant about keeping them, why didn't he simply approach another publisher?"

Gage tilted his head in consideration. "Maybe he did. Maybe they weren't interested, or they *all* insisted he change our names."

"Or he didna want to expose his identity to anyone else," Bonnie Brock interjected, circling us back to his previous comment.

"Then I suppose he chose Rookwood for a reason," I said. There was nothing astonishing in that. We had done our research and knew that Thomas W. Rookwood was an established, well-respected publisher. Even so, he had been publishing fewer books with each passing year, and there was some speculation he would soon retire and sell his assets to another publisher. I wondered what would happen to those assets now.

I studied Bonnie Brock quizzically, wondering just how much he knew, and how much he would share with us. "Did your *source* tell you who found Rookwood?"

"Aye, that assistant o' his. Said he left to run errands sometime after midday and when he returned this evenin' he found his employer dead."

"That must have been a shock. So they presume the murder took place sometime within that space of time." Hopefully they would have a surgeon examine the body to further pinpoint the time of death, and witnesses would step forward to narrow down the window, but for now the possibilities were rather broad.

But Bonnie Brock wasn't finished. "He claimed he found the window wedged open wi' a bronze bird statue and muddy footprints across the floor."

My head reared back at this statement. "You mean . . ." I glanced at Gage, whose expression had turned grim. "Like from the book?"

He arched a single eyebrow in confirmation.

The fact that the bronze bird statue and muddy footprints neatly echoed one murderous scene from *The King of Grassmarket* could not go unremarked upon. Not when the book's publisher had been the man murdered, and the book's protagonist was certain to be the chief suspect.

"That cannot be a coincidence," I murmured.

"No," Gage conceded. "Not unless Kincaid has taken to

carrying bronze bird statues around with him and leaving them like a fool at every murder he commits."

Rather than glare at him as I'd expected, Bonnie Brock's lips actually quirked at this wry bit of humor.

"Then someone staged that scene," I surmised. "To point the finger at you."

"Or the book," Gage reminded us. "After all, there has been plenty written in the newspapers about how harmful and corrupting that book and the subsequent plays are, and now the outcry is only going to grow louder."

"But would one of those people really go so far as to commit a murder to make their point?"

Bonnie Brock shrugged. "I've seen reformers and officials do much worse."

What he meant by this, and what precisely he considered worse than murder, I didn't know, and I wasn't going to ask.

"Then we're looking for someone who not only had a reason to kill Rookwood but also holds a vendetta against you," I summarized. "For I didn't see a bronze bird statue conveniently sitting on a shelf in Rookwood's office when we visited yesterday morning."

"Did you ever figure out who your informant is?" Gage asked. "Who revealed what they knew about your past to the author?"

Bonnie Brock turned his face to the side, showing us his profile, and much of that was hidden by his fall of tawny hair as it slid forward. "Nay," he bit out in a hard voice. "I've accepted it's no' either o' you, and I'm convinced it's no' Locke or Stump, or Maggie for that matter. So perhaps one o' my other men, someone who discovered more than he shoulda. Or someone from a rival gang who somehow put together all the pieces. I didna ken. No' yet."

"Maybe the information came by bits and pieces from several

sources," I suggested, wondering if this would soften the blow of betrayal he felt or make it worse. "They could have even been unwittingly given. Too much drinking and blathering one night at the White Hart or some other pub."

"What about a mistress? I daresay you've had a number of those."

I stiffened in surprise that Gage should be the one to make such a suggestion, even creditable as it was.

Bonnie Brock took no pains to hide his amusement. "I dinna ken what you do in bed wi' a lass, but I dinna do much talkin', least o' all aboot my past."

I scowled at the implication and was about to defend my husband when he spoke up.

"Yes, well, that's a pity for you, then."

I turned to my husband, warmed by his words.

"Ah, weel, maybe when you're basket-makin' 'tis different," Bonnie Brock retorted, but I was not going to allow his vulgar euphemism for making love with the intention of procreation rile me. All the same, I was more than ready to be quit of him for the evening, and thus relieved when our carriage drew to a stop outside our town house.

"You'll understand when I say that I prefer that you not be seen exiting our carriage, and ask that you remain inside until it pulls around to the mews," Gage stated firmly as he reached across me for the door handle.

"Aye, Stump and Locke are already waitin' there for me."

Gage glanced back at Bonnie Brock at this statement, perhaps relieved the criminal wasn't putting up a fight. I was simply grateful he could remember to be considerate when the occasion called for it.

CHAPTER 11

"Rookwood is dead," Gage announced without ceremony once Bree, Anderley, and Jeffers were all gathered with us in the drawing room of our town house.

"The publisher?" Anderley clarified as Bree sank into one of the giltwood chairs, her eyes round with shock.

"Yes. Coshed over the head in his office sometime this afternoon or evening, and the scene set to look like a chapter from *The King of Grassmarket.*"

"Then you're thinking it's not the work of Mr. Kincaid," Jeffers intoned, his manner as unflappable as ever.

"Unfortunately, no." Gage's mouth curled wryly. "Not when he's already under increased scrutiny because of the book and plays, and this is certain to add to it." He looked to me. "I should mention that *we* are also under suspicion, in light of the fact that we might have held a grievance with Mr. Rookwood."

"Weel, that's just ridiculous. I never heard so much gibberish in my life," Bree protested.

"No, it's only logical. After all, we did pay him a visit the day before, and we were certainly irritated with him, at the least, for his publication of *The King of Grassmarket*. But Maclean is no fool. He'll ascertain soon enough we're not the culprits."

From his furrowed brow I could tell he wasn't as sanguine as he wished to appear. He respected Maclean, and the pair of them had a rapport that had served them both well. So I knew this morning's tiff between us all in Mrs. Duffy's tea shop, and then Maclean's treatment of us outside Rookwood's office, must have been weighing heavily on his mind.

In any case, none of us were going to sit around waiting for Maclean to come to the right conclusion when we could help him to it faster by uncovering the truth ourselves. There was no need to even broach the question. Our most trusted staff had already made their way to the same conclusion we had.

"Then who *do* you think did it?" Anderley asked, perching on the rounded arm of a bergère chair. A stance which earned him a pointed glare from Jeffers.

When Gage settled on the arm of the sofa in much the same posture, I thought our butler was going to throw his hands up in exasperation, but he remained stoic.

"We don't know," Gage admitted, crossing his arms over his chest. "Not yet. But we have a number of suspicions. Beginning with a rival publisher. Or someone else who had been besmirched in Mugdock's book." He didn't propose outright that the police were a possibility, but he must have known that his inclusion of this category encompassed them. "Either way, it's even more crucial we uncover who this Mugdock is, once and for all."

"Ye think he might be next?" Bree asked.

"Maybe. But even if not, I think we'll find him wrapped up in this conundrum, whether his book was the cause of his publisher's murder or not."

"We also need to take a closer look into his personal life," I said. "I know Rookwood is a widower, but I'm not certain whether he has children, and if he does, where they're located. Either way, we need to know who stands to inherit his considerable assets and those of his publishing business. The motive for his death may lie there."

Gage nodded in agreement. "You and I need to pay a visit to Mr. Heron tomorrow to find out what he knows. Since he was the one to discover Rookwood, it will be killing two birds with one stone."

Bree cringed.

"My apologies," Gage corrected. "Poor choice of words."

"And what of us?" Anderley leaned forward eagerly. "What do you want us to do?"

"I need you to find out who was seen entering and exiting Rookwood's office today after his assistant departed around midday. The entrance to the markets is across the road, so there shouldn't be any shortage of witnesses. I'm sure the police will be questioning them as well, but some of them may hesitate to share what they saw with them. I'm hoping you can convince them to speak to you instead."

Anderley scratched his chin and nodded, perhaps already plotting his approach.

"There was an oyster cart and a ballad-seller near the entrance yesterday with clear views of Rookwood's door," I told him helpfully. "Perhaps they usually set up in those spots."

"What o' me?" Bree asked, sliding forward in her seat.

"We need you to speak to Rookwood's staff," I supplied. "Find out what they know." I sat taller, having a sudden inspiration. "And find out who cleans Rookwood's publishing office. It's a small enough establishment that I wouldn't be surprised if one of his household staff maintains the office as well."

"Aye. Shouldna be a problem to convince 'em to talk."

I didn't doubt either of them for a moment. Anderley possessed good looks and charm, and the chameleonlike ability to conform to whatever social strata he found himself within, while Bree was so friendly and empathetic that it was impossible not to find yourself pouring your heart out to her.

"Be careful," Gage cautioned them. "Don't draw too much attention to yourselves, and be aware of your surroundings. The cholera may be decreasing, but that doesn't mean it's gone. Beware the food you eat from any carts, or better yet, don't consume any, since the Board of Health suspects that is the likeliest source of contamination."

They both promised to be vigilant, rising from their seats as he dismissed them.

"Jeffers, I have a different matter I need your help with," Gage declared, turning to our butler.

But I was still focused on Bree and Anderley, who shared a flirtatious glance in the doorway as he allowed her to proceed him through the door. I was pleased to see they seemed to be in accord again, but I couldn't halt the unsettling feeling, born of experience, that it wouldn't last.

"You are acquainted with Sir Phineas Riddell, are you not?" Gage asked, reclaiming my attention.

"I am," Jeffers replied, moving several steps nearer.

Lord Phineas was known to be a friend of Lord Drummond, who was Jeffers's previous employer, so it had seemed a safe assumption that Jeffers knew him.

"Apparently, Sir Phineas was the victim of a housebreaking a short time ago. Their jewelry was stolen from their safe," Gage explained, reminding me that there had been no time to discuss what he had learned from the Riddells at Imogen's ball. Just as there had been no time for me to arrange with Lord Henry Kerr when it would be best for him to inform Gage that he was his half brother.

"I believe I heard mention of that somewhere," Jeffers replied evenly.

Of course he had. The best butlers were always well informed. And Jeffers was undoubtedly one of the best.

"See what you can find out about the matter from their staff."

"Anything in particular?"

Gage frowned at the fire burning low in the hearth. "I want to know if they believe a theft actually occurred."

Jeffers bowed his head. "Will that be all?"

"Yes. Mrs. Gage and I will retire shortly," he added distractedly.

Jeffers bowed again before exiting the room.

I shifted closer to where Gage perched on the opposite arm of the settee. "You think Sir Phineas is lying?"

He didn't speak at first, forcing me to grasp his hand and repeat myself in order to pull his thoughts from whatever unhappy place they'd gone.

"Yes. At least I'm fairly certain of it." His gaze dropped to my hand, his long fingers skimming over the skin of each of my knuckles. "When I spoke to him at the ball he suggested perhaps *I* had something to do with it. Said that Kirkcowan had told him that we were responsible for the theft of his jewels last year."

I flushed in acknowledgment that at least part of that statement was true. "What did you say?"

"I questioned why he would believe such an assertion when he must know what an inveterate gambler Kirkcowan is. And not a very good one at that." His eyes lifted to meet mine. "Most surprisingly, Lord Drummond agreed with me."

My eyes widened. "He did?"

There had been no shortage of animosity between me and Lord Drummond a year ago when I had insisted that his wife had met with foul play, and subsequently proved it and unmasked her killer. For a time, I had even believed him to be the culprit, for he had been brutish to her, and his first wife's death from a fall down the stairs still struck me as suspicious. But perhaps time had mellowed his hostility toward me.

"He did." His mouth pursed briefly. "Little good it did. Sir Phineas merely countered with the argument that Kirkcowan never seems to be short of funds."

It was my turn to pucker as if I'd tasted something sour. "You know, he's right. Kirkcowan does always seem to get his hands on money from somewhere. I was just wondering earlier today how he's able to keep his town house here in Edinburgh. Surely it's not entailed. Not like his estate, which his wife told me last year was mortgaged to the hilt."

Gage brushed his fingers over my palm, sending pleasant tingles through my body. "I don't know. But truthfully, I don't wish to discuss any more of this tonight." He hoisted me to my feet, positioning me so that I stood between his legs. With him perched on the high, rounded arm of the settee, our heads were almost the same height. His hands shifted to gently cradle my rounded abdomen between them. "You must be more exhausted than I am."

"I admit, I am looking forward to lying down." I glanced down at my stomach. "Though this little one now makes it difficult to rest."

He smiled tenderly at me before bending his head. "Are you pecking at your mother in there, little Branok?"

I heaved a playfully aggrieved sigh. "Not another of your relatives' names." This was a familiar refrain, his suggesting we name our child after one of his Cornish great-grandfathers, and me demurring.

"No. But Branok means 'raven' or 'crow,' so it seemed apropos."

"Only if you want our child to arrive with raven-dark hair. Personally, I'm hoping he or she looks astonishingly like you."

His pale blue eyes softened with empathy. "That would put an end to all the spiteful gossip, wouldn't it?"

"You would think the known facts about gestation would have already done that," I remarked drolly. "But people seem happy to either live in or feign ignorance."

Gage's arms slipped around my waist, pulling me closer. "Forget them," he murmured, pressing a kiss to my lips. "And they'll forget their ridiculous speculation in time, as well. We won't let it blight our happiness at Meryasek's birth, no matter what he looks like."

I smiled at his persistence in slipping these Cornish names into our discussions about the babe. "What do Meryasek and—what's the other name you've mentioned? Casworan? What do they mean?"

"I believe Meryasek means 'sea lord,' after the founder of Brittany. And Casworan has something to do with a warrior or a battle hero."

I chuckled. "Your father would be pleased with either of those."

"Well, don't let that turn you against them."

I laughed aloud at this quip, and he grinned broadly, a sight that was certain to make me weak in the knees. Skimming my hands up his broad chest, I began to pick at the folds of his cravat, suddenly hesitant to voice my own suggestion. "Actually, if our child is a boy, I wondered if we might name him Will. Well . . . William." I snuck a glance up into his eyes, uncertain what I would see reflected there.

"After William Dalmay?" he asked softly.

I swallowed past the lump that had gathered at the back of my throat at the memory of my friend. "Yes."

William Dalmay had been an old family friend and had served as my drawing instructor one formative summer when I was fifteen. That is, before he had suddenly disappeared. He'd served as an officer during the Napoleonic Wars and had struggled to forget the horrific memories of his time fighting in the Peninsular campaigns, so most of us who had been close to him had believed he'd simply run away, too embarrassed to continue to battle his demons in front of those he loved. But the truth had been much darker. His own father had locked him away in a lunatic asylum for nearly ten years. Only upon his father's death had his younger brother been able to discover the truth and demand his release. But Will had known too much about the terrifying things that occurred at the asylum, and the fanatical doctor who ran it had been determined to silence him. In the end, Will had given his life to save me and others from the doctor's same machinations, and to avenge the woman he'd loved.

I had grieved for Will deeply, and Gage knew this. But he had also accused me of being in love with Will, blind to the fact that I was already in love with *him*. He should have realized the truth by now, but that didn't mean he would want his son to be named in Will's memory.

He brushed his knuckles along my jaw. "I think that's a fine idea."

"You do?"

"Yes, it's a good sturdy name. Very British. And nothing nearly so fanciful as Sebastian."

I smiled at the sight of his wrinkled nose. "I like Sebastian."

He gazed deeper into my eyes. "I like it when *you* say it. But otherwise . . ." He shrugged.

"Why did your parents choose it?"

"My mother was enamored with Shakespeare's *Twelfth Night*."

"Ah," I exhaled.

"And I believe she convinced Father by referring to St. Sebastian, the patron saint of soldiers. But what about you? I'm not sure I've ever asked why you were named Kiera. After a relative?"

"My grandmother named me." I tilted my head to the side in fond remembrance of her. "My mother's mother."

"She was from Ireland?"

"Yes. She always told us that she had the blood of ancient Irish kings flowing through her veins, and I believed it. She was quick-witted, and unique, and beautiful. She had this presence about her. As if she knew exactly who she was and precisely where she was supposed to be, and nothing you could do or say would change that. Because of that, she was keener to accept people as they were. Including me. It was a . . . relief not to have to pretend in her presence." I looked up to find his pale blue eyes studying me intently, the silver flecks near the pupils glinting in the firelight.

"It sounds like you inherited a great deal from her."

I warmed at the compliment. "She attended at my birth, and the moment she saw my crown of dark hair, she insisted I be named Ciera, which means 'little dark one.' My father wanted to name me after his mother, Anne, but my grandmother prevailed, though my father got his way in spelling it with a *K* rather than a *C*. And Anne became my middle name."

"But your hair isn't so very dark," Gage said, twirling one of my side curls around his finger.

I laughed. "No, it fell out soon after I was born and grew back chestnut brown. Something my father never ceased to remind my grandmother of. But she never wavered in her belief it suited me." I shook my head. "I'm not sure I'll ever know what she meant by that. But she was rumored to have the second sight."

The clock on the mantel softly chimed, recalling me to the lateness of the hour and the fact that I had never gotten an opportunity to sample the delectable fare at Imogen's ball. My stomach growled and Gage grinned. "Go on up. I'll ask Jeffers to have a cold tray sent to our bedchamber."

I nodded. "But no red wine." I pressed a hand to my chest, imagining the burning sensation. "I'll never be able to rest tonight if I drink it."

"Noted." He pressed a kiss to my temple, sending me off while he crossed toward the bell-pull.

I slept late the following morning. Much later than I intended, for by the time I emerged from my toilette, Sergeant Maclean had already come and departed.

"Perhaps that was for the better," Gage remarked as our carriage set off for Rookwood's office, in hopes of locating Mr. Heron. "As it was, Maclean was hardly forthcoming with what he knew." He frowned. "He was more interested in questioning me."

"You think he honestly suspects you?" I asked in genuine shock.

"I think he wants me to *think* he does. As to whether he actually does, I don't know. But he certainly has Kincaid at the top of his list."

"What of me?"

Gage turned away from the view outside the window, where the dreary weather from the evening before had turned downright dreich. Anyone with any sense or choice in the matter would have remained curled up in front of the fire and out of the damp, blustery, miserable conditions. "I gather he doesn't believe a woman in your condition could have slipped into the office unnoticed or climbed through the window, *if* that is, in fact, how they gained entry."

I adjusted the capote of terry velvet covering my head, contemplating the distance from the close below Rookwood's office to the window ledge above. "I think I could make it with a ladder."

He stared at me in disbelief.

"Not in this ensemble, of course." I gestured to my mantua of bright cerise gros de Tours fabric. The full shape hid much of my form and all but the bottom hem of my aventurine merino walking dress beneath. "But something dark and less voluminous."

"Well, don't go about informing people of that," he groused. "I considered it a blessing that, at least, he'd crossed you off his suspect list."

I glowered. "I'm not daft, Gage. I'm not informing other people. I'm informing *you.*"

"Well, regardless. Let's not test it out."

I rolled my eyes. "Maclean must have interrogated you in earnest if you're determined to be this stern."

He tapped his fingers in agitation against the head of his walking stick propped beside his leg. "No, not really. I'm more aggravated that he wouldn't share what he knew. Though I suppose I shouldn't fault him for wanting everything in his investigation to be aboveboard. And corroborating with any suspect, even me, isn't that."

"What are you planning to do with that?" I nodded toward his walking stick, which he rarely carried. "Drive away any encroachers?" I knew well that walking sticks often doubled as weapons for gentlemen. I suspected that was why Lord Gage had developed the affectation of carrying one. But Gage usually eschewed this traditional accessory in favor of a pistol tucked into his greatcoat or the back waistband of his trousers.

"Don't worry," he replied, correctly interpreting my thoughts. "I've got my gun, too."

We were venturing into the edge of Old Town, and there were bound to be curious bystanders gathered about the place where a murder had so recently occurred, but his decision to carry two weapons seemed a trifle excessive. Particularly as I also had my Hewson percussion pistol concealed inside my reticule, where I always carried it.

"Well, let's try not to use either, shall we?" I responded tartly.

His brow darkened and he opened his mouth to argue but then stopped, perhaps realizing I was imitating the insulting obviousness of his earlier statement.

However, I was soon grateful for his extreme foresight when I saw the crowd gathered on North Bridge Street. It was worse than the evening before, with people loitering twenty to thirty deep, obstructing traffic, even in the chill rain. I supposed I shouldn't have been surprised. The populace's macabre fascination with murder, along with the victim's connection to the spectacularly popular *The King of Grassmarket*, ensured that the crime would capture the public's interest.

But Gage had the forethought to direct his carriage to approach the office from Calton Low and Leith Wynd, driving past Trinity Hospital and into the old Physic Gardens. On this backside of the row of tenements where Rookwood Publishing stood, there were still a few inquisitive onlookers, but far fewer than on the bridge. Since our carriage could only traverse so far without getting stuck in the narrow lanes, Gage and I soon had to set out on foot.

We picked our way over the slick and uneven cobblestones that paved the steep slope of Carrubbers Close. The walls of the tenements on either side closed around us, leaving only a thin slice of leaden sky overhead, making the umbrella I carried so that Gage's hands remained free to grip his walking stick and steady me almost unnecessary. This close had long been a refuge for Jacobites—those loyal to the exiled King James II and VII and his Stuart descendants. While the quest to restore the Stuart line to the throne was now extinct, the stones still bore the traces of the past, including the image of an oak leaf and acorns etched into the wall near the entrance to a wool merchant's shop.

A pair of men, roughly dressed, idled in the doorway, and Gage stepped between me and them, guiding me toward the rear entrance to the building in which Rookwood's office was located. I could feel their gazes following us as we stepped inside.

The rear of the building being several floors below that of the level facing the bridge, we climbed two dimly lit flights of stairs before approaching the likeliest door. Gage tried the latch, but it would not open, and we soon heard a voice call out from inside. "Go away! I'm no' lettin' any o' you vultures in here. No' if I have any say."

Gage and I shared a speaking glance. Apparently, we weren't the only ones who had attempted to gain entry in this manner. After witnessing how the infamous London Burkers' home had been plucked apart as souvenir hunters descended upon the place after their arrest for the murder of the Italian Boy, even stripping the single tree in their garden of all its bark, I was more resigned to the fact than startled. Had the Burkers' victim had a home, let alone a definitive identity, I suspected it would have been plundered as well.

"Mr. Heron, this is Mr. and Mrs. Gage." Gage turned his ear toward the door to listen. "We were hoping to speak with you."

For several moments these words were met with silence, and I began to think Rookwood's assistant would turn us away. But then his voice replied louder this time, closer to the wooden barrier between us. "Are you alone?"

Gage glanced behind us to be certain. "Yes."

We heard the metal screech of a bolt being thrown back and then the click of a lock before Mr. Heron peered out at us through a narrow crack in the door. His round, stricken eyes searched the shadows behind us until he must have been content we were telling the truth. Then he pulled the door wider, urging us to enter hurriedly. Gage had barely slipped past him before he slammed it shut again, fumbling as he refastened the locks.

CHAPTER 12

If Daniel Heron had gotten any sleep the night before, he certainly didn't look like it. His wide eyes were shadowed by dark circles and his skin pallid. His prematurely silver-white hair was disheveled, standing on end in places, as if he'd been running his hands through it repeatedly. When he spoke, his voice trembled slightly, from either residual fright or the effects of too many cups of tea. "Come this way."

He led us down the corridor and into the larger front room filled with mostly bare desks, save his cluttered bureau. When we'd visited previously, the blinds had been open, allowing light to spill across the gleaming wood. Now they were closed, so only the barest sliver filtered through from the leaden skies outside. I couldn't blame him for keeping them shut, not with the noise of the crowd gathered outside, practically pressed against the glass, penetrating through the cracks and crevices.

An oil lamp burned on Mr. Heron's desk, and he moved it to the empty desk farthest from the windows, casting a small circle of light around the space. Gage helped him move two chairs closer to the table so that we could all be seated while I propped the dripping umbrella against the desk. Unlike last time, Mr. Heron did not offer to take our outer garments, and I was glad of it. A draft of chill air had found its way inside my mantua, and I draped my ermine boa tighter around my throat.

"I s'pose you heard aboot what happened to Mr. Rookwood?" he began, glancing distractedly toward the windows.

"Yes, and first of all, let me say, we're terribly sorry for your loss," Gage replied.

Heron turned to stare at him rather goggle-eyed and then swallowed, making his Adam's apple bob up and down. "I found him, you ken. And yet . . . and yet it hasna really sunk in that he's . . ." He swallowed again. "He's dead."

I noticed his brogue was more pronounced this morning than it had been two days before, but that was understandable. After all, many merchants and businessmen affected a more polished English accent similar to the aristocratic tones the upper class were taught to perfect from an early age, no matter whether they were Scottish, Welsh, or Irish. My brother-in-law Philip's accent was as crisp as any nobleman's, except when he was tired or had too much to drink. Then his Highland brogue rounded his speech.

"That's not an uncommon reaction," I assured him. "It can be difficult to accept something so tragic, so final."

He nodded, his gaze drifting toward the door to Rookwood's office. Until a loud bang at the front of the building made him start. His round eyes swung toward the disturbance.

"I don't expect they'll gather for long," Gage said. "Not when they realize they won't be allowed to tour the premises. Not in this weather."

"You think so?"

The corners of Gage's mouth lifted in a heartening smile. "Most of them must already be soaked and freezing, and not all of them have the resources for coal and a fire to warm themselves by. Poor chaps."

Mr. Heron inhaled a deeper breath than the shallow ones he'd been taking thus far, seeming to derive some hope from Gage's words. Then he spread his hands flat on the desk between us. "I s'pose you heard aboot it from the police, then."

Gage didn't correct him. "Tell us in your words what happened."

"Mr. Rookwood sent me oot to run a number o' errands for him. 'Twasn't uncommon. His gout had started to flare up more often o' late, and so he would send me in his place."

I wondered if Rookwood had also been grooming him to take over, but if Mr. Heron held similar aspirations, they didn't reflect in his voice or demeanor.

"I . . . I didna finish 'til late, and I expected Mr. Rookwood to be gone. He usually left aboot six o'clock. But I noticed the light under his door, so I knocked to see if there was anythin' he wanted. When he didna answer, I thought maybe he'd fallen asleep o'er a manuscript. He'd done so a time or two, and I always roused him. And sure enough, there he was, hunched o'er his desk." His face paled. "But when I stepped closer, I could see the blood and . . . and his Louis XVI ormolu clock. The one wi' the globe at the top that rested on his fireplace mantel."

I recalled seeing the distinctive piece on our previous visit.

"It was lyin' on the floor behind him." He raked his hands through his hair. "I . . . I tried to see if he was breathin', but he was cold to the touch."

I studied his drawn features, his agitated movements, and it was clear to me that Mr. Heron was still suffering from shock. If he had anything at all to do with his employer's demise, he evidently hadn't expected to find his employer killed in such a manner.

"I apologize for making you relive it all, but every detail could be important," Gage told him. His expression was sympathetic, his posture unthreatening, but I could tell by the way he'd laced his fingers together over his flat stomach that he was intently observing Rookwood's assistant. He often adopted such a stance when he was seriously questioning someone, and the manner in which he suppressed his inflection confirmed it. "What errands did Mr. Rookwood ask you to run yesterday?"

"Weel, ahh . . . Mostly the usual." He squinted, squeezing the bridge of his nose. "The bank, the tobacco shop, our printer . . ." He broke off, glancing at Gage in suspicion. "Why are you askin'? Dinna tell me you suspect *me* . . ." He pressed a hand to his chest, his voice strangled as he struggled to find the words. ". . . o' . . . o' . . . *harmin'* Mr. Rookwood?"

That he'd avoided saying the word *murder* spoke volumes.

"I don't think anything," Gage replied calmly. "But the tasks Mr. Rookwood sent you to perform might give us some insight as to what was on his mind, and subsequently who might have killed him."

Mr. Heron's chest rose and fell with each breath as he weighed the candor of Gage's response. He must have found it truthful, for his shoulders slumped and he pressed a hand to the side of his head. "As I said, the bank, the tobacco shop, our printer, a handful o' bookshops, his solicitor, the Theatre Royal." He scowled. "And I had to track doon one o' our authors oot in Leith who's late wi' a manuscript."

If he'd truly visited all those places, I could understand why it might have taken him half a day.

"And you departed here sometime at midday?" Gage clarified.

"Aye. At a quarter after twelve."

"Why the Theatre Royal?"

That location had leapt out at me as well. Particularly as Rookwood had told us that Mugdock had refused to endorse their play.

Mr. Heron shrugged. "I delivered a letter to Mr. Murray, the manager. I dinna ken what it contained."

Didn't know or wouldn't tell us?

"And his solicitor?" Gage asked.

"Same. A sealed letter."

Gage nodded before asking for more specifics about the businesses he'd visited on behalf of Rookwood, as well as their locations, so that we could follow up with them. "Would you mind showing us Rookwood's office?"

His eyes were stricken. "It's no' been cleaned."

"I didn't expect it would."

He rose to his feet shakily before crossing toward Rookwood's door and opening it. The scent of stale tobacco smoke assailed us, smothering some of the more unpleasant smells left behind. I pressed my mantua sleeve against my nose and followed the men inside.

Rookwood's body had, of course, been taken away, but I could see the outline of his head on the blotter where blood and other matter had pooled. I fought down a wave of nausea, my nose being more sensitive and my stomach more prone to queasiness in my condition, and turned away. As there was no corpse to examine where I might use the knowledge I'd acquired from my first husband, Sir Anthony, I elected to allow Gage to search that side of the room, while I surveyed the other.

As far as I could tell, most of the office appeared undisturbed. The chairs had been moved, but that was probably the work of the police. Mr. Heron still hovered to the side of the door, eyeing the desk as if a snake perched atop its surface, ready to strike.

"I understand the window was propped open?" I queried, hoping to distract him, as well as gain more information.

"Aye." He turned to face me. "Wi' a bronze bird."

"Like in the book?"

He nodded. "I didna immediately notice the connection. No' 'til the police asked me aboot it."

I moved closer to the now closed window, discovering that a pool of water still sat on the floorboards directly below it. Muddy footprints trailed away from the window toward the desk, crossing back and forth over each other, but curiously never venturing farther into the room. Had the killer scaled the building with the aid of a rope or a ladder and, finding Rookwood asleep at his desk, climbed through the window and snuck up behind him to deliver the fatal blow? That was the only explanation I could think of for why Rookwood hadn't risen from his seat or at least shown some sort of alarm at the intruder's entrance, as well as why the footprints didn't extend farther into the room.

Unless it was all a ruse, and the killer *hadn't* entered through the window.

I found that scenario far more likely for a number of reasons. For one, surely someone would have noticed a man scaling the wall in broad daylight, even in a dark close like Carrubbers. The killer would have been taking a terrible risk that the alarm wouldn't be raised by his actions. Two, we had seen for ourselves just days before how difficult this window was to open, and Rookwood was unlikely to have propped it open himself in the cool, damp weather. And three, the theatricality of the evidence and the way it pointed a finger at *The King of Grassmarket* and Bonnie Brock Kincaid was far too calculated.

As we'd entered, it was perfectly obvious to me that Rookwood's killer had come through the door—either the front or the back. I could tell from Gage's measured scrutiny and the cynical twist of his lips as he examined the evidence that he was of the same opinion. The question that remained was whether Rookwood had been aware of their arrival or if he had fallen asleep as Mr. Heron claimed he'd done in the past. But the answer to that query would not be found here but on the body. The location of the wound on Rookwood's skull would reveal the position of his head when he was struck.

I wondered how we might obtain this information, whether Sergeant Maclean could be convinced to share it with us. Sometimes the newspapers relayed detailed information about the autopsies of murder victims to the public, but that was not guaranteed. Especially in the case of a respected member of society like Mr. Rookwood.

In any case, that was a matter to be addressed later, and Mr. Heron was once again beginning to look rather green about the gills, so I rejoined him near the door. "Is the back door to the office normally kept locked?"

"No' during business hours. Some o' our staff and suppliers enter that way." He paused, glancing behind him toward the front of the office where outside the crowd was gathered. "Today was different."

I nodded in understanding. "What of Mr. Rookwood's assets? Do you know who stands to inherit?"

He shook his head. "I believe he has a sister who lives near Aberdeen, but I've ne'er met her."

"And the publishing assets? What will be done with them?"

"Well, I . . . I'd hoped we could make an arrangement where I might buy the business from him in installments." His shoulders sank and he turned away. "But I s'pose 'tis too late for that noo."

He looked so dejected, so lost, my heart ached for him.

"Whatever the state of Rookwood's will, may I make a suggestion?" Gage said, clasping the other man on the shoulder. "Hire a few men to help you pack up and clear out of these premises. Before it's too late." He glanced past him toward the windows, where outside a mob still gathered. "Or else you're liable to return tomorrow and find the windows smashed in and the contents looted by souvenir hunters."

Mr. Heron stiffened, his eyes wide with alarm.

"I can recommend a few good men. I can send them to you within the hour, if you like."

He exhaled in relief. "Aye. Aye, I would."

"You've got some unsavory-looking fellows loitering in the close behind here, so I don't recommend leaving until they arrive. And ask anyone who tries to gain entry what my wife's favorite flower is before you let them in." He flicked a glance at me. "It's a bluebell. That way you'll know I really sent them."

Mr. Heron swallowed. "I will. Thank you."

"Now that that's settled," I interjected. "How are *we* going to depart without being accosted?"

Gage moved back across Rookwood's office, peering out through the window and down to the shadowy close below. "I have a plan. But we need to put it into action now before those louts decide it would be a better idea to wait for us on the stairs than in the close."

He explained quickly as we retraced our steps to the back entrance. Then he drew his pistol while Mr. Heron unbolted the door and threw it open. Once he was certain no one was lurking on the dark landing, he crossed to the door on the other side and rapped on the worn wood.

"We're no' Rookwood's, ye bloody midges," an angry woman hollered from the other side. "That's the other door."

"Mrs. Tolliver, it's me, Mr. Heron."

There was a beat of silence and then the sound of footsteps approaching. The lock clicked open, and a gray head and a pair of wary dark eyes appeared in the crack in the door. "What do ye want?"

"Can you let my friends leave through your shop? There are men lurkin' in the close, and they're goin' for help."

Mrs. Tolliver's scrutiny shifted to me and Gage, and it was obvious she recognized us, for her mouth puckered with disfavor.

"Ye sure ye should be trustin' 'em? Heard they been protestin' that book Rookwood published."

"Aye, and who can blame 'em," Mr. Heron surprised me by remonstrating with her. "What wi' Mugdock libelin' 'em, and no proof to his claims. 'Tis pure fiction."

I studied his profile, wondering precisely how much he knew and whether he was privy to Mugdock's real identity. Rookwood had led us to believe not, but perhaps that had been to protect Heron.

"Aye, weel, yer Bonnie Brock's friends, arena ye? That much is true?"

"Acquaintances," I replied, not really certain I could categorize our relationship as a friendship. We were more reluctant allies.

Her gaze dipped to my rounded abdomen concealed by my mantua as she cackled. "Right."

I stiffened.

"Come on, then?" She gestured us forward. "Before those midges return for another try."

I followed the woman inside as Gage shook Mr. Heron's hand. He lingered in the doorway as the publisher's assistant retreated to his office and closed and bolted the door.

"Lock that door, noo," Mrs. Tolliver groused, pushing past me to do so herself. "I dinna need 'em burstin' in here, stealin' Mr. Tolliver's materials."

I glanced around me to discover we were in the back room of a shop. The walls were lined with deep, open cupboards, each stacked with dozens of rolls of fabric in various shades of wool and linen.

"Ye could give my husband some custom for this favor I'm aboot to do ye," she told Gage as she bustled forward again. Her appraising gaze slid over his current frock coat of green superfine and the brown trousers revealed beneath his open greatcoat. "If ye were to sport a suit made from his cloth tha' would drive the apers our way."

"Consider it done," Gage replied. "I'll send my man with my measurements within a few days' time."

"Oh, I can gather those just by lookin' at ye," she declared as she circled him, her gaze roaming to places I'd have preferred it hadn't gone. "But he'll need to select the fabric."

Gage's eyes twinkled with suppressed amusement. "Of course."

"Wait here a moment," she instructed us, brushing through the cloth hanging over a doorway into what I presumed was the front of the shop.

"Mr. Tolliver may be the woolen-draper," I murmured to Gage. "But there's no doubt Mrs. Tolliver runs this shop."

He cracked a smile. "Somehow I feel lucky to escape here with the promise to purchase the fabric for just one set of clothes."

"She's probably hoping your guilt will work on you."

"Come on, then," Mrs. Tolliver ordered, suddenly reappearing. "There's no customers. No' that they can make it to the door through that lot o' midges. Bunch o' ghouls."

We followed her into the front room where a man, presumably Mr. Tolliver, lifted his head from poring over a book and stood blinking at us.

"Right, then. Best cover your faces as best ye can, 'specially in those fancy garments." She held the door for us, gesturing us out as she raised her voice. "Have a lovely day. Please come again. I promise it's no' usually this crowded." This last comment rang with vexation, and was obviously added for the benefit of the mob. She punctuated it with firm closing of the shop's door.

CHAPTER 13

Gage helped me open the umbrella, and then I gripped his arm tightly and lowered my head, trusting him to guide us through the swarm of people. Mrs. Tolliver might have thought our garments ill-advised, but they did the trick as we knew they would. Because they screamed quality, and because Gage oozed quiet authority, the people gathered on North Bridge Street moved out of our way without thought. Even my lowered head was to be expected, given the fact that gentlewomen were supposed to be reserved and demure.

For the most part, the mob was a silent, sullen mass, huddling beneath their drab clothes as they grew damper in the rain. For some, this was the only manner in which they washed themselves, and the smell attested to it. Only the men gathered at the front, near the windows, seemed to be making a disturbance—banging on the glass and shouting from time to time as they tried to intimidate Mr. Heron. In truth, I suspected the two watchmen positioned under an adjoining shop's eaves were all that kept them from hurling a rock through the window.

I felt more at ease once we'd maneuvered through the thickest part of the crowd, but unfortunately we'd been forced to stroll toward High Street, deeper into Old Town. And while we were not near the area that had seen the greatest outbreak of cholera, I couldn't banish it from my thoughts. Just as I knew Gage couldn't either. I felt highly conscious of my breathing and every person who came near me. Most physicians believed it was spread through an influence in the atmosphere, a miasma of bad air, which was more likely to afflict those who had weakened themselves by exposure to certain foods, intemperance, or dissolute behavior. This was why it was believed to linger over certain areas of the city and not others. Cholera morbus seemed to be transmittable without direct personal contact, but that didn't mean that contact with an afflicted person could not also infect you.

At the corner of High Street, Gage steered us to the left, still keeping me close. We hurried past Carrubbers Close and a couple of pubs before veering left into North Gray's Close. This passage was even narrower than Carrubbers, and the buildings overhead seemed to lean inward toward one another, almost blocking out the light completely. Nevertheless, we were mostly alone, and the sound of the crowd gathered on North Bridge Street had receded, absorbed by the craggy stone buildings.

With each step I grew more damp and miserable, the umbrella heavy in my hand as I held it high enough to shelter Gage. Normally, he would have carried it, but it would only have hindered his ability to defend us. An act that might still be needed as we inched our way down the hill of slick cobblestone. When finally we reached our carriage parked near the old Physic Gardens behind Trinity Hospital, I was shivering, my limbs stiff with cold.

"Next time we speak with Mr. Heron, I think we should visit him at his rooms instead," I pronounced as Gage tucked a blanket around me to ward off the chill.

"You're already sure there will be a next time?"

There was no subtlety in the fact that this was a leading question, and I waited until he stopped fussing with the wool covering and looked up at me to answer. "Aren't you?"

"Well, yes." He sat back with a sigh, turning to frown through the curtain of rain at the orphan hospital in the distance. "For one, we forgot to ask him about the sequel."

I'd also realized this once it was too late to turn back and do anything about it. "Do you think he knows who Nathan Mugdock really is?"

Gage leaned forward to lift the opposite bench and retrieve his travel writing desk. "I don't know." He flicked open the brass latch to reveal the smooth mahogany writing surface and slid open the drawer to extract a sheet of paper. He paused, his lips flattening as he mulled over some unsettling thought. "But I do think he knows who killed Rookwood. Or at least he suspects it."

I didn't speak as he jotted off a quick request to the men he'd promised Mr. Heron he would send to help him move Rookwood's things, the scent of ink mixing with wet wool inside the carriage. "Why didn't you press him on it?" I asked as Gage waved the missive in the air to speed the drying.

"Because he never would have given me a straight answer, and then he would have been on his guard about any future questions I put to him on the topic. As you know, it's always best to already know the answers to such questions before you ask them. And at the moment, we haven't the slightest clue as to who the culprit is." He folded the foolscap and then hollered for Peter, our footman, who was perched at the back of the carriage. Leaning through the doorway, he passed him the letter and then issued instructions on its delivery.

168 · *Anna Lee Huber*

Once that task was completed, he put the lap desk aside and turned to me more fully. "Now, shall I deliver you home, or are you determined to accompany me to the businesses Mr. Heron visited yesterday on Rookwood's behalf?"

I arched my eyebrows. "Must you ask?"

His mouth curled at the corners. "I figured it couldn't hurt. Where to first, then?"

The chiming of the bells at nearby Trinity College Church drew my gaze toward New Town. "We're only a short distance from the Theatre Royal. But will the proprietors be there at this hour?"

"I doubt it."

"Then let's visit the printer. This Mr. Lennox may know as much about Rookwood's business as Mr. Heron, if not more."

All trace of humor fled from Gage's expression. "You heard Heron say that Lennox and Company Printers is located at the corner of Cowgate and Blackfriars."

Which was a block south of High Street, just a short distance from our current location, but it plunged us into a very different world. Cowgate stretched to the west, connecting with Grass-market, and hosted many of the poorest residents of Edinburgh, packed together in squalid tenements. We would be stepping up to the very edge of the area of the city hardest hit by the cholera morbus. It was only right that we should pause and evaluate the risk.

"I brought the Chantilly veil that matches this capote so I could drape it over my face if needed," I told him, pulling the delicately folded lace from the pocket of my mantua. "That would offer some extra protection. And I can button my pelerine higher on my throat." I clasped the small cape-like garment draped over my voluminous mantua together at the neck to illustrate.

Gage carefully considered these suggestions before guardedly adding, "I suppose we aren't going to encounter a great deal of people gathered around a print shop. And the fumes from the equipment likely overpower any of the bad air that might waft over from the neighboring tenements." His gaze assessed me once more before he sighed heavily and knocked on the ceiling of the carriage to issue instructions to our coachman.

As the carriage rumbled forward, I reached out to clasp Gage's hand. Though he didn't turn to look at me or speak, he did squeeze back, holding my hand tightly until we reached Cowgate. I buttoned my pelerine to the top and draped the veil over the brim of my capote bonnet before stepping down from the carriage beside Gage. The soot-stained gray stones of the stolid building before us were certainly nothing to look at, but I noted two or three hearty souls clustered around the broadsides posted on the side of the building as Gage hustled me toward the door. A tarnished bronze plaque attached to the wall next to it was all that proclaimed its proprietor.

Inside, we were assaulted by the acrid stench of hot ink and oil, and the click and whirl of the moving metal parts from a trio of steam printing presses. A pair of men stood at each press on either side of it, feeding paper onto the belts that pulled it under the cylinders, while a fourth pair of men stood conferring off to the side. Catching sight of us, the man dressed in gentlemen's attire, sans his frock coat, the white sleeves of his linen shirt rolled up to reveal his forearms, dismissed the man in the leather apron to approach us.

"Mr. Lennox," Gage called out as he neared, raising his voice to be heard above the noise. "My name is Sebastian Gage." He nodded to me at his side. "Might my wife and I have a word with you?"

Lennox gestured broadly toward a door to our right, and we followed him into an office. On first glance, it appeared as if someone had stood in the center of the room and thrown ream after ream of paper into the air so that it floated down to carpet the room. But on closer inspection, I realized the papers were actually organized in some sort of system of neat stacks of various sizes. They covered every available surface, as well as a large square footage of the floor. Even the chairs boasted piles of documents, the uppermost pages ruffling in the breeze caused by Lennox's quick movements.

"There," he declared with a congenial grin as he closed the door. "Now at least we can hear one another without shouting." Although, the clacks and clinks of the presses still penetrated through the door, albeit more softly. He offered Gage his hand. "Welcome to my shop, Mr. and Mrs. Gage." His gaze skimmed over my veil, but he didn't remark upon it. "What can I do for you?" He gestured toward the chairs for us to have a seat, only to realize they were already occupied by the fruits of his trade. "Oh! My apologies."

I took the opportunity to study him as he shifted the stacks of various broadsheets, brochures, and booklets. A tall man of about thirty with a long, thin nose and thick copper red hair, Mr. Lennox appeared to be a sturdy, affable fellow. While he might have hailed from the second or third generation of a wealthy middle-class family, I strongly suspected his ancestors were instead gentry forced to turn to trade. It was somehow evident in the rhythm and accent of his voice—effortless and resonant like a bell.

"We understand you do much of Rookwood Publishing's printing," Gage said.

"Yes, yes, I do. What a sad business," he declared with a shake of his head. "I don't mind telling you I was shocked and dismayed this morning to hear what had happened to him." He plunked down the second stack on the floor and then dusted the chairs with the handkerchief from his pocket. "Is that why you're here? Working with the police, are you?"

I turned to Gage as I settled in the nearest chair, curious how he would answer this query.

"We haven't had a chance to consult with them yet, but that's not uncommon." A half-truth if ever I'd heard one. "When did you last speak with Mr. Rookwood yourself?" he hastened to ask before Mr. Lennox could dwell too long on his last statement.

"Well, let me see." He leaned back in his seat. "He visited me here two, no, three days ago. Wanted to drop off a new manuscript and discuss some contract terms."

"What of his assistant, Mr. Heron?"

Mr. Lennox swiveled in his seat to glance toward one of the piles of documents he'd moved from our chairs and then changed his mind and reached for one at the corner of his desk instead. "Ah, yes. He stopped by with the text for a pamphlet." He nodded once he'd located it, but Gage shook his head, neither of us being interested in seeing it.

"And when you last saw Mr. Rookwood, what was his frame of mind?"

The printer, who had laced his fingers in front of him, gestured with his combined hands. "The same as always, I suppose."

"Then he didn't seem agitated? Or mention that anything particular was vexing him?" Gage asked as Mr. Lennox continued to shake his head at each question.

"Not about business. I can't speak to his personal life, for we never discussed it. Ours was a purely professional relationship."

Gage nodded, his gaze skimming over the piles of papers on the desk. "What of the new manuscript he brought you? Was it anything noteworthy?"

Mr. Lennox's head tilted and a new watchfulness passed over his features. "Yes, in fact." He paused another moment before continuing, as if debating whether to say more. "It was the sequel to *The King of Grassmarket*."

I sat forward, not having expected to hear this. "*You* have it?"

"Yes."

"May we see it?" Gage queried, his gaze once again dipping to the documents separating us from the printer.

Mr. Lennox weighed this question before declining. "No. I placed it in my safe, and there it shall remain until matters can be ironed out with the author. And now, I suppose, the new owner of Rookwood Publishing. Or at least, its assets."

Gage frowned. "What do you mean, 'matters can be ironed out with the author'? Had Rookwood not finished settling terms with the author?"

"I don't know the specifics, of course. But he said there were some wrinkles to be smoothed out. I assumed he meant the author was giving him trouble on the terms or perhaps a bit of editing. Authors can be rather temperamental, you know. Glad I don't have to deal with them."

"And yet he brought you the manuscript."

A slight furrow formed between Mr. Lennox's brows. "Yes. But it's not as if his actions were unheard of. I can recall at least one other occasion when he brought me a manuscript before he was heading out of town, asking me not to print it until I'd received word from him to do so."

Perhaps, but the printer's puzzled expression made it clear that Rookwood's behavior was also far from customary. Had Rookwood intended to leave Edinburgh? To go see the author, Nathan Mugdock, in person? I had been operating under the assumption that Mugdock lived in Edinburgh because of his subject matter, but maybe I was wrong.

Or had Rookwood given Lennox the manuscript for another reason? One much less innocuous. Maybe he had known someone was determined to have it and so had passed it along for safekeeping. If so, things didn't look good for Bonnie Brock, who we all knew had been threatening the publisher.

And yet Rookwood had seemed genuinely vexed by the

ramifications of his publication of *The King of Grassmarket*, despite the money it had brought to him. I would not have wagered on his desire to publish a sequel. But perhaps his frustration had all been a ruse for our benefit. Perhaps he was wary of telling us the truth, lest we cause him as many problems as Bonnie Brock.

"Have you read it? The sequel?" Gage clarified.

Mr. Lennox's lips pursed. "No. At least not past the first two or three sentences."

"It sounds like you're not an admirer."

He turned his head to gaze up at the lone picture on the wall—a rather mediocre landscape of a field dotted with flowers and a hazy, jumbled set of ruins looming in the background. "Not everyone who lives or works along Cowgate is an admirer of Bonnie Brock Kincaid." He nodded toward the main room of his shop. "And what with my prosperous business, I doubt Kincaid is an admirer of mine either."

I found it interesting he had chosen to focus on the subject of the book and not the author as being the topic of Gage's question.

"But then again, I've hardly the time to read everything that comes into my shop to be printed. And I don't have to agree with something in order to be happy to profit from it." He offered us a self-deprecating smile, perhaps trying to ameliorate the bitterness that had tinted his last words.

"Do you know who Mugdock is?" Gage queried lightly.

"I don't. And I didn't want to know. Well, no. I suppose that's not precisely true," he amended, spreading his clasped hands before pressing the palms back together. "I admit I *am* curious. But I didn't ask Rookwood. I know when it's my business to know something, and when it's not."

"If the police come here asking for the sequel, will you give it to them?"

Lennox scoffed. "Not unless they have a warrant. For I can wager what they'll do with it."

Gage nodded, tapping the crown of his hat where it rested in his lap. "Thank you for taking the time to speak with us. I have just one more question. Who do *you* think killed Rookwood?"

Mr. Lennox's eyes narrowed slightly at the corners, and he inhaled a deep breath before speaking. "Well, it seems perfectly obvious to me that it's Kincaid, and just as obvious you don't wish to hear that, but it's true. And I warn you, if I find my shop and my safe broken into, I'll be sending the police to speak to you."

"We are not Kincaid's informants," Gage replied crisply, pushing to his feet. "Rest assured, if he is the killer, we will just as surely see him brought to justice as anyone else."

"Yes, *you* might. But . . ." He broke off even as he glanced my way, making it clear what he had been about to say before he'd thought better of it.

I arched a single eyebrow in disdain as I joined the others in standing. "Was there something you wished to say to me, Mr. Lennox?"

His gaze met mine squarely through the covering of my veil, and for a moment I thought he was actually going to insult me to my face. But then he swallowed, visibly relenting. "No. No, there isn't."

I nodded once. "Good day to you." Turning sharply on my heel, I marched toward the door and opened it without waiting for Gage.

Though he quickly caught up, lacing my arm through his as we made our way back through the noise and stench of the shop, and then hurried to escape out of the rain and into our carriage.

Sinking back against the squabs, I lifted my veil and pressed a hand to my forehead, feeling the mild beginnings of a headache from the shop's fumes. It seemed as if the stink lingered about us, permeating our clothes. How did the employees stand it? I supposed there were worse jobs, but the manner in which the scorched ink seemed to sting one's nostrils was most unpleasant.

"Well, I suppose we now have confirmation that a sequel exists, and where it is." I frowned. "But if Lennox has had it since the day before Rookwood's murder, then what papers did the murderer rip from Rookwood's hands, leaving only the corners of a few pages behind?"

"Maybe there was more than one copy. Or maybe they only thought it was the sequel." He scowled down at his walking stick. "Or maybe they weren't after the sequel but something else entirely."

Something we had no suspicion of. At least, not yet.

Disheartened, I turned to stare through the mist of rain outside the window and down the length of Cowgate to the arch where it passed under South Bridge Street. The squalid buildings on either side, crowded against the bridge, forming the infamous vaults. "Where to now?"

"Well, I think we can leave the tobacco shop and the bookshops to Anderley. He can visit them to make inquiries about Mr. Heron's alibi. The author in Leith as well, for I have no desire to traipse that far north. So that leaves the bank, his solicitor, and the theater."

The hour was still too early for Mr. Murray to be at the Theatre Royal, and as for the former two, I could extrapolate the reason for Gage's stoic expression. "Men who are far more apt to confide in you if I'm not present."

"Unfortunately, yes."

I stifled my annoyance by reminding myself that neither visit was liable to yield much information. Mr. Heron had told us his visit to the bank was simply to make a deposit, and it was doubtful Rookwood's solicitor would share the details of his will without the police present. Though I wouldn't discount Gage's charm and powers of persuasion.

"Then you should deliver me home. No, wait," I amended. "Drop me by Cromarty House instead."

"Have you spoken to your sister since her last unwelcome tirade?" he asked after leaning forward to issue these instructions to our coachman through the small sliding wooden door built into the front wall of the carriage behind the driver's bench.

"No," I replied simply, unwilling to allow myself to dwell on the tangle of emotions her harsh words still caused me, not when I was about to pay her an unexpected visit. "But Alana and Philip are always more knowledgeable of people and connections than I am. Maybe they know something about the characters in this farce that we don't."

He stilled my hands from their unconscious fidgeting with the tassel on my reticule. "Well, don't let her bully you."

I smiled up at him gratefully. "I won't."

"And be sure Cromarty lends you his carriage to drive you home. I don't want you walking in this weather."

I recognized that the last was said more for my benefit than Philip's. My brother-in-law could be courteous to a fault, and if by some chance he neglected to insist I take one of his conveyances, his butler, Figgins, would see to it. "I will," I assured him, having no intention of striking out in such dreich weather on foot.

CHAPTER 14

I found Philip and Alana in their drawing room, gathered close to the roaring fire. Philip was seated in a green brocade wing-back chair with one highly polished boot propped over the other knee, poring over a newspaper. His dark gaze flicked up toward me as I entered unannounced before returning to his paper. "Good afternoon, Kiera."

"Good afternoon," I replied.

Alana reclined on a spring green fainting couch nearby, bouncing her youngest child on her knees. His laughter brought a smile to my face, and I was helpless not to coo at him.

"Oh my, just look at how big you're getting. We won't be able to call you wee Jamie much longer."

His gaze shifted to me as he offered me a broad grin and a dribble of a drool down his chin. Alana lifted the bib draped around his neck to swipe away the slobber.

"I cannot believe he's almost one," I declared.

"Wait until it's your little one aging before your eyes," my sister replied. "But that does remind me, we're hosting a small party on his birthday, and of course, we'd like you and Gage to attend. Trevor said he would try to make it, but they'll soon be in the midst of lambing at Blakelaw, so I'm not counting on it."

Our brother had written me much the same thing in his last letter, saying he hoped he could make it to Edinburgh in time for my child's birth. He had inherited our childhood home from our father, along with its farm and sheep. After some financial setbacks the previous few years, he'd recently added more ewes to his flock, and while he had an excellent estate manager and farmhands to cope with such matters, it was only natural that he should be anxious to ensure that this year's lambing was a successful one. I had told him not to be concerned with being here for the birth. After all, there was nothing he could do, and he could just as easily meet his new niece or nephew when they were a few weeks old.

"We'll be there," I replied as Jamie's brow furrowed with impatience, wiggling in his mother's arms.

She began to bounce him again, earning another giggle of laughter. "Yes, I heard about the murder," she told me, her icy words contrary to her crooning voice and the smile she gave her son. "It's all over the papers, and I've no desire to discuss it."

That she was fuming was obvious, but far be it from me to refuse the opportunity to miss one of her lectures.

"May I see them?" I asked, and she nodded toward Philip. A stack of newspapers covered the table beside his chair.

"The London papers, of course, don't contain word of it yet," he told me as I began to sort through the pile. "But the *Caledonian Mercury*, the *Gazette*, and the *Herald*, as well as a few of the broadsheets, all cover it."

I sat in the chair opposite to scan the headlines. Most of them were short on facts but quick to link the murder to the publication of *The King of Grassmarket*, condemning it and the plays for corrupting the public. That this outcry would only grow in the next few days was all but assured as public figures and people eager to express their opinions in the editorials put in their two pennies' worth. However, two of the publications were also quick to notice that the staging of Rookwood's office to look like the scene in the book might just as assuredly point the finger at someone who wished to discredit the story.

More troubling, most of the papers also didn't fail to mention my and Gage's role as inquiry agents, or our far-too-obvious inclusion in *The King of Grassmarket*. The writer of one of the broadsheets also seemed to be aware that Gage and I had spoken to the police outside Rookwood's office the night before. But providentially, no one was suggesting we were suspects. At least, not yet.

"Are you staying for luncheon?" Alana asked, interrupting my self-absorption with the words before me.

My stomach rumbled at the suggestion, and I caught Philip's answering grin out of the corner of my eye.

"I'll take that as a yes," Alana replied.

I pressed a hand to my stomach. "I can't help it. I'm hungry all the time, but I can never finish a meal without feeling positively stuffed."

Philip chuckled aloud. "Don't worry, Kiera. In my opinion, a rabid appetite in a woman with child must be a good sign."

Alana shook her head. "I wouldn't have the faintest idea. I could never even think of food without feeling nausea while I was expecting my fiendish little darlings." She smothered Jamie's pudgy cheeks with kisses while he giggled. His baby-soft brown hair stood on end. She glanced over her shoulder at her husband. "But your sister was always disgustingly healthy when she was expecting. She claimed it was the only time she could eat whatever and whenever she wanted, so she was going to take full advantage of that fact."

Something jostled the door ajar, and a moment later, in strutted Earl Grey. Catching sight of his sashaying tail, Jamie made a lunge for him, gurgling some inarticulate sound, but the gray mouser ignored him and ambled toward me.

"That cat," Alana derided, restraining her son. "He knows the moment we have guests and comes in here expecting attention. As if he doesn't get more than enough of it in the nursery."

I shook my head at him fondly as he leapt up onto my lap, forcing me to lift aside the broadsheet I'd been perusing. He circled and then settled half on my legs and half on my rounded belly, gazing up at me with slitted eyes. I scratched under his chin, making him purr contentedly, and then stroked a hand down his back, only to pull it away covered in something sticky. Toffee, perhaps?

My sister sighed. "I suppose I shouldn't complain. He's remarkably sweet-tempered. You should see the things the children do to him. All in love and good-natured fun. But children don't always understand their own strength or why a cat doesn't want to be dressed in a bonnet or given a bath. They would be heartbroken if you took him back." She broke off as if the thought had just occurred to her. "You aren't, are you?

I smiled. "No. I wouldn't do that to them. And I think Earl Grey is much happier here with you."

Perhaps the sound of his purring and the manner in which he'd blissfully closed his eyes belied this statement, but I knew it to be true. Once Gage and I had selected a country home, we'd discussed getting a dog or two. Perhaps even a wolfhound like Philip's pair up at Gairloch Castle. But for now we traveled too much to drag an animal about with us to and fro.

The door opened wider and the nursery maid appeared. "Shall I take him noo, m'lady?" she asked my sister. "'Tis time for his nap."

"Yes, despite all his squirming, I can tell he's getting sleepy,"

Alana replied as Jamie made one more lunge toward me and Earl Grey.

"Oh, good day, m'lady. I didna see ye there," the nursery maid said, dipping a curtsy as she caught sight of me.

"Good day, Molly."

She gathered Jamie up in her arms and then turned to glare at the cat. "Shall I herd His Highness along with me, as well?"

Clearly the conceited mouser hadn't made as good of friends with the maids as he had the children.

"No, I'm sure he'll follow along when he feels like it."

"Ain't that the truth," she muttered, and then departed through the door.

I turned to look at Philip, who was still ostensibly reading the newspaper. "Does the prime minister know you have a cat named after him?" I hadn't considered the potential ramifications of this when I named the feline or when I gave him to my nieces and nephews.

"He's quite flattered actually." A smile hovered on his lips as he folded and set aside his paper. "Believes the children christened him."

I couldn't help but laugh. "Well, at least that's one scandal diverted, I suppose."

This was the wrong jest to make, for Alana swiveled to sit upright, spreading her laurel green skirts. Her eyes flashed with repressed anger. "As lovely as it is to see you," she lied, "I well know you've visited us for a reason. So, out with it."

I fought a flush, refusing to feel guilty for coming here to seek their help. The current situation I'd found myself in was not of my making, no matter what my sister might think. I was not responsible for the publication of *The King of Grassmarket* and all of its spurious implications, nor had I killed Rookwood. Even so, I kept my voice carefully controlled.

"Gage and I have already researched Thomas W. Rookwood,

but I wondered if perhaps you or Philip might be privy to any information about him we are not. As well as his assistant, Mr. Daniel Heron, and printer, an Alexander Lennox."

Alana stared stonily at me, but Philip scratched his chin, as if genuinely giving the matter some consideration. "I can't say I'm familiar with this Mr. Heron, but I've met Mr. Rookwood once or twice at various city functions. From what I've heard, he was an honorable businessman. More conscientious than most."

"Yes, that was our impression of him as well."

"Now, this printer chap." He frowned. "There are an awful lot of Lennoxes floating about. Where is his shop located?"

"Blackfriars at Cowgate."

"Kiera," my sister snapped. "Is *that* the pungent odor I smell hanging about you? Did you *go* there?"

"Gage accompanied me."

She pushed to her feet. "Of all the careless, foolish, reckless . . ." She broke off, stomping across the room toward the bow window overlooking Charlotte Square.

I knew she was thinking of the cholera, and my heart surged into my throat in recognition of the worry I'd caused her. But my breast also burned with the indignation that she discounted my own intelligence in taking sensible precautions yet again. And it was that indignation that won out. "Yes, the printer showed me how to work his machines . . ."

Alana gasped, whirling to face me.

"And then I shared a tankard of ale with his employees before Gage and I went for a stroll down Cowgate into Grassmarket," I quipped defiantly.

Her eyes narrowed. "It's no joking matter, Kiera."

"Then you *meant* to imply that I'm a muttonhead, in earnest?"

"Ladies, please," Philip intervened before his wife could voice whatever scathing retort I could see blazing in her eyes. "This is not helping. Alana, you know Gage is as protective of

Kiera as you are. Perhaps more so. I'm sure they took precautions."

She crossed her arms over her chest and turned to stare at the spirits on the sideboard.

"And Kiera, there's no need for such sarcasm. Your sister is merely concerned about you."

I bit my tongue, clenching my hands at my sides to restrain my anger. Of course I knew she cared for me. But she had a funny way of showing it.

But Alana was not to be deterred in her pestering. "Have you hired a nursemaid yet?"

"No, but you know our situation is complicated." We traveled a great deal, rarely remaining in one city for more than a few months, and I didn't see that ending any time soon.

"Kiera, the baby could arrive any day. This should be your priority, not chasing after another murderer."

I flushed at the implication of her statement—that I was already failing as a mother. "We will find one in due time," I retorted. "And in the meantime, it's not as if Gage and I and our staff can't handle caring for one infant. I'm not entirely inexperienced in the matter." Having lived with Alana following two of her births.

"Yes, but . . ."

Fortunately, a light rap on the door halted Alana from saying more as Figgins appeared to announce that luncheon was served and that he'd already taken the liberty of adding a setting for me, as he'd presumed I would be joining them.

"Thank heavens," Philip exhaled in relief. "Shall we, ladies?"

My sister and I both recovered our dignity and preceded him through the door and down the stairs to the dining room. The meal began stiltedly at first but soon progressed with relative ease so that by the end the three of us were conversing as we had during the two years I had lived with them between my marriages. Philip and Alana both had commitments following the meal, but he escorted me upstairs so that I could visit my nieces and nephews in the nursery before I departed. Along the way, he promised to speak to a few people about the men I'd mentioned earlier, and I thanked him.

I found the children to be as boisterous as ever. How wee Jamie managed to slumber in his crib in the corner while they played, I didn't know, but I supposed he'd grown accustomed to the tumult. In any case, Molly, the nursery maid, seemed to place few restrictions on the volume of their antics, as long as they didn't shriek—something my nieces Philipa, at age seven, and Greer, at almost three, excelled at. Though she did protest nine-year-old Malcolm playing me the new song he had learned on his violin until Jamie woke.

When he finally had the opportunity to play it for me, I could only listen in bemusement at the discovery that it was the charming flash song from the Grand's version of *The King of Grassmarket*. The jaunty tune was certainly a hit with his sisters, who twirled about the room. Even Jamie bounced up and down on my lap, clapping in pleasure. There was nothing for it but to give in to the enjoyment of the moment and applaud Malcolm's playing.

A short time later, Philip's carriage delivered me home. As I was climbing the steps, contemplating whether I should send Peter to the Lejeunes' patisserie to purchase some mattentaarts, my attention was suddenly captured by a hulking man lurking at the corner. I might not have noticed him at all, except that he was staring at me, rain dripping from the brim of his hat. It took me a moment to realize he was Stump, one of Bonnie Brock's henchman. He tipped his head toward the right, and I heaved a resigned sigh, able to guess what that meant.

Once inside, I declined to give Jeffers my things, including my umbrella. Our butler was accustomed to our odd behavior, but this proved even too peculiar for him.

"I believe we have a visitor to our garden," I told him before advancing toward the stairs leading to the ground floor.

Exiting through the French doors inside our morning room, I followed the paved stones of the walk which led through our garden. Rain pattered against the umbrella, drowning out any of the sounds that might have carried from the neighboring homes and the street beyond. It still being winter, there was little in the way of new growth, and what greenery there was sagged with the weight of precipitation. The only bright spot was a white trellis, which would be covered with roses come June.

At the rear of the garden stood our carriage house and stables, which led out to the mews. Accordingly, we didn't have a garden gate, but merely a door leading into the outbuildings. This door was opened wide as I approached, revealing Bonnie Brock Kincaid.

I paused a few feet away, knowing Gage would already be furious at the criminal's impudence. We might have been forced into close proximity inside the carriage the evening before, but that didn't mean he would approve of me being close to him now. "You'd better have a good reason for being here," I told him as another figure shuffled her feet just over his shoulder. "Good afternoon, Maggie," I said more politely. The girl already appeared uncomfortable and ready to bolt at any moment.

"What have ye uncovered?" Bonnie Brock demanded, reclaiming my attention.

I scowled at his tone.

"I ken that ye were seen on North Bridge Street." He straightened from his slouched stance, leaning against the doorframe. "Were ye able to talk to Heron?"

Maggie startled, drawing both of our attentions. A horse whinnied somewhere in the stable behind her. I wondered if she might be afraid of the steeds. I doubted she'd had much interaction with such animals. Her shoulders inched up around her ears, and she glanced behind her repeatedly, as if unnerved by her surroundings. I wished I could invite her inside, but that was not possible for several reasons. Chiefly to do with her brother.

I grimaced at the infuriating subject in question. "Yes, we spoke with Mr. Heron. And we were able to confirm that Rookwood's office was almost certainly staged to appear as if the criminal was imitating the crime ascribed to you in *The King of Grassmarket*. But we have a great deal more investigating to do, and your hovering over our every move is not in the least helpful."

"Then your visit to your sister was part o' the investigation?"

I narrowed my eyes at this challenge, anger beginning to bubble in my veins. "Now, see here, Mr. *Kincaid*," I snapped, drawing attention to my use of his last name, as he had insisted upon my calling him Brock for more than a year now, and I normally complied. "I know you are accustomed to ordering your men and your sister about as if they are all pawns in your little kingdom, but I am *not* one of your subjects. And I will not be interrogated as such. Where I go and how I choose to investigate is my own affair. Do I make myself clear?"

Even in the shadows cast by the doorway, I could see that the ridge of scar tissue running along the length of his nose stood out white against his angry flush. This was never a good sign. But I also knew that if I didn't stand firm now, he would take even greater liberties and make even more demands. This was something I was not willing to sacrifice, despite the quavering his glare caused in my stomach. I simply had to trust that his good sense—and the fact that we were standing in *my* garden, with Jeffers and possibly other members of my staff looking on through the windows behind me—would prevail. I would never discount our cook, Mrs. Grady, and her skill with a rolling pin.

Slowly the color faded from his face, and a droll smile hitched one side of his mouth upward. "Lord Avonley always said to beware the woman who can best ye at your ain game. And I realize noo, he was right."

There was little he could have said that would have disarmed me more. I knew how rarely he spoke of his family or his past, including Lord Avonley, his sister's father and his mother's last, and probably dearest, lover. From the expression that transformed Maggie's face, it seemed she was equally flustered. Her eyes shimmered with not only surprise but also anguish and longing. I suspected then that her brother must have also refused to speak of such things even with her. Even when he knew that she had only been three years old when her mother and father had died, so she could not possess many clear memories of them.

"If we uncover anything of importance . . ." *Anything he should know*, I added as a silent qualifier while I adjusted the drape of my boa. "I'll send word to you through your men. I know you still have them following us."

When Bonnie Brock's expression turned contemplative, I began to puzzle as to why.

"Unless you wish me to send it somewhere directly?"

I had never been privy to the location of his home, though I had heard the outrageous rumors that circulated from time to time. That he possessed an underground palace accessed only through the vaults, and filled from floor to ceiling with a treasure more vast than a maharaja's palace. That he lived in an unused wing of the Palace of Holyroodhouse, right beneath the nose of the current resident, the abdicated and exiled former king of France, Charles X. Bonnie Brock having been linked to Charles X's widowed daughter-in-law, the Duchess of Berry, as her lover seemed to add credibility to this theory. But I found the supposition made in *The King of Grassmarket* to be the most credible—that he possessed a number of residences throughout the city that he rotated among.

188 · Anna Lee Huber

A supposition which seemed to be confirmed by his next statement.

"Nay, Maclean and his men are too determined to sniff us oot for me to remain in one place for long." He turned his head to the side, but even in profile I could see the deep lines of anxiety scoring his forehead. "And I canna be certain any longer precisely who I can trust." That this worry extended not only to himself but also his sister was made plain by the look he cast over his shoulder at her.

She crossed her arms over her chest, hugging herself tightly, and I had to wonder if she had already been threatened in some way, or if Bonnie Brock was merely fearful she would be harmed. After all, she was the last family member he possessed and clearly the dearest person in the world to him. The play at the Theatre Royal had purely speculated on Brock's motivations for who he was, but more and more I had to concede they might have been worryingly accurate.

In truth, I was somewhat fearful of what he would do, who he would become, if he lost Maggie. He already skirted the edge of cruelty and ruthlessness in his crimes, and the death of his sister might rob him of any remnant of compassion he had left. An utterly heartless Bonnie Brock would be a terrifying thing indeed.

"Would you like Maggie to stay with us?" I asked before I could think better of it. I knew Gage would be furious I'd made the offer, but I trusted that I could talk him around to my way of thinking.

The quickness with which Bonnie Brock turned his head to look at me told me I'd shocked him. However, it was Maggie's face to which my eyes were drawn. Her shoulders lowered and her mouth gaped, and if I wasn't very much mistaken, I thought I detected a shimmer of wetness in her eyes. But then she blinked, and it was gone.

Bonnie Brock's hands clenched and unclenched by his sides, and his Adam's apple actually bobbed up and down as he swallowed. I'd never seen him as disconcerted as this. Not even when he was lying ill in our guest bedchamber ten months' prior. It seemed for a moment he was considering my offer. But then he shook his head. "Nay, the protection o' my sister is my responsibility. I canna entrust it to anyone else."

I nodded in acceptance, half torn and half relieved. "Well, if you should change your mind, the offer stands." I transferred the handle of the umbrella to my other hand. "Better here than somewhere like the vaults," I tried to quip as the atmosphere among the three of us had grown heavier than the leaden skies.

Bonnie Brock seemed to regain his equilibrium at this comment. He certainly recovered his cocksureness. "No need to worry aboot that. I've ne'er used 'em. 'Tis just a rumor, and a useful one, at that."

Maggie seemed just as intrigued by this comment as I was.

"But I thought some years ago the police discovered an illegal distillery there," I retorted.

"Aye, they did. But 'twasn't mine. I dinna distill whisky." He flashed a wide grin. "I simply broker it."

Broker it, indeed. He was a smuggler, plain and simple.

"Then whose was it?"

"That'd be Geordie McQueen. And he's blamed me ever since. But it's no' my fault he wasna wise enough to realize the pollies would eventually be brave enough to raid the place."

I'd heard of McQueen, and despite Bonnie Brock's carefree demeanor, I didn't believe for one second he was truly so unconcerned about the man commanding one of his rival gangs. Particularly if McQueen's cold-blooded reputation was true.

But his comments also raised another question. "How much of the book is true and how much is fiction?" I asked him bluntly, wiping the amusement from his face. But I was in earnest.

"Truly? How much of *The King of Grassmarket* is accurate? Fifty percent?" I prodded when he didn't reply. "Seventy-five percent? I know it's not all."

But he seemed determined not to answer, staring out into the rain-soaked garden to my left, his jaw tightly locked. So I prodded a little harder.

"What of the speculation about your father's identity? You must know the rumors abound. And yet Mugdock never definitively named him. Why do you think that is? Does he not know, or did he deliberately choose to omit that information?"

"I dinna ken," he finally ground out between his teeth. "Maybe he saved it for the sequel."

That was certainly a possibility, but somehow I didn't think so. It made little sense to keep such a titillating piece of information from the book, from the beginning of Bonnie Brock's story, where it belonged, if the author had intended to reveal it at all.

In any case, it was clear Bonnie Brock wasn't going to share it with me. Not when he was already withdrawing. "Give Gage my regards," he drawled, knowing full well I would do no such thing. Though I could hardly keep Bonnie Brock's visit from him, no matter how much I wished to spare myself the exasperation that would follow.

I frowned as he turned to go, beckoning Maggie to follow him as he disappeared from sight. But even so, her gaze never moved from mine, not until the door swung shut, and I was left to wonder just what she'd wanted to say. I knew she was aware who her brother's father was. She'd admitted as much to me in the past. Was it the critical piece of information we needed to unmask Mugdock? And if so, could she be convinced to share it?

CHAPTER 15

Fortuitously, Gage returned home a short time after I'd emerged pink from the bath, having washed the stench of the printers from me. He had often been disarmed by the sight of me lounging barefoot before the fire, my long chestnut tresses cascading around my shoulders as they dried, and this proved no exception. As a consequence, any fury he felt upon learning that Bonnie Brock had come to our home was soon mitigated. Particularly when I assured him of the precautions I'd taken, and shared with him the fact that Bonnie Brock and Maggie were being hunted.

Gage sank back in the chair across from mine and turned to stare broodingly into the fire. "I suspected the police would make the apprehension of Kincaid their top priority, whether the evidence points to him being the murderer or not. And while we both know he's committed an untold number of crimes." He sighed. "I don't think this time he's the one to blame."

"Did you uncover anything of interest at the bank or via

Rookwood's solicitor?" I asked, adjusting the belt of my indigo silk dressing gown.

He shook his head. "They confirmed Heron's presence at approximately the times he said he was there, but neither visit was lengthy. As I expected, the solicitor wouldn't share Rookwood's will with me, though he did confirm that Rookwood has a sister living in Aberdeen."

"Then it's likely she'll inherit."

"Perhaps. I suppose we'll know soon enough. The will is being read in a week's time." He looked up at me hopefully. "Did you learn anything helpful from Cromarty and your sister?"

"No, but Philip said he would find out what he could."

"Then we're left with little to go on."

"Not unless Anderley's day has been more fruitful." I had been able to tell from Bree's expression while she prepared my bath that hers had been unsatisfying.

Less than an hour later, we were able to find out. The fire in the drawing room had been built up to a blaze, warming the chill room as rain continued to pelt the windows. At times, the sharp strikes of precipitation sounded more like ice or sleet than rain, and I could only be glad we had no obligations for the evening.

"Although it wasn't the most auspicious weather, I was able to speak with a few witnesses from the market, including the owner of that oyster cart you mentioned," Anderley said, rifling his still-damp hair. "Sadly, he claimed he'd been too busy to notice who came and went from any of the shops across the street yesterday. And I must admit, if he was doing as brisk a trade as he was today, then I believe him. As for the ballad-seller, he wasn't there. But that's not entirely unexpected."

"No," I agreed. "His sheet music would have been ruined in this weather."

"I'll try to speak with him tomorrow, or find out where he's gone."

Gage nodded and then turned to Bree. "What of you, Miss McEvoy?"

"I spoke to Mr. Rookwood's staff. There was only four o' 'em, and three o' 'em were happy to help. Though they didna ken much o' note. But they seemed to have genuinely liked their employer." Her mouth twisted. "But the fourth servant, the maid, she wasna as chatty."

"Do you think she had a reason to not want to speak with you, or was she just mistrustful of strangers?" I asked.

Bree surreptitiously kneaded her left thigh through her gown, reminding me that it often ached in damp weather. "I'm no' sure, but she definitely set her back up against me once I started askin' questions. Before that she was friendly enough. And ye were right. She did clean his office, as well. Got that much oot o' her before she became skittish."

"I could try to talk to her, if you like," Anderley offered, his gaze dipping to her hand where it rubbed her leg.

She ceased abruptly, clasping her hands in her lap as a furrow formed between her eyes. "Nay, I'll try again tomorrow." She forced a smile. "I think I ken noo how I can convince her to trust me."

Whether or not it was obvious to the men, I could tell why Bree didn't want Anderley's help. She'd often teased Anderley and groused about his method for convincing females to confide in him, which was tantamount to flirtation, and I could tell by the stiff line of her shoulders that that was exactly what she was envisioning happening. Fortunately, he didn't pursue the matter, instead seeming to become momentarily distracted as Bree reached up to adjust her hairpins for perhaps the fourth time since she'd entered the room. Her normally well-tamed strawberry blond curls had frizzed in the dampness and were threatening to come tumbling down around her shoulders. Apparently, Gage wasn't the only male intrigued by a woman's hair, and the intimacy implied by seeing it down.

"Anderley, I've another task for you anyway," Gage told him, reclaiming his attention. He extracted a piece of paper from his pocket and passed it to him. "I need you to speak to the proprietors of these shops to see if Mr. Heron visited them yesterday, and how long he stayed. Then I need you to track down the author listed. He lives in Leith and is purportedly not the easiest individual to find."

His valet scanned the list before slipping it into the inner pocket of his bottle blue coat.

"Though I'm still not sure all of these stops will account for the full amount of time Heron was absent from the office." Gage lifted his teacup, cradling it before him. "Not to mention the fact that the locations of a number of his errands were in and around North Bridge Street near to Rookwood Publishing. He might have easily slipped in through the rear entrance, murdered his employer, and left again, with no one the wiser."

"That's true, but I don't think he's our culprit," I replied, contemplating his nervous behavior that morning. "He definitely knows something he hasn't yet divulged to us, but I don't think it's that he's the murderer."

"Perhaps he kens Mugdock's identity," Bree suggested.

"Maybe," I conceded, having already wondered the same thing.

Gage tapped his fingers against the arm of his chair. "Rookwood's solicitor proved uncooperative, but he did let slip the name of the executor of Rookwood's will. And I've a mind to track him down this evening at the club." He turned to Anderley. "So you'll need to set out my evening kit."

"Yes, sir."

Given the fact that the only club Gage was a member of here in Edinburgh was the New Club on St. Andrew's Square, and they didn't allow ladies entrance, I knew better than to ask if I could join him. Regardless, I had little desire to stir from the house in such weather, especially not to enter such a bastion of gentlemen smoking cigars and drinking brandy while they played cards and billiards. It was no wonder Gage hadn't yet chosen to bathe away the stench of ink. Not when he would be wading through a cloud of smoke this evening.

For a moment I thought of protesting his absence. Upon my return from my chat in the garden with Bonnie Brock, Jeffers had informed me that Lord Henry Kerr had called while Gage and I were out. What if he returned this evening while Gage wasn't present? But we couldn't very well sit around waiting for him to call again when we had a murder to solve. As much as I wanted the truth to be revealed, I would also be lying if I didn't admit I was relieved to postpone it for at least one more day. Because once Gage realized I'd been keeping this from him, I wasn't certain how he would react, but I knew it would not be in my favor.

"Then I'll spend some time trying to tease out what we do know," I declared. "Maybe one of the books in our library can provide some hints as to why the author chose Mugdock as his nom de plume, or some other possibilities for the *Bo* or *Ba* Rookwood wrote before he died." Though I suspected that list might be long. It wasn't an uncommon beginning to a name. If that was even what it was.

"I can help," Bree offered.

"Then we have our tasks," Gage summed up as he pushed to his feet. He leaned down to press a kiss to my brow. "Don't wait up. I'm not sure how late I'll be."

I caught hold of his hand before he walked away. "Be careful."

He smiled in reassurance. "Always."

Well, that book was singularly unhelpful," I declared some hours later, pushing the tome aside, where it joined a pile of half a dozen other texts. Arching my back, I tried to stretch the muscles cramping along my lower spine. I glowered at the oak shelves filled with books covering three of the walls, many of their contents having been left behind by the previous owner of the house. "One would think the name *Mugdock* was plucked entirely from the air, but I just *know* that it wasn't."

"Aye, m'lady. It's odd. But no' odd enough for that," was Bree's mangled logic. But since I agreed with her, I didn't question it.

I rubbed my tired eyes and sighed. "Perhaps I need a break."

"Perhaps ye need to retire," she suggested, peering up at me from the book in her lap.

I glanced at the clock on the mantel, finding it was an hour later than I'd expected. "Not yet." I was determined to solve at least one mystery tonight.

Pushing to my feet, I strolled toward the windows, peering out through the drapes to discover that rain still lashed the glass. The garden was dark, the outbuildings at the opposite end little more than smudges in the blackness. While inside the fire burned cheerily in the hearth, casting flickering shadows over my portrait of my niece Philipa, curled up in a chair asleep. She held a book open in her lap and pillowed her head on Earl Grey, who gazed out of the painting like a prince humoring his subjects. The aroma of a fresh pot of tea wafted over from the sideboard, and I was tempted to drink another cup, but I suspected it would only make me tense and keep me propped upright much of the night with indigestion.

There was a rap at the door, and I turned as Jeffers entered. "This just arrived for you, my lady."

I accepted the letter perched on the silver salver he held out to me. Its writing was smudged, suggesting the messenger had not succeeded in keeping it dry. I flipped it over, not recognizing the seal, though for it to have been delivered at this hour and in this weather, it must have been urgent indeed. "Thank you, Jeffers."

He bowed his way out, and I crossed toward Gage's desk, taking the letter opener from the drawer to slit it open. Out of the corner of my eye, I could see Bree watching me with curiosity, but she didn't speak.

My gaze immediately skimmed to the bottom. "It's from Lady Kirkcowan."

I sat in one of the ivory damask bergère chairs positioned before the desk at an angle so that Bree could still see me, and then read aloud.

I'm so pleased to hear from you, though I do wish it were under better circumstances. If only my wretch of a husband would cease his foolish recklessness. He has already reduced his son's inheritance to such a state that he shall likely have to resort to trade, and our daughters have no hope of receiving a dowry. But I digress.

No, I did not return a single item to him of the stash you helped me secure. Although some months following your departure from Edinburgh, he did accuse me outright of being involved with their theft. Where he received such an impression, I do not know, but he did his worst to force me to confess.

I pressed a hand to my throat, fearful of what precisely that meant, before continuing.

Soon after, I left Edinburgh with my children and the items mentioned. My father has proven to be more forgiving and supportive than I ever expected, and I'm more grateful than I can say for that. However, his grace does not extend to Kirkcowan, so I feel secure in the wretch not being able to harass us here.

This seemed an urgent matter, so I am sending my reply to you posthaste. I apologize that you must be confronted with Kirkcowan's dissolute behavior yet again. If he is claiming said items were recovered and then stolen yet again, he is unequivo-cally lying. And I wish you all the best in proving it.

Write to me should you require any further information, and please send word when your child is born. It is lonely here in Lanarkshire, and I welcome any correspondence I can get.

"Well, I suppose that answers that," I said as I lowered the missive. Though I still couldn't comprehend how such a scheme helped him. If Kirkcowan had insured the jewelry, wouldn't he have claimed the loss when they were first stolen? But then if they were recovered, he would have had to return the money. Unless he hadn't reported their recovery and had instead insured them the second time with a different company. But then how had he proven they were genuine when he acquired the policy?

I rubbed my temple, certain I was missing something. But my attention was soon diverted by the opening of the library door a second time. Gage strolled inside with the hair at his temples damp and his demeanor serious. When another man appeared in the doorway behind him, I feared I knew why.

My heart clutched in dread at the sight of Lord Henry, whose gaze immediately locked with mine. But I couldn't tell from his reserved expression whether he'd told Gage anything yet.

Sensing that the discussion that would follow might not be meant for her ears, Bree rose from her seat and curtsied as she beat a hasty retreat. Part of me wanted to order her to stay, if only to prolong the inevitable, for neither gentleman would speak openly about such a topic with a servant present.

"Good evening, darling. You know Lord Henry Kerr," Gage began, gesturing to the man behind him. "I believe you spoke to him briefly yesterday evening at Miss Drummond's debut."

"Yes," I replied, struggling to swallow to moisten my throat, which had grown desperately dry. I offered Henry my hand, feeling as if I were taking part in some cruel charade.

"Though he has refused to share his brother's whereabouts, we've come to an understanding," Gage relayed, never removing his firm stare from Henry's face.

I blinked rapidly, my head whirling in confusion before I grasped that he was speaking of Lord John, and the fact that Henry had just returned from escorting him abroad to escape any consequences from his murderous actions at Sunlaws Castle.

"And he is in possession of some information that may be helpful to us."

"Is he?" I replied, feeling ridiculous for uttering such an inane retort.

Fully expecting this information to be the disclosure of his relation to Gage, I felt my stomach flip over in anticipation of his next words. But instead, Gage leaned against his desk and continued to speak.

"I stumbled upon Lord Kirkcowan again tonight, betting as high stakes as ever in the card room at the club."

I was sure I stared at him as if he'd lost his mind. Why was he talking about Kirkcowan? I looked down at the letter I still held in my hands, wondering if I'd fallen asleep and was dreaming. Or worse, perhaps I was hallucinating.

"What?" Gage replied, having noticed my odd demeanor. "Is something wrong?"

"Uh, no." I licked my lips, my gaze cutting to Henry, who now perched at the edge of the chair opposite mine. "Please continue."

He scrutinized my features as I tried to appear unperturbed and then resumed his explanation. "Once again I found myself wondering how Kirkcowan is able to continue financing such a habit, particularly when he loses far more often than he wins."

He nodded at our guest. "That's when Lord Henry approached me, and after our rapprochement, we found ourselves conversing about the baron."

Henry cleared his throat. "Yes, a friend of mine told me that he had been privy to a private wager Lord Kirkcowan had made in the betting book at the club and, being aware of my acquaintance with you, wanted to know if it was true."

I had been on the verge of rolling my eyes at the stupidity and foibles of man. Kirkcowan had gotten himself into trouble numerous times before for his ridiculous and insulting bets in the books at gentlemen's clubs in both London and Edinburgh. The existence of such books was maddening, in and of itself, as they were filled with both degrading and asinine wagers that often reduced women to little more than chattel or broodmares. However, his mention of our connection to it made my ears perk up.

"What was his wager?"

His watchful eyes never moved from my face. "That a sequel to *The King of Grassmarket* would be published before Midsummer's Eve."

CHAPTER 16

My head reared back and then I turned to my husband, whose eyes gleamed with satisfaction at my reaction. "Doesn't that show prior knowledge?"

"My thoughts exactly," he replied. "How is he even aware of such a publication being a possibility, let alone confident enough to place a sizable wager on its occurring?"

"Are you suggesting Kirkcowan is Mugdock?" I asked, suddenly doubtful.

Gage scoffed. "No, I don't think he's capable. But clearly he knows something about him."

My gaze dipped to the missive in my lap. "Lady Kirkcowan replied to my letter."

He straightened. "Did she?"

I looked at Henry, wondering if I should be speaking openly in front of him. "She says she never told Kirkcowan what truly happened to the jewels, *despite* his threatening her, and they are still safely secured. So the necklace people reportedly witnessed Lady Kirkcowan wearing last autumn must have been the paste version of her diamond and sapphire necklace. And as I've mentioned before, I recall it being a very good likeness."

"That also means that any claims Lord Kirkcowan made about any of those pieces being recovered and then restolen are an outright lie," Gage surmised as he ran his index finger over his lips in thought.

"Yes, but the question is why? For the insurance money? Would he actually have been able to insure them again, unexamined, simply based on his title alone?"

"I highly doubt it," Henry said, drawing our attention. "Most insurance companies are highly suspicious. It's their profits at risk, after all, if fraud is perpetuated. Especially on something as expensive and portable as jewelry."

"Henry's right," Gage agreed. "But I do have a thought." He crossed toward the door and stepped out into the hall. "Jeffers, would you come here for a moment?"

Our butler soon followed him back into the room. "Yes, sir?"

"Were you able to speak with anyone on Sir Phineas Riddell's staff yet?"

Jeffers's gaze cut briefly to Lord Henry before he spoke. "Yes, sir. I am acquainted with his butler, and I contrived to encounter him this morning while out on an errand. He joined me here for tea this evening."

Gage smiled at Jeffers's distinct use of the word "contrived." "Were you able to solicit any information from him?"

"I was. Apparently, Sir Phineas and Lady Riddell are rather parsimonious and demanding masters, and he was very affronted, indeed, by what he termed "the incident," for they heavily implied that the theft was his fault. Even though they'd *insisted* he have the night off that evening."

Gage's eyes narrowed in speculation. "Interesting."

"Indeed."

"Then I gather he isn't convinced that everything about the matter is quite straightforward and aboveboard from his employers' standpoint?"

"'Highly suspicious,' that's how he phrased it to me. I believe the other servants are of the same opinion, for none of them have been granted an extra day off in their entire employ by Sir Phineas, and the housekeeper has been with him for close to two decades."

"Thank you, Jeffers. Well done," Gage told him. Though this elicited little response from our stoic butler. He merely bowed at the waist and excused himself, closing the door behind him.

Gage leaned against his desk again, grasping the edge on either side of him with his hands, seemingly to restrain his enthusiasm. "Maybe Kirkcowan didn't attempt to insure his jewels. Maybe he only made it seem like he did."

Henry shifted forward. "You mean, to make it appear like he'd received remuneration?"

"From committing fraud?" I interjected, finishing the thought.

"Yes." Gage leaned forward. "What if his real aim was to convince his acquaintances who might be in dun territory like himself, and close to rolled up, that propagating a similar scheme could save them from ruin, and that he could even show them how to perpetuate such a ploy?"

"For a nominal cut of the profits, of course," I added wryly.

"Of course."

"He's swindling them," Henry stated indignantly. "All of them."

"Yes. But the question is how many people are involved, and can we prove it?" He crossed one leg in front of the other before him, staring at the rug with a frown. "And what, if anything, does this have to do with *The King of Grassmarket*?"

I tapped Lady Kirkcowan's folded missive against my palm.

"Well, clearly he was inspired by the theft a year ago. Perhaps he even suspects Bonnie Brock is involved." I shook my head. "But I don't think Kirkcowan is Mugdock. He's a punter and an indolent bounder. I can't imagine him exerting the effort required to write a pamphlet, let alone an entire book." I frowned, suddenly recalling something Kirkcowan had said the evening prior. "He mentioned he had stumbled upon a new lucrative enterprise." I looked up at Henry. "Last night, when you rescued me from his dubious attentions outside the dining room at Miss Drummond's debut." I turned to Gage. "He warned me that he wasn't going to let us spoil it for him."

But my husband's attention was directed at Henry, assessing him with new eyes after hearing he'd come to my aid. "And you think that means the book?" he finally replied.

"Or the jewel thefts?"

"How can we know which?" Henry interjected.

I didn't fail to note his use of the word "we," and neither did Gage.

A spark lit his eyes. "I have an idea, but we're going to need your help with it. Are you willing?" Gage asked him.

Henry's shoulders went back and his chin lifted slightly. I could sense his desire to please, and it made my heart constrict in my chest. "What do you need?"

Gage's lips curled into a satisfied smile. "First and foremost, those cardsharp abilities I overheard your brothers jesting about." This must have been a conversation I missed at Sunlaws Castle several months ago. "Though I won't ask you to actually cheat."

Henry nodded. "Tell me what to do."

After worship service the following morning, Bree and I resumed our search for the elusive origin of Mugdock, with no more success than the evening before. Conversely, our list of names beginning with *Bo* and *Ba* had grown considerably.

Sometime in the middle of the afternoon, I pushed the books aside and retired to my bedchamber to take a nap. If I was to be of any use at the soiree we were attending that night, where we intended to entrap Kirkcowan, then I needed some rest.

Some time later I was woken by the sound of raised voices. I blinked open bleary eyes to peer around the bedchamber, uncertain of how long I'd slept. The long shadows cast across the ceiling suggested it was growing late, and I would need to dress soon for our engagement. Lifting up on one elbow, I shifted positions so that I could see the door leading to the dressing room. The light beneath and the renewed noises of squabbling suggested it was occupied, and I could quickly surmise by who.

I heaved a sigh, sinking back against my pillows and wondering what Bree and Anderley were fighting about now. Based on the shrill tone of my maid's voice, a pitch I'd never heard her use, it was not a dispute that would resolve itself easily. And yet they had been so amicable and affectionate that morning, their heads bent close together as they strolled to church behind me and Gage in the crisp morning air. The storm the night before had finally blown itself out around three o'clock, ushering in a cold but sunny start to the new day.

The sharp words ended abruptly as the door to the dressing room opened and Bree strode through, her mouth tight with anger. She stumbled to a stop at the sight of me watching her from the bed. I had but a brief glimpse of Anderley through the doorway behind her, his hands clenched at his sides in frustration before the door shut.

Her brow creased in regret. "My apologies, m'lady. I was just comin' to wake ye when I was . . . distracted."

I slowly pushed myself upright, turning to sit on the edge of the bed while she bustled about the room, pouring warm water from the ewer she'd brought with her into the basin on my washstand and readying my garments.

"The iris blue satin," she suggested, laying the gown across the counterpane.

"Yes." It was next in the rotation of the two ball gowns that still fit me, though in a pinch one of my opera or dinner dresses would do. Crossing to the washstand, I splashed water on my face and then blotted it with a towel as I turned to face Bree. She was feigning absorption with my stockings, but I was not about to let what just transpired pass without remarking on it. "Do you want to tell me what that was about?"

She frowned at the ribbon on one of my garters. "I suppose you'll find oot soon enough. *Mister* Anderley managed to charm Mr. Rookwood's maid into revealin' why she was so tight-lipped wi' me."

My heart sank. *Oh, Anderley, you didn't?* And after Bree made it so clear she didn't want his interference.

She slammed the drawer of the dresser and marched across the room to arrange the implements to style my hair with sharp, precise movements. "She was only too happy to cry on his shoulder and tell him how sad she was, and how frightened that the murderer'd come after her next."

I perched on the dressing table bench. "Why would she think that?"

"She says she heard the printer and Mr. Rookwood arguin' the day before he was murdered when she was cleanin' the outer office, though she didna ken what aboot." She scoffed, untying the ribbon securing the bottom of my braid with a tug. "Somethin' I ken I could o' convinced her to share tomorrow if'n he'd kept his nose oot o' it like I asked."

I didn't dispute this, for I knew well how Bree's warmth and empathy could convince one to confide in her. After all, it had worked on me, and I had never regretted it. Though I was beginning to regret the romance which had blossomed between her and my husband's valet, for it was upsetting the balance and easy camaraderie our investigative team had enjoyed since my marriage to Gage. Not that I begrudged either of them finding such happiness, but as it currently stood, their relationship was far from blissful.

"Has Anderley informed Mr. Gage?" I asked as she pulled the brush through my hair, making it crackle.

"Aye. That's how I found oot."

Gage had often counseled me not to insinuate myself into our servants' personal lives, but I couldn't allow the moment to pass without saying something.

"I do wish Anderley had allowed you to handle the matter as he was supposed to."

Bree didn't speak at first, but her strokes of the brush became less forceful. I studied her face in the reflection of the mirror, curious what she was thinking, but she seemed resolved not to divulge it, replying with a simple "Thank you, m'lady." Whether this was to shelter herself or me, I didn't know, but I respected her too much to force the issue.

But that didn't mean I wasn't going to broach it with Gage. "And what did you say to Anderley when he presented you with this information?" I asked as we waited in the line of carriages delivering passengers to St. James Square.

"Well done."

I scowled.

"Surely you didn't expect me to scold him. We needed the information, and he obtained it for us."

"Yes, but that task was assigned to Bree, and she asked him not to interfere."

He tugged at his gloves. "We aren't planning a garden party, Kiera. This is a murder investigation. It doesn't matter who the task is assigned to, so long as we receive results."

"I see," I replied measuredly, fighting to restrain my anger. "So then Anderley has finished checking Heron's alibi?"

"No. He feared many of the shops would be closed."

"Then if I give Bree a list of those same addresses and tell her to feel free to track them down first, you'll be fine with that?"

His expression turned cross. "This isn't a competition."

"And yet your failure to discourage Anderley when he interfered in the exact same manner has set up just such a scenario between our servants."

He glared at me tight-lipped.

"It would be one thing if you'd ordered them to work together, but instead you assigned Anderley his own tasks to accomplish, in addition to finding the ballad-seller."

He turned away, and for a moment I thought he'd decided to concede the field, but I should have known better. "Why does Miss McEvoy care so much that Anderley interfered? He helped her."

I wasn't about to divulge my suspicions about the underlying motive for Bree's upset—Anderley's flirtatious tactics for eliciting information from females—for that was merely secondary to the main reason anyway. "She was given *one* job to do to contribute to this investigation, and he took it from her. Wouldn't you be miffed if, say, your father assigned you one task to complete, and then your cousin accomplished it before you had the chance?" I arched my eyebrows in emphasis. "Just because Bree is a woman doesn't mean she's happy to pass off responsibility." It was my turn to look away, adding in a dry undertone, "We're not all damsels needing rescuing, contrary to popular opinion."

Before Gage could respond, the door to our carriage was opened and the step lowered. A massive mansion loomed before us, occupying the corner where Elder Street met St. James Square on the older side of New Town as it began to incline toward Calton Hill. Lord and Lady Soames had resided here for close to fifty years and, both being about the age of seventy, chose to receive their guests while seated on two high-backed, gilded armchairs before the massive stone hearth in their entry hall. As we inched our way forward in the line, I felt Gage's warm hand press against the small of my back.

"I'm sorry we quarreled," he leaned down to murmur in my ear. "You are right. I should have considered the matter from Miss McEvoy's perspective."

I smiled gratefully up at him, and seeing the warm regard reflected in his eyes, I felt my anger toward him thaw. I was well aware that I was wed to one of the most attractive men in the realm, though much of the time I didn't dwell on such a thing. But once in a while it struck me with the same impact as it had the first time we met, making my insides melt and my knees a little weak. Though I would never have admitted it at the time, even to myself. I'd despised the way women seemed to turn fluttery and foolish at the sight of him. And while it was true that I'd never outwardly lost my senses, inwardly I was nearly overcome.

As I was now. His golden hair gleamed in the light of the chandelier overhead, a burnished halo to his bronzed features, finely sculpted cheekbones, and pale blue eyes. Eyes that communicated his love for me as much as the twinkle in their depths hinted at his anticipation of the plans we'd already set into motion for the evening.

"Oh, my dear. I do so love to see two young people in love," Lady Soames gushed, recalling me to the fact that the receiving line had moved forward. "Oh, and you're in the family way. How lovely." She accepted my hand, pressing it between her own. The servant standing behind the chair bent forward to whisper my name. "You are very welcome to our home, Lady Darby. Oh!" she gasped as if just now recognizing who I was. "Yes, Lady Darby." She smiled archly. "You must come to call. I have questions, so many *questions*."

I smiled tightly, caught between amusement and embarrassment at her novel approach. Most of the ladies who gossiped about *The King of Grassmarket* either glared at me in disapproval—few of them daring to cut me direct because of my husband and father-in-law—or cornered me in an effort to pump me for information about Bonnie Brock. None of them had yet invited me to call. I hurried past her and Lord Soames, who squinted so pronouncedly I doubted he saw more than a blurry wash of color.

Gage took my arm, his social mask firmly in place as we circled the rooms dedicated to the Soameses' soiree. We were some of the last people to arrive, and by any measure it was a crush. So much so that I feared we would never be able to find a place to confront Kirkcowan privately. That is, *if* Lord Henry could succeed in our plan. It wasn't until that moment that I realized how much trust Gage had placed in him, and he didn't even know yet that Henry was his half brother.

When Gage returned to my side later in the evening after a second foray to the gaming room, a satisfied grin stretching his lips, I remarked on it.

"I take it matters are proceeding as planned."

"Yes. Lord Henry is doing splendidly," he tipped his head down to say, as he guided me away from a cluster of ladies with whom I'd been conversing. "Has Kirkcowan tugging at his collar and downing brandy faster than he should, which will only hasten matters in our favor."

We both nodded at an acquaintance strolling past us on the opposite side of the corridor.

"You've entrusted Lord Henry with a great deal in this scheme."

"I have," he admitted in a voice that told me this wasn't the first time *he* had considered that. "I suppose you're wondering why."

I nodded and then elaborated, lest he misunderstand. "Don't get me wrong. I like Lord Henry. I believe I have since the moment

I met him. He has a streak of honorability running through him a mile wide." I jostled my elbow against his side. "Not unlike *some* people I know."

He smiled at my gentle teasing.

"But until yesterday evening, I would have sworn you felt a marked distrust toward him because of all of that business at Sunlaws Castle and his role in escorting his brother abroad."

"It's true. I was still remarkably cross with him. With the duke's entire family. But after speaking to him, I realized what an impossible situation he'd found himself in during our investigation. And in the end, he did the right thing and confessed to you what so troubled him, which helped you put the pieces together to figure out that Lord John was the culprit." He lowered his head. "As for his escorting his brother abroad, Lord Henry apologized to me for the necessity of his actions but confessed he would still make the same choice. That he'd feared that without his calming influence his brother might do something drastic on the voyage."

I looked up in dismay. "You mean . . . ?"

Gage nodded.

I swallowed. "And his other brothers aren't precisely calming influences, are they?" Though I didn't doubt their regard for one another, in truth, his other brothers would have been more likely to drive Lord John to take his life than the other way around.

"Given that, I can't hold Lord Henry's actions against him. Rather, I find them to be commendable."

A pang of empathy tightened my chest imagining Henry trying to navigate such a dilemma. If he escorted his brother abroad, then Gage—the half brother he was anxious to confess his connection to and befriend—would be terribly angry with him, and might never give him the chance. While if he refused and stayed to speak with Gage, then Lord John might throw himself overboard into the sea.

I realized I couldn't hold his actions against him any longer either, no matter what they had cost me. He had made the right choice. And I would give him no more grief for it.

"Mr. Gage?"

We both turned to face the footman addressing my husband.

"Yes?" Gage asked.

"Lord Henry Kerr has asked me to tell you he'll be with you in five minutes."

"Very good. Thank you." He nodded, dismissing him.

A pulse of anticipation quickened through my veins as Gage turned our steps toward the rear of the mansion.

"Apparently, matters have progressed even more quickly than I anticipated. Which is all for the better. If Kirkcowan becomes too sotted, we might not get anything from him." His lip curled upward in scorn. "Last night he nearly passed out under the table."

"That reminds me, whatever became of the executor of Rookwood's will you intended to speak to?"

"He never appeared. I'll call on him at his home if it proves necessary."

That he expected to learn something significant from Kirkcowan tonight was obvious. Perhaps he even thought we'd unmask Mugdock and solve Rookwood's murder. But given how belligerent and difficult Kirkcowan had proven to be in the past, I didn't think it would be so simple.

I glanced behind us before slipping through the door Gage opened on the right at the end of a corridor. It proved to be a private parlor of some sort. One where ladies normally gathered, if the lingering scents of powder and perfume were any indication. Dainty furnishings filled the space, and Chinese silk paper covered the walls. A low fire burned in the hearth, but Gage took the liberty of lighting several candles while my attention was diverted by a portrait of a young Lady Soames hanging on the wall. If I wasn't very much mistaken, it had been painted by Angelica Kauffmann, an artist I greatly admired. Perhaps I would have to pay a call on Lady Soames after all.

So absorbed was I in studying the quietly dramatic pose and the exquisite brushwork that I almost didn't hear the door opening. However, no one could mistake the fury in Kirkcowan's voice.

CHAPTER 17

Now, see here, Kerr. What in blazes is the meaning of this? Just because I now owe you several hundred quid doesn't mean you can haul me about."

My eyebrows arched skyward at the sum Kirkcowan named as he stumbled into the room. His cravat and hair were rumpled, and his sallow complexion was what one would expect of a man who spent his time drinking and gambling, and indulging in other unworthy pursuits. Lord Henry, on the other hand, appeared as fit and strong as any man in the prime of his health, though his expression was foreboding.

When Gage stepped forward to stand beside him, I was struck again by their resemblance. The same strong jawline, the same cleft in their chin, the same thick hair, even though Gage's was golden and Henry's auburn. But I didn't have long to dwell on these facts before Kirkcowan began to bluster in anger.

"Bloody hell. This is *your* doing!" He pointed an accusing finger at Gage before letting out a foul stream of curses.

"Mind your tongue," Henry snapped. "There is a lady present."

Kirkcowan's ruddy face twisted into something particularly ugly before he spat, "All I see is a doxy."

At this insult, Gage seized hold of his lapels, nearly lifting him off his feet. "You will treat my wife with respect or I'll break your jaw so you can never utter such vulgar words again."

But Kirkcowan was far from intimidated, emboldened by the brandy in his belly. "Don't you mean you'll bash my head in," he snarled, clearly referencing Rookwood's murder.

The muscles in my husband's arms rippled beneath the tight cut of his coat as he grappled for control of his temper. My chest constricted at the evidence of his fury, even knowing it was in my defense, even knowing Kirkcowan deserved to be thrashed. So when instead he shoved Kirkcowan away with a look of disgust, making him tumble backward over the arm of one of the settees, I could only be relieved.

"We know you never recovered those jewels you claimed you did," Gage stood over him denouncing. "We know you lied about them being stolen again. And we know you've cooked up some scheme where you've convinced your friends at ebb-water to feign the theft of their own jewels to defraud their insurers. So if you don't want Lord Henry reporting your debt to the police and having you thrown into debtors' prison, you'd better start talking."

"This was all a trick," he grumbled as he tried and failed several times to sit upright. "I'm not paying anything. And I want what money I did have returned to me."

"The gaming was fair and square, as all the gentlemen in that room will attest to if questioned. You're simply a rotten punter."

The sound Kirkcowan made at the back of his throat was more akin to a growl than human speech, and I feared for a moment he would lunge at Gage. But he could barely regain his feet, let alone attack anyone.

"Now, you made a wager that a sequel to *The King of Grassmarket* will be published. How did you come by that information?"

He smiled nastily. "It's just a wager. Doesn't mean it's true. After all, you just said yourself I'm a terrible punter."

"Yes, but I think you *did* learn that somehow. Perhaps directly from the man who styles himself Mugdock."

Neither of these accusations seemed to ruffle Kirkcowan in the least. In fact, he seemed to be enjoying himself as he finally found his balance and tugged on his coat to straighten it, nearly toppling over again.

"And when Rookwood declined to publish the sequel, perhaps you helped Mugdock kill him." This was just a lie meant to provoke a reaction from Kirkcowan, but it jostled something in my brain all the same. Albeit something I couldn't quite place.

Kirkcowan's eyes narrowed.

"I suspect all of this is information the police would be glad to have," Gage threatened.

"Go ahead," he blustered. "They can't detain a man of my station. And they would never dare to toss me into debtors' prison."

"Maybe," Henry conceded. "But what will you do once your illegal source of income has been foiled? How will you pay me and the other gentlemen you've dunned?" He took a step forward to stand in line with Gage. "You might think the police won't dare, but for a dozen or more angry lords, I can assure you, they will."

Perspiration broke out across Kirkcowan's brow, and his hands clenched into fists at his sides, but the same stubbornness which made him such a terrible card player also kept him from folding now. He gave a sharp crack of laughter. "You think that's my only source of income," he retorted, all but admitting that our accusations about fraud were true. "You're not the only one who's good at uncovering other people's secrets." He strode forward, glaring sideways up into Gage's face. "Or putting them to use."

He shouldered his way past them toward the door, and Gage and Henry didn't stop him, apprehending, as I had, that Kirkcowan was not going to tell us anything.

"Bloody fool," Gage spat.

"Yes, but a bloody fool who knows something and is not above using blackmail to profit from it," I said, pressing a hand to my back, which had begun to ache.

"I just hope he doesn't attempt to blackmail the wrong person." He planted his hands on his hips, shaking his head. "He's playing with fire. I'll have to hire someone to follow him and discover where he goes, who he speaks to." Turning away from the door, he offered his hand to Henry. "Thank you for your assistance with this," he declared, shaking his hand. "As reckless as he is, Kirkcowan would never have allowed himself to be goaded into a game of chance with me, and it might have taken me all night to best him as you did so thoroughly."

"My pleasure."

Gage glanced at me. "We're finished here, and I suspect you'd like to go."

"Yes."

"Are you staying, or can we give you a lift to Bowmont House?" he asked Henry.

"I'm leaving, so I'll take you up on that." Lord Henry's gaze flicked toward mine, making my insides flutter with nerves. "Actually, there's something I wished to discuss with you."

Gage nodded, offering me his arm and then guiding me toward the door. "If it's about the blunt Kirkcowan owes you, that's entirely your affair," he spoke over his shoulder. "All I ask is that you wait a few days before attempting to collect it or forgive it to keep the pressure up on him."

"What of the jewel fraud?" Henry murmured, following us closely.

"*That* I intend to inform Sergeant Maclean with the Edinburgh City Police about at the earliest convenience."

Henry's silence seemed to convey his approval, and I was far more preoccupied with the realization that Henry was finally going to tell Gage that they shared a father. It was time. It was *past* time. And yet still I dreaded the knowledge that my husband was going to be startled by the news. There was no bones about it, he was going to be terribly hurt by the discovery of his father's betrayal of his mother. I could only hope that the pleasure of learning he had Henry as a half brother was compensation for some of that pain.

The men conversed cordially about various topics as we drove the short distance through New Town to our town house. While I could barely manage to contribute more than monosyllabic comments to the discussion, I was amazed by Henry's ability to speak seemingly without a trace of nerves. Only the twinges in my back seemed capable of directing my thoughts elsewhere.

Once we arrived home, I excused myself, knowing it would be best to allow them some privacy for such a conversation no matter how much I wanted to be there to lend Gage my support. I worried that my presence would actually be more of a hindrance than a comfort, particularly once he realized I already knew. If Bree noted my distraction, she didn't comment on it, but she did recognize that my lower back was troubling me and brought me a hot water bottle to recline in bed against.

"It's minor," I assured her after thanking her. Nevertheless, a sigh escaped my lips as I sank back against the warmth. "Too much dancing, I suppose." In truth, I'd been surprised by the number of men who had asked me. And I didn't want to examine their motives too closely. Not so long as they'd treated me with respect.

Bree passed me the book resting on my side table, her brown eyes scrutinizing me. "Ring if ye need me."

I nodded, eager for her to depart. It was clear she thought I was about to go into labor, but I knew my body better than she did. Even though I had never given birth, I had witnessed other women doing so, in particular my sister, and Dr. Fenwick had instructed me well. I was aware of the signs to look for. These mild twinges alone indicated nothing.

Although I felt less certain when my abdomen began to tighten and release in small contractions. At first I thought it was the babe moving about inside me, and I pressed my hand to the spot, hoping to feel their tiny heel, fist, or bottom wriggling about. But it soon became evident it wasn't that. The discovery was enough to temporarily divert me from my anxiety over the conversation happening on the floor below.

I was just about to climb from bed and walk about to see if movement would relieve the contractions when they seemed to stop. There, I reclined with my hands clasped on either side of the rounded swell of my stomach, my eyes fastened on the taut white fabric of my nightdress when the door to the dressing room opened. One look at Gage's face told me he was still stunned, and I abandoned my own concerns to reach for him.

He crossed the room and plopped down on the edge of the opposite side of the bed, facing away from me, and I scrambled awkwardly across the counterpane to sit beside him, draping my arms around his shoulders. "Oh, darling," I murmured, struggling to hold back the emotion clogging my throat at witnessing his pain and disenchantment.

His gaze remained trained on the rug, and for a long moment he didn't speak, though he did shift his arm to wrap it around me loosely. I pressed my forehead to his neck, feeling the bristles of facial hair along his jaw. Tears pricked at the back of my eyes, followed by a flush of anger, hot and sharp, that Lord Gage should have done this to him. To his mother.

But then I inhaled a deep breath of Gage's skin and spicy cologne, and tempered my thoughts. What was done was done, and undoing it would only undo Henry's existence. That was a thought too cruel. However, I did curse Lord Gage for being so bloody secretive. If he'd only told his son years ago rather than keeping it from him, some of this anguish could have been avoided. And Henry and Gage might already have established a relationship.

Every time Gage thought he had found himself on steady ground with his father, something occurred to prove it was naught but a shaky foundation. Like the parable of the foolish man who built his house upon sand. Except Gage wasn't accountable for his father's deception, even if he did feel like a fool every time his trust in him was revealed to be undeserved.

"How long have you known?"

The hollow tone of his voice cut me to the quick, and the tears I'd been fighting spilled down my cheeks. I knew I couldn't lie to him, though the impulse was still there to protect him, to protect myself. "Since the day we caught Lord John," I admitted, though forcing the words out made me feel as if I were going to vomit.

No emotion registered on his face, and he had not yet looked at me, so I made myself continue.

"I . . . I'd heard the speculation about the duchess's younger children, and then I recognized the resemblance between Henry and your father. And you," I added shakily, seeing his jaw harden as it had when we were confronting Kirkcowan.

"And so you asked him?" he managed to query in an even voice that was all the more unsettling for the roughness around the edges.

"More or less," I replied quietly.

"And yet you didn't tell me!" He turned to me then, his eyes blazing with such fury that I shrank away from him.

"I . . ."

"I already know that Henry made you promise to let him tell me. That Father is apparently in possession of some damning secrets that secured the duchess's and Henry's silence until now. But fiend seize it, Kiera! I am your husband. Your loyalty should be to me."

"I know. You're right," I sobbed. "I'm sorry. But I knew how much you adored your mother, and you'd . . . you'd just reconciled with your father . . . and I knew how much this would *hurt* you. And I . . ." I hiccupped ". . . I just couldn't seem to bring myself to tell you."

He shook his head angrily, sweeping aside all of my excuses. "You should have told me!"

I nodded, swiping at my cheeks, even as my gaze remained watchful, my muscles tense. "Yes. Yes, you're right, Sebastian."

Gage saw all this. Saw the way I was shrinking into myself. And he hurdled to his feet, rounding on me.

I instinctively jerked away from him, fear flooding me and driving out all other thought.

"I am not Sir Anthony!" he roared. "How many times must I tell you that?"

"I know. I know. I'm sorry," I blubbered. "I can't help it!"

"Did you think I would hurt you?"

"I . . . no. No!" Not in my rational mind. But Gage could read between the lines.

His face twisted with rage and agony, and he whirled away, striding toward the dressing room.

"Sebastian," I called after him. "Sebastian, wait!"

But he was already gone, slamming the door behind him.

I sat staring at the offending portal, trembling with grief and despair. I had doubly hurt him, and worse, I had destroyed his trust. If only I'd ignored Henry's request. If only I'd not been so cowardly and timid. But it was too late now.

I collapsed into the bed and wept bitter, disconsolate tears.

I didn't see Gage again until the next morning while I was seated in the morning room where we took our breakfast, gazing out the French doors, my toast and cup of warm chocolate barely touched. Though my appetite had been ravenous for most of my pregnancy, I found that it had deserted me overnight. The sun shone brightly down on our little garden, but that only seemed to cast my own circumstances even more in the shade. I wanted to shake myself for entertaining such gloomy thoughts. When my husband suddenly appeared in the doorway, I clasped my hands tightly in my lap to stop myself from rushing over to him.

He hesitated for a moment before approaching the table. "Good morning," he stated politely.

So at least I wasn't to be punished with silence.

"Good morning," I replied, matching his even tone, and then forced myself to pick up my cup and take a sip.

He selected a newspaper from the stack on the table, opened it, and began reading. Though his actions were not so different from those he performed every morning, they felt altogether irregular. There was no warmth, no ease. And that made my toast as dry and tasteless as ash on my tongue, and my chocolate as thick and cloying as syrup.

Whether the servants were aware of our disagreement was answered by Jeffers's reticent glances as he brought Gage his usual breakfast of sausages, a hot roll, eggs, and cheese, and then quickly withdrew. First Bree and Anderley, and now me and Gage. I wouldn't be surprised if Jeffers soon gave notice.

Seeing that Gage was determined to remain absorbed in his

paper, I stifled a sigh and resumed my study of the garden in between obligatory bites of my breakfast. I had managed to choke down one slice of bread and was considering abandoning the other so I could end this torture when Jeffers rapped on the door.

"Sergeant Maclean is here to see you."

Gage looked up at me for the first time since he'd entered the room, and I realized he was seeking permission from me. I nodded, feeling a pulse of curiosity. Normally Maclean preferred to meet in neutral territory at his sister-in-law's shop. What had brought him to Albyn Place?

"Send him in," he told our butler.

In short order, Maclean stood before us, seeming to inhabit half the space in our cozy morning room. His jaw sported a new bruise in an alarming constellation of colors.

"Good heavens, Sergeant," I gasped. "What happened to you?"

His gaze cut to Gage. "That's why I'm here."

That didn't sound good. "Oh?"

"Aye."

"Well, then you'd better have a seat," I told him. "Or else you'll give me a crick in my neck from having to look up at you. Have you broken your fast?"

He eyed Gage's sausages hungrily as he sat in the chair indicated, but then declined. "Havena actually fasted. Havena been to bed either."

"There's been a development," Gage surmised.

"I would say that much is obvious," I couldn't halt myself from retorting, earning me a brief narrowing of eyes from my husband.

Maclean glanced back and forth between us, his brow furrowing slightly. "Aye. We surprised some members o' McQueen's gang tryin' to rob another warehouse. Managed to nab a few o' 'em, too."

"Looks like one of them nabbed you as well," I replied, nodding at his jaw.

He scratched at the dark stubble sprouting around it. "Aye, got in a lucky right hook. But 'twas the *only* jab he landed."

"Then do you suspect that McQueen's men are behind the other crimes imitating the scenes in *The King of Grassmarket*?" Gage asked.

"They're no' talkin'. But aye, I'd wager so. Looks like Kincaid is innocent o' at least that." He didn't appear happy about this fact.

"Do you think they murdered Rookwood as well?"

"Nay. Most o' McQueen's men would swipe the shirt off their ain dead granda, but they're no' murderers. Least o' all calculatin' ones."

I wasn't as confident of that as he seemed to be. After all, McQueen had managed to run an illegal whisky distillery out of the vaults for some time before being caught. Surely there must be someone within his gang capable of carrying out such a crime. Perhaps even McQueen himself.

Maclean sat back, crossing his arms over his chest. "Are you the one who helped Heron move Rookwood's things oot o' his offices?"

"Before the scavengers broke in and picked it clean?" Gage replied defiantly. "I am."

"Ye were s'posed to steer clear, *and* keep clear o' Kincaid. But I heard he paid ye a visit the day before last." His stern gaze swung from my husband to me.

"Do you honestly think I would allow Bonnie Brock Kincaid to step foot in this house?" I retorted, wondering where Maclean had gotten his information.

Gage arched his eyebrows at this bit of linguistic wrangling, but when Maclean's glare returned to him, he did not point out the misleading nature of my statement. "Kincaid knows full well what I would do to him if he dared to enter my house uninvited," he replied, sawing off a bite of sausage with his knife almost in illustration.

Maclean chose not to question this, though I could tell from his expression he was far from convinced.

Lest he change his mind, I put to him the question I'd wished to ask him. "Where was the wound located on Rookwood's head?"

"On the top, slightly to the left."

"Then he was seated upright when he was struck?"

He had answered the first question seemingly without thinking, but my second query did not pass by unnoticed. I waited patiently as he pursed his lips in aggravation and then relented. "Aye."

"So he was awake and aware someone was in the room with him. And he trusted that person enough to allow him to stand behind him."

"No' if the killer snuck in through the window," he countered.

Gage and I both turned exasperated looks on him.

"I know very well that you are a superb policeman. So I know you tested the window and realize the impossibility of that," Gage challenged. "It squeals like a stuck pig."

"Aye. But that doesna discount the possibility he was ambushed by more 'an one person."

"All climbing through the window? Or did this duo or trio of killers waltz through the door without anyone on North Bridge Street noticing?"

"Aye. No one *notices* Kincaid and his men doin' anythin'," he replied in a scathing tone.

I frowned at Maclean, for he was being stubborn. I understood his anger at Kincaid for continuing to escape justice, and his frustration that he held such sway over the people of

Edinburgh, but arresting him for a crime he *hadn't* committed was not the way to go. Especially when he would never be convicted on what little proof they did have.

The fact of the matter was that Rookwood would never have allowed Bonnie Brock or any of his men to stand behind him, not after the threats Brock had made. And he certainly wouldn't have sat complacently while they picked up the ormolu clock from his mantel. The location of Rookwood's wound was confirmation for me that not only had the murder scene in his office been staged, but he had been killed by someone he knew and trusted.

Maclean appeared ready to continue arguing this point when there was another rap on the door.

"This just arrived for Sergeant Maclean," Jeffers informed us, stepping forward to hold out the silver salver on which rested a missive.

Maclean picked it up with equanimity, though I doubted he was often confronted with so pretentious a presentation. He unfolded it, reading quickly before rising abruptly to his feet. "My apologies. Somethin' urgent has come up."

"Come now, you're not going to leave us without telling us what it is," Gage protested.

Maclean appeared as if he wanted to do precisely that, but then he relented. "Lord Kirkcowan was attacked. He was found unconscious in his home."

CHAPTER 18

"How bad is it?" I asked several hours later as I settled into our carriage next to Gage.

"Bad," he replied grimly. "The physician isn't sure he'll recover."

I blanched, turning to gaze out the window at the green of the Queen Street Gardens as we rolled past. "I don't like Kirkcowan. He's odious. But . . . no one deserves to be attacked like that."

Gage didn't reply, but I could tell he was in agreement.

He had departed earlier with Maclean, insistent he inform him of our dealings with Kirkcowan the evening before, and his fraud and blackmail schemes. Maclean must have then allowed him to accompany him into Kirkcowan's residence on St. Andrews Lane, for it was now midafternoon. Until Jeffers had told me my husband was waiting for me outside in our carriage, I hadn't known when he would return.

I watched as the carriage turned right onto Hanover Street. "Where are we going?"

"We still need to find out what was contained in Rookwood's letter to Mr. Murray with the Theatre Royal."

I'd noted that Gage hadn't included that on the list of Heron's errands that he'd asked Anderley to verify.

"And I think we should find out why Lennox failed to mention his argument with Rookwood the day before he was murdered."

Even though Gage seemed to be avoiding looking at me, the fact that he'd returned for me when he could have conducted these interviews on his own gave me hope. So I sat quietly, gazing out the window at the smart Georgian architecture and elegantly landscaped streets, determined not to give him any more reason to be angry with me.

Silence had never been a problem for me. I was perfectly content to pass the time wordlessly observing the world around me. During the years I'd been wed to Sir Anthony, I don't think I spoke more than two dozen sentences a day, and most of those were to our staff.

When we arrived at the Theatre Royal, I turned to find that Gage was looking at me. For how long he'd been doing so, I didn't know, but he didn't look particularly pleased. It was on the tip of my tongue to ask if I'd done something wrong, but I was worried that would only provoke another argument about my failure to tell him about Henry's relation to him. So I kept my mouth shut, hoping he would explain his irritation without my having to ask.

Instead he climbed from the carriage as if he couldn't wait to escape the confines, though he did reach up to help me descend rather than leave the duty to our footman. I suspected he'd only done so for appearance's sake, for the pavement in front of the Theatre Royal was thronged with people. A number of them gathered around a broadside advertising the theater's rendition of *The King of Grassmarket*, chattering about the play.

Gage escorted me around the building to the stage door,

where he asked for Mr. Murray. We were then ushered down a corridor whose walls were plastered with old playbills, which smelled strongly of the chalk and lampblack the actors used for their stage makeup. It still being the middle of the afternoon, there were few people about, so a deserted hush seemed to fill the passages which hosted a flurry of activity every night.

The man assisting us rapped peremptorily on a door before opening it to announce us and then hurrying off. Inside sat William Henry Murray, actor and now owner of the Theatre Royal. He had obtained possession of it through his sister, Our Mrs. Siddons—as all of Edinburgh referred to Harriet Siddons, in order to distinguish her from her mother-in-law, the celebrated actress Sarah Siddons. Murray was renowned for his stage management and deserved much of the praise for the success of King George IV's visit to Scotland in 1822, the first visit of a reigning monarch to Scotland in 171 years. Given these facts, it was no surprise he had staged *The King of Grassmarket* to such thrilling effect.

Mr. Murray possessed a head of pale wispy hair, a weak chin, and rather round eyes. Eyes which widened even further as he rose from his chair, holding his hands up, palms out. "If ye have an issue wi' the characters in the play, you'll have to take that up wi' my solicitors. I'm no' gonna discuss it wi' ye."

I realized then that he thought we were there to harangue him for his portrayal of Lady Dalby and Mr. Gale in the theater's adaptation of *The King of Grassmarket*, and possibly sue him for defamation. A case I wasn't certain we could even win given the fact that the actors cast as our characters looked nothing like us. A casting choice that I suspected had been deliberate.

"Mr. Murray, we're not here about the characters or the play," Gage protested calmly.

His hands began to lower, even as his head tilted suspiciously. "You're no'?"

"No. Actually, my wife and I saw it about a week ago, and we can certainly understand why it's a tremendous success."

"The staging was ingenious," I added. "And the actor who played Bonnie Brock was inspired."

His shoulders relaxed. "Aye, Keaton is a marvel." His arms crossed over his chest. "But I thought ye said this wasna aboot the play."

"As I'm sure you know, Thomas Rookwood was murdered three days past."

His brogue deepened. "Aye, sorry bit o' business. Rookwood was a good sort. Easy to work wi' and reasonable. I canna say that aboot all o' his type."

And by *type*, I presumed he meant publishers.

"His assistant, Mr. Heron, told us he delivered a letter to you the day Rookwood died. Can you confirm that?" Gage asked.

"Aye. But surely you dinna suspect Heron? That chap is too chickenhearted by far. And he was dashed fond o' the old fellow, who was fond o' him in return."

"We don't. But much of investigating is following up on each tedious piece of information, for one never knows where it will lead you," Gage explained. "Do you mind telling us what the contents of the letter were?"

A spark of levity lit Murray's eyes. "Aye, is tha' what yer really after? Rookwood wanted to ken if anyone had visited me in the last fortnight, complainin' aboot the play." My puzzlement must have shown, for Murray shrugged. "He dinna explain why he wanted to ken. And I dinna have the chance to ask."

"And had anyone?" Gage prompted.

He scrutinized Gage, perhaps still uncertain if we were trying to gather information to use against him. "Aye, there's been plenty o' complaints. Most o' 'em outraged at the supposed immorality o' the play, though that disna stop 'em from comin' to see it. We've had packed houses every night. We also published a note on the broadsides just for the likes o' 'em, proclaimin' that 'depravity, even masked by daring, is certain to result in guilt and imprisonment.'"

I suspected this was a quote he had been forced to repeat more times than he wished to count.

"Though I s'pose the fact that Kincaid hasna yet been made to pay for his crimes does a great deal to contradict that sentiment," he added under his breath.

While that was in some regards true, I also knew that Bonnie Brock had paid for his crimes in other ways. In truth, the law which had so failed his thirteen-year-old self and his sister had made him into the criminal he'd become. So if there was guilt to be handed out, it went both ways. But no one was going to punish the law or the police for those failures. No one in authority anyway.

"Have *all* of the complaints been about the morality of the play?" Gage asked, clearly following the scent of something I hadn't caught. "Has there been anything different?"

Murray rubbed his chin. "Aye, there was one fellow. Cornered me in the midst o' one o' the performances to complain aboot the discrepancies between the book and the play. Accused me o' deliberately makin' Kincaid into a hero rather than a villain. And o' course he was right. I ken what plays well to an audience, and makin' Kincaid into a villain is no' it. No' to mention the fact that no one could make heads nor tails o' the hodgepodge o' accusatory nonsense made in the book. 'Twas best to leave it oot and shape the script as we did."

"Did you tell him that?"

"Aye, and he accused me o' bein' in Kincaid's pay," he scoffed. "I had 'em tossed oot. Havena seen him since."

"Did you get a good look at him?"

Murray shook his head. "'Twas too dark backstage. But he was tall and had an upper-crust accent—or he feigned it." This was a theater, after all.

We thanked him and then made our way back down the corridor the way we'd come.

"Rookwood told us that Mugdock refused to endorse the Theatre Royal's rendition of *The King of Grassmarket* because it was inaccurate," I murmured so that only Gage could hear me. "He said he was so furious about it that he turned down the money they offered."

"Rookwood must have suspected that his author had gone directly to Murray to complain. But why decide to confirm it? Why would it matter?"

I considered his questions and everything we knew thus far. "Maybe . . . maybe he thought Mugdock was stirring up trouble. And maybe he was worried he would suffer in the repercussions."

Was that why he'd been murdered? Because of something Mugdock had done other than write the book? If only we knew the author's real identity. Then we might be able to answer that. Because whatever the truth, Rookwood had clearly been punished for something, whether justly or unjustly.

Gage and I returned to our carriage and traveled the short distance to Lennox's shop. Here, too, people were gathered outside in front of the broadsides plastered to the side of the building—placards presumably printed by Lennox. Though curious, I didn't inch closer to see what they advertised. I kept my veil over my face and allowed Gage to hustle me inside the building before anyone could approach us. Including the brawny man leaning against the wall just beyond the broadsides, whose eyes followed us into the shop.

Lennox was absent from the main room where the printers ran, throwing off their pungent scent and clinking noises. I wondered if they ran day and night, if they were ever given a rest. Gage led us toward the office, where he knocked on the door.

"Come in!" a voice shouted, which proved to be Mr. Lennox's

when Gage opened the door. "Mr. and Mrs. Gage," he declared, pushing to his feet. "To what do I owe the pleasure?" His expression was a curious jumble of emotions, but chief of them was definitely not pleasure. He forced a smile. "I thought I'd answered all your questions."

"Some information has come to light that we need to ask you about," Gage replied.

"Of course." He gestured for us to take a seat, but my husband declined.

"This shouldn't take long. During our last discussion you told us you'd last seen Rookwood when he visited you here two days before his murder. However, you were overheard arguing with him at Rookwood's office only the day before his death."

Lennox looked away, scraping a hand through his copper red hair.

"What do you have to say to that?"

"It was the maid, wasn't it?" He sighed, shaking his head. "I knew I should have told you, but I thought it would only make me look suspicious." He held his hand out. "And you would jump to just this sort of conclusion."

"Your decision to omit it makes you look far more suspicious."

He nodded, staring broodingly down at his cluttered desk. "I can see that now."

"Why were you arguing?" I pressed.

He grinned shamefacedly. "It seems silly now, but I was angry because I'd found out he recommended another printer to a colleague of his. A big job, too."

"Then he cost you a great deal of profits," Gage construed.

"Yes and no."

I frowned. "What do you mean?"

"Rookwood explained to me that this colleague is fussy, demanding, and notoriously difficult to work with. That whatever profits I expected to make would be eaten up by his demands for adjustments and reprinting, and by the end I would be cursing him for even recommending me. Once he informed me of that, I could hardly remain cross. Especially after I conferred with some of my own colleagues and verified he was telling the truth."

It was a plausible enough explanation. And yet I wasn't certain I believed him.

And I told Gage as much as soon as we returned to our carriage.

"It did seem like an inane reason to make such an omission," Gage agreed. "But innocent people often do absurd things simply because they *fear* they might look guilty."

"True," I conceded, straightening the folds of my skirt. "But there was something about his demeanor. The way he was gripping the back of that chair with his hands, almost as if he might tear it in two. And his facial expression when we arrived. He was not pleased to see us."

"Yes, but people's words and demeanor don't always reveal them to be a liar, do they, Kiera?" The bite in his voice and the hard glitter that entered his eyes left me in no doubt about to whom he was referring.

A bitter taste filled my mouth, momentarily leaving me speechless. The hollow space in the center of my chest—the one that had been ripped open when Gage stormed out of our bedchamber the night before, the one that seemed to rob me of my breath—yawned wider. Tears bit at the back of my eyes as he looked away, almost as if he were dismissing me.

"Sebastian, I . . ."

"No, Kiera," he interrupted before I could squeak out more than that. "I'm not ready to discuss it yet."

I swallowed, choking on the emotions crowding at the back of my throat and then nodded. For what else could I do? He had a right to be angry, and I couldn't force him to talk. Not if he didn't want to. Only that little "yet" he'd tacked on to the end gave me hope he would eventually forgive me. But there was no telling how long I would need to wait.

So I turned aside, subtly swiping at the few tears that had slid down my cheeks so he wouldn't see them and grow angrier. It proved more difficult to sniff quietly, but I tried my best.

"I'll drop you at home, and then I'm going to the New Club to see if I can speak with the executor of Rookwood's will," Gage told me a few minutes later, his voice still tight with residual feeling. "Perhaps he'll have some insight we've missed. But I'll be home in time to dress for your cousin's dinner party."

More than anything I wished we could skip Morven's soirée, but then that would leave us at home, avoiding each other. Or worse, with Gage at his club while I sat alone fretting.

I offered a faint farewell as I climbed from the carriage. One which Gage emotionlessly reciprocated before the door was shut and the coach departed. I stood at the base of the stairs, watching it depart as I tried to compose myself before I faced Jeffers. A movement out of the corner of my eye made me realize I wasn't the only one on the street. Lady Kinnear and another woman stood on the opposite corner, as if strolling to Queen Street Gardens. I raised my hand in greeting and then hurried up the steps, hoping my anguish hadn't been as evident as I feared it was.

I considered venturing up to our bedchamber to lie down for a rest, but I knew I would never sleep. There were books that still needed to be searched in the library, but I knew I would never be able to focus on the pages. So I meandered aimlessly around the drawing room, trying to divert myself, to force my thoughts down a different path, but to no avail.

"My lady, I thought I heard you come in," Anderley said, appearing in the doorway. He glanced around the room. "Is Mr. Gage not with you?"

"He went to the New Club to try to speak to the executor of Rookwood's will again."

"I see." Anderley hesitated, and I wondered at the sudden stiltedness in his demeanor. Whether Gage had told him anything about our fight, or if he'd simply inferred as much from our conduct. After all, it would be impossible to miss the source of the tension that had been introduced into our household. Even Jeffers had been especially cordial upon my arrival, clearly unaware I was the one at fault.

"If you'll excuse me," Anderley finally said, but I called after him.

"Did you learn anything of interest while confirming Mr. Heron's alibi?"

He turned back, his dark eyes scrutinizing my face before he replied, "Unfortunately, no. Though I can attest that the author he visited in Leith was, in fact, difficult to find. Took me half the morning."

"Oh, well, I suppose we all knew it was unlikely they could tell us much."

"I'm still trying to locate the ballad-seller."

"Thank you."

He bowed his head and then turned on his heel to depart, leaving me alone once again.

I soon found myself perched on the seat before our bow window, watching the world pass by outside. I considered asking Peter, our footman, to accompany me to Queen Street Gardens for a stroll in the sunshine, but my lower back was bothering me again. Though I knew Bree would fix me another hot water bottle or some other remedy for it, and offer me all her sympathy, I resisted the urge to ring for her. Somehow, I felt I deserved the discomfort, foolish as that might be. It was a penance of sorts.

So lost was I in my own morose musings that I almost failed to note the carriage pulling up to our door. I didn't recognize the conveyance and was on the brink of retreating to our bedchamber, lest I be forced to receive them, when I caught sight of the occupant emerging. She was a vision of loveliness in a gown of *ver de mer* sea green in figured gros de Tours, with a standing collar and deep epaulettes, and a magnificent hat adorned with a rich plume of white feathers. My heart leapt in eagerness.

Charlotte, the Dowager Countess of Stratford, soon to be wed to my cousin Rye, was one of my dearest friends. Though we hadn't started out that way. She had once viewed me with barely concealed contempt, and I had avoided her with chilly dislike. Until I helped to save her from her late husband's murderous machinations. Since then, we'd both realized we'd misjudged each other and had developed a close friendship, despite the distance that often separated us.

By the time Jeffers opened the drawing room door to introduce her, I was already standing, ready to receive her. He had known not to stand on ceremony where Charlotte and I were concerned, and so she entered behind him. If possible, she looked even more radiant than the last time I'd seen her, which was saying something, as she was one of the most beautiful women in all of Britain.

"Oh, Kiera, my darling," she exclaimed with a laugh as she hurried forward, her soft gray eyes sparkling. "You look as if you are ready to pop."

"Like a champagne cork," I conceded as she touched both sides of my rounded abdomen and then reached up to hug me around the neck. I felt my emotions stir at being embraced so, especially after all of the trials of the past few days, and strove to tamp them down. "Rye must be treating you well. When did you arrive in Edinburgh?"

"Oh, he is a dear." She pulled back to look at me, her hands still clutching my arms, which she squeezed affectionately. "But you know that."

I opened my mouth to reply but then had to close it, for my lip began to quiver.

Charlotte's eyes widened in concern. "Oh, dearest. Whatever is the matter?"

"I . . . I think Gage hates me," I gasped, dissolving into tears.

CHAPTER 19

"Come now. What's this nonsense?" Charlotte coaxed gently sometime later after I'd cried myself out leaning against her shoulder on the settee. "Gage doesn't hate you."

"I know," I sniffed, already recognizing how ridiculous that statement had been. A culmination of fear, and stress, and the overwrought emotions I'd experienced at times during my pregnancy. I'd never been the type of woman who cried easily, but I'd been assured that sentimentality was a natural consequence of my expectant state.

"Then what made you think so, even ever so briefly?"

She listened quietly, her pale blond head tilted to the side, as I explained about Lord Henry Kerr being his half brother, and how I'd kept the secret from Gage. Perhaps I shouldn't have shared that shocking bit of information about Gage and Henry's relation to each other, but I knew Charlotte could be trusted. She might appear as fragile as a china doll, what with her porcelain skin and pale pink lips, but she was strong and resilient, and fiercely loyal—something that I valued highly.

It was such a relief to have someone to talk to, to have someone to listen, I even shared my hurt and bafflement over my sister's treatment of me. I hadn't realized how much I'd missed being able to confide in Alana until that moment, how difficult it was not to have her advice and support. Now, when I needed it. Simply being able to share the burden eased its weight off my shoulders, allowing me to breathe more easily.

When I'd finished, Charlotte smiled at me sympathetically, clutching my one hand while I used the other to dab the remaining tears from my eyes with my handkerchief. "I'm sorry you've been enduring this all alone, and while expecting. But things are not so bleak, Kiera."

"But I kept a secret from Gage I should never have withheld," I protested.

"Yes, you did. But for the very best of reasons. And Gage will see that eventually. He's simply wounded and angry right now. Give him some time to come to terms with what his father has done, with the discovery he has a brother." She lifted her hand to tuck a wayward strand of my hair behind my ear. "If I know anything about Gage, it is how much he loves you. This won't make him stop. In fact, it might make him love you more."

I frowned in puzzlement at this statement, but before I could ask what she meant, she continued speaking.

"As for your sister, I suspect there's more to her behavior than she's telling you." She tapped her chin thoughtfully. "If you can find the reason behind her strong emotions and responses, a reason beyond even the fear she feels for you, I think you will have your answer."

"You know something." It was a statement, not a question, for I could see in her eyes that this wasn't some hypothetical suggestion.

"No. Yes." She frowned. "Maybe. I will think on it. But in the meantime, the next time she attacks you, see if you can probe deeper into her reaction."

I nodded, unsure that I would be able to remain emotionless enough to do so. Or whether Alana would remain in the room long enough. She had the infuriating habit of walking away from an argument once she'd believed she'd won rather than waiting to listen to what I had to say in return.

I twisted my hands in my lap, and Charlotte eyed me patiently, recognizing that there was still something troubling me we hadn't addressed. "But what about the way I flinch from Gage whenever he's angry? I *know* he would never hurt me." I pressed my hands to my chest. "I know it in my heart. And yet I can't seem to help it. My body reacts before I can stop it."

She grasped hold of my hands, waiting for me to look her in the eye. "I'm going to tell you something you told me once. *Your husband's actions are not yours to atone for.*"

I blinked, fighting another wave of tears as she continued in her own words, knowing she was speaking of Sir Anthony.

"Even the wrongs he did to *you*." She shook her head. "It's not your fault any more than it's mine what our late husbands did to us, or that our bodies have longer memories than our conscious thoughts."

I nodded, unable to speak.

"Whatever pain or anger Gage and Rye are feeling when we quail or cringe, it isn't so much *at* us as *on our behalf*. For they know there's nothing they can do to erase the cause of it. All they can do is love us forward."

My lips curled into a trembling smile at the impact that that truth had on me, soothing an ache inside me I hadn't even known I needed to heal. "That's very wise."

"Well, I was helped along to it by the very best of women," she proclaimed, chucking me playfully under the chin.

I smiled wider under her regard.

"Now, other than to see you looking so splendidly fecund . . ."

I laughed as she leaned back to gaze at the evidence of this.

"I really came to invite you to a dinner party my great-aunt is hosting."

"Didn't you and Lady Bearsden just return to Edinburgh?" I gasped in amused wonderment.

"Yesterday. But you underestimate my great-aunt. She has been known to send her staff into a flurry by deciding within an hour of her arrival that she'll be hosting a soiree that very night. This time she's at least giving them three days' notice." She tapped the back of my hand. "It's on Wednesday and is certain to be enjoyable, for rather than inviting a crowd of stuffy society matrons, the dinner is to be a small gathering of theater folk."

This sparked an interest in me, particularly as we'd recently had encounters with such people. I wondered if any of them would have any insights into Rookwood's murder or *The King of Grassmarket*. And whether they would share any of it with me.

"Of course we'll come."

"Excellent. Auntie will be in raptures to see you in such a state."

I searched Charlotte's eyes for any indication that she might be saddened or discomfited by my expectant condition, but I only saw joy reflected there. I knew she had longed to be a mother more than anything, but she had proven to be incapable of conceiving. That was one of the reasons I was so happy she'd found love and companionship with my cousin Rye, for he had two young children of his own, both of whom had taken a great liking to her.

"Tell me about your wedding plans," I urged, and then listened happily as she shared the details of their July ceremony.

They had elected to wed at Barbreck Manor in Argyll, the estate of Rye's great-uncle, the Marquess of Barbreck. It was to be a small ceremony with close family and friends. A decision which did not surprise me. Rye had always been quiet and serious, and Charlotte had endured enough of society's attention to last a lifetime. I was to serve as her attendant, an honor I was pleased to perform, so she spent a great deal of time describing our attire, to most of which I merely nodded. For all my strengths, fashion was not one of them, and it being Charlotte's special day, I would wear whatever she told me to.

I embraced her tightly again when it was time for her to depart. Then I stood at the window, smiling as she issued instructions to her footman to fetch pastries from the Lejeunes' shop. I had just been describing the deliciousness of their macarons in embarrassing detail.

As the footman trotted off and her carriage rolled forward, my interest was caught by the sight of a man standing in the shadow of one of the buildings across the street. At first I assumed it was one of Bonnie Brock's men, who I knew still followed me about the city, for either Brock's edification or my protection. The reason varied depending on who you asked. But something about the man seemed familiar, and after studying him for a moment I realized why. It was the same brawny fellow I'd seen outside Lennox's shop. He wore the same dark brown coat and leaned against the wall with his arms crossed over his chest in the same exact manner. And he was watching our house.

I stepped back, ensuring that the damask drapes shielded me from his sight.

What was he doing here? Was he one of Bonnie Brock's men? Had he followed us from Cowgate? Or had he already known where we lived?

I contemplated what to do. My first instinct was to speak to Gage, but matters were already strained between us. If the man across the street proved to be one of Bonnie Brock's men, I knew it would irritate him to be reminded that I was being shadowed in such a manner. But if the man wasn't, if he was there for another reason, then I wanted to know why. And whether it was connected to Lennox and his shop in any way.

I turned toward the writing desk, but then realized I didn't know whom to pass the message to for Bonnie Brock. Though I could usually spy his men if I looked closely enough for them, they had gotten better at masking themselves in recent months. Once in a while a fresh recruit would appear, one who hadn't yet mastered the art of concealment, and so stood out like a mustard pot in a coal scuttle. Thus, I couldn't judge the brown-coated fellow by that factor alone.

Returning to the window, I tried to detect whether another man was observing the house, but after ten minutes of searching I gave up the effort. I would simply have to keep a note for Bonnie Brock in my pocket, in hopes that I would recognize one of his men and could pass him the message to be delivered to Brock. For once, I hoped that would actually be sooner rather than later.

Despite a promising start to the day the next morning, matters swiftly turned to bad and then worse.

Though we hadn't spoken much the evening prior, I woke in the middle of the night to find Gage asleep in bed beside me. I lay there gazing at his slumbering face in the dark, softened in repose, and felt my heart overflow with affection for him. So when I roused the next morning to discover he was already gone, at least I could comfort myself with the knowledge that he had been there, and at least he'd slept well.

At breakfast he seemed calmer, not simply pretending to be so. So although we didn't speak about anything of substance, he could nonetheless converse about trivial things without the corners of his eyes crinkling or his mouth pursing with repressed anger.

Given that fact, I chose not to mention the strain that was still evident between Bree and Anderley. All in all, I wasn't given much opportunity to observe them together, but what I had seen was not encouraging. And neither was Bree's general mood. A passing comment she'd made the previous evening while readying me for Morven's dinner party had led me to believe they'd both taken sides in my and Gage's disagreement, essentially pitting men versus women. This was not promising for the future harmony of our household or our investigative quartet.

We had nearly finished breakfast when a message was delivered for Gage.

"It's from Maclean," he explained as he began to read. "Kirkcowan is still unconscious. His physician is even less optimistic of his recovery." He exhaled in frustration, crumpling the missive.

I lowered my cup of chocolate. "I suppose we shouldn't hope for any further information from him, then." I felt a pulse of empathy for Lady Kirkcowan and her children. Whatever his failures, he was still their husband and father, and I knew they would grieve him in some capacity if he passed.

"No. Nor from his papers, of which he had few. From what I gathered, he seemed to believe that if he burned the bills and IOUs, then that destroyed all evidence of his debts and obligations. The only thing of interest we found in his safe was the paste copy of that diamond and sapphire necklace he alleged was stolen, recovered, and stolen again." Gage pushed to his feet. "If you'll excuse me. I need to reply to Maclean."

I nodded, watching his retreating figure until it disappeared from sight.

A few moments later I wished him back, for my sister appeared in the doorway, apparently having barreled past Jeffers, who followed close behind. "Still breakfasting?" she demanded without preamble.

"Good morning to you, too, Alana," I replied, and then offered our butler a sympathetic smile. At the best and worst of times, my sister could be a force to reckon with. Butlers might be trained to stop ruffians from entering, or overbearing gentlemen, but I would back my sister in a match against any of those for craftiness.

"Can I offer you anything to drink?" I asked with a saccharine sweet smile, knowing that a scolding was coming. "Tea?"

"No, thank you."

"Coffee?"

"No."

"Chocolate?"

"Kiera, I said *no, thank you*," she snapped.

"I don't think she wants anything," I turned to Jeffers to say.

"Yes, my lady," he replied, a hint of amusement lurking about his mouth. He bowed out of the room, leaving me to my sister's surly company.

"You *know* why I'm here," she accused.

"Of course I do. You practically announced it to the world with that angry stride and scowling visage."

"Lady Kinnear couldn't wait to crow to me and everyone else who would listen last night that you and Gage are quarreling."

I sighed, having known this was coming. I should have slapped the gossiping Lady Kinnear at Alana's dinner party when I had the chance.

"That he practically threw you out of the carriage onto your own doorstep."

I cast her a dismissive glance. "Can you honestly imagine my husband doing such a thing?"

"I can't," she conceded. "But that's beside the point."

"Actually, it's not," I countered evenly.

"It's what everyone *thinks* happened."

"Everyone?"

She plowed on, ignoring me. "Morven told me the two of you barely spoke two words to each other yesterday evening."

"My, our cousin was up and about quite early this morning. She's a busy little bee."

Alana's brow lowered, clearly not appreciating my attempts at levity. "Is it true?"

"No. I distinctly remember saying at least six words to him." I counted them on my fingers. "*Darling, will you fetch me a drink?*' No, seven."

"Kiera!" she practically shrieked. "This is no laughing matter. *People* are talking. And now someone is saying they saw you with Bonnie Brock Kincaid earlier this week."

I arched my eyebrows in surprise, considering the possibility that we were seen while we conversed in my garden, but I quickly dismissed it. Not only was it raining too hard for anyone to have spied us from the neighboring town houses, but Bonnie Brock had stayed inside the stable, out of sight of prying eyes. "Now, that's balderdash."

But once again she wasn't listening. "Is that why Gage is so angry? Is that why you fought?"

I glared at her, as her leap to such an offensive conclusion succeeded in enraging me when none of her previous words had.

She leaned toward me. "You have to stay away from him, Kiera. For the sake of your reputation and your marriage . . ."

"Alana, stop!"

The crack of my voice seemed to grab her attention when nothing else had. She stared back at me in startlement, but I knew it wouldn't last long.

"Do you know how incredibly insulting you're being? Do you honestly think my husband isn't aware of every altercation I might happen to have with Bonnie Brock before, during, and after they occur? Do you honestly think he's threatened by him? Or that he has the least need to even *fear* my involvement with him?" I tossed down my napkin. "Why are you berating me about nonsensical gossip?" I asked, recalling Charlotte's counsel.

She inhaled a deep breath before diving into her typical recriminations. "Your reputation . . ."

"No, no," I cut her off. "Not that. You say it's about my reputation, about your reputation, about conforming to society, but *why* must I do that? Why *personally* must I do that?" I scrutinized her snapping lapis lazuli eyes and the clamped line of her mouth. "Did *you?*"

"Of course I did . . ."

"And what did you give up to do so?"

I hadn't recognized how important this question was until it was out of my mouth. It passed my lips with a feeling of rightness and seemed to hit Alana square in the chest, almost rocking her back on her heels with the impact. I watched her absorb the words, feeling much of my own anger drain away.

I'd never considered whether my sister had given something up when she'd married Philip and become a mother, as most women did because they were expected to. I'd been a self-absorbed seventeen-year-old when they wed and when Malcolm was born nine months later, thinking of little but my art. Morven had known my sister far better at that age than I had. Perhaps that was why my cousin had also understood Alana's reaction better than I had.

"Alana," I prodded more gently.

Her head took on that stubborn tilt I knew so well. "I'm simply trying to help," she retorted crisply, pushing to her feet. "I don't see why you always have to be so selfish and do things the difficult way, but so be it."

However, I could see through her attacks now. There *was* some deeper reason behind her insistence that I cease my involvement with murderous inquiries and conform. Some deeper reason than her fear for my safety. And it was something she didn't want to share with me, perhaps because then she would have to acknowledge it herself.

I watched her storm from the room before turning to gaze out the French doors at the garden. In truth, I'd always thought marriage to Philip—whom she'd been in love with since the age of twelve—and motherhood were all she'd ever wanted. It troubled me to think I might not be aware of another side of Alana, that she might have hidden it from me.

I tapped the side of my cup with my fingernail, wondering if our brother, Trevor, knew. As the middle child and a boy, he had often been privy to things that I, as the youngest, had not. If I wrote to him about it, I wondered whether he would share what he knew, if anything.

I'd just resolved to do so when a movement in the garden captured my attention. The door to the stables opened, and the lad who helped care for our horses came trotting down the garden path. However, it was the man I saw standing in the doorway behind him that truly piqued my interest, for he knew he wasn't supposed to be there. In any case, I knew he wasn't going to be turned away without speaking to me, so I rose from my chair and climbed the stairs to the library-cum-study.

I found Gage bent over his desk, scribbling a note in his nearly illegible scrawl. He glanced up and then lowered his head again to his task. "Did you want something?"

"Always," I replied softly.

His hand halted abruptly, the only indication he'd heard me before he resumed writing.

I inhaled a deep breath that trembled slightly as I stifled my more tender emotions. "But for the moment, it appears we have a visitor."

When I didn't elaborate, Gage looked up. I arched my eyebrows toward the window overlooking the garden, and he glanced toward it in confusion before turning back to me.

When comprehension dawned, his head snapped back around so that he glared at the window. "In the stables again?"

"Yes," I replied. "I saw him out the French doors in the morning room, and I'm anticipating a request for our presence from Jeffers in . . . ah, now," I finished as our butler paused in the doorway.

"Kincaid is in the garden?" Gage snapped.

If Jeffers was surprised by our already being aware of this, he didn't show it. "Yes, sir. He requested an audience with Mrs. Gage."

My lips quirked, having no doubt this phrasing had been chosen by Jeffers and not Bonnie Brock. An audience, indeed.

Gage's scowl darkened. "Fetch our . . ." He broke off at the sight of my forest green cloak and his dark greatcoat already draped over Jeffers's arm. "Yes, thank you."

Once we were appropriately attired against the chill, Gage led me back to the morning room and pushed open the French doors before he offered me his arm to guide me down the steps of the terrace into the garden proper. Sullen, gray clouds scuttled across the sky, blocking much of the sun, while now and then a stray sunbeam pierced through. I would have made light of the downturn in weather after two sunny days without Bonnie Brock's presence, simply to ease the tension, but I decided Gage didn't need any more ammunition to use against him.

The stable door swung inward as we approached, revealing Bonnie Brock standing in the shadows. At first glance he appeared as irritable as Gage and spoiling for a fight. But on closer analysis, the muddled swirl of emotions reflected in the depths of his eyes told me it wasn't simply anger he was feeling, but something more akin to fear.

"Why are you here?" Gage demanded. "I thought I made it clear . . ."

I pressed a hand to his chest, halting his words before speaking to Brock. "What is it? What's happened?"

"Maggie." He took a step closer. "Have ye seen her?"

I shook my head in surprise. "Why? Is she missing?"

He swallowed. "Aye. When I woke this morning, she was gone."

CHAPTER 20

I could hear the panic stretching his voice, see it in the taut stillness of his stance. And so could Gage, who had fallen silent, his anger draining from the muscles of the arm beneath mine that had earlier flexed, ready to lash out.

"I ken it wasna very likely, but I thought . . ." He broke off, shaking his head, unwilling or perhaps unable to finish that thought.

"May-maybe she went for a walk," I suggested hesitantly.

He nodded. "She does that sometimes." A vee formed between his brows. "Least she did before."

Before the threats to him had increased after the publication of *The King of Grassmarket* and his decision to keep her close for her own protection? Or before she'd run off with a former member of his gang and returned to him hollow-eyed, malnourished, and pregnant, only to lose the baby a few weeks later? I didn't ask.

"But she kens no' to go anywhere wi'oot me or Stumps or Locke," he insisted. "She wouldna disobey me."

I wasn't so certain of that. As docile and obedient as Maggie was most of the time, I'd recognized that she had a dogged streak that was just as strong as her brother's. She'd simply been too beaten down from her experiences in the wilds of Northumberland, betrayed by the man she had believed loved her, to summon her will to resist. But she was seventeen and chafing at the tight control her brother exerted over her life and his failure to acknowledge her needs. It was only a matter of time before she rebelled again.

"What time did you notice she was gone?"

"A little before sunrise."

I felt a pulse of alarm, for that was almost four hours ago. Even if Maggie had dared to go for a walk alone, she would never have been gone that long.

"Are your men searching for her?" Gage asked.

"Aye, as we speak." He glanced behind him, his jaw hardening. "Though I've a fair idea noo who has her."

His thunderous expression and the red suffusing his features alarmed me. "Who?"

He turned to look at me, hesitating to say the name as if I might try to dispute him. "Who else but McQueen." He fairly spat the word. "No' that he was directly responsible. McQueen never gets his hands dirty."

"Don't be rash, Kincaid."

He turned to glare at Gage, who held his hands up palms out.

"I know you don't want my advice, but you need to hear it anyway. It could be McQueen or it could not, but you need confirmation before you send your men after him. Who do you think will be the first person McQueen will harm if your men start attacking his?"

Bonnie Brock's chest rose up and down with each angry, heaving breath, but he appeared to be listening.

"You also need to consider that all of this might easily be a trap to catch you. If you're killed or arrested, that won't help your sister."

Brock looked away, struggling to master his emotions, and then nodded.

"Let us help look," Gage surprised me by offering. "And if it turns out McQueen, or someone else with nefarious intentions, has Maggie, let me help you get her back. Safely."

His eyes narrowed in obvious mistrust.

"It may shock you to know, I have some experience with recovering captives," he retorted. "And I doubt McQueen's men could possibly be more vicious than the Turks. Or the Greeks for that matter," he added in an undertone.

Gage almost never talked about his time fighting in the Greeks' struggle of independence from the Ottoman Empire. It had taken me months to convince him to share even the smallest detail with me. So to hear him speak of it now, and to help Bonnie Brock no less, made my heart swell with love for him.

When Bonnie Brock still didn't speak, Gage retorted impatiently, "I'm not about to let your sister come to harm. Regardless of her relationship to you."

At this derisive quip, he seemed to regain some of his self-possession, nodding stiffly. "Aye."

I knew it would be too much to suppose he would thank us, so I added my input before Gage began to expect it. "I'll tell our staff to admit her if she comes here. My maid will know what to do."

He began to turn away, but then I remembered I still had a question to pose.

"Don't take offense, but I need to ask you about the men you have watching the house."

He didn't sneer mockingly as I'd expected. "Aye."

"Is one of them a brawny fellow in a brown coat? Perhaps a new recruit?"

His frown deepened. "Nay. That's no' my man." His eyes narrowed. "But it sounds like one o' McQueen's. Has scars from smallpox and a dark smudge beside his eye here." He tapped his right temple.

"I didn't get a good look at his face," I admitted, looking up at Gage, who was listening intently. "But he was standing across the street watching our house yesterday afternoon." I didn't add that I'd seen him outside Lennox's shop as well, not wanting to tip that hand to Bonnie Brock.

"I'll speak to my men," he promised. "But I can tell ye it's no' the first time they've noticed McQueen's men shadowin' ye."

"And you're just telling us this now?" Gage protested.

Bonnie Brock shrugged. "Ye didna seem to want to ken."

What he really meant was that he didn't want us to know precisely how much he was monitoring our movements. He probably already knew about Lennox and every other place we'd visited since returning to Edinburgh in early February.

"Dinna fash. My men'll keep 'im in line." His brow furrowed, perhaps recognizing that these were the same men he had also been relying on to keep Maggie safe, and they'd failed at that.

This time when he turned to go, I halted him with a single word: "Brock."

He glanced over his shoulder.

"We'll find her."

He didn't speak, but I could sense the distress rippling through his features. It was in the angle of his head and the tight restraint of his shoulders. A moment later he walked away, allowing the door to shut behind him.

I turned to look up at Gage, his eyes a bluer shade than the patch of sky peeking through the clouds behind him.

"When were you going to tell me about the man watching our house?" His words weren't accusatory, but I could sense his annoyance nonetheless.

"Just as soon as I knew he was something to concern you with," I replied as I turned to stroll back toward the house.

"And how precisely were you going to discover that?" he asked, catching up with me.

I struggled to stifle my own irritation that he insisted on pressing me on this and decided distraction was the best tactic. "Observation, my dear. I saw him outside Lennox's shop yesterday as well."

A small pucker formed between his eyes.

"Has Anderley been able to track down that ballad-seller yet?" I inquired as we reached the terrace.

"Not that he's informed me."

"Don't you think that's odd?" I posited as Gage opened the door. "We had two sunny days. You would think that old man would have positioned himself at one corner or another, if not in front of the market." He didn't seem like he could afford to go many days without working. That thought settled like a heavy weight on my chest. "I hope nothing has happened to him."

"Maybe he did see something. Maybe he's afraid to be asked about it. If so, perhaps Anderley can coax it out of him."

I nodded, thinking that would be one of the better outcomes.

Gage ordered our coachman to drive in a griddle pattern through the streets north of High Street and Canongate, deducing that Bonnie Brock and his men would have already searched to the south. I hadn't a great deal of confidence we would be the ones to find her. In truth, I hoped she had already returned to wherever she and Bonnie Brock were currently staying. Regardless, we rolled slowly through the streets, each peering out opposite windows as we searched for a slight young woman with brown hair and big green eyes.

I was watching the washerwomen on Calton Hill as we traveled down the North Back of the Canongate when astoundingly

I spied her. She had come striding out of a narrow close between two buildings, her shoulders hunched and her head down. "Stop!" I hollered as we drove past her, and the coachman brought the horses to a halt.

Wary of startling her, I opened the carriage door and leaned forward as far as my expectant state would allow, to find her staring at me with wide, frightened eyes. "Miss Kincaid, don't be alarmed. It's merely us."

But my words didn't seem to relieve her. Contrary to my expectations, she seemed even more distressed. Her gaze darted behind her anxiously, her feet seeming glued to the cobblestones.

Gage helped me descend into the dusty road, and I hastened toward her, worried she would dash off before I could speak with her. "Are you well?" I asked in concern, scouring her features. "As I'm sure you can guess, your brother came to us when he couldn't find you this morning."

"I-I dinna mean to be gone so long," she stammered, clutching her cloak tightly around her.

"Of course," I agreed readily. "He was worried something bad had befallen you. But you are unharmed?"

"Oh, I dinna mean to cause so much trouble." She inched away a step, as if prepared to flee.

I hadn't failed to notice she hadn't answered my question, but I was more anxious to keep her from running. "We don't have to take you back to your brother, if you don't wish. We can take you anywhere else that's safe." It was the same promise I'd made to her after we'd saved her from her folly in Northumberland, risking Bonnie Brock's wrath.

I searched her eyes. Was he the reason she was so wary? Was she was afraid to confront her brother? After all, she had a history of running from him rather than talking to him. Though, admittedly, Bonnie Brock wasn't the best listener, especially to his sister. Maggie had spent too many years feeling beholden to her brother because of what happened in their childhood, and Brock had never recovered from the guilt he felt at having failed to protect her.

But this offer also did nothing to calm her. "Nay, I'm returning noo. There's no need for ye to go to such bother." She glanced behind her again, though I couldn't tell what she was looking at or for. Did she think she was being followed?

I had just opened my mouth to ask her when a man darted across the road, between passing carts, to join us. I realized it was Locke—the taller of Bonnie Brock's two right-hand men.

"Maggie, are ye off yer head?" he demanded to know, though I could tell by the way his posture softened that he was relieved to find her hale and whole. "Yer brother is fair tearin' apart the city lookin' for ye."

"I didna mean to cause trouble," she repeated, and I began to wonder if she was apologizing for more than her slipping away from her brother's watchful eye this morning.

Locke nodded to us, then firmly pulled her arm through his to lead her away.

I watched them go, still wrestling with the reason behind Maggie's agitation. Locke's presence hadn't seemed to trouble her as much as mine, and that was strange to me. "That was curious," I finally stated aloud before turning to look at Gage standing by our carriage. "Wasn't that curious?"

He nodded. "And you know what's even more curious? I just realized Mr. Heron's lodgings are nearby."

I whirled around to gaze in the direction he was looking. "Where?"

He nodded toward the close Maggie had emerged from. "There."

Gage and I shared a look heavily laden with mutual speculation.

He arched his eyebrows. "Shall we pay him a visit?"

"I think that's an excellent suggestion."

He stepped forward to take my arm, leading me into the narrow close, which proved to be merely a gap between two buildings. The hill behind these two buildings began to rise too precipitously for more abodes to be built, and a hundred yards or more above rested the terrace on which Regent Road had been constructed into the side of Calton Hill. Its traffic clattered past, and on particularly dry days must have cast up a plume of dust and debris over these dwellings.

The buildings on either side of the close were made of dark stone with slate roofs—the same as much of the city—with narrow dormer windows along the roofline. Gage guided us to the left around a wooden barrel positioned to catch rainwater from the roof. A rutted lane extended along the base of the hill between the structures and the slope—a spot which I imagined flooded during heavy rains from the runoff from the hill. Dried mud coated much of the lower steps of the staircase leading to the story above, seeming to prove this. Even the rails were covered with mire, as if tenants attempted to wipe away the worst of the grime before ascending.

Mr. Heron's rooms were at the top of the house at the back of the building, facing the hill, so he'd probably not witnessed our meeting in the road with Maggie. A fact which seemed to bear out when his eyes flared wide at the sight of us standing outside his door.

"Mr. Gage, Lady Darby," he spluttered. "What brings you here?"

"Good day, Mr. Heron," Gage replied genially. "May we speak with you?"

"O-o' course." He stepped back. "Come in."

In terms of abodes, it certainly wasn't the most lavish I'd

seen, but it was also far from the meanest. What furniture there was appeared to be good quality, and the space was clean and tidy, but for the boxes stacked along the far wall, presumably cleared from Mr. Rookwood's office.

"I assume the men I sent were helpful in extracting Rookwood's things?" Gage asked, noting them as I had.

"Oh, aye! Thank ye. I dinna ken if you've been by to see the office, but the window was smashed just as ye predicted." He turned away, his profile troubled. "I hadna the heart to look inside and see what other damage they'd wrought."

"It isn't the first time we've seen it happen. Nor will it likely be the last."

Mr. Heron turned back toward us, and as if just now realizing we were still standing, he offered us seats. "Can I get ye somethin' to drink?" he asked me.

"No, thank you," I replied, choosing the armchair near the window so that I would have leverage to help me rise again. "But I do believe we may have met an acquaintance of yours along the road."

He straightened, nearly choking on his next word. "Oh?"

"Miss Maggie Kincaid?"

He shifted in his seat. "Nay, I dinna believe I ken anyone o' that name. Wait, isna that Bonnie Brock Kincaid's sister." He shook his head. "Nay, I . . ." He coughed. "I definitely dinna ken her."

Except it was perfectly obvious he did. And why lie about it unless there was a reason he didn't wish the association to become known? Or perhaps Maggie was the one who didn't want their relationship revealed?

Either way, his connection to Maggie, Rookwood, and the publication of *The King of Grassmarket* was suspicious. However, I didn't press the issue. Not yet. Not until I knew more.

"No? My mistake, then," I replied breezily.

"Once you began sorting through Rookwood's things, did you find anything of interest?" Gage said, switching topics before Heron could dwell too long on how much we knew.

His gaze shifted to the side as he sifted through his memory. "No' that I recall. Nothing that would suggest why . . . why someone would harm him anyway."

"What of the sequel to *The King of Grassmarket*?"

He frowned in confusion. "I thought ye believed that was what was taken from Rookwood when he was . . . killed?"

"We did. But we've since learned Mr. Lennox, the printer, possesses it."

Deep grooves scored Mr. Heron's forehead. "But Mr. Rookwood rejected the sequel."

Gage and I looked at each other in surprise.

"You're certain?" he clarified.

"Aye. Rather emphatically, I might add. Told me it was mostly a diatribe o' Kincaid's crimes and faults. A personal vendetta. That it wasna even disguised in story form. No' successfully anyway. And that much o' it wasna even based in fact."

"Did you read it?"

He shook his head. "Nay, I only ken what I just told ye. But I'm certain Rookwood wouldna changed his mind. He was that adamant aboot it."

Then why did Lennox have a copy? Or did he? After all, we hadn't been allowed to see it. Perhaps he was only claiming to possess it. But why?

Whatever the case, I knew who we were going to be visiting next. But Gage still had one more question.

"Have you accounted for all your time during the afternoon Mr. Rookwood was murdered? Have you forgotten to inform us of anything?"

Mr. Heron stiffened. "I didna do it."

"We aren't saying you did, but if we can definitively rule you out, that makes all of this easier."

He glowered at Gage, clearly not believing him, and clearly still withholding something from us. "I may o' stopped for dinner. But it wasna an errand."

That this was an obvious thing he should have mentioned earlier made the corner of Gage's jaw tick, but he managed to reply calmly. "And where did you stop?"

A sudden sharp twinge in my back made me miss the answer. I pushed to my feet and turned toward the window, ignoring the men's looks. Pressing against my back, I breathed deep as another pain stabbed through me there. After a moment, the ache eased, and when another didn't replace it, I turned to face the men again. Gage was taking leave for us, and I added my farewell before exiting onto the landing.

"Is anything wrong?" Gage asked as we descended the stairs.

I glanced up at his concerned expression. "Oh, no," I demurred, trying to diminish the incident. "It's simply that at this stage, sometimes sitting is as uncomfortable as standing." Which wasn't false. "In truth, no position truly feels comfortable right now," I added with a sigh. "Bree says that's merely nature's way of helping us forget our fear of labor and make us eager for the birth."

He nodded. "Do you think Bree is enough? Or should we ask if you can borrow Alana's maid when the time comes? After all, she has helped with four of Alana's births."

I laughed. "And Bree has helped at births since she was old enough to fetch water. You forget, she did a marvelous job assisting Dr. Fenwick with Jamie's birth when Jenny was poisoned, and she'll do just fine for me."

"If you're certain?"

I smiled up at him, finding his concern endearing. "I am."

He helped me into the carriage before he issued instructions to our coachman. I rested my hands against the taut skin covering the child inside me, anxious that the aches in my back not begin again. For regardless of my air of unconcern, I couldn't brush them off entirely. Not when the first one had been so sharp it had neatly stolen my breath.

CHAPTER 21

When we arrived at Lennox's shop, he was standing outside with his hands on his hips, directing a pair of men putting up new broadsides on the wall of the building. He turned to look at us when our carriage drew up to the side of the building, and this time he wasn't so careful to mask his irritation with our presence.

"You again," he stated with a look of mild chagrin. "More questions? Come on, then." He led us inside to his office and closed the door behind us but didn't bother rounding his desk to his chair, communicating this would be a short interview. "I don't know what else I can possibly tell you."

"Mr. Heron told us that Rookwood emphatically rejected the sequel to *The King of Grassmarket*," Gage informed him. "That he refused to publish it. And yet you told us he had already brought you the manuscript to do that very thing."

Lennox's face rippled with exasperation. "How should I know what Rookwood told Heron? Nor do I care. All I know is that Rookwood brought me the manuscript and told me to hold on to it and await further instructions. His implication to me was that he intended to publish it." He threw his hands up. "We even discussed the type and layout, and whether there would be any illustrations. A man does not do that unless he intends for me to print it."

"Would you allow us to see it, simply to prove that what you say is true?" Gage asked evenly.

Lennox's eyes narrowed for a moment, as if he were considering this request, but then he arched his chin upward obstinately. "No. Not until Rookwood's estate is settled and I'm told what to do with it."

"I see," Gage replied.

Though from my standpoint, I couldn't see anything. Did Lennox actually have the sequel in his possession or not? And if not, why would he lie about it? For that matter, why would Heron lie? Or if neither man was lying, why had Rookwood changed his mind about publishing the sequel?

"We won't take any more of your time, then." Gage reached for the door handle. "But don't be surprised when the executor of Rookwood's will comes by to collect the manuscript from you."

With this parting shot, he pressed his hand to my lower back and urged me from the room, but not before I caught the glower of dislike Lennox directed at him.

Once back inside our carriage, I turned to my husband with interest. "You spoke with Rookwood's executor?"

"Yes, and he was shocked and bemused by the entire affair. Said Rookwood was the man he would have least likely expected to be murdered."

"And you think he'll try to secure the manuscript from Lennox?"

"I don't."

My head reared back in surprise.

Gage smiled weakly. "Rookwood's friend is a fine enough man, but he's a pudding heart. He'll no more confront Lennox than sail to the Arctic." He turned to gaze out the window at the group of people gathered under the vaulted bridge over Cowgate. "The man will do precisely what Rookwood's solicitor instructs him to do and no more."

"Then might the solicitor collect the manuscript?"

"He might. But I've already uncovered much of what I intended to."

"Which is?"

He looked back at me. "Lennox doesn't intend for anyone to take it from him. Not now, not ever. At least, not until he's printed it. Which makes me think he possesses something." A hard glint entered his eyes. "And he might be willing to go to great lengths to keep it."

"Including murder," I added, boldly stating the implication.

"Yes."

"But why? For money?"

Gage shrugged. "Money can be a strong motivator."

And yet I could tell he found that answer no more satisfying than I did.

I gritted my teeth as another sharp pain stabbed me in my back, turning away lest Gage see it. But he was much too attuned to me, even when we were at odds.

"You truly are uncomfortable, aren't you?"

"Yes," I replied, shifting in my seat to try to find a better position.

"What can I do?"

I lifted my gaze to his, caught off guard by the offer, though I shouldn't have been. Seeing the tenderness in his eyes, I had to swallow the lump rising in my throat before I could reply. "Will you rub my back?"

"Of course."

"Lower," I directed as I turned my back to him as best I could in the confined space. I nearly groaned aloud when he began to knead my muscles there. When he eased up, I realized he feared he'd exerted too much pressure. "No, harder," I urged him, closing my eyes at the bliss of the relief I felt when he pressed firmly against my spine.

"Better?" he asked, and I nodded.

Gage continued until we reached Albyn Place, though I knew his hands must have ached from the effort. He stretched his fingers as our carriage rolled to a stop before our town house, just in time to encounter Sergeant Maclean descending our stairs.

"Were you looking for me?" Gage asked as he greeted him, and then turned to help me descend on unsteady legs.

"Aye. There's been a development." His grim expression and the manner in which his eyes had slid toward me before he made his second statement made me suspect that whatever it was would not be good for me.

"Kirkcowan?"

"No. He's still hangin' on. By a thread."

"Then?" Gage prodded when he still seemed hesitant to speak.

"The unclaimed bodies o' three cholera victims were stolen from the cholera hospital last night."

My heart surged in my chest at the implication.

"Pointing another finger at Kincaid," Gage surmised.

"Aye, if it's no' Kincaid himself."

"It's not," Gage stated firmly.

"Has the matter been made public yet?" I asked, wary of the city's reaction. After all, this was the same city in which Burke and Hare's murders had occurred just three short years ago. And now with the legislation for an Anatomy Reform Act being discussed by Parliament, one which would make the unclaimed bodies of the deceased in poorhouses and other institutions available to medical schools, there was a great deal of anxiety and uncertainty surrounding the entire issue. Thus by stealing the unclaimed bodies of cholera victims, the culprits stirred up the public's fears over not only the cholera and the resurrectionists but also the proposed Anatomy Reform Act.

But had any of that been their intention, or were the culprits purely trying to make further trouble for Bonnie Brock?

"Nay, but 'tis only a matter o' time," Maclean replied.

Gage looked up from the spot he'd been frowning at on the pavement. "Could it be McQueen's men?" Plainly thinking of their recent arrests for robbing warehouses where whisky was stored.

"Aye, maybe." His gaze slid toward me again. "I just thought ye should ken."

That he was thinking of my late husband and his involvement with the questionable procurement of bodies for his anatomical studies, and my enforced participation, was obvious. Not to mention the mob incited against me and Gage in Grassmarket just a year ago because of my macabre reputation.

"Yes, thank you," Gage said as the sergeant doffed his hat and strode away. Then he turned to me as we began to ascend our steps. "I know that was not easy to hear."

"No," I agreed, inhaling a deep settling breath. "But it was not as upsetting as it once might have been." And no one was more astonished than I to realize it was true. While I doubted I would ever be able to hear about stolen bodies or body snatchers without feeling a pang of uneasiness, I was no longer terrified by it. Not like in the past.

Gage pressed a consoling hand over mine where it rested against his other arm and offered me a proud smile, fully aware of how far I'd come.

Jeffers greeted us both in the entry with correspondence.

Mine was the invitation for Lady Bearsden's dinner party the following evening, while Gage's appeared to be of greater significance. He paused to read it in the doorway to the drawing room rather than following me all the way inside, the furrow in his brow deepening the further he read. When he'd finished, his gaze lifted to find me already waiting for him to speak.

"I must go out. To see Henry," he added, struggling with the words as he wrangled with something inside himself. "I . . . didn't receive his news as . . . equably as perhaps I should have."

The heartache in his eyes, the uncertainty stamped across his features made me long to go to him, but I could tell from his tense shoulders that he did not want that. That he would not accept it. Not yet. "How could you have?" I said instead. "I know it must have been both shocking and painful to hear."

His gaze dipped to the rug. "Yes, but . . . I should have behaved better."

I realized what he meant then, felt it resonate through me, and I blinked back tears for him, for Henry, and for myself. "It's not his fault, Gage. I know you know that. Just as I know you know it's not his fault he was forced to keep the secret."

"That's why I must talk to him." He took a step backward before looking up at me. "And after . . . we'll talk, too."

I nodded, not trusting my voice to remain steady if I spoke.

When he had gone, I went to the window, watching as he descended our stairs. Catching sight of me, he lifted his hand in farewell and then strode down the pavement. Only then did I allow myself to collapse on the window seat, wincing in pain.

Bree found me there some minutes later, sent either by Jeffers or by her own intuition. "M'lady?" she asked in concern as she crossed to me.

I offered her a weak smile. "I think it would be best to send for Dr. Fenwick. Just to be cautious."

"O' course," she agreed, helping me to my feet. "And in the

meantime, let's get ye to bed wi' a hot water bottle. I ken yer back was botherin' ye more than ye wanted to admit."

Late sunlight streamed through the windows, forming patterns across the counterpane when Gage returned. I reclined in bed, half seated, with my head tilted sideways to rest against one of my pillows as I studied the portrait I'd painted of Gage, which hung over our fireplace. I had sketched and painted him numerous times since then, but it was still my favorite. Perhaps because I'd managed to complete it after weeks of inability to paint even a flower correctly, fearing I'd lost the ability to create. Or perhaps because it captured him so perfectly—his good looks, his impressive physique, and his charm, but more importantly, his sincerity, his honorability, and his steadfastness. He was nearly tangible, his vulnerability drawing the viewer toward him and his strength.

Just as the vulnerability stamped across his features drew me toward him now when he entered the room.

"Dr. Fenwick was here?"

"Yes," I replied, holding my hand out to him.

He hurried forward to perch on the side of the bed, clutching my hand tightly with his.

I smiled gently. "There's no cause for concern. Dr. Fenwick said the back pain and false labor pains I've been feeling are perfectly normal."

"False labor pains?"

"Yes." I didn't protest my reasons for not telling him, especially as the last round had occurred just before he learned about Henry. "He said the baby was turned the wrong direction, which could be causing me the pain, but that he or she will more than likely right themselves before I go into labor."

His pale eyes searched mine. "Then . . . it's normal?"

"Yes. Although, he did caution me to take it a bit easier than

I have been," I admitted with a sheepish grin. "Not that I should remain in bed all day, which will only make my labor harder when the time comes. But that I might be putting a bit more stress on myself than I should."

Though I'd spoken the words as lightheartedly as I could, I could tell from the pale flush rising in his cheeks that they'd caused him guilt nonetheless. "And I certainly haven't been helping that," he said with such remorse that my heart cracked a little.

"Oh, no, Sebastian. It's *my* fault. You were right. My first loyalty *is* to you, and I should have told you. If not immediately, then the moment I realized Henry had departed Sunlaws with his brother."

He squeezed my hand between his. "But I understand why you didn't. I do. And I didn't react any better with you than I did with Henry. I'm sorry for that. I just . . ." His gaze trailed away, stamped with pain. "I didn't want to believe, *couldn't* believe it."

"I know." Tears filled my eyes as I gazed at his beloved face. "I'm so terribly sorry your father hurt you like this."

"Oh, darling, I know you are." He shifted closer, using his thumbs to swipe away the tears spilling down my cheeks. "I don't know why I keep being surprised by anything my father has done." He sighed heavily. "I suppose if there's any blessing in this, it's that my mother isn't alive to learn of his duplicity."

Except I wondered if that was really true. If Emma Gage had truly not known precisely what kind of man her husband was. But I kept those thoughts to myself.

"Did you speak with Henry?"

He turned his head, staring unseeing at the book resting beside me on the counterpane. "Yes, and I listened this time."

"He's a good man," I ventured hesitantly.

"He is." He lifted his gaze to meet mine. "And in time, I hope we'll grow close."

I offered him an encouraging smile. "I know Henry would like that. He said as much to me."

"Did he?" The note of forlorn hope at the edge of his voice brought on another swell of emotion I tamped down.

"Yes."

"Well, I've invited him to luncheon tomorrow."

"Good."

He nodded, as if uncertain what else to say.

"What will you say to your father?"

His expression darkened. "I don't know. If he were here, I would confront him. But he's in London, and given his threats to the duchess and Henry, I will need to think on it."

I squeezed his hand in support.

He sat very still, contemplating something significant, and I waited patiently for him to speak. "I asked Henry if his mother had named him Henry deliberately."

I frowned in confusion. "Aren't all the Kerr children named after former kings and queens?" Then I gasped, realizing something I hadn't before. "Your grandfather."

"Yes, my father's father was named Henry. Sir Henry Gage. That's why it's one of my middle names."

I searched his face, trying to decipher what he was feeling. "Does it bother you that he's named Henry?"

"Actually, no. In truth, it seems rather fitting. Father might have tried to hide from the truth, but in her own way, the Duchess of Bowmont made sure he would never forget it."

I couldn't help but smile in approval. "Yes, that does sound like Her Grace."

Gage reached for my face then, cradling it between his hands before he pressed his lips to mine tenderly, once, twice, and a third time. "Are you in pain now?"

"No. Bree's application of hot water bottles has helped."

One of his hands dropped to rest on my abdomen. "When does Dr. Fenwick expect the baby to arrive now?"

"He said it would be at least another week."

He smiled sympathetically. "So a little more discomfort."

"Yes. But I can manage."

"And I will help," he pledged, kissing me even more deeply. And he certainly did.

I had decided to make it my goal the following day at luncheon to direct our discussion to the lightest topics possible, but Gage and Henry seemed determined to discuss Rookwood's murder. Eventually I gave up trying to introduce a different conversational gambit and sat back to smile at their mutual enthusiasm. There was no doubt they were brothers, despite their only having known each other for such a short time.

I didn't venture many of my own theories, curious to hear what they thought instead. Gage had been so silent the past few days, I hadn't been as privy to his impressions as I normally was. And even Henry appeared to have followed along as best he could, even from a distance.

"If only Kirkcowan had cooperated with us," Gage lamented. "Or if he would wake so I could question him now."

Henry paused with a bite of jam tart halfway to his mouth. "Then, you haven't heard? Lord Kirkcowan passed away. Sometime in the middle of the night."

I set down my fork, thinking of Lady Kirkcowan and her children. I would write her that afternoon, though I didn't know what I could possibly say.

Gage took a drink from his glass of wine and set it on the table before speaking. "I suppose we knew it was inevitable." He twirled the stem. "His bad conduct caught up with him. I do wonder if there's any way to find out where his money was coming from. He was blackmailing someone. Possibly several someones. But I can only imagine they paid him in cash."

"Let me look into it," Henry offered. "I might be able to find out something."

Gage gazed at his half brother in approval. "If so, I'd be grateful."

CHAPTER 22

While I generally dreaded society events—finding them to be tedious and the other guests to be overcritical—dinner parties were often the exception. Especially when they were hosted by Lady Bearsden. Charlotte's great-aunt was not only acquainted with a wide range of interesting people, who invariably had more fascinating things to discuss than the usual small talk and petty gossip, but she also despised cruelty in all forms.

The fact that she was a collector of such gossip would seem to contradict this, but she'd admitted to me once that she only gathered tittle-tattle because it was amusing to be informed of everyone's foibles, particularly at her age. In any case, since her niece and I had become friends, I knew I needn't worry about suffering any slights from her other guests. She wouldn't stand for it. And so I entered the drawing room of the town house she often rented off St. Andrew's Square with great anticipation.

"My dear Mrs. Gage," she exclaimed with delight from her

chair near the door. Her white hair was piled up on top of her head in a style that seemed reminiscent of the wigs worn sixty years prior. She pushed to her feet with the aid of her gold figure-headed cane and then grasped both of my hands with her own, holding them wide so that she could examine me from head to toe, expectant abdomen and all. "You are looking positively radiant and as ripe as a cherry."

"A very large cherry," I quipped, blushing at her approval and the attention she was drawing.

She laughed brightly. "Any day now, isn't it? I'm so very pleased you could come. And your doting husband, as well." She beckoned him forward, releasing my hands so that she could offer them to Gage. "My Lumpy couldn't hold a candle to you or your father in looks, but he was a good man nonetheless," she proclaimed with a sigh, referring to her late husband with the mildly insulting nickname she always used.

Seeing that she'd latched on to Gage and would likely be monopolizing him for the foreseeable future, I turned to greet Charlotte as she approached. She shook her head at the sight of Lady Bearsden incorrigibly flirting with Gage. "Auntie does love the attention of a handsome young swain. She kept poor Mr. Aldridge at her side for a quarter of an hour before you arrived." She nodded toward a man with the copper complexion associated with the African continent.

"I doubt it's a hardship," I replied, my interest returning to the other young man. His tall bearing and tailored evening garments matched that of any gentleman of my acquaintance, but the mobile expressiveness of his face as he spoke to another guest suggested another noble profession. "Mr. Aldridge . . . why, do you mean the American actor?" I asked, recalling that Charlotte had told me many of the guests at tonight's dinner party would be connected to the theater.

"Yes, have you seen him onstage?"

"No, but I've heard his portrayal of Othello is magnificent."

"It is. I saw him for the first time at the Royal Coburg in London, and Auntie saw him in Manchester. He'll be performing the role here in Edinburgh shortly." She turned to look at me, though I was still distracted by Mr. Aldridge and the pair of people he was talking to, whom I recognized to be Mr. Murray from the Theatre Royal and his sister, Our Mrs. Siddons. "I've seated him next to you at dinner. I hope you don't mind."

"Of course. Why would I mind?" I asked, a moment before I realized what she meant. Although the slave trade had been prohibited in Britain over two decades earlier, and all enslavement within the British Isles effectively abolished, slavery in the British colonies was still legal, and many members of society still held very prejudicial views. A gentleman of color might be good enough to grace the stage or serve as a merchant, but not to dine at the table with them, or worse, their wives.

"No, I don't mind," I repeated.

She smiled. "I thought not. And he is a delightful conversationalist."

She glanced at Gage in consideration.

"And neither will he."

"Good." She pulled my arm through hers, leaning in to murmur, "And has he forgiven you?"

My heart warmed at her concern and the memories of my and Gage's reconciliation. "Yes."

"I thought so. Now, come." She urged me forward. "Let me introduce you to our guests."

It was a small but lively soiree of about a dozen guests. Among which I was by far the least gregarious. However, I was content to listen to their amusing banter, particularly when a trio of the actors—present and former—initiated a witty exchange which turned into a sort of prandial parlor game similar to Consequences, where the last word of the previous Shakespeare quote had to be used as the first word of the next quote spoken. Soon, almost all of the guests were participating, including Gage.

By the time we adjoined to the dining room for dinner, we were a merry party indeed. The vivid arrangements of camellias, daffodils, and pale yellow pears gracing the table between glimmering settings of silver and crystal only heightened the sparkling atmosphere. The flickering firelight in the candelabras above was reflected in the mirrors hung about the room between paintings by Flemish artists, forming a warm glow around the party.

While bowls of chestnut soup were placed before us, I took the opportunity to address Mr. Aldridge directly. "Lady Stratford told me you'll be performing the role of Othello here in Edinburgh. I look forward to seeing it."

"Yes, our opening night should be in about a month's time. There's been a delay because of the success of *The King of Grassmarket*. They've extended its number of performances by a few additional weeks."

"Oh, I hadn't heard that," I replied. "Though I suppose I'm not surprised. But that must be inconvenient, if not vexing for you."

He smiled, his warm brown eyes crinkling at the corners. "Not at all. Actually, I welcome the respite. I've only just come from Dublin, and before that Bath."

"And you're originally from New York?" I asked, before eating a spoonful of the silky soup.

"Yes. Have you been to America, my lady?"

I shook my head.

"Let's just say there aren't many career prospects there for a man like me."

I offered him a sympathetic smile, able to read between the lines but uncertain what to say. It wasn't just unfair but morally wrong that he and others were treated differently because of the color of their skin. My Irish grandmother had held very strong views about such matters, and she had made certain all of her grandchildren were well aware of them. I'd been fortunate to have the benefit of her wisdom.

"Well, I am glad your prospects are better here," I finally said. "Their loss is our gain."

He cast me a look of mutual regard, and I hoped he knew I wasn't simply being polite.

"Have you attended any of the performances of *The King of Grassmarket*?" he asked after taking a drink of his wine.

"Yes." I nodded toward where Mr. Murray sat across the table. "At the Theatre Royal."

"And what did you think?"

Though I wasn't certain where this question was leading—for surely he must apprehend, as all of Edinburgh did, that I was the inspiration for Lady Dalby—I decided to answer him candidly. "The staging is brilliant and the acting impressive. It's no wonder it's become a sensation."

"Yes, but what of the story?"

"You mean the book?" I asked in confusion. "The script is certainly immeasurably better."

He nodded, but I could tell it wasn't in agreement but rather acceptance that I did not and perhaps could not comprehend him. It left me feeling as if somehow I had failed, if not him precisely, then in some other aspect. And I found it very hard to swallow my next spoonful of soup.

"What did you think?" I asked after a moment of silence, wondering if he would try to explain what I'd misunderstood or if he would simply dismiss it, dismiss me.

From the manner in which his gaze cut to mine, I could tell he was debating that very thing. He set his glass down precisely, taking care with his words.

"I thought it . . . illuminating." He looked up at me to see if I was following. "The manner in which it explored the plight of the lower classes here in Edinburgh. The unfairness of society and the justice system under which they must live. The manner in which they've tried to right some of that wrong by establishing their own hierarchy and laws. Perhaps not laws the Scottish government would uphold, but which the citizens are happy to abide by because they seem just and honorable and sensible, when much of the social and legal structure under which they're forced to live is not."

My heart stilled at his words, and I felt my thoughts shift to another level of understanding. I had recognized the corruption and unfairness amid the levels of society long ago, and I had easily comprehended why Bonnie Brock and his code of honor so appealed to the inhabitants of Edinburgh. And yet I hadn't grasped the fullness of it, or its relation to the popularity of *The King of Grassmarket*, until that very moment.

I lifted my gaze to meet Mr. Aldridge's, wondering if he'd seen it so readily because he could draw the same parallels to the life he had lived. The life he continued to live.

I inhaled a deep breath, willing to admit my failings. "I hadn't considered it that way, but you're right. Viewed in that regard, it is illuminating." I frowned, thinking of the man who'd authored it, and the vendetta he held against Bonnie Brock. "Although I don't believe the author held such a noble intent."

"You don't think it's Kincaid himself?"

"Oh no," I protested, aware that others were also now listening. "Definitely not. And he certainly didn't give permission for the publication either."

His head tilted to the side as he considered this new piece of information while our soup bowls were whisked away to be replaced by plates of mackerel with fennel and mint. "That is more problematic, then, isn't it? For essentially the author is profiting from his hardships and successes, without Kincaid deriving any benefit."

My gaze flicked toward Mr. Murray, for the same could be said about the theaters to a certain extent. Although at least they employed people from the social classes Bonnie Brock seemed to champion. But the theater manager kept his head down, making it difficult for me to deduce what he might be thinking.

"Not deriving any benefit?" one of the other actors protested. "He's the hero of the city, lauded on every corner."

"Not by everyone," Gage replied around a bite of fish, swallowing before he continued. "The police are now more determined than ever to apprehend him for making them look foolish. And rival gangs are intent on seeing that their own crimes are blamed on him. In short, he now has a very large target on him. Even larger than before."

I had seen the same reports in some of the newspapers that the actor was referring to. Claims that Bonnie Brock was strutting about Grassmarket and Cowgate like a conquering hero, but nothing could be further from the truth. He was hiding, skulking, shifting from place to place. I imagined he felt safest among those citizens who had always protected him, but the police knew that and were not above trying to leverage that to their advantage.

"Then who is this Mugdock character?" Lady Bearsden demanded to know from her seat at the head of the table. "Not someone *I've* ever met."

"We believe it's an alias, a nom de plume," Gage explained.

"Ah, yes. That *does* make sense." She tapped her chin. "But why Mugdock? It's not a very illustrious name."

"Perhaps he was trying to identify in some way with something," Mrs. Siddons suggested.

"Or he simply picked it out of a book or off a map," Mr. Aldridge said.

That had been my theory, but I hadn't yet been able to find it.

"Hmmm," Lady Bearsden hummed, speculating aloud in her

musical voice. "Well, there *is* a Mugdock Castle, over in Dunbartonshire or somewhere." She gestured vaguely with her fork in that direction. "Not far from my estate."

"There is?" I asked in surprise.

"Yes. Most of it's a heap. My Lumpy mentioned it to me once. Some childhood memory involving his cousins. I can't quite recall now." Which only meant that it hadn't interested her, otherwise she would have all the details locked away in her brain. She took a sip of her wine, seeming to swirl it around in her mouth as she thought. An odd mannerism which seemed to help dislodge whatever she was trying to recall, for her next words proved remarkable. "Come to think of it, I seem to recall May Kincaid being born there."

I stilled with my glass halfway to my lips. "You mean Bonnie Brock's mother?"

Gage's gaze met mine down the table, wondering the same thing I had. Why hadn't Bonnie Brock mentioned this?

"Yes, I think that's right. Her father was a third brother of a third brother, or some such connection, so he and his family lived in one of the less prestigious properties owned by his uncle." Because true gentlemen were not supposed to work for a living or undertake any employment save the military or the church. "She was a beautiful woman," Lady Bearsden continued to muse. "Which only caused her heartache. For she became involved with one of her second or third cousins—a married man—and it ruined her. Her parents cast her out, so her lover set her up in a cottage somewhere as his *chère-amie*, for what else was she to do. And then he abandoned her. It was after that she first made her way to Edinburgh, with Bonnie Brock naught but a babe in arms."

"She couldn't have had an easy time of it establishing herself with a child, even as a cyprian," Mrs. Siddons remarked.

"No, indeed. But she was very beautiful and charming. And fortunately so was her son."

Bonnie Brock. Bonnie, bonnie Brock.

I wondered for the first time whether that nickname had not come from an incident during his time in jail but from his mother. After all, it had always struck me as an odd choice in a sobriquet for the head of a criminal gang. But from a mother, that made much more sense.

This insight caused a resounding sense of rightness within me, as well as an unbearable ache. He might have transformed the moniker into a term of deceptive menace, but it had begun as a loving epithet from mother to son.

Mrs. Siddons shook her head sadly, laying her fork down. "Then this cousin is Bonnie Brock's father?"

I perked up at this question.

"Most likely," Lady Bearsden replied as her glass of wine was refilled.

"Do you know who he is?" I asked.

"Well, the trouble is there are a number of possibilities, and the family has remained rather closemouthed about the entire affair. But the cousin was certainly older than her, and he was already wed, so he couldn't be forced to do the honorable thing and marry her, which narrows down the possibilities. Perhaps Graham of Strathblane or the Duke of Montrose." She rattled off a few more names, but none of them meant anything to me. A duke would certainly have the prestige which seemed to be indicated, but from what I recalled of Montrose, he wouldn't have taken a great deal of interest in a young cousin in Dunbartonshire, no matter how beautiful she was.

Either way, Bonnie Brock certainly had some explaining to do.

After rolling over in bed for approximately the tenth time—a not inconsiderable effort when one was heavy with child— I accepted that sleep was determined to elude me. The rich meal combined with the aches in my own body—particularly my hips, which clasping a pillow between my thighs didn't even ease— and the weight of my thoughts all contrived against me. So I slid as gracefully from the bed as I could while being roughly the size of a gray seal, donned my warmest dressing gown, and crept from the room.

I wasn't surprised when my steps led me unconsciously to my studio at the top of the house. Pulling aside the drapes, I allowed moonlight to spill over the shrouded easels, their forms almost spectral in the hallowed light. Given the contents underneath, it wasn't difficult to imagine them taking on a life of their own, as I tried so ardently to imbue life into my portraits.

I hesitated a moment, breathing the chill night air tinged with the lingering scents of linseed oil, turpentine, and gesso deep into my lungs. Then I reached out to carefully remove the covers from each of the canvases, exposing them to the light. They were at various stages of completion, each unique in their composition. Two were commissioned portraits, one a rough sketch of a portrait of myself and our as yet unborn child that I hoped to give Gage for his birthday in late July, and the last three were paintings for my proposed exhibit of the *Faces of Ireland*.

It was to these last three that I turned, not so much examining my brushstrokes as my intentions behind them. I had been touched by the plight of the Irish people, and the hatred and discrimination the largely Catholic population received at the hands of their Anglo-Protestant leaders, as well as the rest of the population of Britain. And so I'd conceived of this exhibit to illustrate how much they were not so different from us.

But the truth was there were faces in every corner of Britain, every corner of the world that deserved to be better seen—their joys, their pains, their struggles, their *humanity* illuminated on canvas. And yet I'd largely turned a blind eye to the people in my own part of Scotland who most needed to be noticed. It was a humbling and sobering realization. One that I'd been stumbling toward but had needed my conversation at dinner with Mr. Aldridge to help me to see more clearly.

My thoughts turned once again to my grandmother, who'd often been called eccentric, and at times had been viewed with disdain simply because of her Irish blood and her firm convictions. While I'd always appreciated her wisdom and acceptance—both of herself and others—I hadn't fully respected how she'd become the woman she was or the adversities she'd faced. I hadn't fully embraced the things she'd taught me, content to abide by many of the norms of society because I was already seen as so unnatural in other ways.

I saw now that that was wrong. Perhaps it had been understandable given the slights I'd endured because of my peculiarity, but now that I was aware of what I'd chosen to ignore, I couldn't continue to go on doing so. Not without shaming myself and my grandmother, and our faith. She had done her part, both big and small, to try to enlighten those around her, and now it was my turn—small and insignificant though it might be. I had to try.

I traced the brushstrokes of the old Irish woman I'd nearly finished painting, realizing one of the reasons she had so captured my imagination when I'd first seen her on the street in Rathfarnham was that she reminded me of my grandmother. Her gentle smile, her strength, her resilience. It brought a not unhappy tear to my eye.

"Kiera, what are you doing up here?"

I turned to find Gage standing bleary-eyed in the doorway, his hair standing up in tufts about his head.

"And crying?"

I dashed away the tear and offered him a reassuring smile. "I couldn't sleep."

"Obviously." He looked around the room, noticing that the sailcloths had been removed from the canvases. "You aren't going to try to paint now, are you?"

"No," I replied in gentle amusement at his still-sleepy voice. "Just thinking."

He nodded slowly, as if not quite comprehending. "About art?"

"Partly." I nibbled my bottom lip, considering the artwork around me and the decision I had just come to. "I'm not going to accept any more portrait commissions. After I finish these two, I'm done with them."

"Are you sure?" he asked in astonishment.

"Yes. I no longer need the income from the commissions, so there's really no reason to continue them."

"But Kiera, you love your art," Gage said aghast. "I know how much it means to you."

"Oh, I'm not going to stop painting," I reassured him, recognizing now the reason for his confusion. "I'm simply not going to paint wealthy clients who already have more portraits of themselves than they probably need."

"Then . . ." he prompted.

"I'm going to paint the unseen. The people who move about us every day, making our lives, our city, our country work, and yet are all but overlooked and dismissed. I'm going to meet them where they are, and observe how life plays across their faces, and paint them in truth. But with dignity and grace," I amended, determined that they should not be exploited by me—not intellectually or monetarily.

I looked up from the portrait of the Irish grandmother I'd been studying as Gage stepped forward to rest his hands on my shoulders. His features were softened by the moonlight. "This was not a decision made lightly."

"No," I admitted. Giving up my commissions of the wealthy would mean very few of my portraits would ever grace the walls of stately homes across the country or the galleries in London and elsewhere. They might only be exhibited by me. I would likely never receive the praise and esteem other portraitists received, but being a woman, I had known that was unlikely anyway.

I inhaled a deep breath. Deeper than I'd seemed to be able to inhale in a long time. "But it's the right one."

And one that would not have been possible had I not wed a wealthy man. I was in a unique position—fortunate that I didn't need income and prestige to support me or my family. The vast majority of artists could not say the same. Thus, the creation of my art was solely at my discretion.

He smiled in acceptance. "When did this decision come about?"

"Tonight. Though I've been grappling with it for some time. Since we went to Ireland. No, before that. Perhaps when we were last in Edinburgh."

He studied my features. "I suspect your discussion with Mr. Aldridge this evening may have had something to do with it."

"Yes," I admitted, lifting my hands to cup his elbows. "He helped me to see I'd been willfully ignoring some things." I pictured him seated beside me, his expression patient and controlled despite my obtuseness, his graceful features steady and assured despite the injustice of the world he must live in. "What did you tell Philip about the plan the prime minister and the other cabinet members are hatching?"

I could see in Gage's eyes that he understood at once why I was asking. "That if they convince the king to create new peerages in order to pass the Reform Bill, they can rely on me. For that, and for the passage of the Anatomy Reform Act. And the Slave Abolition Act," he added, having recognized where I was leading.

Three critical pieces of legislation. Three essential issues.

And in many ways, they all relied on the Reform Bill. For many of the wealthy West Indian plantation owners had essentially purchased the rotten boroughs that the Reform Bill sought to eliminate, thwarting and manipulating Parliament on the matter.

"Good," I told him. "They need you."

He nodded distractedly, and I wondered if he was thinking of his father. Of what he would say if his son was granted a title separate from the one he would inherit from him. Of what his father truly thought of these issues, which I knew was certain to be complicated. Of his lies and betrayals and failure to tell him he had a half brother.

I wrapped my arms around his torso and turned to the side so I could rest my head against his heart. If possible, I would wrap the heart beating inside his chest with silk and surround it with armor, standing guard against any who might hurt it. But such a thing was impossible. Had I not injured it myself only a few short days ago? So all I could do was try my best to soothe it with all the love I possessed. To let him know he was not alone.

His arms embraced me in return, and a few short minutes later I felt his warm breath against my forehead. "Little dark one."

I looked up at him in question, uncertain why he was referring to the meaning of my name.

"I know why your grandmother insisted that be your name. Because somehow she knew you would dare to plumb the darkest recesses of the human heart and shine a light there." His pale blue eyes were two liquid pools in the moonlight. "You certainly plumbed mine."

The love I saw reflected in his face made the tears that always seemed to be so near the surface these days threaten. So before they could fall, I arched up onto my tiptoes and kissed him.

Sometime later Gage pulled his mouth from mine, and I

began to trace the line of his jaw with my lips. His voice was rough as he spoke. "As delightful as this is, perhaps we might move this to an alternative location. I think my feet are turning numb."

I giggled. "You should have worn slippers."

"Had I known that seeking out my wife in the middle of the night would lead me up to her glacial studio, I would have."

"Fair enough," I replied, reaching for one of the sailcloths to recover the portraits.

But Gage's hand captured my wrist. "It can wait until morning."

I nodded. A few hours' exposure would do them no harm.

However, Gage did turn back and twitch the drapes shut just for good measure, remembering how sunlight could damage the pigments, and my heart surged with even more love for him.

CHAPTER 23

Unsurprisingly, I slept late the following morning and then took breakfast in bed. When I finally arose, I found that Gage had already replaced all of the covers over my portraits. I smiled as I made my way to the library to see if I could find Mugdock Castle on one of our maps. Even with Lady Bearsden's helpful indicators in mind, it was not easy to locate, but once I did, I allowed my eyes to wander every direction of the compass for other landmarks.

One immediately leapt out at me. Lennox Castle. At approximately five miles distance, the two castles were practically part of the same estate, and perhaps at one time had been.

I frowned, wondering if Lennox the printer was also a relation. In all likelihood, not a close one, but still the coincidence could not be ignored. After all, I'd noted his upper-class elocution and carriage. It was true, it could have been learned, but I didn't think so.

I was searching for further information on the Earl of Lennox and the offshoots of his family when the door to the library opened to admit Gage and Henry.

"Henry has news," Gage declared without preamble. "Guess whose shop Kirkcowan was seen visiting multiple times over the past six weeks?"

I shook my head, looking to Henry, whose pride at having uncovered this information shone clearly on his face.

"Lennox and Company Printers."

I lowered the book I'd been perusing. "And I've just discovered that Lennox Castle stands no more than five miles from Mugdock."

They hurried over, peering down at the places on the map I pointed to.

"Do you think that means Lennox is Mugdock?" I asked as Gage leaned closer, searching the surrounding countryside as I had done.

"Maybe." He glanced at Henry. "He's certainly involved in some way. *And* it would explain why he has a copy of the sequel. But Kirkcowan might just as easily have been blackmailing him for another reason." He frowned in determination, pressing his fist against the table. "We need more information before we question him, or else I'm afraid we'll tip our hand too soon."

I nodded in agreement. "How is he related to the Earl of Lennox, if at all? Why would he have a vendetta against Bonnie Brock?"

"How did he get his information about his past? I doubt it's part of the Lennox family lore." He turned to Henry again. "Do you think your sources would speak to me?"

"I can ask," he replied. "You think they may know more than they're telling?"

"I do."

"Then let's try."

I warmed at the sight of their anxiousness to please and include each other. It was too soon for them to have reached the

292 · Anna Lee Huber

point in their relationship where they were entirely comfortable with each other, especially given the fraught nature of its start. But they were both expending equal effort, and I was relieved and heartened to see it. Perhaps Gage's relationship with his father had been forever strained and broken by this latest discovery of betrayal, but at least he had gained a brother in the bargain. And a good one.

After they departed, I sat down to resume my scrutiny of *Debrett's Peerage*, only to be interrupted again. This time by Anderley.

"I'm afraid he's just departed," I told him, assuming he was looking for Gage, and then turned back to the page I was examining.

"Actually, my lady, I believe you are the person I need to speak to."

I looked up in surprise before pushing the book aside and swiveling to face him. "Of course, Anderley. What is it?"

Seeing the anxiety etched across his brow, I thought perhaps he wanted to discuss his relationship with Bree. But I was wrong again.

He cleared his throat, clasping his hands behind his back. "I found the ballad-seller."

"Yes," I replied eagerly. "And did he witness anyone entering Mr. Rookwood's shop?"

"He did," he began more tentatively than I would have thought the answer warranted. "A woman. A lady," he corrected. "She entered the shop about an hour after his assistant departed."

I felt the first quaver of misgiving. "Did he recognize her?"

"No, but he described her to me, and her coach."

The more he hesitated, the more nervous I became. "And?"

"She was wearing a fashionable gown of some purplish-pink shade, and her carriage bore the crest of a crown with an arm lifted, holding a sword."

I blinked at him for a moment, trying to come to terms with this information, before pressing a hand to my forehead. "That sounds like the Earl of Cromarty's crest." I lifted my hand, gesturing with it rather needlessly, but I felt somewhat unmoored. "Or rather the Mathesan clan crest. But the earldom's crest has a similar design."

"Yes, my lady."

I turned to the side, not wanting to face the compassion in his eyes. Not when I was already fighting the nausea that accompanied my rising certainty that Alana had paid a visit to Rookwood, and on the day he had been killed. It explained why she had arrived so uncharacteristically late that day to my appointment, long after Dr. Fenwick had departed. And she had been wearing a Parnassus rose gown, her hair slightly in disarray.

Swallowing forcefully, I refused to even entertain the possibility that she'd killed him. But *why* had she gone to see him in the first place? And why hadn't she told me? She must know she was one of the last people, if not the very last person, to see him alive besides his killer.

There was nothing for it. I would simply have to talk to her and hope she hadn't done anything more foolish than keep such a revelation from me.

"Thank you for telling me," I told Anderley. "Did Mr. Gage take the carriage?"

"No, my lady."

"Then please ask that it be brought around for me. And should Mr. Gage return before I do, tell him where I've gone."

He bowed and exited the room while I gathered up my scattered wits. I would need them all for this confrontation.

Alana was not home when I arrived, but Figgins assured me she should return soon, so I elected to wait for her. I was thus ensconced on the spring green fainting couch near the window overlooking Charlotte Square when she entered the room, fluffing her chestnut side curls as if to ensure they weren't wilted. The intricacy of her chintz muslin gown, which was shaded the color of evening primrose and boasted a full skirt, as well as gold and amethyst agraffe and bracelets, told me she had not simply gone out for a stroll.

"Figgins said you were anxious to see me. Had I known you were coming, I . . ." Her footsteps faltered, clearly inferring from my expression that this wasn't merely a social visit. "Is it the baby?" she asked, hastening closer, and then ruined any softening I might have felt toward her at this display of genuine concern. "I *told* you not to go traipsing about the city. I told you . . ."

"I know you paid a visit to Rookwood Publishing," I interrupted, cutting off her diatribe.

Her eyes widened, and for once she seemed to be at a loss for words.

"I know you called on him the very day he was murdered. That's why you were so flustered when you arrived late to my appointment with Dr. Fenwick."

She clamped her mouth shut and turned away.

"What were you doing there, Alana? And why didn't you tell me?" When she didn't answer, I shifted on the couch, lowering my feet to the ground as I sat upright. "Did you go to confront him? Did Philip accompany you?" My breath tightened seeing the way her back heaved in and out with each of her agitated breaths. "Did something happen? Did . . . did he attack you?" But then I remembered how Rookwood's body had been found. "Did you lose your temper?"

"No, I did not lose my temper!" she whirled around to shriek at me. "How could you even *think* . . . ?" She stamped her foot, her face flushed as she struggled to restrain her anger. "He was alive when I left him."

"But why did you go . . . ?"

"To clean up your mess. *Again.* To demand he tell me who Mugdock is, so he can be made to retract his nonsense before your child is born. With our luck the baby will have a crown of hair as dark as yours was, and no one will ever believe the child is Gage's."

I shook my head. "Alana, people are going to choose to believe whatever they wish to, no matter what shade of hair our child is born with. But those closest to us, those who genuinely care for us know what utter nonsense that book's suppositions are. And the rest can go hang."

"So you say, but what about in eight or nine years' time, when your son goes off to school and the other boys make slanderous accusations about his parentage. Or when your daughter makes her debut and the other debutantes taunt her."

I frowned, unsettled by the prospect, but more so that she should wave it in my face when there was nothing to be done about it. "That is many years from now. Plenty of time for the truth to be made evident." After all, the child wasn't likely to be an exact replica of me.

She swiveled away from me abruptly, marching across the rug with her hands clenched into fists before turning on her heel to once again face me. "Don't you understand? They only view all this as proof they were right about you all along. That this is your due."

I stiffened, shocked to hear her state such a thing so baldly. I knew there were people who didn't like me, who were determined to think the worst of me simply because I'd never seemed to be able to behave in the prescribed manner, especially when I was younger. In general, I didn't like balls and soirees, or fashion, or small talk. I didn't care for the same things that other young ladies seemed to. But most people who genuinely tried to get to know me seemed to like me well enough. It was merely my public awkwardness which repelled or offended people. But Alana was implying it went deeper than that.

"When the scandal about your involvement with Sir Anthony came to light, they expected you to go into hiding, to live out the rest of your days meek and remorseful," she continued, mistaking my astonishment for confusion. "And you did, for a time. But you proved yourself to be stronger and more resilient than they could have ever imagined. I was so proud of you for that." She sat beside me, taking hold of my hand. Her face softened. "You regained your footing, and you embarked on these investigations with Gage, and I encouraged it because I thought it was helping. And it did. And your courage was rewarded when Gage fell in love with you, giving you a second chance at the life you should have had all along."

"But . . . ?" I prompted, unwilling to be mollified by her display of affection when I knew there were more hurtful things to come.

"But there are those who think it's unfair that you were rewarded for your unorthodox behavior. They would like nothing more than to see you receive your just deserts. And help that along, if necessary."

"And you?" I asked, feeling a heaviness in my heart. "What do you think?"

She reared back as if I'd slapped her. "How can you even ask that? I've supported you in everything. Championed you. Encouraged your relationship with Gage. Even praised your inquiry efforts."

"Until now."

"Yes, but that's different."

"Because I'm going to be a mother?"

"*Yes.* You can't merely be thinking of yourself now. You have your child to consider."

I clasped my hands together in my lap, staring at the swirled pattern of the rug before me. "Even though I'm simply trying to make the world a better, safer, fairer place? For my child? For my nieces and nephews? For everyone?"

"Well, I . . . that's not your place now."

"Yes, but isn't it? If it's not a mother's place, then whose is it?" I turned to look my sister straight in the eye, allowing her to see all the hurt her words had caused me, both those spoken and only hinted at. "I don't solve murders for a lark, Alana. I do it because someone has to see that the truth is brought to light. Yes, I could leave the task to others, but *I* happen to be very good at it." I pressed a hand to my abdomen. "If my child has something he, or she, is good at, something that benefits society—whether it's painting, or growing plants, or studying the stars, or unmasking criminals—I would hope I would encourage them to do it. I would hope I would be proud of them for it."

"And if you're not around to do so?" Alana snapped, pushing to her feet. "If one of these murderers catches you before you catch them, what then?"

I stared back at her evenly. "I can understand your fear, Alana. But that's not what's making you lash out at me so angrily. That's not what's kept us at odds these past two and a half months."

"No, it's because you won't *listen*!"

"No, it's because I won't do what you want. I hear you perfectly well, Alana."

My calm only seemed to infuriate her more.

"Fine. Do whatever you want," she exploded. "Get yourself killed. Just don't expect me to mourn you." She turned to stomp from the room.

"Alana, wait," I called after her, waiting until she turned to look at me. "What if the life I've led, the *entire* life, was the one I was supposed to have all along? The good and the bad." I held up a hand. "I'm not saying I'm glad Sir Anthony mistreated me or that Will had to die as he did, or that God wished for any of it to happen. But . . . what if it was the only way I could become who I am right now? What if it was the only way I could become the mother this child needs?" I breathed deeply, feeling something loosen inside me, some deep source of pain I'd been harboring. "Then, I can accept that."

Alana stood there frowning, and I could tell she was considering what I'd said.

So I decided to press my advantage. "Do you remember how our grandmother used to say, 'Just because that's the way things are, doesn't mean that's the way they always have to be'?" I shrugged one shoulder, hoping she inferred from that what I was trying to say.

The movement caused a few tendrils of my hair to slip from their pins and cascade down around my neck. Something my unruly tresses were forever doing, being too thick and heavy to behave. I reached back to fix them, stabbing the pin they'd fallen from into my scalp, but that wasn't enough to erase Alana's suddenly fierce scowl.

"Did Bonnie Brock stay with you last May, just a fortnight after your wedding?"

I stilled at this accusation, shocked into silence.

She advanced closer. "Did you truly enter his room with your hair down?"

"Who told you that?" I demanded, scrambling to comprehend how she could know about that. Of course, it was framed in the most terrible light possible. Bonnie Brock had been poisoned, barely able to lift his head, let alone rise from his sickbed to ravish me, as she seemed to be implying.

"Rookwood. He wouldn't tell me Mugdock's name. But he wanted me to tell him whether any of the things written about you in *the sequel* were true."

Why would Rookwood ask her those things? I couldn't comprehend it. Unless he wanted to rile her. Unless he wanted her to abet him in his goal to keep the manuscript unpublished. If the Earl and Countess of Cromarty filed a suit for libel on my behalf, that would certainly gain the court's attention and possibly force the revelation of Mugdock's identity.

However, that was not what suddenly horrified me to my core. For I'd realized who Mugdock's informant was. There was but one person who had both known about Bonnie Brock's stay in our home the previous May and witnessed me in the guest room where he was convalescing with my hair down. It was also the person whose betrayal would hurt him the most.

I was sick in my heart at the thought of the pain this was going to cause him. But he had to be told. His betrayer had to be confronted—so we could understand why, so we could discover whom they'd told.

There had to be a good explanation. There simply had to be.

"I need to go," I declared abruptly, pushing to my feet.

"Where are you going?" Alana asked as I hurried past her.

A sudden impulse made me turn back and throw my arms around her neck. She staggered back a step before regaining her footing and awkwardly returning the embrace. Pressing a swift kiss to her cheek, I took my leave.

I spent the rest of the day in an agony of waiting. Upon my return from Alana's, I'd penned a brief missive to Bonnie Brock and instructed our footman to pass it to Brock's henchman currently observing the house. I had no doubt that Brock had purposely arranged for the lackeys now watching us to be men I was already familiar with and for them to remain better visible so there would be no confusion with McQueen's men. The brawny man in a brown coat had not returned, but I didn't know whether that was because Bonnie Brock's men had driven him off or his orders had changed.

However, it would be hours before we could securely meet

with him unobserved, and then only if he obeyed my summons. For all my faith that he would come—knowing that I would never have sent for him had it not been important—I also knew that Bonnie Brock was nothing if not contradictory. Increasingly so. Since the publication of *The King of Grassmarket*, his erratic and volatile moods and behavior had been exacerbated.

Gage was in low spirits when he returned from his hunting expedition with Henry, having not turned up any new information that would be helpful to our inquiry. So when I told him what I'd learned and the meeting I'd arranged, I expected him to berate me. Instead, he received the news equably, I supposed realizing there was really no better option.

Thus, that evening we both found ourselves ensconced in the drawing room, anxiously waiting to learn Bonnie Brock's response. Or rather, *I* was anxiously waiting, reading the same page in my book ten times without comprehension and glancing up at every creak and groan of the house to see if Jeffers was approaching. Gage, on the other hand, relaxed in his chair, perusing his own book and drinking from a glass of whisky, seemingly oblivious to any sort of tension in the air.

When the clock on the mantel chimed the hour of ten, I began to fear they weren't coming, and I would have to try to sleep with this knowledge swirling about inside my brain. But then there was a light rap on the door—one which surprised me, for I had not heard footsteps approaching.

"Yes, Jeffers?" Gage asked as our butler appeared in the doorway.

"Your guests have arrived."

My heart leapt into my throat.

If our butler had any such opinion on the matter—good or bad—his expression did not reveal it. "I've left them in the morning room, as requested."

"Very good," Gage replied.

Jeffers bowed and departed, leaving me with Gage.

"Shall we?" he asked.

I smiled tightly and took his proffered arm.

We entered the room as a united front, finding both of them still standing. Bonnie Brock leaned against the sideboard, his arms crossed over his chest. Though he was seemingly at ease, I could sense the tension racketing his frame. While Maggie hovered near the French doors, looking as if she wished she could flee. It was clear she'd deduced why she was here, and I felt a pulse of empathy for her, having found myself in a similar circumstance recently.

"Given the fact that your husband used some rather colorful language to swear I'd never enter your home again, I gather this is verra important," Bonnie Brock drawled as Gage closed the door, granting us privacy. "Weel, then, I'm all ears."

I turned to Maggie, her face pale in the candlelight, and spoke gently. "Do you want to tell him or shall I?"

CHAPTER 24

B onnie Brock straightened from his slouch. "Tell me what?"
I kept my eyes trained on Maggie, watching as her shoulders hunched and she tried to shrink into the eyelet curtains behind her. When she didn't answer, I took that as my cue, moving a step closer to the frightened, uncertain young woman, but staying far enough away that Gage wouldn't protest the proximity. "Maggie is the informant. Though I strongly suspect she didn't do it to hurt you," I hastened to add.

Maggie's gaze darted between me and her brother before finally settling on Brock as obviously the greater threat.

"Nay. That canna be true," he denied, the muscles in his arms rippling with restrained anger. "My sister wouldna betray me."

"I don't think she intended to betray you," I said, still speaking in a quiet, even voice. "I think she thought she was confiding in someone she could trust."

Her wide green eyes flicked to mine and held.

"Isn't that right?"

She slowly nodded.

At this first tentative admission of her guilt, Bonnie Brock exploded away from the sideboard, but fortunately the round table was positioned between them. "How could ye do this to me?" he demanded to know as Maggie cowered against the wall. I edged a step closer to her even as Gage moved to intercept Brock should he try to come nearer. "Our secrets. Our past. Ye ken why I kept it quiet. Why I dinna tell *anyone*." His face twisted with dark emotions. "My ain sister!" He whirled away with a snarl of disgust and fury, struggling to absorb this act of perfidy. "Did ye help to write that book, too?"

"Nay," Maggie gasped, speaking for the first time as tears streamed down her cheeks. "Nay, o' course I didna."

"There's no o' course aboot it."

She flinched at the harsh words but continued. "I had no idea they'd be used in a book. I had no idea he would ever . . ."

Betray her. Those were the words she seemed to choke on, her own pain shimmering in her eyes.

"You're speaking of Mr. Heron," I deduced. "That's the man who betrayed you?"

"Heron?" Bonnie Brock repeated before she could speak. "Ye mean Rookwood's silver-headed assistant? Why, I'll kill him."

"No!" Maggie cried as he turned to charge toward the door, but Gage held up his hands, stopping him.

"Get oot o' my way, Gage."

My breath caught at the dangerous glitter in his eyes and the way his hand hovered inside his loose greatcoat, where I knew he concealed weapons.

But Gage was not so easily intimidated. "Not until you hear what your sister has to say. Heron isn't going anywhere," he rationalized. "So listen to her first and then decide whether he deserves to die."

Maggie stiffened, and even I was taken aback by this cool

statement, but then I realized what my husband was doing. He was bartering with Bonnie Brock, knowing it would be easier to convince him to back down by suggesting he delay his intentions instead of abandon them.

When he looked as if he still might argue, Gage tempered his stance. "She's your sister. At least give her the chance to explain." His gaze darted briefly to mine, perhaps recognizing that was more than he'd given me upon discovering that Henry was his half brother.

Bonnie Brock grunted, turning back to face his sister. "Then talk. Tell me why ye betrayed me."

But the manner in which he was ferociously scowling at her, impatiently waiting for her to speak, was of no use. Maggie would never be able to get her words out around her trembling sobs. So I pivoted, partially blocking her brother from her sight. "Tell me, Maggie," I coaxed. "Tell me what happened."

She sniffed, swiping her hand under her nose, and reminding me of how young she still was. I passed her my handkerchief, waiting while she dabbed at her nose and the wetness on her cheeks, seeming at a loss for where to begin.

"When did you meet Mr. Heron?"

"Last summer. He . . . he was eatin' on a bench in the Trinity Hospital Physic Gardens. I like to walk there." She shrugged one shoulder self-consciously. "It's no' so busy as other places in the city. It was blustery that day and my bonnet blew off. He ran after it to catch it for me."

It was a familiar enough story. A chance meeting. A kindly gesture. The rest I could guess.

"And so you struck up a conversation and then continued to meet there."

"Aye, but at first 'twas merely be chance. I mean . . ." She flushed and lowered her gaze. "I looked for him, but 'twasn't planned."

"And then it was."

She nodded. Her gaze slid over my shoulder as if to see how her brother was taking this news before returning to mine. "At first, Daniel didna ken who I was. I mean, he didna ken I was Brock's sister. And when he did, he got upset. Accused me o' lyin' to him." Her brow furrowed. "But then he apologized. Said 'twasn't my fault who my brother was. He seemed to think Brock was some sort o' monster, and that was even worse." Her eyes dropped to where she was worrying my handkerchief between her hands. "So I . . . I started to tell him things, aboot my life, aboot our past. He was a good listener." A tear slid from her eye. "I didna ken he would tell anyone." Her voice lowered to a whisper. "I thought I could trust him."

"Then Heron didn't write the book?"

She shook her head. "Nay. Said he was tricked into tellin' Mugdock all he ken. That he thought he was helpin' me and Brock. And when he found oot the truth, 'twas too late."

I didn't see how that could be, but I wasn't going to question Heron's motivations to Maggie. Not when it was clear from the soft look in her eyes when she spoke about him and the way she used his given name that she was in love with him.

I glanced at her brother to see if he was softening, but his jaw was clamped as tight as ever, his eyes as hard as flint.

"It's lonely being Bonnie Brock's sister, isn't it?"

Out of the corner of my eye, I could see his angry gaze shift to me, but I had a point to make, so I kept my attention squarely on Maggie.

She sniffed again and then nodded.

"I imagine you're surrounded by people nearly all the time, what with his men guarding over you, and yet none of them are really your friends. And when you do meet someone, you have to wonder why they're befriending you. Whether it's because of Brock or because of you."

"Aye. A lot o' the lasses who've pretended to like me in the past were only after Brock's attention."

"But Mr. Heron was different."

"He didna even ken who I was, but he still liked me." Her voice conveyed that this was almost a wondrous thing.

"So he says," her brother grumbled beneath his breath.

I turned to glower at him, for he was missing the reason for this confession.

"Did Mr. Heron tell you who he was tricked into telling?" I asked, harking back to an earlier statement.

She lifted her hands in a futile gesture. "I asked, but he said it was safer if I didna ken."

Bonne Brock made a noise between a harrumph and a growl, and I couldn't say I disagreed with him. It sounded like Heron had been protecting himself more than he'd been protecting Maggie.

But now that we knew how Mugdock had learned about Bonnie Brock's past, I wanted to know why Bonnie Brock had chosen to conceal an important piece of information from us, lest he think his sister was the only person who had lied by omission.

"Gage and I have been puzzling and puzzling, trying to figure out why on earth the author of *The King of Grassmarket* chose such an odd surname. Mugdock." I tapped my chin, pretending to ruminate on the answer. "It's not exactly common."

Maggie glanced at her brother ruefully, though his face remained stoic.

"But then last night we learned of the existence of a Mugdock Castle. One where *curiously* your mother was born. And yet you didn't see *fit* to tell us?" I snapped the last, enunciating harshly.

But Bonnie Brock was unmoved by guilt, his scowl remaining as black as ever. "Aye. And what's that to do with anythin'?"

I glanced at Gage to see if he shared my exasperation. "Obviously it was chosen to rub salt into the wound, for the man has a vendetta against you. The question is, why? Why strike out at you through that book? Why try to damage your reputation among the populace of Edinburgh? Why use your mother's birthplace as his pen name?"

Brock's gaze dipped to the table as if actually giving these questions some consideration.

"What is his goal? What does he gain?" I persisted.

But neither Brock nor Maggie—who watched him silently, following his lead—offered any answers.

"Brock, who is your father?" I demanded to know. "Does the Lennox family have anything to do with this?"

He looked up at me then, scrutinizing me as if I were the one under interrogation and not him. "Are ye thinkin' that printer named Lennox is involved?"

I wanted to bite my tongue for offering him any piece of information, particularly when I knew he was bound to thrash the person and ask questions later.

"Oh, aye. I ken you've been to his shop more than once."

Of course he had.

"We don't know what to think," Gage groused, answering for me. "Lennox worked for Rookwood. He printed *The King of Grassmarket.* But the name Lennox also keeps cropping up in relation to your mother. Rumor has it your father was her cousin, possibly a Lennox. And since you won't share with us what, if anything, the name Lennox has to do with all of this, we can't tell for certain whether the printer is pertinent or not. There are, after all, a lot of Scots named Lennox."

Bonnie Brock's voice rang with quiet menace. "Then I'll just have to find oot for ye."

"No, you won't," Gage stated in a tone that would not brook disobedience, and I could practically see Brock's hackles rise in response. "You will stay away from Lennox and Heron and let us question them. In addition to being Mugdock, one of them could very well be a murderer."

Maggie gasped in objection to Heron being called such, but Gage ignored her.

"We won't be able to uncover the truth, recover the sequel, and clear your name if you go about pummeling people, or worse, killing them. You *have* to stay out of this. For now," he added in appeasement.

Regrettably, we had no way of forcing him to listen, and the stubborn clamp of his jaw told me he was already planning on confronting both men. My anger, which I'd kept tamped down through so much of this ordeal, suddenly reared its head.

"Fiend seize it," I snapped, borrowing Gage's favorite curse. "You bloody blackguard! Do you know what you've put me through? Do you think I enjoy being winked at and observed slyly from the side, as if I've done something wrong? This is *your* fault." I stabbed my finger at Brock, advancing on him. "If you hadn't abducted me from the theater, or insinuated yourself into our lives, or provoked yet another person into wanting revenge against you, I wouldn't be in this predicament." Gage reached out to restrain me before I got too close, and I stamped my foot in emphasis. "And I am *not* going to allow my child to be born into the world with people believing I cuckolded my husband simply because *you* can't be made to see reason. So for once in your life, listen to directions and stay out of it. So we can fix this mess you've gotten us into."

I glared up at Bonnie Brock, making sure he understood how serious I was. But far from being chastened or intimidated, he actually smiled.

"No' just a bloodthirsty wench, you're also a hellcat," he quipped, his gaze roaming over my face. "Best get your wife away from me, Gage, or I really will kiss her."

"Try it and I'll scratch your eyes out," I hissed as Gage pulled me farther away.

"That's enough, Kincaid," Gage reproached. "She's right. You've been a selfish wretch through all of this. The least you can do is help instead of hinder us."

I turned away, unable to stomach the sight of him after he'd treated me so shockingly, and with no remorse.

"So be it," he grumbled a few moments later. "I'll stay away for a day or two. But after that, I'll make no promises."

"Two," Gage demanded, knowing full well that Brock would grant us the smallest concession possible.

"Aye, two."

I looked to the side at Maggie, still unwilling to face her brother. "Perhaps you should stay here tonight," I suggested, not wanting him to take his anger and frustration out on her. I didn't care if such an implication insulted Brock.

"Noo, see here. I've never laid a hand on my sister," he protested.

I ignored his bluster, keeping my gaze locked with Maggie's.

"He's right. He's never hurt me," she replied, though her cowering posture seemed to belie her words. Perhaps he had never struck her, but clearly she was frightened and intimidated by him.

"The offer still stands," I told her.

Her eyes flitted from me to her brother and back, and I could sense her hesitation.

And this, above everything else, seemed to have the power to subdue Brock. Although I wasn't looking at him, I could sense the shift in his temperament, for it altered the atmosphere of the room. It was as if a piper had released the mouthpiece on his bagpipe, and suddenly the instrument had begun to deflate of all its air.

I peered over my shoulder, finding his eyes locked on his sister, stark with pain. I wanted to look away, for it seemed like something I shouldn't witness. It was too intimate, too personal, and the sight of such vulnerability—especially coming from Bonnie Brock—tore at something inside me. Yet I continued to watch as he leaned across the table toward her.

"You ken I would never let harm come to ye, Magpie. No' willingly." He spread his hands in supplication. "Why, I woulda given my left and right arm if it woulda prevented Sore John from misusin' ye like he did. And the bairn . . ." His voice ached at the word, and Maggie's eyes flooded with tears. "If I coulda saved your bairn for ye, ye ken I woulda done anythin'. *Anythin'.*"

I felt Gage's hand press warm against my back, not having noticed he'd moved closer. It was only when I looked up at him, seeing him through a wash of tears, that I realized I was also quietly weeping.

Brock's brow furrowed. "So, aye, I may be angry wi' ye noo for what you've done." He lowered his hands to his sides. "But I'll no' raise my hand to ye." His lip curled upward at one corner in self-deprecation. "Just maybe my voice."

The corners of Maggie's lips lifted in a watery smile.

"And I'm sorry I ever made ye think I would."

I swiped at the wetness on my cheeks, and Gage passed me his handkerchief, for Maggie still had mine.

Brock held out his hand to her, even though his posture was uncertain. "Will ye come home wi' me, lass? Wherever home may be tonight."

Maggie sniffed and nodded, taking several steps to meet her brother halfway around the table. When she was near enough, he pulled her into his side and dropped a kiss on the matted hair of her forehead, murmuring something I could not hear but which seemed to settle her. Then he led her from the room toward the French doors, opening them to the chill night air. But not before directing a look of firm determination at me and Gage. One which seemed to say, *Resolve this.*

Thus, as soon as the doors closed behind them, I said to Gage. "Promise or no promise. We'd better visit Mr. Heron at first light."

Knock again," I told Gage. "He has to be here."

This time my husband banged on the door, using more force than the times before. "Mr. Heron," he called into the wood. "It's important we speak with you. We're not going away until we do."

I turned as a door farther along the corridor opened and a woman peered out through the crack, clearly wondering who was making such a racket at this hour.

Gage scowled when Heron's door remained shut.

"Do you think Bonnie Brock got to him first?" I whispered, tugging my fur collar higher around my chin. Had we made a mistake trusting him? Maybe we should have come at midnight.

Gage shook his head, pounding once more. "Mr. Heron, we aren't the only ones who wish to speak to you, but I promise we're the nicest."

This at last seemed to achieve results, for I heard something scrape across the floor within and then a lock being turned. The door inched open to reveal one of Heron's dark eyes. "What do you want?" he hissed in fright.

Gage pushed on the door, forcing Heron backward in astonishment, and then muscled his way inside. "Good morning, Mr. Heron." He ushered me inside, past a ladder-back chair that I wondered whether Heron had propped beneath the latch. "I do believe you will prefer to have this discussion in your parlor rather than in your doorway where all of your neighbors can hear." Once I had glided past, he closed the door firmly and positioned himself in front of it.

Not that I anticipated Heron trying to make an escape. Not when he was still dressed in his nightclothes with a dark brown cotton banyan draped over top. A nightcap even covered his prematurely silver-white tresses; however, when he caught the direction of my gaze he removed it.

"I've told ye everythin' I ken," he protested.

"Really?" Gage asked in a leading voice, one whose lightness seemed to confound Heron.

So much so that he actually answered in a question. "Aye?"

Gage tilted his head, studying the man before he continued. "Do you recall that we told you we met Miss Maggie Kincaid on the road outside your home the last time we called?"

He blinked and then forced a laugh. "Oh, aye. But I'm sure many people traverse the North Back o' the Canongate. 'Tis well trod."

"Yes, but more pointedly, she emerged from the lane leading to *your* door."

He shrugged. "More than a dozen sets o' rooms lead off the same lane. She mighta visited any one o' 'em." His words were nonchalant, but the manner in which he was wringing the life out of his hat certainly was not.

"She *might* have," Gage conceded. "But we've already spoken to Miss Kincaid."

"You have?"

He nodded, and Heron's eyes widened with dismay.

"She told us everything," I said, growing tired of Heron's stunned silence and Gage toying with him. I'd been unable to sleep much the night before from nerves, and now that the opportunity to speak with Heron was before us, I refused to waste any more time beating around the bush. I cut him off with a slice of my hand as he began to utter another nonsensical question in response. "About your meeting in the Physic Gardens, and her confiding in you about her and her brother's past, and your telling the information to someone else." I narrowed my eyes. "Or did you sell it?"

"Nay! Nay, I dinna sell it."

"Then whom did you tell? And why?"

He lifted his hand to his head, scraping his fingers through his hair and then tugging on it.

"You betrayed her, you know?" I added, grinding the ax in further. "She trusted you."

"I ken. I ken." He sank down in a chair and cradled his head in his hands. "She says she's forgiven me, but I dinna ken if I'll ever forgive myself. Or if God will."

"Or if Bonnie Brock will," I replied, perhaps a trifle mean-spiritedly. But I didn't come here to listen to him wallow in self-pity. That got us nowhere.

He sat upright in alarm. "Does he ken?"

"Yes. So out with it, before he comes to extract the answer from you himself."

Heron shrank backward.

"Whom did you tell? And why?" I repeated more stridently.

His eyes darted between me and Gage, who now stood beyond my shoulder, his arms crossed over his chest, allowing me to take the lead. "Mr. Lennox. Our printer."

I shared a speaking look with Gage, for he had been the name at the top of both of our lists of suspects.

"He . . . he told me he'd seen me wi' Maggie. That he ken who she was. And then he invited me to have a drink."

I frowned, not understanding where this was leading.

"He asked if he could take me into his confidence. Said he believed that Maggie was his cousin. Her brother, too. Through their mother. Said the family had been searchin' for 'em because there was an inheritance owed to 'em. But given Kincaid's reputation, he needed to be certain." He gestured with his hand. "Many o' the Kincaids are descended from the ancient Earls o' Lennox."

This was a piece of information I had not been aware of, but it helped fill in the larger picture.

"So it seemed feasible that they could be related. Lennox has always claimed his ancestors were more than tradesmen."

"So you told him what you knew," I surmised. "What Maggie had told you in confidence."

"Aye. Wi' the help o' a few too many glasses o' whisky." His head hung in shame. "I dinna realize how much I'd actually told him until he brought *The King o' Grassmarket* to Mr. Rookwood. When I read it, I wanted to put a pistol to my head."

I scowled. "Spare us the dramatics. Did you confront Lennox?"

"Sure, I did. But he just laughed in my face. Told me there was nothin' I could do aboot it wi'oot tellin' the world, the lass I loved, and her blackguard o' a brother what I'd done. That my only choice was to keep my gob shut." He sighed. "So I did."

"But Maggie figured it out anyway."

"Aye. Confronted me." He pressed a hand to his heart. "Told me she hated me. But after I told her why I'd done it, she said she understood." He shook his head. "I dinna ken how she was able to—"

"The day Rookwood died," I interrupted before he could dither on, taking us on another melodramatic tangent. "When you couldn't account for all of the time you spent on errands. That's because you met with Maggie that day, isn't it?"

He flushed. "Aye."

"And the sequel? Was that a surprise?"

"Aye, it was. When Rookwood showed it to me, I was gobsmacked. And furious. But o' course I couldna tell him why. It's filled wi' nothin' but lies. I told Rookwood no' to publish it, and he told me he'd already decided no' to." His brow lowered thunderously. "But Lennox wouldna take no for an answer. Threatened him even." He pounded his fist down onto his open palm like a gavel. "So I decided to threaten him in return. That's why

I really went to see him on the afternoon Mr. Rookwood was killed." His shoulders deflated. "But he wasna there."

My head reared back and I turned to Gage.

"Did you say he wasn't there?" he repeated.

"Aye," Heron replied. "His foreman didna ken when he'd return, so I left."

Lennox had misled us. He'd told us that Mr. Heron had stopped by to deliver a pamphlet for Mr. Rookwood, but he hadn't actually said he'd seen him. He'd been deliberately vague. Which made me wonder if there was anything else he'd misled us about.

CHAPTER 25

That confirms it, then," I declared when we returned to our carriage. "Lennox is Mugdock."

Gage slumped deeper into the squabs, the folds of his many-caped greatcoat draping around him. "It was the perfect arrangement, really. Lennox could have published the book himself, without Rookwood's assistance. The subject matter alone would have sold it. But he needed the concealment that the name of Thomas W. Rookwood Publishing provided, so that all the questions and pressure and suspicions would be directed toward Rookwood instead of him, the lowly printer."

"He could come and go, visiting with Rookwood in his guise as printer without any suspicions attached to it, and without the fear of their correspondence being intercepted or their meetings being discovered."

"Which also explains why he agreed to change our names at Rookwood's insistence," he mused, rubbing his index finger over his bottom lip as he pondered. "If he took the book to another publisher, he would sacrifice the concealment and convenience Rookwood provided."

"Plus the fact that Mr. Heron knew," I pointed out. "Perhaps Lennox saw funneling the publication through Rookwood, and thus bolstering Heron's income, as extra incentive for him to remain quiet." I shifted in my seat, trying to find a more comfortable position. "Though I still don't understand why Lennox holds such a vendetta against Bonnie Brock. Or us, for that matter."

"Maybe there is no vendetta. Maybe Lennox simply saw an opportunity to make a great deal of money."

I considered Gage's suggestion. "It doesn't feel impersonal."

He sighed. "No, it doesn't."

"And what of Lord Kirkcowan? Why was Lennox being blackmailed by him, as we speculate?"

"I think Kirkcowan knew he was Mugdock. Though I'm not certain how." He frowned. "Or if that was truly what got him killed."

I pivoted to face him more fully. "Right, then. Here's a more vital question. We now have confirmation Lennox is Mugdock, but is he a murderer?"

"Well, he had the ability and the opportunity. Heron told us he wasn't in his shop when he called, and as Rookwood's printer he probably would have been aware of the rear entrance off Carrubbers Close. Rookwood knew him, possibly well enough not only to allow him into his office but also to turn his back to him."

"But *why*? Simply because he refused to print his sequel?" I asked doubtfully.

"I suppose it's possible that was his sole motivation, but you're right. It does seem rather weak."

I changed positions again, in hopes that sitting upright

would ease some of the strain on my back. "I still think we're missing something. What about everything Mr. Heron told us about Lennox claiming Bonnie Brock might be owed an inheritance? Do you think there might be any truth to it, or was it purely a ploy to convince Heron to talk?"

"That I don't know, but I strongly suspect the latter. Not only because it proved to be a persuasive ruse to convince Heron—who seemingly isn't prone to tale-telling—to talk, but also because Kincaid was born out of wedlock. Most inheritances only pass to legitimate offspring." His eyes surveyed me with concern as I changed seated positions again. "Kiera, are you in pain?"

"It's my back," I groaned. "I thought perhaps the baby had shifted, because I've felt like I could breathe easier the past few days, but apparently not."

Gage urged me to turn around as he stripped off his gloves. When his hands began to knead my lower spine, I thought I might weep at how wonderful it felt.

His voice was a low rumble in my ear as he pressed deeply into the muscles in my back. "I think it might be best if I return you home before I venture out to speak with someone who may be able to explain the tangled web of the Lennox family and all the clans with which it intermixes."

"No, I can manage," I assured him. "I want to pay a call on Lady Bearsden first. She seemed to know a great deal about May Kincaid. More than anyone else I know. Than anyone else who is willing to share," I amended drolly, thinking of Bonnie Brock and his stubborn silence.

"Are you certain?"

"Yes, and I'm equally certain she'll lend me her carriage to drive me home when we're done." I turned my head to glance at him over my shoulder. "Who are you going to see?"

"Knighton. If I'm not greatly mistaken, his mother was a Lennox."

"Oh," I exclaimed, for I was rather fond of Gage's friend from his Cambridge days. And perhaps more importantly, I trusted whatever he had to tell us. "Is he still staying at his home in Hermiston?"

"Yes, so I won't return until late this afternoon."

I nodded. "Give Mr. Knighton my best."

"The same to Lady Bearsden and Lady Stratford. And Kiera?" He paused in his ministrations to lean forward so he could look me in the eye. "Don't put on too brave of a face. If you're in pain, go home. And have Jeffers send for Dr. Fenwick."

"I will," I promised, pressing a kiss to his lips. "Don't worry about me."

He nodded, but I could tell he didn't quite believe me.

And well, he shouldn't. For I had no intention of ceasing this investigation—short of actually going into labor—until it was over. The last thing I wanted hanging over my head was the knowledge that Rookwood's murderer was still out there, and that Lennox's sequel might cause me and my child more damage than even the original.

Two hours later, I arrived home tired and dispirited, for this time, Lady Bearsden's encyclopedic knowledge of all of society's gossip had failed to produce the answers we sought. She recalled the fact that May Kincaid had possessed a number of Lennox cousins, but she couldn't remember precisely which ones would have been of the appropriate age and rank to have potentially ruined her and then set her up in a cottage, before abandoning her after Bonnie Brock's birth.

I knew it was unfair to expect her to recollect every tidbit of gossip from the past thirty years, but I was disappointed nonetheless. A fact Charlotte hadn't missed, for she'd promised to pay me a call on Monday, or sooner, if her great-aunt remembered anything.

"Unfruitful morning, my lady?" Jeffers asked as he took my bonnet.

"Not fruitful enough," I replied with a forced smile. "Is Miss McEvoy in?"

"I believe she is."

I paused in the removal of my gloves, trying to figure out why his voice sounded strained around the edges. However, his expression was as unruffled as ever. "Please have her bring up a hot water bottle," I told him before moving toward the stairs.

Once inside my bedchamber, I sank down on the edge of the bed with a long sigh. Closing my eyes, I leaned forward so that the muscles in my back stretched taut. But I could only lean so far without the risk of toppling forward. So I slid my feet back to the floor and turned to stand facing the bed, before bending over in a rather undignified pose. Indecorous though it might have been, it relieved the pressure in my back.

Which was why, a short time later when Bree entered the room, she found me with my face and forearms pressed into the bedding and my bottom hoisted in the air. When she didn't speak immediately, I turned my face against the counterpane, wondering if I'd been mistaken. Perhaps Gage had returned and was even now ogling me as if I weren't nine months heavy with child. By now, I well understood the idiosyncrasies of the male mind and their curious affinity for the shape of a woman in such a position.

Bree, indeed, stood inside the door, but she hadn't yet pivoted to face me. And if I wasn't very much mistaken, she was gathering herself. My chest tightened as I pondered why.

I buried my face back in the bedding as she turned, not wanting to disconcert her with the knowledge that I'd been observing her.

"Aye, that'll do the trick," she remarked with her customary frankness as she observed my posture. "But I assume ye were wantin' this." I lifted my head to find her brandishing the hot water bottle I'd requested. "So let's get ye oot o' that gown."

She helped me to stand, swiftly undoing the buttons down the back of my dress before lifting it over my head. Then she removed my stays and helped me to crawl up onto the bed. Positioning my pillows and the hot water bottle at my back, I shifted until it rested in just the right position, sinking deeper with a contented breath.

"Better?" she asked, allowing me my first chance to see her fully. Her eyes were rimmed in red and her cheeks were splotchy, telling me she'd been crying. And not just a few tears, but great heaving sobs.

"Yes."

She began to turn away, but I caught hold of her hand before she could do so.

"Bree, what's happened?" I knew I was breaking a rule to ask, but I couldn't see her looking so miserable without at least attempting to help.

She shook her head, forcing a smile. "It's nothin', m'lady." But the tears glittering at the back of her eyes told me that was a lie.

"It's not nothing," I argued gently. "Please, will you tell me?"

Her head swiveled to the side as she tried to hide her distress. But her throat worked as she swallowed, and her jaw alternately tightened and softened as she struggled to master her emotions.

"Is it Anderley?" I asked, deciding to wager a guess.

She turned to blink at me. "How'd ye ken?" she asked in a raspy voice.

"Because he's typically the cause of your grief."

She frowned, as if uncertain whether to defend him. "That's no' really true."

"Lately, it is," I disputed not unkindly. When she offered no rebuttal, I decided to press harder. "You two do seem to argue a great deal."

Her hands smoothed the fabric of the counterpane before her over and over as she considered my words. "Maybe."

"What happened this time?"

"He . . . he told me I expect too much o' him. That I canna expect him to stop doin' all he can to help Mr. Gage wi' his investigations."

"You asked him to stop investigating?" I inquired in tempered surprise.

"Nay. I never said that. I *dinna* want him to stop." She pressed a hand to her chest. "*I* dinna want to stop myself. I like helpin' you and Mr. Gage. We both do." Her face contorted. "I only want him to stop flirtin' wi' every girl who crosses his path in order to get information."

"Does he do that?"

"Aye. The actress at the play, Rookwood's maid, and who kens how many others." She crossed her arms over her chest. "Ye forget, we've been, more or less, part o' the same household noo for fifteen months. I've seen him work his charm on dozens o' lasses—old and young."

"Anderley is an attractive man, and I suspect that's the method that's proven most effective in the past." I thought back to when I first met Gage at Gairloch Castle. How he'd flirted and charmed every female in his vicinity. How they'd fawned and fluttered. How vexed it had made me before *and* after I'd realized I was attracted to him as well. Until I'd realized that his roguish persona was a mask, his charisma wielded as a shield and a weapon.

"Aye. Too attractive for his own good." Her entire body flexed with frustration. "But is it truly too much for me to ask that he no' flirt so much, that he develop some different tactics?"

"No, it's not," I agreed. "Although Gage still uses his charm to gain information from time to time, and to interact socially, I know I can trust him never to cross the line." I tilted my head. "It seems like you're saying you can't say that about Anderley." I had never personally observed such behavior in my husband's valet, but then our interactions were limited. I rarely witnessed his dealings with other servants or his methods of investigation unless he was assisting Gage in questioning a suspect.

She pressed a hand to her forehead, rubbing it fretfully. "I dinna ken what I'm sayin'. I should be able to trust him, shouldna I? But I just dinna ken." She began to pace a tight circle. "Whenever I see him talkin' to another lass like that, it just makes my stomach churn and my palms sweat."

"Other than the flirtations you've witnessed, has he given you any other reason to believe he's playing you false?"

She shook her head. "Nay, I s'pose no'." She inhaled a swift breath before blurting, "But how can I be sure? My mam believed my da could be trusted, until it was too late. I dinna want to wind up wi' a man like that."

This statement seemed to slice straight to the heart of the matter, for I hadn't known Bree's father had apparently been unfaithful to her mother.

"Bree, look at me," I urged.

She halted her steps abruptly and turned to face me, though her body still thrummed with frantic energy.

"Be careful you're not tarring Anderley with the same brush as your father. Not all men are scoundrels." I knew from experience that this was no way to begin a relationship, looking for the same faults in one man as another.

"Am I doin' that?" she asked meekly.

"Maybe," I replied, hesitant to dismiss her concerns completely. "But Bree, it's obvious you haven't been happy."

She lowered her head as if in shame.

"That doesn't mean that anyone is to blame. But you can't tell me that, in general, you've been more contented, more joyful in the past few months than you were before. In fact, at times I've never seen you more miserable and discomposed. Love should make your life better, not worse."

Her expression registered the truth of this statement.

"Whether your discontent has been caused by your suspicions, or whether there are deeper issues of mistrust and incompatibility, I can't say. But you have most definitely been out of sorts."

She lowered her arms, considering my words. "You're right. But what should I do?" Her brown eyes glittered with uncertainty.

"To begin with, talk to Anderley. *Calmly*," I emphasized. "And be more forthcoming with him about why you feel the way you do. Then decide together. As of now, things haven't grown so contentious between you that if you agreed to it, you couldn't simply return to being just friends. It might be awkward at first, but I'm sure things would improve with time."

She swallowed. "I will."

I smiled in encouragement, hoping I was right. For if things had grown more contentious than I suspected, then matters might be more difficult not only for them but for our entire household.

The leaden skies continued the next morning—an inauspicious start to wee Jamie's birthday. But given the excitement and terror surrounding his birth a year before, I would choose the gray weather over that any time.

As seemed to be my custom of late, I was running behind schedule. Having already donned my claret pelisse and hat, I'd just bustled into the entry hall where Gage was waiting when there was a knock at the door. Sliding my hands into my tan kid leather gloves, I glanced to Gage in question as Jeffers moved forward to answer the door. He shook his head, as bewildered as I until a familiar face appeared beyond our butler's shoulder.

"Knighton," Gage exclaimed as Jeffers allowed his friend into the entry. "Good to see you, old chum. But tell me you didn't travel all the way into Edinburgh just to see me."

"I had business in town, and when I learned you'd paid me a call yesterday, I decided I would return the courtesy." Mr. Knighton clasped my proffered hand, bowing over it as his emerald green eyes twinkled down at me. "Mrs. Gage, you are looking as lovely as ever." He glanced at our traveling attire. "But apparently I've caught you as you are leaving."

"Yes, to a gathering for my nephew's first birthday," I replied.

He smiled. "Then I must not keep you."

"But I do have a somewhat urgent question to ask you," Gage told him. "Will you ride with us?"

"Of course. I'll instruct my carriage to follow."

We hurried from the town house and were soon ensconced in the comfortable confines of our carriage and setting off on the short distance to Charlotte Square.

"Now, what is this urgent question?" Mr. Knighton prompted.

Gage adjusted the angle of his hat. "Bear with me, as I may have to work my way around to it. Am I correct in recalling that your mother was a Lennox?"

"Yes."

"We've been given to understand that the Kincaids and Lennoxes often marry. Is that true?"

His brow quirked quizzically. "Yes, again. They share neighboring lands, so it's to be expected."

"Then are you familiar with May Kincaid?"

He began to shake his head, but at Gage's next words he stopped.

"Bonnie Brock Kincaid's mother."

His eyes sparked with interest. "I've heard tell of her. But what specifically are you wanting to know?"

Gage glanced at me and I spoke. "There are rumors that Bonnie Brock's father may have been a Lennox. A cousin who was already wed when he trifled with Miss Kincaid."

Mr. Knighton turned to peer out the window at the Georgian façades lining the street, but I could tell from his sudden reticence that he knew something. "I heard a tale from one of *my* cousins when I was a lad. Though, to hear a Lennox tell it, May Kincaid wasn't so innocent in the affair," he remarked ruefully.

Of course they would say so.

"Did your cousin name Miss Kincaid's lover?" Gage pressed.

"The Wolf of Badenoch. At least, that was the sobriquet my cousin used. I'm not certain how widely he was called that. But from the tales I heard about him, it wasn't difficult to deduce why it became his nickname. Though not as notorious as the late fourteenth-century Wolf of Badenoch, he was still undoubtedly a hellion."

Notorious was right. The earlier Wolf of Badenoch referred to Alexander Stewart, the Earl of Buchan, the third surviving son of King Robert II of Scotland. He'd earned the nickname because of his cruelty and malice throughout his lifetime. He'd burned, sacked, and looted parts of the Highlands when out of temper for one slight or another, including the royal burgh of Elgin and its cathedral. That legends said his death occurred when he'd played chess with the devil and lost was really no surprise.

I frowned in puzzlement. The book and play had both included allusions to lions, not wolves, being part of Bonnie Brock's father's identity, as in the lion-headed walking stick he carried. An allusion that had seemed fitting given Bonnie Brock's hair. His thick tawny tresses often seemed akin to a lion's mane. But perhaps the author had recognized this and sought to exploit it. After all, Maggie let slip a year ago that her brother looked nothing like his father. I had recalled this and just as easily forgotten it, buying into the easier illusion.

If Bonnie Brock's father was the nineteenth-century Wolf of Badenoch, that might explain how Mugdock had been inspired to make use of such a ploy. It also suggested how determined he was to throw suspicion away from the truth.

"I don't recall a Lord Badenoch. What was the Wolf of Badenoch's full name?" Gage asked.

"It's unlikely you would," Knighton replied. "In any case, it's a feudal barony of Scottish origin." So the holder was not necessarily considered a peer, but a nobleman of lesser rank, and they held no seat in the House of Lords at Parliament.

"This chap was from a minor branch of the family. His name was Alexander Lennox of Badenoch."

I felt a tightening in my abdomen, whether from a false labor pain or because my body sensed how important this was before my mind could catch up. "Then he's not still alive?"

"No." Mr. Knighton tilted his head upward in thought. "And if my memory serves me correctly, he didn't leave his family in a very good position upon his death. Not only had he tarnished the title, but much of his fortune was also depleted. I believe his son had to take up a trade of some sort."

When Gage asked his next question, I could tell he'd been struck by the same suspicion I had. "What was his son's name?"

"The same as his father. Alexander Lennox of Badenoch."

CHAPTER 26

It took everything in me not to curse roundly. We finally had the final piece to our puzzle, and yet we were on our way to my nephew's birthday party, which we could not miss short of my being in advanced labor. Though I could tell from Gage's expression that he was considering making his excuses.

"Don't even think it," I told him. If I couldn't go, then he certainly wasn't going either. Besides, there was little risk that Lennox would be fleeing Edinburgh. Not when he was still unaware of how much we knew. And even then I had the distinct impression he was the type of man who believed he could brazen his way through anything.

Mr. Knighton's mouth creased with humor. "I take it this information has been helpful in some way."

"Yes, thank you," Gage told him, offering him his hand as our carriage rolled to a stop. "Let me know next time you're in town, and we'll invite you to dinner."

He shook his hand. "Message me with the happy news when

your child arrives." He turned his warm smile on me. "I anticipate it will be soon."

"We will," Gage replied, helping me from the carriage. Once
inside the entry hall of Cromarty House, I tugged loose the
ribbon securing my bonnet and whispered in Gage's ear. "Badenoch. 'Ba.' That's what Rookwood was writing. Not Bonnie
Brock."

Gage tilted his head nearer to mine as he stripped off his
gloves. "It makes sense. Writing 'Lennox' would have been too
ambiguous. But there is only one Badenoch."

"He's his half brother," I marveled. And yet he was doing
everything in his power to destroy him. Not unlike the man who
had shared their father's sobriquet.

Gage's brow furrowed as he shrugged out of his coat, and I
wondered if he was thinking of his own newly discovered half
brother. Of his very different reaction.

"Kiera, Gage, there you are," my sister proclaimed, addressing us from the landing above. "I was just beginning to worry."

"My apologies," Gage said, before I could speak. "Mr.
Knighton paid me a call just as we were leaving our town house."

"Oh, well, you should have invited him to join us," she declared, her voice softening in regard, but then bustled off before
he could reply, calling over her shoulder. "Come and join us."

Gage offered me his arm, and we climbed the stairs toward
the sounds of children merrily playing and the accompanying
hum of their parents' conversation. True to her intentions, Alana
had kept the party small and intimate, with naught but family
and a few friends. I exchanged greetings with a few of the adults
but then had to pause beside a chair as I felt another tightening
in my lower abdomen. It wasn't painful, merely uncomfortable,
but it did give me pause, for in the past my moving about had
always halted such contractions.

However, I was soon diverted by my niece Philipa's broad

grin as she hurried over to show me a picture she'd drawn. At age seven, she was all elbows and knees, and prone to mothering her almost-three-year-old sister, who followed in her wake, flinging her arms around my legs in a hug. Then just as swiftly they darted away, eager to take part in the next game. Even Jamie, who fearlessly crawled around after the older children.

I did my best to join in the conversation of the other women, who each seemed eager to discuss my heavily expectant state, but I found myself distracted, unable to stop contemplating Lennox and his motivation for his actions. My eyes sought out Gage across the room, but he seemed to be doing a much better job of ignoring the matter. When another contraction began—false or not—I turned my steps toward the round table in the corner where Jamie's gifts were lined up in pretty boxes with bows. Alana had also decided to display a small portrait of Jamie I had painted soon after his birth, and a small framed pressed flower. She had made one for each of her children with the flower associated with their birth month. Jamie's was a yellow daffodil, and it was inscribed with his full name—James Kieran Matheson—and a short line of verse. I picked up the picture to read it, smiling at the words.

"Yes, Alana captured him perfectly, didn't she?"

I glanced up at my cousin Morven as she read over my shoulder.

I must have looked a question for she explained. "The verse. Alana wrote it."

"She did?" I replied, reading it again.

"Yes." She gestured toward the curio cabinet where the other three pictures were propped. "She wrote the verses on all of her children's." She gave a short laugh. "You didn't know that?"

"No," I replied in bafflement, and then turned to gaze across the room at Alana, who stood near the hearth conversing with

Morven's husband. Why hadn't she ever told me? Or had she simply expected me to know?

"Your sister used to write a great deal of poetry. She was quite good, too," Morven remarked.

I met her gaze, realizing this was what she and Charlotte had hinted at in my conversations with them, even if no one had spoken outright. "Why did she stop?" I asked, though I suspected I already knew the answer.

Morven shrugged one shoulder, as if it were self-explanatory. "She married and then Malcolm was born."

I set the picture down carefully on the table as a dawning realization filled me, followed by a swift flash of anger. This was why Alana was so insistent that I give up my inquiry work. This was why she was determined I follow the rules of decorum. Because she had.

But why had she done so? Why had she stopped writing poetry? Surely she could have continued to do so even after she had children. Unless Philip forbade it.

I lifted my gaze to study my brother-in-law, who was bent over explaining something to a pouting Philipa. No, I didn't believe that. Philip might be traditional in many senses, but he would never have forbidden Alana from doing something she loved, something so harmless.

Alana must have elected to do so herself, ever the perfect countess and politician's wife.

I kept my gaze on the table before me, struggling to understand. No, there must be more to the matter than that. After all, Alana had always supported my art—she still did—and poetry was not so very different. There must be something else to account for her ferocity toward me in continuing my investigations. Something beyond her concerns for my safety. Something to explain her frustration and fury at my flouting society's dictates, at my persistence in intruding into what most saw as the rightful domain of men.

I pressed a hand to the amethyst fabric draped over my rounded abdomen. It was contemplations like these that, at times, made me wish the child inside me was a boy. But swiftly upon the heels of that thought would come another, the desire to have the chance to raise a daughter who knew she didn't have to submit to such ridiculous standards. That she could be strong, courageous, intelligent, talented, ambitious, and still a faithful, devoted wife and mother, if she so chose.

Lifting my gaze to the wall where a portrait of our parents I had painted after their death hung, I wondered for perhaps the hundredth time how our mother would have counseled us. Would she have urged Alana to do what she'd done? Or would she have encouraged her the way Alana had encouraged me when I was younger, before I'd become great with child?

The truth was, I would never know. I would never have the chance to experience that. So perhaps I needed to stop asking the wrong question. Perhaps it no longer mattered what our mother would have said. Perhaps it only mattered what I would decide to say instead.

You're awfully quiet."

I looked up from my contemplation of the carriage seat across from us to look into Gage's concerned face. "I'm just thinking about Lennox and our impending conversation with Mr. Heron," I replied. An answer which wasn't entirely honest, for I was also thinking about the contractions that had returned. For a time during the party they had ceased, making me suspect that once again they were merely false labor pains. But now— some three or four hours later—they were back. They were still some distance apart, and I wasn't truly in pain, so there was no reason to be alarmed. Particularly as a woman's first childbirth often took half a day or longer. Alana had labored for nearly twelve hours with Malcolm, and Morven for fourteen with her first child.

If that was what was happening. After all, by no means were the contractions regular, and they had stopped and started. So perhaps this was just another form of false labor.

Either way, I'd decided that if they continued as they were, I would wait to tell Gage until after Lennox was taken into custody. Otherwise he would rush me home to pace the floors, anxious to hear what was happening. In any case, we had just a few more questions for Mr. Heron before we reported everything we'd learned to Sergeant Maclean and allowed him to handle the interrogation and arrest.

"Yes, but you were also quiet at Jamie's party," Gage remarked, plainly suspecting I wasn't telling him all. "Did Morven say something upsetting?"

So he'd noted my conversation with her over Jamie's pressed-flower picture. But now was not the time to delve into my strained relationship with my sister, and I told him so. "Ask me later."

His gaze searched mine as if uncertain whether this was some sort of test he was about to fail if he didn't immediately press for answers.

I smiled. "Truly. We're almost to Mr. Heron's, and I don't want to become preoccupied."

"You mean, any more than you already are?" he teased.

"Believe me, I'll be focused once we're standing before him."

And I was. Even though Heron seemed more unsettled by our appearance—if such a thing was possible—than he had been before.

"I-I've told ye everythin' I ken," he stammered, waving his hands as if he might be able to shoo us from the room simply by flapping them.

"You may think you have," Gage replied in an even tone.

"But we just have a few more questions we need answered. Lennox's sequel. You said Rookwood rejected it because it was filled with lies and half-truths. But what lies specifically?"

"Y-you want to ken what lies it told?" he asked in confusion.

"Yes. For instance, did it mention anything more about Kincaid's father, or his father's family?"

Heron's head reared back slightly and he blinked. "Well, aye. He alleged that Kincaid stole from and blackmailed his own father, bankruptin' him and stealin' his legitimate son's inheritance."

Gage turned to me, the look in his eyes conceding that I had been right. The inheritance did have something to do with this.

"But he provided no proof for this. No' even Kincaid's father's name. And the scheme he implied made little to no sense."

Of course it didn't, for he'd almost certainly made it up out of whole cloth.

"Did you know that Lennox is Kincaid's half brother?" I inquired bluntly.

His eyes widened and his mouth gaped before he stumbled through a response. "I . . . That . . . Are you in earnest?"

"Yes."

He scraped his hand back through his silver hair, pivoting in a circle. "But that doesna make any sense. Why would he write such things . . . oh!" he gasped, finally realizing that Lennox had been accusing Kincaid of stealing his own inheritance. He frowned. "But then, why did he make him such a hero in *The King of Grassmarket*?"

"He didn't intend to. Remember how he highlighted the body snatching and then accused him of fraud. He was trying to discredit Bonnie Brock. But the plays changed the narrative . . ."

"Which infuriated him," Gage continued with a look of mild inquiry as I broke off, momentarily silenced by the sharp pain of a contraction located in my lower back. "They left out the most damning parts."

"And the accusations only get worse in the sequel," Heron informed us as I breathed deeply until the pain passed. "Not only does he assert that Kincaid stole his inheritance, but he also claims that Kincaid collaborated wi' anatomists and the government to steal unclaimed cholera victims to be used by the anatomy schools for dissection. That is, until the Anatomy Reform Act passes in Parliament. Then that step willna be necessary."

Good heavens! Lennox was playing on the worst fears of Edinburgh's populace. I'd seen some of the broadsheets, heard some of the rumbles, that the doctors were letting the poor die of the cholera so that there would be a ready source of bodies. That the passage of the Anatomy Reform Act—which seemed almost a foregone conclusion—would exacerbate the problem. The idea of such a coordinated conspiracy had not yet captured the entire country's attention, but it was only a matter of time if Lennox published a book espousing it.

"Can you imagine what will happen if the sequel is read aloud in the pubs and other gathering places throughout Grassmarket and Cowgate?" Gage posited, for books and broadsheets were often shared in such a manner among those who couldn't read and could little afford books even if they could. "Can you imagine if they believed the accusations?"

"They would storm the cholera hospital and drag out the patients, spreading the disease even farther," I answered in horror. "They would ransack the anatomy schools and hang Bonnie Brock themselves for his part. His reputation as the people's champion would be destroyed."

He nodded. "Riots, sedition, and worse."

"Mr. Rookwood understood all this," Heron explained. "He wanted no part o' it. Said he'd never have published *The King o' Grassmarket* if he'd kent what it would lead to."

"Did he know that Lennox was related to Kincaid?"

This question seemed to rouse Heron from his morose hand-wringing, for he looked up at me in shock. "Nay, how could . . . ?" His mouth flattened as if he'd thought of something. "Maybe. He . . . he was pretty emphatic about his actions bein' a betrayal, but I thought he just meant to the city, or law and order."

Gage had pulled aside his greatcoat, planting his hands on his hips as he contemplated this new information. "Did you truly not hear any part of their argument the day before Rookwood was murdered?"

Heron shook his head. "But they were both furious. When Lennox stormed out, I thought he was gonna smash something."

"Do you think Rookwood would have threatened to expose him if he tried to publish it elsewhere or simply printed it himself?"

"I dinna ken."

"Of course," I gasped. "Lennox must have realized he didn't need the shield of Rookwood's name anymore. He could print the book himself, with everyone remaining ignorant of the fact that *he* was Mugdock."

"And so he resolved to get rid of the threat, throw some more suspicion at Kincaid, and create a diversion, if you will, from his publication of the sequel," Gage surmised.

"Which he's already doin'."

We both turned to Heron in some alarm. "How do you know that?" Gage demanded.

His shoulders hunched and he swallowed nervously. "Because he came to see me."

My heart leapt in my chest.

"When?" Gage barked.

"Yesterday. After ye left. He . . . he wanted to ken what I'd told ye."

We must have been followed. By McQueen's men, I wagered.

After all, one of them had followed us home from Lennox's shop. It only made sense that they had also trailed us to Heron's.

"And did you tell him?"

Heron shook his head emphatically until Gage loomed closer. Then he squeaked out the truth. "Only that ye were suspicious he was Mugdock because o' his possessin' the sequel. None o' the rest aboot Maggie and such."

Gage moved toward the window, peering out through the curtains at the lane backed by the steep slope of the hillside. "You do know he's probably having you watched."

No wonder he'd been so anxious when we first arrived.

He swallowed again. "Aye."

"And you're just now telling us this?"

He was smart enough not to respond to this query.

"Is there another way out of your building?" Gage asked.

He nodded.

"Then I suggest you pack a bag after we leave and use it. Stay elsewhere until this matter is resolved." He peered out the window again before rejoining us. "With any luck, that will be in but a matter of hours. Especially if Lennox is already printing the sequel."

Heron's face had visibly paled, and he seemed unable to speak. I only hoped he heeded Gage's advice.

"We have enough to take to Maclean," my husband told me. "Enough to get the printing of that sequel stopped at the outset."

I agreed, taking his proffered arm as we moved toward the door. Once in the corridor outside, we had taken but two steps toward the stairs, when suddenly an arm grabbed me from behind. It hauled me backward as I cried out in protest. But it was too late. Less than a second later, Gage crumpled to the ground.

CHAPTER 27

Terror shot through me and I shrieked. "Let me go! Get your hands off me. Gage!"

But he didn't move or respond, not even with a groan. Blood began to mat the back of his blond hair, his hat having been knocked off. At first I feared they'd shot him in the head, and a bolt of sickening panic nearly paralyzed me. But then I saw the crude cudgel one of the other men was brandishing. By his hulking size, his brown coat, and the smallpox scars Bonnie Brock had described, I knew him to be the man who had followed us from Lennox's several days ago. McQueen's man.

I kicked out, struggling against the man who had my arms pinned behind my back, but in my expectant condition I was awkward and clumsy at best. My Hewson percussion pistol was nestled inside my reticule still attached to my wrist, but I couldn't reach it with my hands restrained. The door across the corridor cracked open, and the woman who had spied on us the day before peered out. I screamed at her to help, but she merely slammed the door.

"Shut your gob," the man behind me ordered. "Or I'll throw ye doon these stairs, and we'll see how much ye like that."

Knowing that such an act would likely kill me and the child in my womb, I bit my lip. My eyes darted around us, trying to find some way out of this situation. But without anyone's help, there was little I could do but obey their commands. The two other men lifted Gage's body, carrying him unceremoniously down the stairs, while I was hustled after them.

I considered elbowing the man restraining me in the gut and trying to run once we reached the bottom of the stairs, but another contraction ended any such attempt before I could even try it. I stumbled forward, wishing I'd taken the pains more seriously earlier. They were still paced well apart, but if I was truly going into labor, they would only get worse. Much worse. And who knew where these men intended to take us.

Rather than turn right to return to the street where our carriage awaited us, they hustled us to the left along the lane at the base of the hillside to a wider close some one hundred yards farther west. There, an old hackney carriage stood waiting. Gage was tossed into its confines before I was pushed toward its dilapidated step. I wasn't even certain it would hold my weight. But before I could begin to climb, the man who had restrained me wrenched me back around to face him.

"Noo, just a moment. We was warned ye might be armed." He yanked my reticule from my wrist, feeling through the velvet the clear indentation of my weapon. His dark eyes glinted with satisfaction before trailing over my pelisse. "Ye got anythin' else concealed under there?"

I scowled at him to no avail.

"Open it, lass." He leered, revealing a large gap between his front teeth. "Or I'll do it for ye."

I unfastened the buttons in sharp tugs, angry that I was being treated so, and frightened for Gage, myself, and our child.

Once I'd parted the claret fabric, his gaze ran over me insultingly before focusing on my neck.

"Noo, what do we have here," he drawled, reaching for the gold chain draped around my neck. He pulled the amethyst pendant my mother had given me from beneath the bodice of my gown. "Take it off."

My heart squeezed at the idea of doing so. I wore it so often, not only because it was the most special thing she'd ever given me but also because she'd said it was for my protection. And even though rationally I knew that it wasn't imbued with any magical powers, I still felt vulnerable and exposed at the thought of not possessing it.

"Take it off," he repeated sharply, leaving me with no doubt he would rip it from my neck if I didn't.

I lifted my shaking hands to undo the clasp before passing it to him. He stuffed it into his pocket and then gestured for me to get inside the carriage. Fighting a wave of panic, I did as I was told. Surely our coachman would realize something was wrong when we didn't return. Surely Heron had heard us being attacked outside his rooms and would go for help. Or maybe the woman peering at us through her door would take pity on us and run for a watchman.

I rearranged Gage's limp body as best I could, resting his head in my lap. His wound bled profusely, but his skull didn't seem broken. So I did what I could to stanch the flow of blood with the skirts of my gown while the fingers of my other hand searched the side of his neck for a pulse. I found it beating strong and steady and released a shuddering breath. Then as unobtrusively as possible, I searched the pockets of Gage's greatcoat but found that his pistol had also been taken.

The gap-toothed man climbed into the carriage and sat across from us, the harsh stench of his person mixing with the acrid smells that had leached into the tattered leather of the hackney and the metallic odor of Gage's blood. I breathed shallowly through my nose, reminding myself I'd suffered through fouler aromas, but my stomach rebelled nonetheless. So much so that sweat broke out across my brow, and I was forced to swallow repeatedly.

The faded curtains were pulled tightly shut, and I wasn't allowed to see where we were going, but fortunately our destination was not far. We pulled to a stop, and my muscles strained with the desire to flee. But when the door was wrenched open unceremoniously, flooding the carriage with light, it was to allow someone to peer inside, not for me to exit.

Lennox's sharp gaze took in the sight of Gage bleeding in my lap and my pale, distressed face blinking back at him, but he didn't spare us an iota of remorse. "You should have steered clear of this one, Lady Darby. You should have let Kincaid have his due."

He turned abruptly to the gap-toothed man. "Don't leave the job undone this time. Had Kirkcowan revived . . ."

"Costs extra," the man replied.

"I paid plenty," Lennox snapped. "If you've a problem with your cut, speak to McQueen."

Then the door was slammed shut, taking with it all the fresh air that had rushed inside, and a shout went up for us to roll forward.

I warred with myself over whether to try to reason with the gap-toothed man. To ask where we were going. To offer more money for him not to harm us. But speaking meant breathing more air, and I was perilously close to vomiting all over Gage and myself.

When we jerked to a halt a short distance away, I wasn't sure what it meant until the gap-toothed man descended from the conveyance. "Get down," he ordered me, crowding close, but not offering me any assistance as I struggled to descend without tripping and falling.

The other men hauled Gage from the hackney while I turned to look around me. We were in a dark enclosed space between two tall buildings of some kind. They appeared to be tenements, for I saw a number of faces staring cautiously from the windows above down at us below. None of them interfered. They simply watched. A group of lads clustered nearby, and I stared at them, begging them with my eyes to help us lest my words earn me a blow to the stomach.

"Isna that the butcher's wife?" I heard one of them murmur.

I felt a pulse of hope, not even caring that he'd called me by one of the cruel epithets the papers had dubbed me with following the revelations of my assisting Sir Anthony. If they knew who I was, perhaps they would go for help. But one of Mc-Queen's men barked at them, and they backed away, lowering their gazes.

My right arm was clasped in a tight grip, which would leave a bruise, and I was propelled through a doorway and down a dark, cramped corridor and up a staircase. Another contraction rippled through me, and some of my attention was pulled away from my surroundings as I breathed through it, despite the air here not being much sweeter than in the carriage. We entered a dim chamber, passing through it into another room, and then what I thought would be another, but the scent and the feel of the air around us alerted me to the change. I gazed around me at the dark rugged stone arching overhead, at the uneven colors and textures revealed in the light of the battered lantern the gap-toothed man was given by one of his men, and I suddenly realized where we were.

Horror lanced through me. We were being led into the vaults below South Bridge—that underground labyrinth of damp, darkness, and disease. Even now, the sour stench of dank stone and musty air assailed my nostrils. I resisted the gap-toothed man's efforts to pull me forward, my feet rooted to the spot in fright. But he tugged harder, nearly pulling me off my feet as he led me through the tunnels of rock.

My heart fluttered in my chest as I tried to memorize the path he led us on through the warren of rooms and tunnels, but I soon lost track. Occasionally hollow-eyed faces would stare back at us from the darkness, or a groan or cough would reach my ears, but as before, no one spoke to us, no one interfered.

The farther we walked, the lower my hopes became, for how would anyone ever find us? And if they did, would they find us alive or merely corpses? Lennox had ordered them to finish the job, and I held no illusions about what that meant. I cringed as a fat rat scampered down the corridor past us with seemingly little concern about being seen.

In my panic, I couldn't tell how long we'd been walking, but we appeared to have reached the bowels of the place. The deeper we'd gone, the fewer people there had been, and I soon understood why. The floors were damp, the corners black with foul growth. Even the rats didn't appear to want to live here. I shivered in my pelisse, not simply from revulsion but also the cold.

A wall loomed up before us, and I could see now that we'd come to the end. Along the far edge, a stagnant puddle had formed into which the water running down the walls from above dripped. The men dumped Gage onto the floor, and I turned to face them, wary of what was to happen next. But it appeared they had no stomach to actually kill us. Or perhaps they'd decided the effort was unnecessary.

My throat constricted with fear as they began to back out of the chamber.

"Best pray it doesna rain," the man in the brown coat quipped in a rough voice, making me stiffen with dread that perhaps this area actually flooded to above our heads.

I turned my wide eyes to the gap-toothed man, who was the last to leave, taking his lantern with him. I was petrified with the realization that there would be no light without it, leaving Gage and me alone in the pitch blackness. Something of my terror must have penetrated his heart, for he paused and reluctantly returned to pass me the light.

He hesitated a moment longer, reaching into his pocket before tossing something on the floor. "Ye may wish for this afore the end."

Then he turned his back to me and strode from the room.

"Please," I finally squeaked. "Please, don't leave us down here."

But even as I begged, the door slammed shut, and a bar dropped into place, locking us inside.

I trembled, perilously close to dissolving into hysterics. It was all I could do simply to breathe and keep my legs beneath me. Especially when I realized the item he had thrown onto the floor was my reticule with my pistol tucked inside.

Tiny spots formed in my vision, and I closed my eyes, telling myself to focus. But they quickly popped open again at the recognition that the lantern would not last forever, and I would be facing the darkness soon enough.

Ignoring my bag, I turned slowly to examine the contents of the room, of which there were few. Nothing but a broken bottle, a few sticks, and a dented horseshoe. The stone was etched with crude drawings, but nothing of help. Perhaps I would be etching my own words into the stone soon—my name and Gage's, and that of our unborn child.

I grimaced as another contraction swept through me. I hadn't any concept of time, but they still seemed far enough apart, and the pain was not much greater than a discomfort. However, I no longer denied the truth. I was in labor, and the pain would only get worse. And soon.

I studied the construction of the door, finding it sturdier than I'd hoped. Glancing down at the light flickering inside the lantern, I considered attempting to set the door ablaze. But I worried the wood was too damp to catch fire, or that it might suffocate us before we could ever escape.

The sound of a groan behind me pulled me from my musings, and I hurried over to kneel beside Gage. Lifting his head into my lap again, I did my best to brush aside the dirt and debris that had caught in his blood-matted hair and smeared across his face. When he blinked open his eyes, it was all I could do not to sob in relief. "Sebastian. Darling," I croaked, gently stroking his face.

He stared up at me as if struggling to focus. "Kiera?"

I nodded, dashing the wetness from my eyes.

He flinched, lifting a hand toward his hair. "My head . . ." He inhaled a sharp breath through his teeth. "What . . . ?" Then his eyes opened wider as he peered around him. "Where are we?"

"The vaults."

He struggled to sit upright with my assistance, his face blanching in pain.

"McQueen's men ambushed us outside Heron's rooms. They hit you over the head and brought us here and locked us in."

He glanced at the door.

"I'm sorry. They took my pistol and . . ." I pressed a hand to my neck, now devoid of my mother's pendant, and then shook my head, for it was of no consequence at the moment.

Gage reached into his greatcoat pockets, finding them as empty as I had.

I swallowed, eyeing my reticule like a snake coiled to strike. "Though they've since given it back."

His face registered the meaning of this gesture with the same revulsion and horror I had felt.

"They threatened to harm the baby if I screamed or fought. I didn't know what to do," I told him, distress seeping into my voice. "I-I'm sorry."

"Shhh," he murmured, pulling me into his arms. "Hush, now. There's no cause to blame yourself. You were protecting our child, and I was unconscious." He heaved a sigh, pressing my head to his heart, where I could hear it beating steadily through his linen shirt. "Joe will have alerted someone by now," Gage told me, displaying faith in our coachman. "They will be looking for us."

"Yes, but they've no idea where we've been taken. And we're so deep inside the vaults. How will they ever find us?"

"They will," he said with a greater confidence than I felt. "You'll see."

I could only cling to him and pray.

Three hours later—a passage of time I could only tell because I'd asked Gage to let me hold his pocket watch—our lantern was running low on oil, and I could no longer pretend my labor wasn't steadily progressing. While Gage had prowled around the room, searching for some way to contrive our escape, I had been praying. Bargaining with God, really. Begging him to make the labor stop, to calm the child inside me for just a little while longer. But this, it appeared, was denied, and nature would have its way.

That Gage had not yet noticed my discomfort when the contractions struck I credited to his preoccupation with our situation and determination to rescue us from an unescapable situation. Even now he was examining the door for approximately the sixth time, as if its construction and mechanics had somehow changed. Meanwhile, I continued to shift positions—standing, sitting, slouching, walking—trying to find the most comfortable stance in which to endure. I kept taking my pelisse off and then putting it back on, alternating between hot and cold, sweating and shivering.

Eventually, I could remain silent no longer. "Gage."

When he didn't turn but continued to examine the door, I tried again.

"Gage, could you come over here?"

"If only we could contrive a lever of some kind," he ruminated aloud, giving no indication he'd even heard me.

"Sebastian," I groused, finally capturing his attention as he pivoted to look at me. "Could you please come here?"

He crossed the room, studying my face in the flickering light. His eyes dipped to the lantern before he knelt to examine it. "You're right. It will be out of oil soon," he said, answering a question I hadn't asked.

"I know. But we also have another problem." I turned his watch toward him, but before I could speak, another contraction swept up through my lower back and around to the front.

This time Gage recognized that I was in pain and reached for me in alarm. "Kiera?"

"It's a contraction," I bit out between clenched teeth. "They're coming faster now . . . and more intense."

His eyes widened in apparent fear, but then he sank down next to me. "Tell me what to do."

As the contraction subsided, I relaxed in relief, taking several deep breaths before answering. "Let me lean back against you."

He gathered me between his legs, and I melted into him, laying my head against his strong chest. His arms wrapped around me, cradling me close, as his hands rested against my abdomen. "How long has this been happening?"

"I started to notice them when we were on our way to Mr. Heron's, but I thought they were false labor pains like before."

"Why didn't you tell me?"

My nerves ruffled at the irritation in his tone. "I told you. I thought they were false labor pains. I didn't know I was actually going into labor. And the plan was to take everything to Maclean after speaking to Mr. Heron. I wasn't anticipating any danger."

He moved his hands to my arms, rubbing them soothingly up and down. "You're right."

"I didn't know this was going to happen." My voice cracked with emotion. "I didn't know we were going to be trapped in the vaults."

"I know, Kiera," he murmured, pressing a kiss to my temple. "Don't fret. Everything will be well in the end."

"How?"

"I don't know, but it will. Trust me." His fingers brushed my disheveled hair away from my face. "You do trust me, don't you?"

"Yes," I replied without hesitation.

"Then let me worry about all of that. You just focus on yourself and telling me what to do. I'm at your command," he attempted to jest.

My lips curled into a little smile. "That might be how I got into this situation in the first place."

Gage laughed, a deep hearty sound that shook the firm muscles of his abdomen, jostling me in the process. I flushed with the pleasure of knowing I'd been the one to cause him such merriment even in the depths of our bleak circumstances.

"Touché. But the offer still stands."

For the moment I was simply content to be supported by his embrace, and the knowledge that at least I wouldn't have to go through this alone.

And with that thought, the flame in the lantern flickered and went out.

CHAPTER 28

I lost track of time then. What there was of it became measured in breaths and heartbeats between contractions. I could tell they were growing steadily closer together and increasing in intensity even though we couldn't see the dial of Gage's watch in the darkness. Each time I thought the pain was unbearable, I would discover I was wrong, for the ache that tore through me would suddenly increase.

Through it all, Gage remained by my side—stroking my hair, rubbing my back, coaxing me with words of encouragement and affection, helping me to breathe. Even when my water broke, soaking his bottom as well as mine, he merely carried me to a dry area of the stone floor and resettled us.

I knew his head must be pounding from the blow he received, but he never complained, never wavered. Had I the wherewithal to thank him, I would have, but all I could do was lean into him in gratitude. That was, when I wasn't cursing and groaning in pain. Somewhere, in the depths of me, I knew that everything I was going through was normal. Everything except being trapped underground in the vaults. But that was little comfort given our circumstances.

I began to doze briefly between contractions, too weary to remain fully awake even under our dire circumstances. So when Gage startled me out of my daze, struggling to rise to his feet as he gently eased me back against the wall, I knew something important was happening.

"What is it?" I croaked through a dry throat.

He shushed me, and I strained to listen along with him. At first I heard nothing but the steady drip of water and feared Gage had begun imagining things in the darkness. But then the distant echo of a voice reached my ears, too.

"Here!" Gage shouted, making the stone chamber ring with the sound of his voice. "We're here!" I heard him wince. The sound of his own voice must be piercing his injured head like needles, but he continued to yell.

For some time after that, I was overwhelmed by another contraction, but once it subsided, I could hear the voices moving closer, and then hands banging on the door. I began to weep softly in gratitude. When the bar was finally removed and the door swung open, Gage and I both flinched from the brilliance of the light of their lanterns.

"Thank God, you've found us," Gage gasped, revealing for the first time to me how anxious he'd been. "Kiera. She's gone into labor. And I don't think it will be long now. Can you help me carry her?"

I looked up at their faces as they moved closer, Gage's streaked with blood and dirt, and then Bonnie Brock and Anderley. "Wait," I cautioned them as I felt another contraction coming on.

Gage clasped my hands, breathing with me through the pain even as it knifed through me. When it waned and I could open my eyes, I could see how pale Anderley appeared. But Bonnie Brock's jaw seemed to lock in determination.

"I'll carry her," he stated bluntly. "Yer head must be poundin', and yer liable to drop her should ye become dizzy."

Whether Gage attempted to argue, I didn't hear, for Bonnie Brock swept me up into his arms without preamble and strode from the room. Stump and Locke stood waiting for us with lanterns and set off ahead of him to light the way. I lay limp and pliant in his arms, too weary and relieved to remain aloof, trusting him to guide us out of the darkness, and Gage with Anderley's aid to follow.

Each time a contraction would sweep through me, I heard Bonnie Brock softly encouraging me. "T'won't be long noo, lass. We're almost there." But he never broke stride, recognizing that what I needed most was to escape the vaults. I wondered briefly if he thought of Maggie, of the child she'd miscarried, but then another contraction swept every other thought aside.

When at last we emerged from the vaults and then from the tenement building where the entrance had been concealed, I peered around me in startlement to discover that it was night. I breathed deep of the fresh air—its cleanliness relative to where we'd been. Faces crowded near to watch us—Sergeant Maclean, Henry, Philip, and other citizens of this part of Edinburgh. But there was only one my heart leapt at the sight of.

"I hear you've had a bit o' a misadventure, my lady," Dr. Fenwick proclaimed as Bonnie Brock lifted me into our carriage before melting away.

"She's in labor," Gage told him, stumbling up behind us.

"Aye," he responded calmly, pushing his spectacles up the bridge of his nose. "And it seems you've received a wee bump to the head. Best go see the surgeon o'er there." Then he began to climb into our carriage. "Noo, my lady, let's have a look."

I inhaled a deep breath as another contraction swept through me. He waited through it before urging me to recline on the seat so he could lift my skirt to examine me. Rolling my head to the side, I could see Gage standing stubbornly in the doorway, his face haggard and his eyes bright with concern.

"Are you feelin' the urge to push?" Dr. Fenwick asked me.

"Yes. Desperately."

"Aye. Then there's no time to wait. Bring me the blankets and supplies from my coach, Mr. Gage. You're aboot to become a father."

I focused on Dr. Fenwick's voice and my breathing as matters were arranged around and under me. Then the door was shut, and Gage was seated beside me, holding my hand as the physician urged me to push.

The details are not necessary. It is sufficient to say that finally, in the fullness of time, our child was born, giving out a lusty cry. To which those outside answered with a hearty cheer.

I smiled wearily as Dr. Fenwick cleaned and examined our baby.

"Mr. and Mrs. Gage, you have a healthy little girl," he declared before passing her to me.

Tears of joy and relief pricked my eyes as I swaddled her close and stared down into her beloved face screwed up into a furious scowl as she wailed. "Oh, my darling," I crooned. Words of love and affection spilled from my lips without conscious thought, as I tried to warm and soothe her. Gage wrapped his arm around me, gazing down at her in such adoration that my smile spread so wide I thought it might crack my face.

"She's beautiful. Perfect," he proclaimed in awe before pressing his lips to my forehead. I could feel his throat ripple against my cheek as he swallowed, and I knew he was struggling to master his emotions.

"I love you," I murmured.

He lifted his head so he could gaze down at me, his pale blue eyes swimming with affection. "I love you, too."

Several days later, Philip, Alana, Charlotte, Henry, Gage, and I congregated in our drawing room as our daughter, Emma, was passed around. Thus far, she'd proven fondest of sleeping, eating, and making her father hop to her every whim with the tiniest of cries. I teased Gage mercilessly about it, but then I suspected I was just as bad. It didn't help that with her blue eyes and blond hair, she looked so much like her father.

"Well, there will be no more ridiculous rumors about your paternity," Alana cooed as she pressed her lips to Emma's downy head.

Philip looked up from where he had been gazing over his wife's shoulder at his new niece. "I hear they apprehended Lennox and confiscated all of his manuscripts."

"Yes. Maclean acted swiftly once Mr. Heron came forward with his information," Gage replied from his position perched on the arm of the chair where I sat.

"He also sent them looking for us," I chimed in.

After Heron realized that McQueen's men had taken us captive, he'd run straight to the nearest police house with everything he knew. Joe, our coachman, had begun questioning the other residents of Heron's building and discovered we'd been taken. Then he rushed home to inform the members of our household, who had scattered to tell Philip and Henry and organize a search.

"There were people scouring all over Edinburgh looking for you," Philip replied.

"But it's the residents of Blair Street to whom we owe the most gratitude," I said quietly. "Had they not notified Bonnie Brock when they realized who we were and what was happening, we might never have been found."

Charlotte shivered at the implications.

Henry nodded at Philip. "We tried to venture in after Kincaid and Anderley, but after just a few turns, we had to retrace our steps for fear we would never find our way back out and they would have to send a search party in after *us*."

"What of McQueen's men?" Alana glanced up from Emma's face to ask. "Were they arrested?"

"Not that we've been made aware of," Gage said.

Though I was thinking of Bonnie Brock's pledge to handle the matter, despite my insistence that he leave it to the police. He and Maggie had paid us one more visit the evening prior, conferring with us in the morning room as before. Gage had been somewhat hesitant to allow them to see Emma, but I'd reminded him we probably owed Bonnie Brock our lives and hers. Particularly as he'd risked his own life and freedom by working in full view of Sergeant Maclean and his men. Had he not slipped away the moment after he'd deposited me in our carriage, I had no doubt he would have been apprehended.

In any case, Bonnie Brock had been rather subdued during our conversation, and somewhat cowed by the baby. Maggie had been doting, her eyes lighting with a delight that I had never seen reflected there. It even brought a smile to her brother's mouth. Whatever his feelings the night her betrayal had been revealed, he seemed to have forgiven her, and I could only hope that if she was still enamored of Mr. Heron, he might give the young man a chance to prove himself worthy.

"So Mr. Lennox is Bonnie Brock Kincaid's half brother?" Alana remarked.

I noticed Henry and Gage exchanging a glance, perhaps thinking of their own kinship. "Yes, the late Alexander Lennox of Badenoch was their father." A fact Bonnie Brock had confirmed, however begrudgingly. Though he still wouldn't tell me how he'd gotten hold of the Kincaid seal. "Badenoch squandered away his wealth, leaving his legitimate son with a pittance for his inheritance. As best we can work out, when Badenoch the younger realized how much wealth and influence his bastard half brother, the infamous criminal Bonnie Brock, had amassed for himself, he grew angry and jealous. He became convinced that Bonnie Brock had somehow stolen his inheritance and became determined to see him not only executed but disgraced."

"But why include those accusations against you?"

"Partly for titillation, I imagine," Gage replied, draping his arm over the back of the chair behind me. "And partly because his friend, Lord Kirkcowan, had vented his spleen about us. Kiera, in particular." Because of my interference with his wife, and my role in helping her save her jewels. "But unfortunately that also opened him up to Kirkcowan's blackmail and made the baron another loose end he had to tie up."

"Because he knew too much? Like Rookwood?" Charlotte verified.

"Yes."

Emma made a small sighing gurgle sound, raising her fist, and then settled back into sleep in Alana's arms. At the sight of her contented slumbering, I relaxed back in my chair again as Gage brushed his thumb over my collarbone in reassurance. Five days following our ordeal, and none of us had yet shown symptoms of contracting the cholera morbus from our time in the squalid vaults, but I was still vigilant, alert for the signs.

It certainly didn't help that the newspapers were filled with reports of the deadly infection's spread elsewhere. In a little over two weeks, cholera had already claimed the lives of more than thirteen thousand people in Paris, and the numbers of victims continued to increase. Meanwhile, the outbreak in Glasgow was now expected to be far worse than Edinburgh's. And despite the cessation of the printing of Lennox's sequel, there were continued suspicions regarding the bodies of cholera victims, and whether the surgeons and physicians were colluding to cause more death. Only time would tell whether these rumblings grew louder or reason prevailed.

There was a rap at the door followed by Jeffers's entry. "This just arrived for you, my lady," he said, handing me a small box.

"Thank you," I replied as he departed, but not before he passed a fond glance over our sleeping Emma.

"From Trevor?" Alana guessed.

"I don't think so. Our brother sent me his best wishes two days ago." I lifted the lid of the box and then stilled in astonishment. Inside was nestled my mother's amethyst pendant.

Gage sat forward in equal disbelief, for I'd confided in him how McQueen's men had taken it from me. I lifted the necklace from the box to examine it, noticing a small card underneath marked solely with the letters *BB*.

I supposed that answered the question whether McQueen's men had been punished. I shied away from pondering precisely how.

Gripping the amethyst in my hand, I touched Gage's leg in reassurance before rising to my feet. While the others conversed, I crossed the room toward the mirror near our hearth, affixing the pendant around my neck again.

"That's Mother's pendant," Alana said softly, coming up behind me. I glanced over my shoulder toward the others to discover that she'd passed baby Emma to Charlotte.

"Yes. McQueen's men took it," I answered, forced to explain.

She nodded slowly. "And Bonnie Brock Kincaid retrieved it for you."

"I don't know," I hedged, and then sighed. "But yes, probably."

"You lead a complicated life." She straightened the neckline of my naval blue gown. "But I suppose it's good to have friends in high and low places."

"I'm sure you view all of this as confirmation that you were right," I challenged in a low voice, determined to have it out with her now if she thought Emma's birth or our abduction had changed my mind about assisting with any investigations in the future.

"Actually, no."

I turned to her in genuine surprise.

"Don't mistake me. I still worry about you. I still hate the way the other ladies gossip. But I also know you don't go chasing down every murderer or thief, willy-nilly." She grabbed hold of my hands. "So I'll simply have to trust your judgment on this."

Though grateful for her change of heart, I knew this hadn't come about on its own. "How did you . . ."

"Lady Hollingsworth called on me," she explained, already anticipating my question.

"I see," I replied, though I didn't. Philip's Aunt Jane was arrogant, controlling, and a stickler for propriety. She also disapproved of me—albeit a shade less since I'd wed Gage—and often went out of her way to find fault with Alana. She was not an easy person to converse with, even in the best of circumstances, and these were not those. I would have expected her patented blend of vitriol to make matters worse for me.

"She was asking after you and baby Emma, but what she was really after was gossip about your ordeal."

"Naturally."

Alana's lips curled into a commiserating smile. "I expected her to bemoan your lack of decorum, as she always does. But . . . instead she focused all of her contempt on Mr. Lennox. Or rather, Lord Badenoch, as he should be called."

"Does she know him?"

"Apparently, a few years ago he attempted to court her daughter, Caroline, just as she was making her debut. She even welcomed it. That is, until her eldest son, James, uncovered that Badenoch was a fortune hunter. That he'd been brought to *point non plus*, with only his name to recommend him." She dipped her head closer. "But it wasn't only that. She claims he had the prettiest manners, but even so, she noticed *disturbing tendencies* in him, though she wouldn't elaborate what precisely that meant. That she feared he might follow in his libertine father's footsteps. But she never suspected he would go so far as murder. She decried his shocking behavior and said she could only be glad that you and Gage had exposed him for what he really was."

As refreshing as it was to hear Lady Hollingsworth praising instead of berating me for once, I didn't take it too much to heart. It sounded to me like her pride was smarting from allowing the man to court her only daughter, and she saw his crimes as confirmation of her intuition. But I kept my tongue behind my teeth, for if somehow her words had convinced Alana to stop chiding me, then I would be glad of them.

But Alana wasn't finished. "It made me think of what you told me the other day." She fidgeted with the lace along her sleeve. "How you said you were only trying to make the world safer, fairer, more just. And I realized, how can I object to that?" She arched her eyebrows imperiously. "So long as you're not being a ninnyhammer."

"You do say the sweetest things," I muttered wryly.

"When I try." Her answering smile was somewhat brittle, and her eyes filled with tears. She blinked them away. "I couldn't do what you do, Kiera," she confessed in a broken voice. "I couldn't stomach the sight of murder, or untangle the clues, or confront the danger of it all. And do so while ignoring the censure of society." Her gaze dropped. "And seeing how brave and determined you are has forced me to confront my own shortcomings. How I've bowed to convention my entire life . . ."

I squeezed her hands where I still gripped them. "No, Alana. Don't do that to yourself." I leaned forward, forcing her gaze to meet mine. "Our lives, our paths are not the same. And mine is certainly no more noble than yours is. You are a wonderful wife, and countess, and mother. And I know you've faced your own difficulties. Do not give yourself such short shrift."

She sniffed and nodded.

"Besides, you can't tell me that if you had to do it all over again, you wouldn't have chosen this life every time."

"You're right. I would have." She released my hands to pull the handkerchief from its place tucked inside her sleeve and dabbed at her nose. "But I feel rather ashamed of myself for trying so mightily to force you to fit into the same box simply to make myself feel better about my own choices."

I studied her splotchy face and then reached out to tuck a stray strand of chestnut hair behind her ear. "Well, I won't pretend I wasn't hurt by your attempts to browbeat me. But perhaps I needed it. To recognize how strong I've truly become. Two years ago I could never have withstood such an onslaught. I was so broken. But now . . ." I inhaled a deep breath, glancing toward my daughter and husband. "Now, I have strength enough for three. And a large reason for that is you." I took hold of Alana's hand again. "You stood by me when I needed you desperately. And now I need you to stand by me even though I don't."

Her lips curled upward in an attempt at a smile.

"Can you do that?"

"Yes. You'll always have me, Kiera. Whether you need me or not."

I pulled her close, wrapping my arms around her and pressing my cheek to hers, relieved to have this disagreement between us resolved. Although there was one more thing I needed to know.

"Why did you stop writing poetry?"

Alana exhaled a weary breath as she stepped back from our embrace.

"And don't tell me it's because Malcolm was born. You could have gone on doing so."

A tiny furrow formed between her brows. "Perhaps." She turned to the mirror, dabbing at her eyes and nose and then adjusting the topaz and gold agraffe at the center of her bodice. "But Philip has responsibilities and ambitions, and he needs my support with them. I knew that when I wed him."

"Did he ask you to stop writing?"

"Of course not."

I gripped her arm, forcing her to look at me. "Then surely supporting him and caring for your children doesn't preclude you from writing."

"No, it doesn't. And perhaps someday I will do more than pen a short verse to my children now and again. But for now . . ." She shook her head.

So I relented, despite the conflicting emotions I saw in her eyes. For what could I say? The decision was hers to make. Yet I was still intensely curious.

"Will you let me read any of your poems?"

She laughed softly. "Maybe. Though I'm afraid your expectations of my talents may be overstated if you're judging them by your own artistic merits."

I squeezed her arm. "I'm sure they're lovely."

Her shoulders shrugged as if to brush off their worth, but I could tell from the manner in which she seemed determined to pretend she didn't care that they were not so meaningless to her. Even so, I allowed her to coax me back over to join the others.

Charlotte looked up from her scrutiny of Emma, a happy smile on her lips. And I knew it wasn't simply because she was holding a baby, but also because my sister and I seemed to have resolved our differences. I promised myself we would journey to Barbreck Manor just as soon as it was safe to do so, in order to help her prepare for her wedding to my cousin Rye and to allow her extra time with her infant godchild.

CHAPTER 29

I looked up from Emma's sleeping face as Bree slipped into the room. She brandished my amethyst gown triumphantly before her, and even in the low light of the room, I could see that she'd somehow contrived to remove all the stains from it.

"Bree, you are a wonder," I gasped softly, having written the dress off as not salvable with all the blood and dirt from our ordeal and Emma's birth covering it.

"Had ye been wearing the jonquil one, I'm no' sure I coulda saved it," she admitted, hanging the gown in the wardrobe.

"Well, no matter. I'm still amazed."

She twitched the drapes shut against the dark of night and then stepped closer to peer over my shoulder at Emma slumbering contentedly in my arms, the tiny hand she refused to keep swaddled tucked by her chin. A dribble of milk pooled in the corner of her mouth, and I lifted the corner of her blanket to dab it away.

"Do ye want me to lay her in her cradle for ye?" she asked eagerly, as enamored of the child as Gage and I already were.

"No, not yet," I replied, wanting to hold her a bit longer.

Bree nodded in understanding. "Jeffers said ye may have found a nursemaid."

"Maybe," I replied tentatively. It had been difficult to find someone who not only was qualified and met with our approval, but was also willing to travel with us from place to place, for I had no desire to leave my child behind when we journeyed about the country. Though we owned homes in Edinburgh and London, and had talked of purchasing or leasing a small estate somewhere, thus far our circumstances since our marriage had been very transient. This type of existence required just the right sort of person for the position.

"She'll turn up," Bree declared encouragingly.

The door behind us opened, and I glanced over my shoulder to see Gage entering the room on cat's feet. Through the gap in the dressing room door, I caught sight of Anderley. To my knowledge he hadn't yet held Emma, but he seemed more curious about her than perhaps he would like to admit.

"If you've no more need o' me, I'll take my leave," Bree said, backing away.

"Good night, Bree."

She dipped a shallow curtsy and disappeared into the dressing room, saying something to Anderley that I couldn't quite catch before she shut the door. She had confided in me that she had taken my advice to talk with him, and they had decided to return to being merely friends. However, I didn't think that was necessarily the end of it, not when I saw the way they both looked at each other when they thought the other wasn't looking.

My gaze lifted to Gage, who was bent over watching our daughter sleep with a look of such serene adoration I could only smile.

"Shall I lay her in the cradle for you?"

I chuckled at everyone's keenness to hold Emma, even if for but a brief time. "Yes," I relented, knowing she would never learn to sleep in her own bed if we always held her.

She protested with a soft grunt when he lifted her gently from my arms but then subsided. Moving ever so slowly, he placed her in the beautiful wooden cradle he had presented to me the day after her birth. He'd been waiting for the right moment to give it to me before the birth, but that had never come. No matter. I still cherished it because he'd made it with his own two hands.

I rose to my feet and crossed to stand next to him where he stood gazing down at our sleeping daughter. His arm wrapped around me, and I leaned into him, resting my head against his chest.

"I never knew I could be this happy," he said softly, wondrously.

My heart flooded with so much love at his words that I thought it would burst. I clutched him tighter, wanting him to feel it, and I could tell by the way he held me in return that he did.

But then a sadness crept into his voice. "Do you think my father ever felt this way? About me? About Henry?"

I lifted my face to his, and seeing the pain etched across his brow, I urged him away from the cradle so that our voices wouldn't wake Emma. He perched on the edge of the bed, and I stood between his legs so that I could see him more clearly, cradling his jaw in my hands. His bristles rubbed the skin of my palms.

"I don't know," I confessed. "In many ways, your father is an enigma to me. But . . . I do know that if he wasn't joyful at your birth, or Henry's for that matter, then that was *his* failing . . ." I shook my head ". . . and not yours."

His pale blue eyes searched mine as if looking for answers I couldn't give him, for I had no way of knowing them.

"Have you written to him?"

"No." His hands lifted to rest lightly on my waist, his fingers brushing over the silk of my dressing gown. "I don't know what to say."

I draped my arms around his neck, combing my fingers through the hair at the nape of his neck. "How about the truth." I smiled ruefully. "After all, at this point, you have nothing to lose."

His gaze dipped to the hollow of my throat. "I suppose you're right. I can't continue as we have. And if he can't be honest with me, then there's really nothing more to say."

"You need to inform him of his granddaughter's birth anyway," I said, thinking this might provide him the impetus to start.

He nodded woodenly. "He'll be pleased we named her Emma."

I suspected that was true, but I also couldn't help wondering whether he would be displeased she hadn't been a boy, another heir to his lineage and title. It was just the sort of thing Lord Gage would decide to take exception to, another tally point on his long list of my faults. Just because we'd seemed to turn a corner in our relationship when last we were with him did not mean he accepted or approved of me.

Gage's eyes lifted to meet mine, warming at the affection I knew he would see reflected there. "I'll write tomorrow." His mouth took on a roguish tilt as he pulled me closer. "But for tonight . . ." He exhaled a weary breath. "How about we sleep?"

I laughed softly, the same fatigue dragging at my bones. No one had ever said that parenthood was for the well rested. "That sounds . . . heavenly."

He smiled and then pressed his lips to mine, kissing me long and deep. But just as we both turned to crawl beneath the covers, a tiny cry sounded from the cradle. My head dropped forward in defeat.

He touched my hand gently. "I'll get her."

I smiled at him in gratitude before lowering my head to my pillow. I decided I'd never loved him more.

As my eyes drifted shut, I briefly wondered if the events surrounding Emma's birth would be the end to our misadventures, but as always, time would only tell. Given our history, I wouldn't have wagered on it. And while I silently resolved that Charlotte and Rye's wedding should be peaceful and merry, I had learned long ago that such things were rarely in my control. Even when it came to matters of art.

HISTORICAL NOTE

So first up, let's address the elephant in the room—the cholera pandemic. Prior to the 1820s, cholera had largely been confined to the Indian subcontinent. But beginning in that decade, it started to spread, first along trade routes and then farther afield. In December 1831, it reached Britain, despite a mandatory quarantine placed on ships and their crews arriving from ports in afflicted areas. It quickly spread north and south and continued to advance around the globe.

Britain would experience multiple outbreaks of cholera throughout the nineteenth century until they finally addressed the underlying causes of the spread of the disease. But in 1831–1832, the majority of physicians believed people were infected by either something they ate or a miasma.

For decades before the actual bacteria which causes cholera reached Britain, people used the term loosely to describe anything that gave them digestive problems and loose stools. This was why when cholera actually struck, the medical community persisted in linking it to something ingested, whether it was rotten food, a mineral poison, or a bad combination of items. Intemperance was also linked to it in this way, and for other reasons.

Miasma theory was the predominant medical theory by the brightest minds of the age to explain how diseases spread. The belief was that bad, noxious air emanating from things like rotting corpses, marshy land areas, and other putrid matter actually exhaled vapors which caused people to fall ill. This "influence in the atmosphere" was also believed to afflict those who had weakened themselves by exposure to certain behaviors, places, or "exciting causes." In this way, they promoted the idea that only people of "irregular habits" should fear diseases like cholera. So as long as you were good, clean, and temperate, you could escape the scourge.

Thus, it wasn't difficult to see how the concept of contagion was confused and correlated with religion, piety, sin, and the idea that cholera was God's punishment for certain people's intemperance and immorality. Multiple pamphlets from the time period rail against people's sinful natures and call on the government to make changes to the laws to save people from their iniquities.

Some useful measures were actually undertaken. A Central Board of Health was first established, based in London, and other cities throughout Britain formed their own boards of health that reported to the central branch. In this way, they were able to disseminate information to the public in a more organized manner through the *Cholera Gazette*. Broadsides were also posted, advising people of things like what foods to eat, how to clean themselves and their homes, and to be mindful of the weather and the suitability of their clothing for it. The buildings in infected areas were whitewashed and cleaned. However, these efforts could only do so much when, in their ignorance, they failed to address the true cause of the disease: the open cesspools contaminating the sources of their drinking water. Rarely were quarantine measures recommended because cholera didn't seem to spread by contagion but more often by indirect personal contact.

It wasn't until 1854, when Dr. John Snow was able to trace the source of a single cholera outbreak in London to a specific water pump, and then a decades-long fight for germ theory to overtake that of the miasma theory, that the real cause of cholera was pinpointed and accepted. Once significant sanitation improvements were made and clean water supplies were secured, then cholera was largely eradicated from many parts of the world. Though today there are still areas of the globe without these two crucial elements that struggle with the disease.

The mindset and general knowledge of the populace was unsettled at this time, and there was great fear among some citizens that doctors were allowing or causing people to die of the cholera in order to use their bodies for dissection in the anatomy schools. A fear that would continue to grow into the summer of 1832 and result in multiple cholera riots.

The plot of *A Wicked Conceit* was greatly inspired by the book *Murder by the Book* by Claire Harman, and the murder of Lord William Russell in May 1840. The man executed for Lord William's murder was his valet, François Courvoisier, who claimed he'd been inspired by one of the plays staged from the book *Jack Sheppard*, which were a smashing success in 1840 London. Novels about criminals were all the rage in this era, forming a new genre of "Newgate novels," as they were called, after the infamous prison. And none more so than *Jack Sheppard*, the tale of the eighteenth-century unabashed thief, who escaped jail numerous times, written by William Harrison Ainsworth. The book had already inspired a minor crime wave across London, drawing heavy criticism, but the gruesome murder of a nobleman catapulted its infamy to an entirely new level.

I also borrowed the title of the immensely popular flash song from the Adelphi's production of *Jack Sheppard*. The words for "Nix My Dolly, Pals, Fake Away" were taken from Ainsworth's earlier novel *Rookwood* and were set to music by G. Herbert Rodwell to rousing success. Though written in thieves' cant, it proved to be a favorite among all classes and was one of the most popular songs of the decade, even if the upper classes little understood the words they were singing. The tune was played in music boxes, used as sheet music for children learning to play the violin, and even arranged as a chime for the bells of the cathedral in Edinburgh. "Nix My Dolly" was everywhere.

In 1832, UK theaters did not have to pay authors for the use of the material in their books. They were not yet protected by copyright law. So authors had no choice but to accept it. Sometimes a theater manager would offer a one-off payment to the author, more out of guilt than any other reason, but they were not required to do so.

In this time period, the Theatre Royal in Edinburgh was owned by actor-turned-manager William Henry Murray and his sister, actress Harriet Siddons. Harriet was, in fact, styled "Our Mrs. Siddons" by the people of Edinburgh to differentiate her from her more famous mother-in-law, actress Sarah Siddons. The Wolf of Badenoch was also a real fourteenth-century figure, considered by some to be the most notorious and vile man in Scottish history.

I discovered the African American actor Ira Aldridge while learning about his portrait by James Northcote hanging in the Manchester Art Gallery. A fascinating figure in his own right, he left a lasting legacy in theater and through the accomplishments of his children. He is currently the only actor of African American descent honored with a plaque at the Shakespeare Memorial Theatre in Stratford-upon-Avon, UK. He toured widely in the UK at this time period, particularly in his role as Shakespeare's Othello.

Earl Grey and the Whigs genuinely did plot to ask the king to create a large enough number of new Whig peers in order to pass the third attempt at the Reform Act through the House of Lords, believing this was their only alternative. However, King William IV initially balked at this measure, leading Lord Grey to resign as prime minister. The king then invited the Tory Duke of Wellington to form a new government. This resulted in the "Days of May," a period of revolt and great unrest, which many feared would culminate in outright revolution. Uneasy lies the state of Britain in these days following the birth of Kiera and Gage's child.

ACKNOWLEDGMENTS

As always, I'm so grateful to everyone involved with the creation of this book and those who helped me in various ways to complete it. This was the first book I finished writing during the COVID-19 pandemic, and as such, the experience was both somewhat unique and also fraught with more difficulties. So I want to offer an extra helping of thanks to all who are named below.

My amazing team at Berkley Prime Crime, including, but not limited to, my fabulous editor Michelle Vega, Jenn Snyder, Brittanie Black, Jessica Mangicaro, Stacy Edwards, and Amy J. Schneider, as well as the artists and designers who always create such stunning covers.

My incomparable agent, Kevan Lyon, and her team.

My husband—I don't know what I would do without his love and encouragement, and my daughters for filling me up and making me want to be the best I can be.

My eldest daughter's teachers, as well as educational staff everywhere. Having to assist her through the last nine weeks of kindergarten by remote learning was certainly eye-opening and definitely made me even more grateful for everything teachers do every day, and how much of themselves they pour into their students.

My friends and beta readers, Jackie Musser and Stacie Roth Miller, whose guidance never steers me wrong.

My extraordinary circle of friends and family, whose care and support always means so much.

And God, who never leaves or forsakes me, and from whom all blessings flow.

Ready to find
your next great read?

Let us help.

Visit prh.com/nextread